MORE...

When a Man Loves a Weapon

Toni McGee Causey

St. Martin's Paperbacks

This is a work of fiction. All of the characters, organizations and events portrayed in this novel are either products of the author's imagination or are used fictitiously.

WHEN A MAN LOVES A WEAPON

Copyright © 2009 by Toni McGee Causey.

Cover photo © Herman Estevez.

For information address St. Martin's Press, 175 Fifth Avenue, New York, NY 10010.

ISBN: 0-312-35851-2
EAN: 978-0-312-35851-8

Printed in the United States of America

St. Martin's Paperbacks edition / August 2009

St. Martin's Paperbacks are published by St. Martin's Press, 175 Fifth Avenue, New York, NY 10010.

10 9 8 7 6 5 4 3 2 1

For my girls:

Amanda, Nicole, and Angela Grace

CONSISTENCY. It's only a virtue if you're not a screw-up.
—bumper sticker seen in Lake Charles, LA

One

Bobbie Faye Sumrall lay flat on her back on the thick blue mat in the sparring ring, and if she weren't so exhausted, she'd kill him. If she could just roll over and push her rancid sweaty self up, she'd crawl out of the room, pride be damned, and find the gun. It might take days to load because she'd probably have to load it with her teeth, her arms were so tired, and then she'd probably have to prop the damned thing up on something and ask Trevor to please move within range because she was too worn out to aim properly. And then she'd shoot him, assuming she had the strength left to pull the trigger.

If she thought hard enough, maybe she could come up with a good argument that "lying in a slobbering heap" was the same thing as "being prepared for the next disaster." There had to be some rationalization *some*where she could use, dammit. Because Trevor seemed to believe that another disaster was imminent and that she needed to be all prepared and shit.

He leaned over her and the light from the rafters of the old converted barn gave him a halo. He grinned, white teeth against tan skin, biceps bulging and forearms cording as he crossed his arms against his tight black t-shirt, and his wavy brown shoulder-length hair fell into his Satan-blue eyes. The *least* he could have done was broken a sweat.

"You're improving," he said. "You almost managed to land a kick that time."

"I hate you."

His grin went from merely smug to completely obnoxious. "You did not hate me before breakfast. Which reminds me, we need to add strawberry jam to the shopping list."

Her eyesight fuzzed for a moment as her brain just skipped right on away from the subject of how much of a pain he was being, making her work out for hours every day, and frolicked over to exactly what he'd done with that strawberry jam. Now her favorite food on the planet. She hadn't even known you could *do* that with a topping, and she had a friend who ran an S&M magazine.

"We could have stayed in bed all day," she pointed out. "I'm on vacation. You're on leave. Allllll weeeeeek."

"And you," he said, squatting next to her, "are still hesitating. You're not firing as fast, you're not hitting as fast, and you're thinking too damned much."

"I don't think anyone's ever actually accused me of thinking too damned much."

He glowered at her.

He was right. What was worse was that he knew that she knew that he was right. She really *really* hated that.

She needed a temporary amnesia potion.

Of course, she did not dare tell that to her boss, Ce Ce, who had a little voodoo side business to her Cajun Outfitter and Feng Shui Emporium where Bobbie Faye manned the gun counter. Ce Ce's potions often had unexpected side effects. With Bobbie Faye's luck, a "temporary amnesia potion" would probably erase way more than just the stuff she wanted to forget. She studied the man waiting next to her, his blue eyes heated like someone had turned on a blaze as his gaze roved over her body, and there were just some things she was not willing to sacrifice, no matter how much sleep amnesia might give her.

"C'mon, slacker. Up. You have at least thirty more minutes of sparring, and then we're going to run."

"Did you have to pinky-swear you'd be a relentless, impossible hard-ass when you joined the FBI?"

"No," he said, his eyes crinkling at the corners as he

stood up, smiling. "Pinky-swearing was all the rage back in Spec Ops. The Feds are big on promise rings." He offered her a hand to help her up. "You can do this."

"Ugh. Just shoot me now." She saw him shift, and she might as well have slapped his face, the way his relaxed stance stiffened, and she felt her own body tense in response. The tightening of the muscle in his jaw was infinitesimally small; most anyone else wouldn't have noticed it, but she did and she knew what fury flashed through him when that little muscle quirked. Fury on her behalf.

Four months ago. Three shots. Meant for him.

Bobbie Faye had jumped in the way.

They didn't talk about it. At all. Every single morning, he kissed the scars, and every single night he held her, his long, lean fingers splayed out over that area as if he could ward them off, shove away the memory.

"Hey," she coaxed, tugging his hand, trying to dispel the mood, "he's a metric buttload of miles away."

"MacGreggor escaped." He bit the words out with the same harsh disgust as the first time he'd told her. He'd damned near gone feral, his protective instincts kicking into full gear those first few weeks, and she'd had to fight him to keep him from putting them into complete lockdown mode. He'd have put armed guards on her if she'd have let him, and he'd vetoed traveling to meet his family and his family traveling to meet her. Hell, he'd have vetoed going to the grocery store and Ce Ce's and ever seeing the sunlight again if she'd have listened to him. Good thing she'd patented "titanium-level stubborn" years earlier.

"He escaped three months ago." She was going to put a happy spin on it, if it fucking killed her. "And he's heading toward Canada. We know that from the tips and witnesses calling in." There was a BOLO out on Sean on every continent—a "be on the lookout for" notice that went out internationally, at all levels of law enforcement. "He's trying to get home." To Ireland, she hoped. Well, she *hoped* for *Hell*, because Ireland had never done anything to deserve Sean MacGreggor, either.

She watched Trevor tamp down his fury, that ice-cold hatred he had for Sean MacGreggor, the man Trevor had shot. The man who'd promised to come back and "claim" Bobbie Faye.

She'd been studiously ignoring that little nugget of information. Trying to be normal, whatever the hell that was. She'd actually slept a whole night. Well, sort of a whole night. Okay, four hours without waking up ready to fight someone and accidentally smacking the crap out of Trevor.

Still, she'd been working her ass off to convince him she was okay. "Hey," she said when he didn't answer, "everything is back to normal . . . in fact, better than normal, all flowers and sunshine and fluffy clouds. I have set a whole new record of no one trying to kill me. I think I should get a trophy."

"C'mon." He reached for her again, not smiling at her attempt, his perfect poker face back in place. For an absolutely hot man . . . her Hormones took their own little detour at that moment to wander over his muscled thighs, nearly derailing her entire brain with an Ode to Man . . . he could go granite cold, a veneer he carefully adopted whenever he was undercover. It had become something of a personal goal to make him forget how to use that mask, particularly with her.

He pulled her to her feet, his sparring gloves smooth against her arms, and they stood face-to-face—er, eyes to chin, technically, since he was nearly six inches taller at six foot. She gave him a big grin, which inspired his suspicious appraisal.

"You realize," she poked him playfully in the ribs, "that as soon as we get me in prime fighting form, I'll get flattened by a bus instead."

And just as he started to retort, she landed a punch and didn't take the time to revel in his surprised expression, though he did manage to block her next flurry of moves. Damn freaking man. Two steps later, she nailed his thigh with a kick and they were suddenly *game on*, sparring, and she came very very close a few times to almost landing another one. Close enough to make Trevor's eyes narrow, and he had to concentrate and not merely bat her away. *Ha.* Girl power.

She maneuvered him the way he'd taught her and, in one sweet move, the angels sang and the Universe was distracted from bringing on her total abject humiliation and she managed to take him down. They slammed against the padded floor mat, and if he hadn't immediately rolled and pinned her beneath him, she'd have danced around the ring like a winning prizefighter.

Instead, she kissed him. Which made him relax. Whereupon she flipped him over and straddled him.

She'd have paid big money to have a photo of his expression—half shock, half pride. She wriggled on top of him and leaned down, kissing the corner of his mouth.

"You need to focus," he said, the words grinding out against her lips.

"I *am* focused." She smiled and kissed him again, and reminded herself that she was getting to marry this man.

"You planning on using this technique on everyone you take down? Because that's a lot of guys I'll have to kill."

"I'm not sure whether to be annoyed that you're obsessing again, Mr. FBI, or happy that you think I'm capable of taking down multiple men. I landed a punch *and* a kick *and* a take-down. I think we need to celebrate." She grinned, running her fingers through his hair and wiggled just enough for him to be absolutely certain that sparring practice was over.

"Let's go with happy."

He yanked off his shirt as he rolled over onto her, his hard body pressed along her own, his skin against hers delicious and warm against the cool air in the barn, like safety somehow sheathed in danger. Her body hummed as he braced on one arm and slid the other hand over her, a knuckle rasping just beneath her breast while he kissed her, possessing, dominating. She liked that he could be bossy and strong and rough and gentle at the same time and she wasn't quite sure how he managed it, this treating her like an equal, *but still his*. Then she quit thinking completely as she burned beneath the fire of his kisses trailing down the line of her throat. She wasn't entirely sure when he'd unhooked her workout bra, but she shivered beneath the scratch of his days-old stubble against her breast as he raked his teeth across her nipples, biting, then his tongue soothing, her body flooding with heat and want and need.

"Up," he commanded, and she arched her bottom and he stripped off her shorts—thank God for military efficiency—and she was bare to him. The mat warmed beneath her, the rough calluses of his palm sliding down her hip, past the little birth control patch that she'd checked with the religious fervor of a born-again zealot. His hand slid up her inner thigh until his thumb brushed her, his fingers sliding inside, his mouth taking hers, fast, hard, at the same time, and she nearly came undone at his searing attack of her body.

Then he lifted off her for a moment, a brief heartbeat of loss and cold, and just as suddenly, he was there again, having stripped off his shorts, and he lay down beside her, his blue eyes dark, serious. He seemed lost in the curves of her hip, the angle of her knee, studying her as if all the answers lay there, in the bend of her elbow or the place where he knew she was ticklish just beneath her ear. His face was all confidence and darkness, and she'd seen that hunger before on card sharks in a room full of thieves, a look that was patience and determination and secrets, his fingers sliding with knowledge and skill and when she moved to touch him, he stilled her with a *shhhhhh*.

"Let me," he whispered, and then he took his ever-loving time about it, 'til she felt taut and aching and scattered all at the same time, cards spread on the table, *play me*.

There may have been whimpering. Possibly a little begging.

Okay, a *lot* of begging, and she tried to urge him to move faster, but he was ruthless, and he shut her up with an entire repertoire of kisses that tilted her world, and she shuddered beneath his utter control just as—

—his cell phone rang. The Bureau calling. She recognized,

and loathed, the specific "urgent" ring tone he'd assigned so that he'd know the difference between pure administrative crap that could wait and the life-threatening other crap that could not. She'd itched many times to pick up that damned tyrant of a phone and "accidentally" lose it in the garbage disposal, but the freaky thing was so sophisticated, she wouldn't be a bit surprised if it not only resurrected itself, but videotaped her and ran and tattled.

He kissed her and she forgot about the phone for a second, or ten, and then it stopped ringing. He took his time at the corner of her mouth, braced on one elbow, leaning over her, his other hand playing intricate patterns, weaving through her long hair, its dark, rich browns like dark coffee against her ivory no-tan-for-you-this-summer skin.

The phone rang again. The damned thing went everywhere with him. Even to this barn behind the tiny house he'd found out in the middle of nowhere, south Louisiana. The frayed old house, worn at the edges like her favorite boots, tossed almost absently beneath great sprawling trees on acres of land—land bordered by a massive swamp that spilled into an enormous lake. Another ring. They were at the end of the world out here, somewhere back in primordial time, in the Mesozoic era, if she could judge by the size of the damned alligators she'd seen when he'd taken her on a boat ride to show her the property boundaries.

He tried to ignore the call, his hand guiding her into turning toward him, bringing her back to him as he hung onto his control, trying to keep them right there, in that moment, just them together, no duty intruding, but the phone kept shrilling, echoing off the barn walls, and Trevor sighed, touching his forehead to her own as she flopped her arms out against the mat, resigning herself.

"Sonofabitch," he muttered, knowing he had to answer.

He was supposed to be on leave for another two weeks. The damned FBI had called him every single day. Sometimes, several times a day. She didn't know what exactly he did, but he was assigned to freaking south Louisiana. How busy could they possibly be?

He rolled off her and crossed the sparring ring to grab the phone, and she listened to his very brief, tense side of the conversation.

"What?" he asked. Then, "No, it's—"

He stood, back rigid, muscles granite. Silent. There was a stillness to him that made her very very nervous, as if he were a predator about to spring, and she held her breath. "I'll be there," he said, then snapped his phone shut.

He didn't tell her what the call was about, and Bobbie Faye knew better than to ask, but it fucking killed her. Fucking FBI and fucking missions and fucking going away and he'd only be leaving right now if it was bad. And didn't *that* response have all the maturity of a rabid teenager. *Gah.*

She stood in the empty living room of this tiny house he'd bought . . . *they'd* bought, she corrected herself, as he packed his overnight bag. He had a "go bag" in the bedroom for emergencies—extra clothes, phone, boots, and enough survival crap to make a Sherpa orgasmic, but this bag had more civilized stuff, like his shaving kit, nice jeans, and shirts. She didn't even want to know what was in the hanging bag draped over the card table they used as a dining set.

She wanted to hit something, but there was nothing to hit, kick, throw, slam, or smash. She glanced around at the emptiness: white walls, white trim, no furniture, not a single item, no rugs, just hardwood floors in desperate need of repair and refinishing. She toed one of the warped boards.

"We'll sand that when I get back," he said, a little too chipper for anyone talking about a home improvement project.

She threw him a skeptical glance. "Can you imagine me holding onto one of those big floor sanders? We'll be lucky if I don't take out a couple of walls with that thing."

"I plan on aiming you at the two we need to take out anyway."

"Very economical of you."

"Just wait 'til you see how we remove the tile in the kitchen."

He looked oddly happy at the thought. The man was

clearly a masochist. Of course, that explained an awful lot about their relationship.

"You're just trying to con me into thinking you need more power tools," she said.

"I'm adding it to the vows—love, honor, and router, 'til death do us part."

"You just made a hand tool sound dirty."

"Good to know," he said, grinning.

There was phenomenal woodwork for such a tiny house, and she focused on the Craftsman-styled shelves at the other end of the living room. They were empty, like the rest of the place. A couple of shelves had gone missing and someone had let their kid paste all sorts of stickers on the inside of the bottom cabinet. She had expected the big bad federal agent to scoff at the blasphemy of Teenage Mutant Ninja Turtles rubbed to a mottled gray pattern on "quality woodwork," but he'd squatted in front of that cabinet and smiled as he traced Michaelangelo (he laughed when she knew the name) and said, "This stays, when we refinish. People were happy here. They were a family here."

She still, a month later, couldn't figure out how in the hell he'd found this property, especially at a price they could afford. He couldn't have created a more private home if he'd carved the place out of the swamp himself. He'd found it after she'd gotten out of the hospital—he hated the vulnerability of her trailer. Too many prying neighbors, too easy to rip the door open, too hard to protect. Hard to be a federal agent with just anyone able to tiptoe up to the trailer, unobserved, and overhear everything through the too-thin walls. She'd sold the trailer and most of her stuff to afford her half of the down payment, and they'd only just moved in a couple of weeks ago. There were a few boxes—very few—to unpack. She had almost nothing left from when they'd met and her trailer had flooded (and then fallen over, and then ripped in half) and he'd moved around so much, he hadn't bothered to ever accumulate things.

He put two folded t-shirts on top of a photo. He'd packed the snapshot Ce Ce had taken of the two of them the day she'd first said yes. Bobbie Faye hadn't even realized he'd had a copy made. And it was framed. When had he done that? Did a man really need a photo if he was only going to be gone a short while? She inhaled, sharply, and had to turn away from the satchel, look away from his own too-serious face. She practically vibrated in place. He thought he was distracting her with the remodeling talk, but she wasn't fooled.

She wanted to know what that call was about.

By the time she was seven, she'd been the kind of kid who'd unwrapped her presents before Christmas, played with them each night, and then rewrapped them before her mom realized what she'd done. How on earth did anyone else actually *wait*? And it didn't matter what the hell was inside the box. It could be bricks. It only mattered that she didn't *know* what was inside the box.

She should ask Trevor about that call.

No. That would be *wrong*. And immature.

Maybe she could hint? She could definitely hint. He'd feel guilty about leaving, and he'd probably tell her something to make her feel better. She could adopt a puppy-dog pathetic schmoopy-face but she wouldn't be playing fair. Right? Right. But really, hinting wasn't all that bad.

"Shut *up*."

Dammit, that was out loud.

Trevor glanced her direction as she sighed. "I'm not sure what's scarier, Sundance. That you argue with yourself, or that you lose the arguments."

She would have answered, but instead, she just stood there in the empty living room, fiddling with the ring on her left hand, staring at the socks that she'd given him that he was about to put in his bag. She skirted the edge of such a deep well of emotion, it threatened her, an abyss. Questions logjammed inside her throat: *Is this dangerous? Will you be gone long? How do you know if you'll be safe? How am I supposed to just stand here and say good-bye?*

How could she give him anything less?

Hell, *she* was probably a bigger risk for him. She'd been

in the middle of so many disasters that various state agencies now tracked her, and he'd helped her survive the last two. Which had put his life at risk.

He glanced up when she didn't answer, and stopped his packing to pull her to him. She tried to memorize everything: the cut of the black t-shirt against his biceps, the faded scar just under his eye, the brush of his hair against her cheek, the smell of his skin and soap and something that was always reminiscent of the fresh, earthy scent after a rain. The stubble from his chin scratched against her temple, reminding her of just how rough he'd appeared, all edgy and darkness, the first day she'd met him. When she'd sort of taken him hostage. And she remembered that she'd learned that he'd worked undercover as a mercenary for *many, many months*. Oh, *fuck*.

"Months?" she asked, finally focusing on the one possibility that was driving a spike through her.

"No. Not at all. I'm not going to be long." He massaged the tension out of her shoulders. "Couple of days. Probably not even that, but worst-case scenario, three. I'll be fine. I've done a lot more dangerous things, including running around exploding silos with you."

"Oh, good, *that's* a calming image to leave me with, thank you."

He kissed her temple as he held her. "Seriously. This won't be bad."

"Yeah, because good luck has always worked out for me."

"You don't have anything to worry about. Except the sander I've reserved for next week."

"I've changed my mind. You're not a masochist. You're a sadist."

"Meanwhile," he said, ignoring her, "pick a damned date."

"See? Entirely my point."

"I'm serious."

She couldn't afford a wedding yet. She'd sold everything she could sell for her half of the house down payment. It wasn't fair or right to make him pay for everything. Why in the hell couldn't he see that?

"Maybe when I get—" overlapped, because he already knew the argument, with him saying:

"It's my wedding, too, I'll pay—"

Someone hammered on the door, and they both stopped abruptly as Trevor winced.

Wait. He *winced*. The man had stood in front of loaded guns without so much as a *flicker* of concern, and now he winced?

"Damn, he's early."

"He?" she asked, but Trevor had already crossed to the door.

A disheveled man loitered on their doorstep. Slightly shorter than Trevor, he had gray eyes and salt-and-pepper hair, half of which stood on end as though he'd run his hands through it and it had decided, *fuck it, I'll just stand up straight and be done with it.* Bobbie Faye placed him as slightly older than Trevor's thirty-seven, though that was probably deceiving since it was the color of the hair and the lines around his eyes that gave that impression. The rest of him seemed fit enough. It was hard to tell beneath the wrinkles in the khakis and the ugliest, stained, green and yellow plaid shirt she'd ever laid eyes on.

"Bobbie Faye Sumrall," Trevor said, by way of introduction, "this is Berneke Rilestone. Riles for short."

The man stared at her as he rocked on his heels, an odd self-satisfied expression canting across his bland face . . . she might have thought him the average good-ol'-boy since having a couple of loose screws seemed to be a prerequisite. But oh, he was smug about something, all cat-swimming-in-the-cream smug, and it set her on edge. Maybe it was his violently clashing attire that implied a future when he went batshit psycho and people interviewed the neighbors, who would call him "colorful" and "interesting." Or maybe it was because there was something bleak and confrontational that hovered in the air around him, like too much garlic after a heavy meal. Trevor had mentioned Riles in the context of Spec Ops friends, and since everything they'd done had been pretty much classified, she'd never heard much more than a few bar stories.

She'd never gotten to meet an actual friend of Trevor's. Other agents, sure. Sometimes in the context of almost blowing them up, which did not put her in the "must have" for the Christmas party invites, she knew. His military buddies were spread out over the world. His family—geez, just the thought of having to meet them one day—well, she just wouldn't think about that. Now, however, an actual friend had shown up, and her nerves swamped her, her pulse raced. Hell, she'd had a calmer time dealing that day when the bear was intent on making her its midday snack.

Sonofabitch. Trevor did not want to do this. He didn't want her to meet Riles this way.

But he couldn't tell her what was going on.

And it was all fucking compounded by the fact that he hadn't finished installing the surveillance equipment. The closing of this house, the move—all in the last month— fixing a few minor repairs before they moved in. He thought he'd have more time. Hell, he'd hoped to never have to do this—to leave without knowing for sure he'd make it back.

She pasted on a big smile, stepped out with her hand thrust forward, tougher than she thought she was, braver, too, and said, "Hi, Riles. It's great to meet you."

Riles, the bastard, didn't shake her hand. Instead, he glanced at her with a quick appraisal, and then back to Trevor. "You didn't tell Nutcakes here, did you?"

She stiffened, her wide smiling gaze downshifting into incredulous mode and Trevor shook his head at Riles. "Quit being an ass. And I was getting to that part."

"Why," she asked, enunciating the words carefully, dropping her hand to her side, "are you and the walking pile of laundry talking about me as if I'm not here?" She focused on Trevor and he could practically see the adrenaline pump into her system. "Tell. Me. What?"

Trevor crossed back to her and gave her a direct *you're*

not going to argue with this look. "Riles is a very good friend of mine. He's going to hang here while I'm gone, just to make sure everything stays safe and calm."

She blinked. Waiting for the punch line. Then he saw the moment she realized *he was serious*. "You . . . got me . . . a *baby*-sitter?"

"No," he said, carefully. "Think of Riles as a bodyguard. A watchdog."

"Woof," his friend said in a deep baritone.

Trevor slanted an aggravated glance at Riles. "You're not helping."

Riles beamed, his hands shoved in his khakis as he rocked on his heels, clearly enjoying the moment. "Hey, *I'm* not the idiot who decided to marry a woman with a basket full of crazy."

Trevor put a hand on his friend's shoulder. It was a warning move, and Riles knew it. Bobbie Faye's glance bounced back and forth between the friends as Trevor said, "Insult her again and I'll let her shoot you."

Riles *hmphed*, condescending, not the least bit intimidated, and Trevor noted how Bobbie Faye sized up exactly where she could put a bullet that would wound but not permanently damage him. *If* Riles was lucky.

"She's a better shot than you, you ass, so quit provoking her."

Riles's eyes narrowed, clearly questioning Trevor, and Trevor nodded—Riles had been his sniper in Afghanistan and there really weren't that many people alive better than Riles, and Riles knew it.

Which made Riles reassess Bobbie Faye, his expression grinding into a combination of curiosity and disgust, which Trevor knew his fiancée read as clearly as he did.

"I don't know what your problem is with me," she said to Riles, then lower, almost as an afterthought, "although it *is* Tuesday."

Trevor glanced at her, confused.

She shrugged. "Sometimes that's all it takes. Meanwhile, you had better be kidding about this."

"Not even close." The empty room amplified her breathing. Or maybe that rushing sound was her rising blood pressure. He was leaning toward the latter as her expression tilted into oh *fuck* no.

"I have had my fill of being watched." Especially by him. He had surveilled her for the better part of a year before they met (while he was undercover). She still wasn't happy about the fact that he'd had the chance to know her intimately before they'd ever gotten together.

"I need you to do this." His warm hands held her as he ducked his head a bit to meet her gaze. If he'd had time, he'd have gotten the surveillance equipment set up and she'd have had time to fully recover and he'd have made sure she was at fighting strength and shooting without hesitation and . . . fuck it, he was kidding himself. Even if he'd had months to prepare, he wouldn't want to do this. Hated leaving her more than he could tell her. He would have thought he wouldn't do this even under gunpoint.

Well, this mission was officially the gunpoint of the FBI saying, "You Will Come." He had no choice, especially considering what and who they were tracking.

"I thought you said this job isn't dangerous."

"Not to me. Not right now. And I need to keep it that way. I'm asking you to trust me."

"I'm *fine*."

He arched an eyebrow. She was far from *fine* and she knew he knew it.

"We have two former casserole dishes, eleven broken plates, and three shattered glasses that beg to differ." He did not have to mention the two kitchen fires or the time last week when she shot out the kitchen window because a branch scraped against the side of the house. (He'd pruned all of the trees since then.)

"I am not jumpy," she said, picking up on what he was implying. "Those casserole dishes were just committing hari kari, I can't help that part. And I'm *not* hurting. I can even spar with you."

"One takedown does not make you ready for prime time."

"She got a takedown? On you?" Riles asked, practically swimming in incredulity. "Wuss."

She shot Trevor an *are you* sure *he's your* friend? look after Trevor pointedly glared at the man and Riles wandered off to gaze out the living room window.

"You can't expect to give me a baby-sitter every single time you have to go to work, Trevor," she said, putting a little distance between them, her arms crossed. "I mean, Jesus, what's he supposed to do? Blind people?" She waved toward Riles's outfit.

"You should see the armadillo pants." Trevor reached for her, touching his forehead to hers. "Would you humor me?" He dropped his voice, pitched just for her hearing, though he knew Riles was eavesdropping. "You *are* still jumpy, and with good reason, and the security system here isn't finished."

What he didn't say was, "And you're still having nightmares."

He knew she couldn't stay with her sister. Lori Ann was impossible to live with, though he knew Bobbie Faye missed her niece. She couldn't stay at Nina's—she had contractors in and out, remodeling, which made security iffy, and Trevor was not able to screen multiple laborers right now. He knew Ce Ce's was out—Bobbie Faye still felt guilty over the cost of the last disaster and Ce Ce had just now finished all of the repairs to the store.

Bobbie Faye stewed.

Then she glanced over at Riles as he ambled around the small room, scanning the barren white walls with an affectation as if he were at the Louvre. "*Love* what you did with the place," he said, ever so cheerful. "Minimalist. I *like* it."

Bobbie Faye glared at Trevor, who said, "Promise me you won't shoot him." Riles snorted behind them and Trevor angled a *for God's sake, behave* stare his direction.

"How about I just poison his kibble?"

Trevor's cell phone pinged a text message. He glanced at it and grimaced. "I have to go." He turned to Bobbie Faye. "Will you do this for me?"

He wasn't going to be able to think clearly if he didn't know for sure that she was safe. He let her see that in his expression.

She gazed at him, memorizing his face, and he wanted to reassure her that there was absolutely nothing to worry about. He pushed away from the temptation to tell her what he thought she'd like to hear, when he'd know it was a lie.

"Three days?"

"Three days."

"How bad can it be?" she muttered.

"I like gourmet kibble, by the way," Riles said from the other side of the room. "And room service."

"You'll get used to him," Trevor suggested. "No killing him. And no drugging." When she didn't answer, he leaned forward, cradling her face in his hands. "Promise."

She thought about it and sighed. Then rolled her eyes as she said, not-quite-convincingly, "Fine. I promise not to kill or drug your friend." And then as she glanced over at Riles, who was doing the cameraman frame-the-shot thing with his hands as he mocked their card table, she added, pointedly, "for three days."

He kissed her, then tugged her little t-shirt up, and, bending forward, kissed her scars. He grabbed his duffle bag and turned for the door before she could see his face.

"All employees being transferred to 'Bobbie Faye territory' will immediately cease referring to it as 'hell'—there is no crying in the FBI."

—Brandee Crisp, in an internal HR memo

Two

The mechanic examined the modified gas tank with care. Most people who knew him today would probably have been surprised that he actually had mechanic skills, since he went to the trouble of having his car serviced instead of doing it himself. After all these years, he couldn't tolerate grease underneath his fingernails, the deep stains embedded in the lines of his knuckles or coloring the tips of his fingers, his prints standing out in sharp relief like a drunken crosshatch etching. Even when he'd made a living as a mechanic, he'd hated the sharp, gagging smell of the gas; it reminded him of too much—too much pain, too much work to overcome, too much bitterness. Now he wore gloves, a Tyvek jumpsuit, and kept the work area in immaculate, surgical conditions.

He wasn't worried about being caught. He *planned* on being caught.

No, the precautions were for the new detonators, computerized versions which needed to be installed under pristine conditions.

He could have hired this installation job out, but loyalty was getting more and more difficult to buy and frankly, there was too much at stake. There was no way he'd risk someone else catching on to what he was doing to the gas tanks of the various pieces of equipment he'd rented. Rentals that would, eventually, have been traced back to him regardless of whether or not he was caught initially. He had no doubt about the ATF's ability to trace connections, tunnel through corporate veils, and find out that he owned a piece of the companies who regularly used this type of rental equipment. As soon as his name surfaced in that search, red flags would sprout all over the place—they would immediately suspect his involvement with the bombs. He had the motive. And now, the means. The ATF would be fools not to suspect him and he knew the ATF were no fools.

It had taken him years to set it up—he wasn't about to be sloppy about the technique now. It was essential that each tank appear to be completely normal. He only trusted his own eyes, his own sense of smell. His own attention to the smallest detail.

The gas tank lay on the workbench in front of him. It was a precision job; once the placement of his modification was complete, he'd reassemble the tank. Carefully, he attached the wires he'd cut to length to the C-4. After he had them connected, he'd work his magic, attaching the other ends to the relays, the backups, the trip wires, the computer timer, and ultimately, the detonator. He'd been a bomb tech, years ago. He'd made it a point to keep up with the latest technology, the latest methodology of stopping a device, and he knew how to take a normal bomb squad's expectations and use them. If someone tried to defuse his creation, they would end up hastening their own end. Oh, he'd leave warnings, inside the bombs. They'd be there, plain as day, a professional courtesy.

It didn't have to be this way. He knew that. He'd tried to solve the problem by other methods. Using every other legal channel, in fact. But he'd been left with no choice.

And now there was absolutely nothing that was going to stop him.

He glanced up and over to Chloë's urn, and thought, for the ten-thousandth time, that she would have at least loved the color: cobalt blue, like her eyes. He had to stop for a moment to breathe. Eleven years, and he still had to remind himself to breathe in, breathe out, put one foot in front of the other, try not to worry the family. Try not to be a burden to his friends. His employees. Chloë had faded to a dim memory for so many, even her closest friends, and the sharp, jagged truth of that sickened him.

He placed the tank back into the machine, screwing it into place, and worked for an hour with an airbrush technique to spread the grease and dirt until he was satisfied the tank looked identical to any normal tank with typical usage and wear and tear. He closed the lid of the machine and stood there, contemplating his perfect plan.

He pulled out a cross and said a prayer, asking God to please guide home the souls this machine would kill, to please keep them in His loving care, each and every one of them, because they didn't deserve this.

"How much trouble can that wan be?" Sean had said all those months ago. Fucking eejit, Lonan thought again for the millionth time. He'd tried to go with the crew on the last run, going after the diamonds. But Sean had been insistent he stay behind in Dublin and handle the Castle Brothers problem. They had been properly buried (if one could call being dumped in a low bog being *buried*), just in time for Lonan to learn Sean's crew had been shot and killed. In fucking Baton Rouge, Louisiana.

He hadn't even been able to claim their bodies.

And someone was going to pay for that.

Someone about five-foot-six, long brunette hair.

The crew was the only family he knew. Lonan had been Sean's right hand long enough to know how to make their organization work. Growing up in Tallaght, west of Dublin, Sean had taught them everything. They'd fought hard, fought dirty, and won. They were on the verge of international leverage in the arms business and the money—and lifestyle— that came with it. There were a couple of members of the team who seemed to think he'd take over Sean's enterprise, when Sean was first arrested, but those feckless idiots did not understand family.

Lonan owed Bobbie Faye. He was very *very* good with payback.

* * *

"Six gross of nipple rings," Gilda said, and Nina looked up from the subtle display of her S&M magazine, *Branded*, fanned out on the ebony foyer table. "Are we giving these things away as prizes somewhere I should know about?"

Nina eyed her assistant, who was sleek in her gray Armani suit, her jet-black hair slicked back into a chignon. "Is this the same company that sent us three extra gross of butt plugs last month?"

Gilda nodded. "All extra large."

"Extra large? That says something about either their perception of the South or of us specifically, but either way, I think I'm insulted."

"You want me to return them?"

"You checked the boxes already?" Nina meant checking for bugs, the electronic kind. This relatively new little S&M club, an offshoot of her magazine, was a cover—deeply hidden for a government agency which would pretend to be completely appalled and which would disavow the club (and the magazine's) existence as a covert entity, should anyone suggest a connection. And given the nature of their business, she wouldn't put it a bit past an enemy trying to record the conversations that went on in this ultra-private enclave. Although a butt plug as a recorder would just be *wrong*.

"All clear."

Nina followed Gilda from the opulent foyer with its creamy butter walls and black granite floors and into the warm honeyed tones of the living room. The Chagall on the opposite wall still soothed Nina. It had hung there for the three years of the magazine's reign and, when they'd expanded four months ago to include the club, she'd savored the juxtaposition of its class versus the business done just yards away from it.

"What would you like me to do with them?" Gilda asked, her pen poised above her clipboard.

"Send 'em back. And tell them that if they're determined to send me extra merchandise for use in the club, or for endorsement in the magazine, they have to clear it with you, first."

Gilda checked off that item on her clipboard and moved on to the next order of business.

"About Lavey's sister . . ."

"No."

Gilda grimaced at the abruptness of the answer, the small frown barely creasing her round baby face. Nina smoothed her own Versace suit—mostly nude sheathing with daring crisscross undergarments. "Absolutely not. She's abusive of our employees. I won't have her back."

"But Lavey's offering twice the fee." Two hundred thousand to buy his sister back into Nina's good graces.

"Tell him no, thank you, and not even at ten times the amount. I don't need the money." And this wasn't an ordinary business. The elite clientele only got in by referral, a very large fee, and because Nina wanted them there. Specifically, because there was *one man* she wanted there, and he had to believe the club was real, that there were other patrons, and that she was extraordinarily exclusive.

And that he was safe from blackmail.

She was there today because his appointment was in fifteen minutes. This was his third, and she was afraid they were running out of time.

"You have a call," Gilda said as the cell phone cupped against the clipboard chirped. She glanced at the caller ID and handed Nina the phone. "Your friend."

There was only one person in the world Gilda knew to accept calls from during business hours.

"Hey B," she said into the phone as the front buzzer rang early—the client—and Gilda moved to answer it, "Please tell me you're not hanging off something, about to plunge to your death."

"Sadly, not today. Am I interrupting any hot guys posing for photos?"

"No, not exactly," Nina said, as Gilda escorted the client in through the foyer. This client was middle-aged, fifty-six, white-haired, slight paunch but mostly fit, and fairly wealthy. He would be leaving through the one-way-only private elevator in the back of the club—preferred by the clientele because they were usually exhausted and had welts on them they had not had when entering. She sometimes wondered how the clients explained away the bruises to family or business associates. She returned her attention to Bobbie Faye. "I'm actually cooking."

"*Really*?"

"It happens." She'd already run the man's prints through every known law agency she had access to, but he seemed clean. She just had a pretty good hunch he wasn't. "A soufflé." Gilda escorted the man to the holding area, where he voluntarily disrobed in the glass booth. "We ran long on a shoot, and I'm in a friend's apartment. I'm trying to show off my mad skills and see if it's going to rise." Gilda put the cuffs on the man, his hands behind his back.

"You're kidding me."

Nina laughed. "Yeah."

"Okay, that was scary. And mean. Don't ever do that again."

"Not a problem." They shared a moment of silence, and Nina regretted not being able to tell her friend exactly what she was doing and hear the creative mockage she'd come up with. "So, you okay?"

"Sure. Except for Trevor getting called in and leaving me with a baby-sitter, I'm just peachy."

"A baby-sitter? Does Trevor have a death wish?"

"That's what *I* said." Nina listened while Bobbie Faye filled her in.

Damn. Trevor had called in Riles. *Fuck*.

"You can't paint the entire inside of the house while he's gone," Riles said. "Besides, we have to stay here and I don't want to smell it. Paint stinks."

"It does not stink. It's odorless paint." She rolled on the red. It was a deep red, very satisfying against the white trim. An old barn sort of red. "Though the smell's making me think of butter-cream icing."

"Which means it has a smell, you nut job, which means it stinks."

"Look, if you can't be helpful, you can leave."

"I was helpful."

"Patting down that poor eighty-year-old man in Home Depot was not helpful. I'm pretty sure he damned near had a stroke."

"He came at you with a drill. I'm supposed to keep you alive. And you missed a spot."

She turned to him, the paint roller in her hand. He sat in a lawn chair he'd bought—a chair he'd positioned just outside of her arm's reach with the roller—and boy, had he learned that the hard way. Though she was pretty sure the red blotch had improved the grotesque orange and green shirt. He sat there drinking water and spitting sunflower seeds on the drop cloth.

Trevor had been gone a whole day and already she'd had to lock up the duct tape and her own ammo to keep from using it on Riles. She was hoping that having to go through the extra steps of getting the key out of the barn to unlock the gun safe in the closet would give her a couple of minutes to remember that she'd promised Trevor that she wouldn't kill Riles.

She was beginning to think, though, that she could make that trek to the barn and back in under thirty seconds.

"Can't you do something else useful?"

"Sure, I could. But then I wouldn't be here to tell you that you missed another spot."

"What time is it?" she asked him, and when he didn't answer, she frowned at him. Many more days of Riles and her face was going to be stuck that way. It was day three. *Three.* Trevor would be home soon, and she could quit worrying. She wasn't worrying. She didn't want him to think she'd been worrying. She didn't want him to take that as lack of faith in his ability, because that wasn't it at all. Trevor had ability out the wazoo. She was simply concerned. Worrying? No. Maybe.

Manic. Maybe she was manic. She probably should have slept. But the bed seemed huge and empty and wrong and she hadn't been able to get comfortable. Painting was good.

"Time?" she asked again.

"Fifteen minutes after you asked last time. And twenty-five from the time before that. And you missed a spot."

"Thank you, Big Ben."

She rolled the paint on, a nice *schick shick shick* of fresh wet hopefulness onto the wall. Pale gray green was perfect for a living room. She'd changed her mind from the red. The red was too dark for a room this small; she didn't know what she'd been thinking. Neither had the Home Depot people, who sold her the primer she'd had to use to cover the red. Two coats of green. Pale gray green. Yeah, Trevor would like this.

"He's going to hate this color," Riles said.

"Shut up."

"It's the color of camo. He lived in camo for years. Trust me, he's going to hate it."

"It's the color of my eyes, he'll love it. What time is it?"

Why in the fuck she'd thought green was the right color, she didn't know. Butter cream—a perfect color. A "neutral." That's what she should have gone with. It was day four, and this was the right color and maybe yeah, maybe she should have slept, but really, who could sleep with walls the color of dying grass, it was a depressing color, and she didn't need 'depressing' right now, she was tense enough. Not that she was, you know, really tense but maybe sometimes, yeah, sometimes she was, and maybe she should have painted the primer again, but it had seemed like the butter-cream color was going to cover that stupid green well enough, except now the green showed through the hint of yellow in the "creamy" color and the whole room looked like it had been splattered with baby poo, but maybe one more coat would work and what time was it?

She rubbed her eyes and squinted at Riles and he intoned, "Six-thirteen," without her having to ask. Okay, good. Six-thirteen. Six. Thirteen. She looked back at him.

"A.M."

Okay, morning. Morning was good. Right? Right. Trevor

had said two days, and maybe three, and yeah, it was tipping over into the fourth, but she wasn't going to worry. She wasn't going to let herself even get to the same zip code as Worry because that might bring on an avalanche of bad karma, and she had already stacked up enough for a few lifetimes. Day four didn't mean that something horrible had happened, because really, he was fine.

She just had a bad feeling, that was all.

Please God, don't let her be starting down the shiny happy insanity of "visions" that her Aunt V'rai had. Don't let it be hereditary.

One more coat. That's all this needed, one more. Trevor was fine.

Riles, on the other hand, was not fine. That he was even still alive was a sheer freaking miracle and she wanted brownie points with someone, somewhere, dammit. He had followed her everywhere—to the kitchen, to the mailbox, to the bathroom—where he had stood outside (facing away) for her "protection"—and had sat in that fucking lawn chair while she painted.

"You missed a spot," he said again, and pointed.

She picked up the can of butter-cream paint, pivoted, and dumped it on his head.

Yeah, maybe she should have slept.

The mechanic parked across the street from the equipment rental shop, bouncing to a stop in the broken-asphalt lot of the sleazy strip club conveniently situated on the only road in and out of this area of chemical plants and parts houses, welding services and bolt suppliers. Dozers and backhoes and twelve-ton cranes rested shoulder-to-shoulder in a line on the white shale of the equipment yard. He watched as the rental company's employee off-loaded the last of the mechanic's modified pieces of equipment from the delivery truck. The employee snagged a clipboard from his dash and reviewed a checklist on the equipment, verifying it was ready to go out to the next customer.

Of course it was. The mechanic had made sure of that—

no problems, adequate number of hours added to the meter to give the appearance that it had been used—properly—but not overused, not in need of maintenance. Gassed up, oil at the appropriate level, ready to go.

Seven pieces of equipment. Seven bombs. He knew exactly where they'd been earmarked to go—he'd made sure of that himself. Once he'd had the idea, it had taken four years to work his way into ownership of the kinds of companies who'd use the same type of equipment that PF used. Four years to acquire enough ownership position to mandate which rental companies were used. Another year after that to cultivate the right sort of connections who could hack into PF and make sure that any orders for rentals were sent to the rental companies the mechanic's companies used.

Over the last three weeks, he'd made sure there were orders for seven pieces of equipment by PF. The requirements of each piece were very specific and not terribly common. He'd made sure his own companies had rented each piece first—and that the "release" date—the day he'd turn them in—coincided with the rental request from PF.

His modifications to each piece were nearly complete.

The bastards at PF were already dead. They just didn't know it yet.

PF. Poly-Ferosia. One of the biggest liquid chlorine producers in the state. A plant which was also one of the sole producers in the U.S. of two other chemicals used in plastics.

The plant that had killed Chloë.

Irony, he mused. Plastique explosives taking out the plastics plant.

PF was about to cycle up for a turnaround—a very intensive weekend of maintenance where they took the plant offline, replaced worn parts, valves, pipes, or whatever was needed—and did so as quickly as possible in order to get the plant back up and running in the shortest amount of time. One day of being offline cost the plant around fifteen million. Three days' maintenance was a staggering cost and companies sometimes put off the maintenance longer than they should in order to keep that profit rolling.

Maintenance was a necessary evil, though. Without it, there were leaks and safety problems—the very kind it had been Chloë's job to find. If PF had done the proper maintenance when they were supposed to, Chloë would be alive today. So it was fitting they were going to go out in a blaze doing what they should have done regularly . . . and had been doing regularly after Chloë's death—and the controversy his lawsuit stirred up—gave the media a bone to gnaw on and made the PF owners nervous about cutting corners again. Now, PF would be pulling in extra equipment all week long, getting all of their orders filled so that there'd be no delays once the turnaround began.

He'd studied them, over the years, studied everything about them. His attorney had done more than a hundred depositions on methodology and processes and, thanks to enough documents to fill an entire room, the two of them knew the plant better than anyone alive.

He knew the plant managers would be on location for the turnaround. He was going to notify them minutes before the first bomb blew—and he knew they would attempt to evacuate. Protocol, though, meant they'd be the last to leave. And he knew exactly where they'd be as they marshaled everyone else out of the plant and shut down all of the plant's processors and implemented their disaster plan.

Only then would he let them know they were trapped—with their only hope to admit what they'd done to Chloë.

Of course, that would be his one lie. There was nothing they could do to save themselves.

The plant's own first responders might figure out what was happening once it began, but by then, it would be too late.

Seven bombs.

He'd wanted eleven. He'd had everything in place, except the specific computerized detonators he'd wanted. He'd almost despaired of putting his final plan into place—he couldn't exactly take out an ad on Craigslist: DETONATORS WANTED. When the opportunity had finally fallen in his lap, he'd pushed for eleven—one for each year Chloë had been gone—but the financier could only get seven, and so he'd had to make do.

He'd put word out on the street. Word with one person, specifically, who knew the underworld, knew the arms market, and who was not in a position to double-cross him. And finally, his contact had brought him good news: someone had access to a supplier. They had the money to buy the detonators, and they were willing to do so as long as he completely blew the plant he'd proposed.

He'd examined the financier's motives. They'd make money, once the bombs blew and the market was affected, and he didn't even give a damn. If someone profited off PF's misery? Fine with him. He wouldn't be around to know about it anyway.

He watched as the rental company worker finished his checklist, tagged the equipment ready to go. Just as he walked back inside, the mechanic dialed the company from his cell phone, his number blocked so that it would show up as "unknown" on the rental company's caller ID.

"GPC Rental," a clerk answered on the first ring. One of the things he liked about them—they were prompt and efficient. Out here in the middle of a long stretch of highway, an area nicknamed the "chemical corridor," they were the only rental company left in business after the bad economy a couple of years ago. They could have farted around and taken advantage of their customers. They hadn't—they'd stayed prompt and competitive. If you were going to depend on timing, the last thing you want is an inefficient company who might screw it all up.

"Yeah, this is Talbot at PF," he said. "I've got a work order here says you're gonna be delivering a crane in the morning and I'm double-checking to make sure it's gonna be here."

"Just a second, sir, let me check."

The mechanic, his eyes closed, pictured the man pulling up the information on his computer screen, the purchase order confirming the order that, sure enough, a Mr. Jack A. Talbot had placed a couple of weeks ago. The crane would arrive a little early—a couple of days ahead of when it was needed—but Talbot—the mechanic's fictional type-A purchasing agent inside a company so big entire divisions were oblivious to the existence of entire other divisions (not entirely unlike the government)—would want it there on Thursday so he didn't have to spend Friday chasing it and worrying that his weekend plopped in front of the game would be ruined. It would be delivered and parked exactly where PF intended to use a crane next week. Only they wouldn't be around next week.

"Yes, sir," the clerk said, coming back onto the line, "we just got it in on the lot. It's checked and ready to go."

"You'll have it here by seven?"

"Yes, sir. Anything else I can get you?"

"Nope, son, that's all I need. Thanks."

He severed the call, tossed the phone onto the seat next to him, and pulled out the parking lot.

> "The judge wants to know why we let Bobbie Faye graduate the anger management class."
>
> "We liked breathing?"
>
> —Court clerks Jackie Kessler and Dakota Cassidy

Three

"Is the lot of it done?" the voice with the Irish lilt asked him an hour later, and the mechanic switched the prepaid cell phone to his good ear; he barely heard the lilt as he checked his hands and found a line of grease underneath his index finger. He needed to wash his hands.

"Yes, they're finished. The last piece was returned this morning."

"Sure, an' that's good work."

They hung up, and he ran the water in his sink. He scrubbed, pulling out a brush with stiff, short bristles and used it to dislodge the stubborn mark. Then he dried his hands, and washed them once more, for good measure.

They would remember Chloë; *remember, remember, remember* set up a resonance in his head. He knew they would remember him, as well. It's not how he'd intended to be memorialized, and some would be shocked. Horrified. His family would grieve.

It was what he had to do. He finally had an opportunity for justice, and he took it.

This was the first time in eleven years he couldn't bear to salute her photograph when he left the room. He hoped she'd understand.

Lonan leaned over the shoulder of Ian, their computer expert. The beautiful thing about technology was that money usually won the race, and he'd had money to burn on this project.

"He's placed the final order," Ian said, tapping the screen. His hands dropped to the keyboard, "An' I'm rerouting . . . now."

With a few keystrokes, the final piece of equipment's destination was changed. It wouldn't do to have their bomb-maker aware of the change yet—that would come in time and then they'd have to deal with the mechanic. But for now, he'd served his purpose.

The most important part of his plan—to have someone as a scapegoat for the bombs. Someone to deflect potential suspicion from Sean.

"You've the bomb techs?" Sean asked, triple-checking. They were going to get a little creative with the mechanic's bombs.

"In place," Ian nodded.

Why in the hell she hadn't thought of blue earlier, Bobbie Faye didn't know, but the blue rolled on over the (new) primer, which was over the butter cream, over green, over red, and finally, *finally*, she thought it might be working. Blue was *soothing*. The color of Trevor's eyes. That sort of blue that rocked you to sleep at night, soft swells on a peaceful lake, the kind of blue that—

"Bobbie Faye?" Nina asked from the speakerphone of Bobbie Faye's cordless. "B? You still there?"

"Oh. Uh. Yeah. Sorry. Distracted."

"You have to stop painting, B. Or at least start on another room."

"I think the blue works."

"Which you've said about a dozen times. When was the last time you ate anything?"

Bobbie Faye dipped the roller into the paint tray and made sure it was covered, then squished it onto the wall and rolled a "W" pattern. That's what those stupid home porn networks said to make—a "W" pattern—although why a "Z" pattern wouldn't work just as well, she didn't know. Or an "M" or an—

"B? Where's Riles?"

"Wednesday," Bobbie Faye said.

"What?"

"Wednesday. Ate some Godawful concoction Riles made. Really, the man is trying to kill me."

"B, Wednesday was *yesterday*. Put the roller down and go eat something."

"I will in a minute. I'm almost done."

"Where's Riles?" Nina asked again.

Bobbie Faye had to think about that for a minute . . . she peered around, and he wasn't in his chair. Then she remembered. "Oh, yeah. He's talking to the sheriff. Something about me making the Home Depot people cry."

"B, if I could come over there right now, I would."

"It's Thursday."

"I know."

"Six days."

"I know."

"He said three, *tops*. Three. He's very meticulous."

"I know, B."

"He's always early."

"I know."

"Pathologically early."

"He is a little scary that way," Nina agreed.

"He would know I'd be worried. And no one will tell me anything."

"I know. But I'm guessing that sometimes these things can take longer."

She tried to remember how many times Nina had said just that. "He'd have let me know, Nina. No way he wouldn't have let me know."

Nina didn't answer that one right away and Bobbie Faye stopped rolling. Stopped, right there, halfway through the latest "W" on the wall and listened to the silence on the other end of that phone. She could hear the crickets outside the house, hear the fucking birds *chirping*, hear Riles somewhere down the driveway talking to the sheriff, but Nina was silent. Because it was true—Trevor would have let her know if he wasn't coming home in three days. He'd have gotten word to her somehow.

"I think he'll be okay, B. Go eat something. Stop painting. Get some sleep. He's going to need you sane when he gets home."

"I don't think she was sane before he left," Riles muttered as he came in the door, making sure he stood outside the distance it would take for her to smack him with the roller brush.

Lonan, Ian, the rest of the crew, and especially Sean, watched the camera angle from the computer monitor as one of their hijacked pieces of equipment was delivered. The camera had been set atop the metal structure and Ian could control how it pivoted with a little joystick. They watched as the delivery truck backed in, and the final security checkpoint belched out two guards who examined the paperwork the rental company driver provided.

The paperwork would be in order. The mechanic would believe this piece was on its way to Poly-Ferosia, and he would see paperwork on line confirming that order. Ian had made sure of that—hacking into the mechanic's computer. Meanwhile, these guards would see a purchase order to replace a broken piece of equipment inside the facility.

"It's a fine piece of gear, Lonan," Sean said, eyeing the screen. "They'll never look inside—right?"

"Not likely. This one's too new, and the crowd's already building."

"And this is where the magic's done," Ian said, pointing to the screen as the guard reviewed the purchase order the driver provided. "He'll check his computer . . ." and Ian typed into his own, sending a signal to the facility's maintenance program—something so easily hacked, Ian had wanted to call and gloat. Facilities like this often firewalled their financial data with the best encryption and often thought of maintenance as a necessary evil, but certainly not a department vulnerable—or interesting to—hackers. "And there— he'll see the confirmation. And now he'll see where it's already been inspected by the dogs at the outer checkpoint." An invented report, Lonan knew.

They'd waited 'til today to make the delivery of this big piece of equipment—it would have been too interesting to the bomb-sniffing dogs which had been scheduled for the day before. Once the dogs were done, it was up to security to keep the place clear of any unlabeled, unexpected, nasty items that could be a potential bomb.

Oops.

One of the guards compared the order to his computer, nodded to the other guard, and they waved the driver in. Lonan could hear the *beep beep beep* of the reverse-engine warning as the big diesel truck backed into the shadow of the cavernous bay and he glanced over at Sean, who was wearing the first genuine smile Lonan had seen since the surgery to save Sean's hands.

Sean flexed his fingers now around an exercise ball in his right hand, his left grabbing Lonan's shoulder.

"Good job, me lad," he said, and Lonan nodded.

When Riles slept, Bobbie Faye showered, changed into jeans, and then chose one of Trevor's shirts—a startling blue that matched his eyes, and now the living room—to wear over a pretty lacy cami he'd given her. She sat for a while on the cold tile floor in front of the pantry, her head leaning on the doorframe. The shirt still had a lingering Trevor smell, and she crossed her arms on her knees, propped her chin there and breathed.

He'd alphabetized the food. Categories, subcategories. She closed her eyes, saw him standing in the cramped closet in his raggedy "Kiss the Cook" t-shirt, moving all of the chicken soup under "C"—not, God forbid, under "S" for soup or, had she had her way about it when carrying in the groceries, shoved onto the same shelf as the juice boxes because there was more room there . . . and then when he was done, she'd followed his t-shirt instructions. (They were going to have to replace that old tile on that rickety island with something a little more substantial.)

She wandered into the living room, napped on the floor, then woke and stayed there, trying to decide if the blue was such a great idea. It had *seemed* like the perfect choice, but maybe it was too predictable? Maybe the butter cream was better because it was a neutral. The Home Depot paint department manager had said the butter cream was a neutral (sometime before she'd caused the manager to hide in the storeroom, and she really was sorry about that), but what if she was just saying that to get Bobbie Faye out of her department? Or what if a woman saying "neutral" was really girl-code for "something guys resign themselves to" instead of actually being neutral, like beige? Would Trevor like the blue? What if he didn't, what if he thought it was awful? What had she been thinking? Maybe one more coat? One more? Maybe that would work, make it richer, more striking, and she wondered what time it was.

Some time later, she wasn't sure how long, she was aware of movement in the house again. "He'd have called," she said loudly, so that Riles could hear her—he was in the kitchen, making a sandwich from the sound of it. She wasn't sure how many hours she'd been lying on the floor, staring at the walls. She couldn't keep doing this. She'd have been better off at work. Shooting things. That was exactly what she needed to be doing right now, holding a loaded weapon while she was sleep-deprived and exhausted.

"He'll call you when he wants you to know something. If he wanted to come home, he'd come home, though at this rate, I'll be damned if he's not halfway across the U.S. by now, changing his name to hide from your female version of Jackson Pollock in there."

Bobbie Faye was absolutely certain she was going to break her promise to Trevor. It was not a question of *if* but *when*. "It's day *seven*. Something's wrong. I'm calling the Feds back."

"Didn't the last guy call you the Devil's Spawn?"

"He's gotta be off duty by now. I'm trying again."

She grabbed the cordless lying on the floor next to her and dialed. She'd gone through six people—all of whom assured her that they were not going to tell her a Single Damned

Thing—when Riles came into the living room, flapping paper at her. She hadn't bothered to get up from the floor yet, and he stood there, quite a few feet from the trajectory of a well-aimed cordless phone, and asked, "What's this?"

"What?"

He turned the piece of paper toward her and said, "This was on the refrigerator under your 'to-do' list."

"Oh. Ways to kill you. I brainstormed a bit."

He spread the pages out where she could see all three. Lots of diagramming involved.

"I was inspired."

He flipped it back, pulled out a red pen from his pocket, and doodled on her list. "Oh, look, you misspelled *hanged*. It's just one 'g' like *deranged*, a word I'm willing to bet you're familiar with."

"I was going for emphasis."

"Glad to know you have a hobby." He sat at the card table and pretended to consider the papers in a thoughtful, almost academic manner. "Yes, yes. I'm sure you need some sort of psychiatric help."

"I'm too busy with my murder-by-correspondence course, but I'll look into it." She needed to think about something else. Something that would shove the panic rising in her chest back down. "How'd you meet Trevor?"

"I believe someone said *hello* and we probably shook hands. Exciting stuff. You should be writing this down."

When Trevor came home, which had better be in the next five minutes or Riles was toast, she was going to ask him just exactly when he'd lost his mind and thought Riles being anywhere in the state of Louisiana was a good idea, much less driving her crazy in what was supposed to be her own home. Dipping her in a big vat of acid would have made more sense at this point.

"I'm going in to work," she said, getting up and heading into the kitchen to find her purse, "and you can be all super psycho guy over in a corner somewhere."

He followed her. "You're supposed to stay here. You're on vacation."

"Only if we spell 'vacation' 'h-e-l-l.' If I stay here, I'm going to paint that living room again."

"That's not going to work, by the way," he said, nodding toward her keys, indicating her car. "I disabled the battery."

She stopped, keys hovering midair. "You did what?"

"I disabled your car. You're staying home."

She slowly scanned the small kitchen, seeing without really registering the surroundings. A white (of course) curtain hung at the small kitchen window over the (white) sink, a set of (white) empty open shelves on each side, which Trevor had yet to fill with whatever it was that people used when they were the kind of people who cooked instead of making sandwiches for every meal, and there was a small clock she'd brought with her from her old place—a crazy plastic crawfish clock Stacey had loved. Then she saw what she'd been subconsciously searching for: the knife rack.

"Here's the thing," she said, all reasonable and virtuous as she turned back to Riles, "I agreed to three days. It's four clicks of crazy past that. I can't stay here."

"This is what he does, Batgirl, and you need to get used to it. He can't afford for you to go apeshit every time he's a few minutes late. It's part of the job—if you can't hack it, you need to do him the favor of getting the fuck out of his life."

"Annnnnnnnnnnd I've officially had enough. You want to keep me here? You'll have to stomp my ass to do it."

He scowled at her, grabbing the cordless as she attempted to call for a ride. Clearly, the Neanderthal had believed that talking tough would make her cave. Then he shrugged. "I'm not going to fight you. I, however, did not promise not to tie you up and gag you."

Bobbie Faye leaned forward on the cracked kitchen island, propping her chin in her hand, trying to plaster an innocent expression on her face. "Tell ya what. I'll agree not to go anywhere—today—if you win the toss."

"I'm not tossing a coin with you. The odds are too even."

"No, I meant a knife toss. You, Mr. Big Bad 'I was a sniper' Guy, *can* throw a knife, can't you?"

"Like I'm going to let you arm yourself."

"Oh. Sure. Okay." She shrugged. "Chicken."

Riles frowned at her again, knowing she was up to something. "So I'm assuming you have some talent throwing knives."

"I'm not too shabby. And I did promise not to kill you, so what have you got to lose? I haven't slept much, so surely with your training, you stand a small chance of winning."

If she'd known he was going to sulk so freaking much, she'd have let Riles get a little closer to winning that seventh round. They went two out of three, then three out of five, then five out of seven, and when she'd beaten him at every single round (they played fifteen), Riles finally had to concede. And Jesus, could the man whine. She was pretty sure, though, that it was the humiliating double-or-nothing round where she bet him the trip out against him having to wear normal jeans and a normal shirt that was irking the hell out of him. She probably shouldn't have humiliated him quite so much.

Maybe she could do it again tomorrow.

They stood now in Ce Ce's Outfitter store, a battered old repurposed Acadian-styled house complete with a porch spanning the front and about two billion little rooms added on haphazardly, half of which were accessed through a closet or by standing on one foot and singing the "Hokey Pokey" while rubbing one's ear. It was packed with more merchandise than most stores four times its size.

At the front near the door, was the checkout counter, where biscuits and gravy were homemade for the early morning fishermen. She'd been in charge of cooking the biscuits. Once. Ten fishermen getting their stomachs pumped later, Ce Ce had decided that Bobbie Faye's talents definitely lay elsewhere.

Off to the right of the counter leaned a few old red, chipped Formica booths, the red worn past the undercoat down to faded yellow plywood underneath. Ce Ce had an ancient TV mounted to the wall, usually tuned to the news and weather, but it was getting to the point that someone had to smack it every few minutes when it went all fuzzy.

Sometimes, she felt a little too much like that TV, as if the Universe thought she might not be focused enough and therefore needed to be smacked around regularly. She and the Universe? Not exactly on speaking terms right now.

Riles hovered.

If she thought the customer might like a Glock, Riles countered with a Kimber 1911.

If she said SIG, he said, "Walther P. Don't listen to her, she doesn't know what she's talking about."

When she tried to explain how to unload a Ruger, he took it away to demonstrate.

Trevor had still not called. The hours were ticking away. How the hell did people *do* this?

She picked up the phone to make another call and Riles took the phone away. The only thing that saved her from ripping his arms off and beating him with them was a timorous woman's voice warbling behind him, asking, "Am I dangerous enough yet?"

Bobbie Faye leaned a little to see around him to octogenarian Mabel Gill, who stood stoop-shouldered, propped on her walker, holding a spatula from the BBQ section.

"I could smack her with it," she explained to Riles, who appeared, for the first time, a little helpless.

Bobbie Faye would give up her next paycheck to see that expression permanently etched on his face. As it was, she settled for the temporary revenge. "Oh, of course, Miz Mabel could definitely hurt me," Bobbie Faye said, smiling sweetly at Riles. "You have to frisk her again."

"Payback is going to be a bitch," Riles muttered just within her hearing as he turned to the woman. "Arms forward, Mrs. Gill," he said and the woman beamed.

"Be careful," Bobbie Faye added. "She hides stuff in her girdle all the time."

Riles scowled at her, and Bobbie Faye made a mental note to tell Miz Mabel where the flyswatters were located.

Four

She wanted to throw the damned phone across the store and watch the pieces rain down onto the floor, except for the tiny little detail of it then *really* not working, which just was not an option. *Maturity fucking* sucked. It was near the end of the day and she still didn't have any answers. Friday. Everyone going home for the weekend, no one on duty for her to harass for answers.

Bobbie Faye eased backward just enough to glance out of the storeroom doors and into the main store area, where Riles was surrounded by more than twenty little old ladies and their walkers. Miz Mabel had apparently called in friends, who closed in on him, demanding to be frisked. *Ha*.

"I can't scry for Trevor," Ce Ce said, grabbing her attention back to the moment, "because he's not a demon or a zombie."

Bobbie Faye looked in askance at her boss. "That's one of those 'good news/bad news' things all rolled into one, isn't it? Wait. Do I want to know why you started scrying for demons?"

"Probably not, hon. Luckily, I've only found three since I've been trying," Ce Ce gathered up the potions that she'd rummaged through. She and Bobbie Faye were in Ce Ce's storage room while Riles terrorized the customers.

"Yeah, but she's found seven zombies," Monique said, tagging along behind Ce Ce, catching vials as they fell from the crooks of Ce Ce's arms. Monique was Ce Ce's best friend, a pudgy, redheaded, freckled mom of four who had a wobbly sense of morality and a firm belief that mimosas were not just for breakfast anymore.

Bobbie Faye glanced from Monique, who always seemed earnest, even when she was trying to convince Ce Ce that she should add a stripper club to the store, back to Ce Ce, who carefully placed vials back in their unlabeled boxes. Only Ce Ce knew which vial contained what potion—a little anti-theft plan she'd devised because people were too afraid to experiment.

"Seven zombies? Seriously?"

"Only six." Ce Ce pursed her lips together, her black braids shimmying as she shook her head.

"I still think the governor cheated somehow," Monique added, pouting. "One little zap. Wouldn't have hurt much."

Bobbie Faye wasn't about to ask how they'd gotten in to see the governor, or why they weren't already sitting in jail. Some things were just better left vague.

"Here," Ce Ce said, holding a measuring cup to Bobbie Faye's lips, "spit in this."

There was something . . . gangrenous . . . about the inch-thick icky gel hunched in the bottom of that container. "You're kidding, right?" And when Ce Ce pressed the cup forward, Bobbie Faye leaned away a little and asked, "I'm not going to have to smear this on anyplace embarrassing, am I?"

"Trust me," Ce Ce said.

Bobbie Faye scowled, suspicious. The last time she'd trusted Ce Ce, she'd wound up painted *blue*.

"Hey, it protected you, don't argue with the juju."

Bobbie Faye spit into the cup, wherein the gel turned a nasty shade of orange. "Is that a bad sign?"

"Oh, hush. I'll be out there in a minute. I think you need to rescue Riles."

Bobbie Faye glanced back out at the gun counter, where the Ladies Auxiliary had just shown up in full force—thirty more women, all ranging from the ages of twenty-three to ninety-six—vying for Riles to frisk them.

It was the only thing getting Bobbie Faye through the worry about Trevor.

"Hon," Ce Ce said, waddling over to the gun counter, "wear this." Ce Ce snapped a stretchy bracelet around Bobbie Faye's wrist faster than she could say "ewwww" and Bobbie Faye gaped—there was a chicken foot attached. It was light yellow with an orangey tinge and smelled like the awful gel. "This is a bad juju detector," Ce Ce explained, showing her the match to it on her own wrist. "It'll turn black when you're in deep trouble."

"So, it's like a mood ring for the Criminally Stupid?" Riles asked, and Bobbie Faye zinged a gun safety pamphlet at his head. He ducked and she missed. Damned asshole had great reflexes.

Ce Ce frowned. "I know Trevor meant well, keeping you all protected with Riles, but this is going to work *much* better." She glared at Riles, who pretended to be mortally wounded and staggered around, clutching at his heart.

"I'll be fine. In fact," she nodded toward Riles, "he's probably the only one here who'd really like to see me dead or maimed."

"*Here* being the operative word in that sentence."

Monique plopped a bunch of fabric sample cases on the glass gun countertop and made flirty googly eyes at Riles. Of course, Monique was probably four flasks to the wind at that point, so no accounting for taste. "Can you wait to maim her 'til after the wedding?"

Ce Ce immediately shushed her best friend, scooped up the sample cases, and led Monique away with, "So, how are we on supplies?" and Bobbie Faye knew Trouble had just handed her a special delivery.

"What wedding?" she called after their retreating figures.

"Oh, nothing, nothing, hon," Ce Ce said, and Monique slapped her hand over her mouth (Monique had Compulsive

Disclosure Syndrome), and Bobbie Faye knew Something
Bad Was Up.

"Monique? Spill."

"Hon," Ce Ce said, "remember that time in eighth grade
when you were just absolutely positively sure you wanted to
know whether or not Mark had been out behind the school
kissing Emmy Lou? This is like that. You'd rather not know.
Monique and I will just . . . go over here," she waved toward
the other side of the store, "and, uh, sort. Merchandise. Got
a lot that needs sorting."

They tried scurrying off, but Bobbie Faye asked, "Monique? Wedding?"

Monique squeezed her pudgy fingers over her mouth, and
all Bobbie Faye had to do was lean forward as if she were
going to ask again when the woman blurted, "Marcel says
he's driving you to his and Lori Ann's wedding!"

"What? Lori Ann and Marcel? What the *hell* is she thinking?" Bobbie Faye didn't even know her sister was *dating*
Marcel. The (supposedly) former right-hand man to Bobbie
Faye's gunrunning ex, Alex. Alex, the original Boyfriend
from Hell. Marcel had started tricking out monster trucks—
he'd said it didn't pay as well as being a gunrunner, but not
quite as many people shot at him anymore.

"He's having one of the trucks specially painted to deliver you to the church. Something about a white Godzilla."
Ce Ce smacked her arm. "Or something, I maybe got that
part wrong," Monique amended.

"I am *not* riding in a truck with Marcel." Fuck. Fuck fuck
shit fuckity *fuck*. Because right, let's focus on the important
part, the truck. Geez. Lori Ann was engaged? "How in the
hell had this happened?"

"He's a lot better than the rodeo clown," Ce Ce offered,
trying to help put a positive spin on the notion.

"That one was annulled," Bobbie Faye said.

Ce Ce kept going with the helpful reminders. "Her second husband—that encyclopedia salesman—was a lot worse
than Marcel."

"When Marcel caught the flu and couldn't buy ammo for

a couple of weeks, the bullet manufacturers sent 'get-well' hookers," Bobbie Faye reminded them. "Not exactly brother-in-law material, there."

"True, hon, but at least he doesn't think aliens are using non-dairy products to take over the world."

"Yeah," Monique agreed, "that second husband was a real firm believer in butter. I think I still have some he gave out. He wasn't that good of an encyclopedia salesman, but he had real good butter."

"I'll bet they just hand out incompetency hearings like candy around here," Riles said, not really under his breath. He still hadn't given her ten feet of breathing space.

"But Marcel quit," Ce Ce continued, trying to argue Lori Ann's case. Bobbie Faye had a sneaking suspicion that Lori Ann had promised Ce Ce she could do the decorations if Ceece could convince Bobbie Faye not to go ballistic over the news. "He's not a gunrunner anymore."

"Oh, yeah, that's a huge plus for the guy who might be helping to raise my niece: not having a stash of automatic weapons in the back of the minivan is everyone's idea of a good stepdad. Not to mention that being a former gunrunner means he's *entirely safe* from all of those pesky other gunrunner competitors who wouldn't possibly hold a grudge because they're all so kind and loving and hug-the-world types. At least his school excuses could be creative: Dear Mrs. Alexander, please excuse Stacey from school today—she's helping me oil all of the AK-47s."

It was not as if Marcel had had some shining epiphany about being a law-abiding citizen and just quite his little entrepreneurial endeavor out of the goodness of his heart. She'd feel a whole lot better about Marcel quitting moving guns if it hadn't conveniently happened at about the same time Trevor and a few of his FBI colleagues, along with the ATF, disappeared into the swamp and came out with Alex, in cuffs. Alex, who'd eluded the police and Feds for-freaking-ever. She was pretty sure *that* had something to do with the fact that she'd sort of inadvertently exposed a couple of Alex's hideouts when she first met Trevor. (Oops. Except, you know, *not*).

Bobbie Faye had exactly zero love lost for Alex. In fact, she sort of wished she'd known about his arrest ahead of time, because she would have hand-decorated the cuffs.

"Oh, that reminds me," Monique added, "Marcel said everything but the tires will be bulletproof! Isn't that great?"

Bobbie Faye would have followed up on that, except she saw a familiar someone lurking in the camping gear aisle.

"Oh, hell no," she muttered as Riles surprised her and went on super-alert, his gun out and up and aimed at the young man hovering nearby in the faded purple LSU shirt. Nick.

Nina sat in the control booth, observing. Gilda took notes as they watched the live video spooling from the various rooms. There was enough betrayal and self-loathing pouring out to overfill the moon and slop a bit on nearby stars.

They winced in unison at screen #5.

"That hurt," Gilda mumbled.

"Yes, it did," Nina agreed.

They turned their heads sideways, tracking the action on the screen.

Nina leaned forward and keyed a microphone. "Heidi, we kinda want him still alive."

The Amazon-sized Heidi, near-to-bursting from her tight leather dominatrix costume, barely paused from the pain she was inflicting to nod at the camera.

Nina leaned back as Gilda said, "Heidi may have anger management issues."

"Don't we all."

"She's up for psych eval."

"She gets results. That's what I need." Then she heard something on screen that sent a chill through her. "What was that?"

"I'm not sure." Gilda turned to the computer, rewound and replayed the footage. "I think he said something about bombs."

Nina drummed her manicured nails on the desk. She'd been waiting for this. Waiting for the man to shatter. He was looking for an excuse to, he was plate glass lining himself up with a wrecker ball. She was pretty sure it was guilt pushing him. His background was a little too immaculate. He'd been powerful too long to give in easily; he wanted to be forced.

He'd said *bombs*. Specifically, he'd supplied detonators for bombs. Computerized detonators, Nina suspected, given what the man did for a living.

Then he said another word . . . this time a name, and Nina sat forward again, every single cell intent. He'd said *Bobbie Faye*.

Nick the bookie was more chubby-cheeked dimples and blue-eyed wholesomeness than your average boy-next-door, and came complete with a tan left over from a summer of fishing and a bright smile that would con the underwear off even the most conservative Southern belle. His gee-whiz aw-shucks tucked-chin manner had gotten him out of high school detentions on a regular basis and, Bobbie Faye knew, gave him that air of complete trustworthiness that had cata-pulted him to wealth with his not-so-tiny bookie business. Right then, he stood on the business end of Riles's Kimber 1911 and was coming to the sudden and complete epiphany that fake innocence did not make him bulletproof. For just one itty-bitty moment there, she had the completely evil thought about encouraging Riles to make that point even clearcr, except that Nick wasn't a physical threat as much as he was a pain in her ass. No, he was just the scum-sucking wart of a dirtbag, the pus of a giant zit on the ass of a rat, aka the guy who made book, Vegas-style, on her during every disaster. He'd gotten his start, in fact, keeping odds on her—whether she would live or die, and if it was "die," then exactly how, to the minute, and the bettor had to be specific— thank God. There was a growing contingent of disgruntled gamblers who had been sending her nasty notes because she had the audaciousness not to croak in their preferred manner.

"Oh shit," Nick said, bouncing on his toes, nerves jangling

louder than the change in his pocket. "Oh shit. Don't shoot. Oh shit."

"What the hell are you doing here?"

"Look," Nick said, swallowing hard and trying to pretend the end of Riles's Kimber wasn't perfectly lined up with his brain, "I just had to see why the bets were up." When she blinked blankly at him, he leaned in a little, twitching. "You know. The *odds*."

"What odds?"

"Um, well. You know." His voice dropped lower. "The *bets*." Sweat beaded on his brow and trickled down his neck. "Usually, you're all over the news before the betting gets really heavy, but now, it's super quiet and I can't tell what you're up to, so I can't tell just how to cover the spread."

"Oh, I'm sure she's the kind of woman who always covers the spread," Riles said.

She went rigid, glaring, fingers flexing, tingling to pick up the loaded Ruger from behind the display case.

"New rule!" Ce Ce called from a couple of aisles over. "No shooting in the store!"

Bobbie Faye turned her attention back to the vacant spot where Nick had been. She saw his fingers white-knuckling the top edge of the counter and she leaned over to get a better view of him as he crouched. "Get up, Lucy. You have some 'splainin' to do."

He stood, and his hands shook. He tried to hide them in his pockets. He'd never, ever, been insane enough to show his lying, cheating, gambling, lowlife, lucky-to-still-have-all-his-parts face since he'd become a bookie. Nick darted his gaze between her and Riles.

"Talk." She could smell the fear on him from three feet away.

"There may be a few big bets against you," he half-whispered.

"You came all the way over here for just a few bets?"

He flinched and bowed his head. A guilty puppy would have been more aggressive. "Um. Maybe more than a few."

She spread her arms, palms down on the countertop to

keep from shooting him, and she leaned forward a little and asked, "How bad is it, Nick?"

"Oh, not too bad," he lied, licking his lips again.

"Against?" Riles asked. "And how does one get in on this action?"

"Shut up." Like that would have an effect on Riles. Short of duct tape (which, come to think of it, wasn't a bad idea), she hadn't been able to get the man to be quiet. "Last time I'm asking you nicely, Nick. How bad?"

She was just off balance enough to use him for target practice. Maybe it was the worry over Trevor, she wasn't sure, but if there were a lot of bets going on right now when things were quiet, then something was deadly wrong. Couple that with Trevor's radio silence, and it could not be a good thing.

"Um, pretty bad," he finally answered her.

"What the hell is going on that a bunch of people think I'm going to croak?"

There was an odd hesitation in Nick, and his gaze hopscotched over everything except Bobbie Faye. He even settled a moment on Riles's gun, as if he would almost prefer to be shot right then instead of having to answer that question, and Bobbie Faye seriously considered obliging him.

"You've had big bets against me in the past. Still here, still ticking." The only thing that saved her—and which saved his ass right now—was that the bets had to be super-specific— an unusual death or dismemberment in a certain way at a certain time—and Nick was careful that it had to be an accident, not a hit, or she'd have been dead a long time ago.

As would he, because Cam—her ex, a state police detective—would have probably killed him. If Trevor didn't do so first.

"You need a new line of business." He wisely nodded, but the situation didn't add up, him being here, telling her this. Now. "So why's this time different?"

He shook his head, lips clamped closed, knowing that exposing his clientele was a line he'd be very wise not to cross, because as a bookie, one of the things he guaranteed was his clients' anonymity.

"You know I can't tell you that, Bobbie Faye," Nick said, pleading. He'd probably end up with his own kneecaps broken.

"Sure you can."

"He'll shoot me."

"What makes you think he won't shoot you if you don't talk?" she asked.

"Oh, not *him*," Nick answered quickly, nodding toward Riles. "A different *him*."

Bobbie Faye propped her elbow on the counter, giving Nick a good imitation of relaxed, all while her hand closed on that Ruger. "I don't think your odds are a lot better here if you *don't* answer. And if you're afraid to tell me the name, then I must know him."

Nick's eyes widened, his jaw dropped open, and then he slammed his mouth closed. So that was a *yes*.

"Is it someone who recently tried to blow me up?"

Riles snorted. "I'm sensing that wouldn't really narrow it down for you." But he stepped up and put some sort of Ninja warrior whathootsie hold on Nick's shoulder and Nick slammed to his knees. "Tell the Walking Disaster what she wants to know."

"He knows where I live," Nick said, genuinely scared.

Who did she know who had enough money to place big bets, big enough to worry Nick? Who knew where Nick lived?

One person came glaringly to mind. "Alex?" she asked, and Nick turtled his neck down and arms and legs in, trying to make himself as small as humanly possible, which wasn't all that easy for a guy who was probably five-ten and two hundred thirty pounds.

"Oh, you have got to be fucking kidding me." Alex.

"I didn't say a name," Nick pointed out. "If anyone asks, I never said a name. You guessed. I can't help what you guess."

"This time he is so dead." Or maybe she finally would publish those love poems to her he'd written and was now humiliated over. The local paper had a blog. They would soooooooo put up poems from a gunrunner. (She had given back the originals as promised. She never promised not to make copies.)

"*This* time?" Riles asked. "You've tried to kill him other times?"

"No," she said, but Nick nodded. "No," she re-emphasized.

"You blew up his car," Nick pointed out. "On purpose. When you were aiming for his house."

"I knew he wasn't in the house. Or the car. And frankly, he's lucky that's all I did." She felt she'd been all restraint and merciful.

Riles gaped at her. Horrified. He was a former sniper for Special Ops and he had the nerve to look at her as if she was some sort of aberrant quirk of human nature.

"He's her ex," Nick supplied for Riles.

"Her ex? Hold on . . . *you* tried to kill *a cop*?" Riles asked, apparently having been filled in by Trevor on just who her most recent ex was. Detective Cameron Moreau, state police, and weirdly, still in her life. Once they had been best friends, then lovers, then furious enemies, and now? Now, he wanted her back, and she was so confused about him, just thinking his name made her head hurt.

"No, not *that* ex," Nick said, helpfully. "The *other* one."

"You have more than one angry ex you want to kill?" Riles asked. "Do you like, what? Get a free toaster oven when you reach a half a dozen?"

There was a collective gasp from the staff and customers hidden in the aisles, and then a couple of nervous giggles, then dead silence. The hum of the ancient overhead fans chopped through the air, but not a single other thing dared make a sound. It was as if the whole world needed CPR.

She glanced around and sure enough, every customer plus Ce Ce, Monique, and the twins who worked the front counter, Allison and Alicia, were all diligently examining goods on the aisles around her gun counter. In fact, the word "diligent" would have been quite proud just then, because they were collectively holding their breaths, waiting for Bobbie Faye to spontaneously combust, and while they didn't want to be in close proximity, they definitely wanted to be witnesses.

"No, not *Cam*. *Alex*," Nick explained when Riles looked over at him for an explanation. "Alex is a gunrunner. Pretty scary. They had a very bad break-up."

"You dated a gunrunner?" He'd tossed her looks of disgust with the regularity that a machine gun spit bullets. It was getting so that she was immune. "And then a cop? And now *my friend*?"

"It wasn't like I was asking for their résumés and references."

"Is there some sort of Excel spreadsheet to keep track?"

She ignored Riles and asked Nick, "Where is he?"

"I don't know," Nick said. "No, really, Bobbie Faye, you know how Alex is. He shows up when he shows up."

"Yeah, kinda like cancer."

"But that's not the weird part," Nick mumbled, staring down at his shoes.

"It gets weirder?" Riles asked.

Ce Ce moved out of the aisle, giving up all pretense of stacking shelves, too eaten up with curiosity to risk missing a syllable. "Oh, hon, it always gets weirder."

Bobbie Faye leaned forward, eyes narrowed on Nick. This was going to be bad. She could tell from the way he twitched and avoided her gaze, sweat now running in rivulets down his tanned neck, into his shirt collar.

"There's also a bunch of bets against your fiancé."

Five

Cam would not answer his phone. Three billion calls to him went straight to his voice mail. She didn't know when it was declared National Ignore Your Phone Week, but really, she wanted to beat the living shit out of the person who organized it.

Sure, dispatch had said he'd been working late nights and early mornings, but usually he answered his private cell number.

They rode in Riles's Jaguar. The pumpkin-orange Jaguar. She doubted even Jemy or Claude would have stolen this one, back when they five-finger-discounted car parts. Riles hung up his cell and was quiet. Too quiet.

"They're not telling you anything either, are they?"

He'd worked with Trevor. He was a sniper. She knew he had federal connections.

"They don't know where he is. Or, put it this way, they don't know for sure why I'm calling, or why I don't already know, so they're not going to volunteer his location."

They'd already gone by the FBI satellite office—nary a soul in sight—and now they pulled up to Cam's gray-in-the-twilight house. It was in a sweet little neighborhood that backed up to a horseshoe lake, dark now except for evenly spaced gas lamps installed by the neighborhood along the walking path that surrounded the lake's perimeter. Of course, the lake brought with it snakes and mosquitoes. Cam had been especially proud to have killed a couple of rather large water moccasins in his backyard the first couple of months they'd dated. Until she refused to set foot outside. He suddenly, miraculously, never saw another snake again. They had all magically migrated to the house a few lots down, where that guy and his shotgun were best friends.

"So this is where your boyfriend lives?"

"*Ex*, you jerk. And wait here. I'll only be a few minutes."

Riles climbed out of his car and met her on the sidewalk before she'd gone two steps. She stopped, glaring at him. Not that a serious poisonous glare would actually work on a sniper.

"Look, the Feds aren't telling you a damned thing, no matter how fancy schmancy your stupid clearance was, and they're not talking to me. Cam might get some answers, but he's not going to put himself out on a limb if you're hovering. Back. Off."

She couldn't squelch the horrible feeling that Trevor's life hung in the balance and there was nothing she could do about it. That the Universe thought she was just going to stand around and wait, all damsel in distress, "Why sorry, sir, I'll kindly fret over here in the corner so as to not disturb you."

Not. Going. To. Happen. She might as well plan to sprout wings.

Agents *died*. It was a fact of life. For someone to be placing heavy bets against Trevor suggested his cover had been blown. And usually when someone's cover was blown, they were the last to know, hence the whole "blown" manner of speaking.

"Ten minutes," Riles snapped, and she ignored him as she approached and then knocked on Cam's door. No answer. No conveniently un-draperied window to peer into. She walked around the side of the house, stood on tippy-toes to see into the garage and made sure his truck was indeed parked there.

Which was odd. He never slept that soundly and he wasn't currently mad at her. He didn't want her to marry Trevor, but he was definitely still speaking to her. She thought.

In fact, he was being downright sneaky, because he was being *nice*. And *fun*. And *charming*.

She went to the back door, knocked, and there was still no answer, which—seriously?—just freaked her out. He was as bad as Trevor for his ability to hear a spider hiccup at thirty yards, much less her banging on the back door. Hell, just a car in his driveway should have gotten him out of bed. She keyed her old code into the alarm system, banking on the fact that Cam would have changed his own personal code fairly frequently, but not hers.

He'd said she could always move out, move away from Trevor, if she changed her mind. Come "home."

The alarm flashed to green. When she stepped inside, the kitchen was pretty much as she remembered: it smelled like coffee (Community Coffee, dark roast, no sugar). There were light-colored oak cabinets, deep green tile that registered as black in the late evening light, and randomly stacked batches of mail, tools, and camping crap on every flat surface. "Cam?"

She flipped on the light as soon as she stepped inside, hoping like hell Cam wasn't about to spring out and surprise his "intruder," but it was silent, except for the steady hum of the refrigerator. She eased past piles of junk (holy geez, he was always bad, but this was worse), guns, gun parts, computer guts, and catalogs for every conceivable thing that could be purchased under the sun.

"Cam?" she called again, louder this time, spooked, easing through the kitchen into the dining room where fishing gear covered the old antique table he'd gotten from his grandmother's estate when she passed. His grandmother would have been horrified to see the sharp hooks dangling off the sides of that beautiful wood, just inches away from her polished-to-a-gleam finish. Next to the hooks: a fifth of Jack, empty, at the end of the table where he'd cleared a spot to eat. A single spot, amidst the lures. She turned away, feeling a pressure in her chest she didn't quite want to identify.

He didn't normally drink, and if he did, it might be a beer or two. Well, he didn't used to drink. And maybe that had been on her account, since he knew she was always waiting, always holding her breath that she was going to have to pour someone else into bed and mop up the disasters in their wake. Of course, *used to* were the operative words there. A lot had changed.

Hurry, she thought, calling his name again, knocking on the wall along the hallway, flipping on lights as she went. He must be freaking dead to the world to not hear her and have come storming out. . . .

Dead . . . hung there in the air in a little bubble over her head as her brain crunched out inarticulate syllables, trying to process what she saw as she stood in the doorway to the master bedroom: Cam, dark hair nearly jet black, longer than usual, grown long enough now to flop over his brow as he lay sprawled on his bed face-up, half covered by wine-colored sheets, his long frame catty-cornered to the head-board, his right arm dangling off the side. Motionless. There was no rise and fall to his chest, no hint of hearing her, no flinching at all when she turned on the overhead light.

Panic said *welcome to here* and maniacally mainlined adrenaline as Bobbie Faye shot across the room, her hand automatically reaching for the center of Cam's bare chest. Warm. A slight rise as he pulled in air. *Thank God*. Relief flooded her as she reached her other hand up to stroke his cheek, and said, "Cam?" so lightly, afraid of—

—holy shit. He yanked, hard, flipping her over, the room spinning as she fell and slammed against his mattress. She struggled to get away from his whiskey-warm breath against her face. She muttered "Ugnf," and "Cam, dammit, wake up!" and tried to push off his body, his very naked, *completely devoid of clothes* body, long and lean and *hard* against her—a hard body that reacted to every move she had with a countermove that locked her more and more firmly beneath him.

Holy freaking *geez*, she'd forgotten he'd been on the wrestling team every year in high school, once the football season ended.

He stilled, suddenly, as he finally, groggily, swam back to

awareness, up through the whiskey blur, trying to focus his brown eyes on her face as she fought to squirm out from under him, and then he whispered, "Aw, baby, you're home," and she knew he wasn't completely awake yet as he kissed her.

"Cam!" she snapped as his lips grazed hers, her body stiff with consternation and shock and familiarity and guilt *and shock* and *she was going to have to explain this to Trevor* and *oh, God, Trevor would kill him*, "Wake up, dammit!"

And he did.

She watched his gaze shift from fuzzy to clear, brows slanted in confusion and then for a brief second, pleasure, then Reality slammed a home run as he became aware that he was not only holding her down, pinned, but that he was naked and aroused and she was angry.

"Jesus," he said, pushing away as she sprang from the bed. "Sonofabitch." He rolled up into a sitting position, still not covered, shaking his head as if trying to dislodge the grogginess. "What the hell are you doing here?"

"You didn't answer the door." Way to state the obvious. She could still feel heat where his lips had grazed hers, still feel the fear pumping through her body that he was dead, adrenaline racing around her heart like a trapped wild animal, gnawing its way out.

"Was I expecting you?" He glanced at his bedside clock, the one she'd given him six Christmases ago.

"Since when have you been drinking so much that you don't hear someone knocking on the door, Cam? I knocked all the way through the freaking house." She shook, she was so angry.

A *you know since when* look settled in his brown eyes as he glanced at her left hand and yep, the ring was still there, and with all of those diamonds and rubies, it felt like it weighed about eleven billion pounds just then. She was surprised the entire planet didn't just tip over. *Way to lead with the stupid question first.* Because he didn't owe her that explanation, and she was hyperaware of it.

Without a stitch of shyness, he let the sheet drop as he reached for his jeans at the foot of his bed. And then, whoa, she pinged on the fact that he was still naked, sweet baby Jesus, and she yelped as she spun around to face the wall.

He laughed, low, wistful. "You've seen me naked plenty of times, baby." She could hear the slide of his legs into the jeans.

"I'm not supposed to see you naked." She didn't add the automatic "anymore" to the end of that sentence because it felt like turning a knife, and she'd done enough damage for the night.

"So I repeat, was I expecting you?"

"No. Well, I don't know, in your crazy macho-cop know-it-all world, maybe you did this, maybe you know what's going on and you're having a great laugh here, but really, I'm so going to kick your ass if you are."

"Okay, that was English and actual words and I think it may have even been a sentence, but what the hell it meant, I have no idea."

She heard him zip the jeans and she turned around, try-ing not to let her gaze drift over the acres of muscles of his well-toned upper body, because clearly he'd been working out, working off some of his excess energy, since she knew he wasn't dating. He reached for a shirt and muscles rippled and her brain sent up warning flares to *stick to the point, you moron.* "I need your help." She watched him go from *sur-prised* to *pleased* to *what's the catch* in about a nanosecond. "I think Trevor's in trouble."

Cam held a chocolate-brown button-down shirt in his hand, frozen midway to reaching an arm into a sleeve, and he stared at her. The hard *you gotta be fucking kidding me* cop stare. She'd hated it ever since he'd used it on her when he was in tenth grade and he found out she'd kinda sorta deflated Shelley Henderson's tires (Shelley kept trying to get Bobbie Faye framed for extravagant misdeeds so she'd get detention—mostly because Bobbie Faye's boobs were bigger).

Bobbie Faye really hated that glare.

He stood there motionless for nearly a full minute, anger boiling beneath the cold landscape of his expression. She could practically see the smoke billowing from his ears as the gears ground.

"So you came *here*." He finally moved to slide his arm into the shirt, and looped it over his back, pushing the other arm through, flexing his shoulders, battling the tension. The glare he gave her—hot and hard—made her throat ache from slamming back the emotion. He didn't bother to keep the incredulity out of his voice, pitched with the intimacy only a former lover could use. "Just so I'm clear here, you are asking me . . . your ex . . . who should not be your ex, by the way, to *help you find* your current *fiancé*? Am I getting this right?"

She swallowed hard. She knew what she was doing to him. Hated it. Couldn't stop.

"Yes."

He studied her then with a hot liquid gaze that ran from her toes to the crown of her head, warmth flooding her as his eyes held the memories of them making love right here, in this room—hell, all over this house—the memory of fitting together. He knew all of her and everything and sometimes, he knew nothing at all of who she was, and she saw that, too, as the warmth of his expression plunged to icy. Their break-up had been bad and mean and cutting, the way two people can do when they know each other's vulnerabilities and want the other person to do the changing. There should be a Richter scale for that level of fury, and he'd been the one to reject her first, had been the one to push her away when she'd later approached him. He'd told her, point-blank, he hadn't wanted to love her.

Until he realized he did. And wanted her back. Wanted her to think of Trevor as rebound, as a rushed, awful choice because he'd shut down.

He took a step forward, proprietary, angry that she hadn't come to her senses, the dullness of the whiskey cut away by his fury.

"Have you noticed yet that he's an FBI agent? With about ten thousand other agents and another thirty thousand in support staff that you could go to, and instead, you come here?"

"They won't talk to me."

"They're probably busy custom-designing your butterfly net right now."

"Yeah, Cam, go ahead and make this easy." She crossed her arms, returning his glare.

He sighed, running his hands through his hair, which was, thankfully, long enough to not stick up in Riles's perfected constant *holy fuck, who me?* surprised 'do. The cop in him battled the man—the part of him that was still her friend—and she could see that battle at work, him shoving the emotion aside for a moment as he asked, "What do you mean, he's in trouble?"

"He was only supposed to be gone a couple of days, and it's almost eight days now. Tomorrow morning will be eight. He hasn't checked in with me at all. And you know how he is about that damned phone going everywhere with him."

"That's not enough time to—"

"And Alex is apparently betting against me again. And against Trevor."

"Wait! Alex? You went to *Alex* before you came to *me*?"

She threw his disgusted scowl back at him and raised him an annoyed head shake. "I'm not insane, Cam. I'd never go to Alex for help. But I heard he's betting huge. And you know Alex—he only ever bets on what he thinks are sure things."

"And you know this because . . . ?"

"Nick showed up. Worried that he couldn't cover the bets."

Cam cursed. Hands on his hips, shirt hanging open, looking for all the world like he'd breathe fire on Nick the next chance he got. "I told him I'd arrest him if I had a single witness that could come forward."

"Well, you have a store full of them now, because everyone heard the conversation. Although it's all highly suspicious, for Nick to put himself in that position. There's no way for Alex to know what Trevor's doing, unless Trevor's cover really has been blown. And if Nick was going to make book on the fact that Trevor's cover was blown, why would he let me know that?"

"Unless he's hoping to spread the word, have other people start betting for Trevor, evening out the odds. Covering his ass."

"That's not a good enough reason to come tell *me*. Me, Cam. Think about it."

He tensed, comprehension dawning.

"It's an FBI case. Tell them what you know and they'll take care of this," he warned, moving to stand in front of her.

"Right, because I have such a great relationship with the FBI, they're sure to jump all over any tip I give them."

"Can you blame them?"

No, she could not blame them, but that did not mean she was going to wait around until something had already happened to Trevor. Cam clearly read her determination.

"Damn it!" He slapped his palm against the doorframe. "You *cannot* go blundering around into an ongoing FBI investigation."

"I won't be blundering, you idiot, if you're helping."

"No. Fucking. Way." He leaned a little closer. "I am *not* helping you get killed. And Alex is probably messing with you. Alex doesn't do a goddamned *thing* without an ulterior motive, and you know that."

"Are you going to help me, or what?" God, it galled her to have to ask him. Killed her.

And something in him snapped. She saw it with the way his eyes flared, just like when he'd been out on the football field, calling the last possible play of a game, coming from behind, digging in, *furious*. He put both hands on either side of where she stood, trapping her there as he angled in really close.

"*Or what*," he repeated, "I like that choice," his brown eyes black with pain. He dropped the tone of his voice, low and husky, reeking of sex. "Tell you what: you let me finish that kiss, and then I'll call anybody you want me to call."

She inhaled so sharply, she practically vacuumed the room. She wasn't sure what to feel first—pissed off that he would be such an asshole, knowing there was no way in the world she'd ever betray Trevor, or her mortification at her own deep, shoved-down-to-the-bottom-of-the-ocean, completely-until-this-point ignored awareness that they had too damned much chemistry. History. Connection.

"See," he continued, before she formed the appropriate withering remark, "I know you, baby. I know your body and I know your mind. When I started to kiss you in bed? *You remembered*. You remember how we were and you know what we could be and"—he pushed in a little closer to stop her from interrupting as he invaded her space—"you know that if you had no feelings about kissing me and if kissing me would get your fiancé back, you'd kiss me in a heartbeat to save him and never think twice. And the fact that you have doubts, Bobbie Faye, the fact that you know what is here between us, means you're marrying the wrong guy. You think about that."

He levered off the wall and walked out of the room while her head spun and ears burned and she wished she'd hit him.

"You're being a bastard," she called after him, and he laughed. "And quit calling me *baby*!" she snapped, following him down the hall, losing sight of him just as he entered the living room.

"Who the *fuck* are *you*?" he asked, as she rounded through the archway and nearly slammed into his backside.

Riles sat on the sofa, playing with one of the fishing poles he'd gotten off the dining room table.

Six

Cam cursed that last fucking shot of Jack—he should have been more alert, should have grabbed his spare gun from his bedroom the minute Bobbie Faye showed up because Trouble always followed her, and clearly, it was sitting on his sofa with a gun by his side. Not in his hand, or Cam would have gone for a weapon of his own, but close enough so that the man was a threat. Cam moved to keep Bobbie Faye behind him as she stepped through the hall arch. He felt her falter.

"How the hell did you get in?" she snapped at his uninvited guest, and the man shrugged. "You were supposed to wait! I locked the door! I set the code!"

"You know this guy?" He looked from his ex—who was flushed, livid—to the belligerent composure of the man on his sofa. Had to be military. Or ex-cop. The guy had his feet propped up on Cam's coffee table—as much of an announcement that he had a second weapon as for comfort, and Cam knew that was on purpose. If he'd wanted to be covert, he'd have waited, hidden, or at the least, not shown his weapons. The too-casual attitude he had told Cam this guy knew what the hell to do with the guns, and how to do it quickly, without nerves getting in the way.

"My job's to watch you." Clear, succinct, scathing. *He'd seen the kiss.* And this mattered to him? Who the hell was he?

"So you broke *in*?" She turned to Cam, a tsunami of fury. "He broke in. To your house."

"I noticed."

"Can't you arrest him? Breaking and entering and general shitheadedness?"

The man snorted, derisive. "I don't think they'll put me away for annoying the living crap out of you. I'd probably get a medal. Besides, once he hears why I'm here, he's not going to object."

"You want to fill me in?" Cam asked Bobbie Faye, who clenched her fist on the back of the overstuffed chair just to keep from sidling up to Riles and smacking the ever-lovin' smartass out of him.

"This," she said, pointing to the man, who'd continued to cast the line and reel it in, "is Riles. Former Spec Ops friend of Trevor's, supposedly an excellent sniper and definitely a class-A Asshole. Riles, this is Cam. State police detective. Minoring in Asshole, but has potential. Holds grudges. You two should get along well."

"Why are you in my house? And how long have you been here?" *And what, exactly, did he overhear?* Cam felt like a complete, stupid dick. Sure, he wanted Bobbie Faye to realize she was making a mistake. She didn't admit mistakes—she dug in. Fierce and determined, she'd burrow down into that mistake and build a wall around it like a beaver damming a river. He'd seen her do it over and over again, and he was running out of time; he was going to have to make her face her mistake. He was going to do it for her, for him. Hell, for their future, because dammit, they had a chance. Still, if he'd known the man was here, Cam wouldn't have ever jeopardized her reputation for being honest. It was, sometimes, all she thought she had. She was wrong, but he knew it was important. "Well?" he said again when Riles didn't answer.

Riles shrugged. "Few minutes." He slid his unhappy gaze back to Bobbie Faye. "Long enough."

Cam started forward. No way was this prick going to give Bobbie Faye a hard time for something he'd done. She shook her head, putting a hand on his arm, digging her fingers in as a sign to let Riles's smirk go, to let the implications go, that this was *her deal*. She'd handle it.

He felt the surge in his blood of *pissed-off boyfriend* and then the whiplash of the fact of how that wasn't his job anymore. That's not who he was to Bobbie Faye. Not yet. And he didn't want to make whatever-the-hell-this-was worse for her, so he forced himself to check it at the gate, his teeth grinding against the desire to rip the guy a new one.

"Fine. He's here because?"

Bobbie Faye glanced at him with those big green eyes, her expression resigned, annoyed, and about a hundred other things he knew intimately, and his palms itched to just pull her over to him and push away the world. That's what he should be doing. If he hadn't been such a fucking idiot in the first place and created the chasm that ripped them apart.

"He's a friend of Trevor's." As if repeating the fact was an explanation. He scoured her with his *get to the point* glare. He had an entire repertoire of glares, and it haunted him just a little that the majority of them had been perfected on Bobbie Faye during their college years.

"Quit stalling."

She seemed fascinated with the window drapes all of a sudden. "He's supposed to be watching out for me. Trevor asked him to make sure I was safe while he had to work."

The entire time she spoke, Riles fixed Bobbie Faye with a cold smile of icy dislike—or maybe even hatred—in his eyes. Cam loathed him pretty much instantly. And then Bobbie Faye's full meaning hit him.

"You mean . . . Trevor got you a *baby*-sitter?"

"Apparently. Fido here was supposed to be more of a guard dog, and he's enjoying the hell out of using that assignment to annoy the living fuck out of me."

"Perks of the job," Riles said, shrugging again.

"Are you gonna make those calls?" she asked, ignoring Riles, which only seemed to amuse him.

"You don't have any contact with Trevor?" Cam asked the man.

It seemed to pain him to say no, but Riles shook his head. "Not since his first day. And before you ask, yes, I've tried checking with all of my old buddies and sources and everything else. If I really thought he wasn't in trouble, I'd have chained her"—he nodded toward Bobbie Faye—"to the floor and kept her at home, where it was much easier to do my job and shut her up at the same time."

Bobbie Faye lunged forward and Cam blocked her from kicking the living crap out of Riles. "I've always heard Spec Ops people had death wishes," Cam said, more to himself, and then he regretted it when she flinched beneath his hands; Trevor had been Spec Ops at some point before FBI. Cam did not need Bobbie Faye going all batshit crazy, zipping down the bunny path of hysteria.

"I'll make some calls," he told her. "Try not to kill Trevor's friend in my house."

"Mamma!" Stacey chimed. "Mamma mamma mammam-mammammmamma!"

Lori Ann held onto her five-year-old daughter who'd jumped up on the beginning of every word, and at the rate she was going, would be the first child to orbit the moon unassisted.

"Stacey," Lori Ann laughed, "Stacey Stacey StaceyStaceyStaceyStaceyStacey!" And she jumped with her.

Tiger Stadium. Lori Ann's eyes were nearly as wide as her five-year-old daughter's. They stood a few yards away from the immense stadium, a new cobblestone path absolutely hell on her low kitten heels. She held Stacey's hand as they crossed the street—Marcel had a VIP pass that allowed him to park next to the stadium—and she guided Stacey over to the newly, gorgeous renovated Mike the Tiger's cage. Mike, who was just a big cub, really, lounged at the edge of his spacious pool, half in, half out, thoroughly sated and happy. How he wasn't up, pacing, jittery with nerves with the noise of the crowds all over the various parking lots surrounding the stadium, Lori Ann just did not know, but she was glad he didn't look too scary.

They were going to be pulling him around the football field in twenty-four hours.

She hoped like hell they had something like Tiger Xanax. LSU games had been known to register on the Richter scale for the noise and pounding of fans' feet, and the last thing she wanted to be around was a nervous tiger.

She watched her daughter, who now waved her little purple LSU pom-poms and wanted to do somersaults in her little LSU cheerleader outfit Marcel had bought for her. "No, honey," Lori Ann cautioned. "There's all kinds of crap in that grass that I don't want you to wear." People were barbequing all over the freaking place and dropping things and spilling things. "You'll look like a walking condiment aisle."

Whereupon Stacey started cheering for "Condomees Condomees" and every single family looked over at her as if she'd failed the "good mom" pop quiz.

"Y'all okay?" Marcel called, and she turned to see the bandy-legged man, short, kinda stumpy, as he moved around the big monster truck he'd tricked out with the Eye of the Tiger. She knew he was nervous—this was a big moment for his little fledgling company, getting to pull the tiger around in front of nearly ninety-three thousand people on the inside of the stadium, and of course, the insane forty thousand tailgating outside would see his truck, too. He'd gotten lucky, since the original truck and driver were in a wreck a few days ago. They weren't hurt, thank goodness, but they were out of commission for the game. The truck was the centerpiece of a big raffle—someone would win the truck, provided by a vendor for LSU—and Marcel was going to get the free publicity for having killed himself getting the paint job done on time. Now he circled the truck, attaching the poles to the truck bed to which he'd later attach big LSU and American flags.

He smiled, a little shyly, as she nodded and waved—he'd quit chewing the tobacco that stained his chin and teeth, had gotten his teeth whitened (ended up, he had a nice smile), and had started wearing nicer jeans and shirts that Lori Ann helped him pick out. He called it his personal "upgrade" but Lori Ann thought it was maybe that nobody had ever really taken an interest in him before. Well, not including the one-night stands who were happy as hell to do whatever one of

Alex's gunrunning team wanted them to do because all of the gunrunners were rolling in money. Marcel, though, had been tired of running, tired of hiding, and wanted to build a life.

She felt her phone vibrate, and saw it was Bobbie Faye. She sighed.

Just as she started to answer, one of the tailgaters pumped up the volume of Marc Broussard's "Home" and everybody at their barbeque pits, their grills, their coolers, their RVs, and their tents started dancing. It was just that kind of song, and Stacey got into the rhythm immediately, holding out her hands for Lori Ann to join in.

Lori Ann shoved the cell phone into her pocket and started dancing with Stacey; she wouldn't be able to hear Bobbie Faye, anyway.

It was easily still ninety degrees outside in the early dark of October and the shushing of the air conditioner kicked on for a cycle as Cam made the calls. Bobbie Faye tried to keep busy, but Lori Ann hadn't answered. Nina hadn't answered. Her Aunt V'rai hadn't answered (they talked nearly every other day now, and Bobbie Faye thought V'rai was pretty determined to close the chasm between Bobbie Faye and her family . . . which was a little bit like being ushered into an insane asylum with open arms and LSD-laced brownies). The only one who'd answered had been her brother Roy, and that was only because he had a hot poker game he wanted to sneak into if she would only—please, pretty please, promise to change the oil in her car for the next two years—loan him some money. She didn't bother to remind him that her car had blown up on the bridge four months ago. Roy didn't exactly hold onto itty-bitty details like bombs and lost cars.

Cam's voice rumbled on the phone in the other room— he'd pointedly closed the door when she had paced a loop too close to where he talked. She fidgeted around the living room, straightening up, storing crap in proper cabinets, moving in fits and starts, getting distracted by piles on the other side of the room like a squirrel with ADD, all while

Riles's frowns grew more and more severe. It seemed like every cabinet of Cam's that she opened, every magazine she straightened, was an indictment that there was still something going on between her and Cam, that she was intimately a part of Cam's household, and if she could have sat down without fidgeting, she would have.

Cam cursed as he re-entered the room. Riles jumped to his feet before Cam reached her, and the expression in Cam's dark brown eyes washed ice through her: fear. Regret. Compassion.

"Baby," he said, low, "I'm not getting hard facts. In fact, I'm getting conflicting reports—some say he's fine, just undercover, and others say his cover's been compromised."

So this is what hell feels like. She doubled over, the pain radiating through her, sucking all the oxygen with it, and her hands went numb. Cam laced his fingers through her hair, clasping onto her shoulder as he helped her to stand upright again.

"I'll make more calls," Riles said, pulling out his cell. "I have a few markers I can pull in, maybe, for something like this."

"You do whatever you want. I'm not waiting. I'm finding Alex."

"No way in hell," Cam said, his fingers still laced through her hair, tightening a little, and she shrugged him off as Riles glared.

"I know where he is—Roy says there's a high-stakes poker game at Suds's place that Alex was going to sit in tonight, but Alex wouldn't let him go." Alex was awaiting trial and, technically, shouldn't be within twenty feet of a poker game—he was supposed to be behaving himself at home, but technicalities had never slowed him down before.

"You don't even know if Roy's information is up to date. He's still hiding from Kim Drake's boyfriend. Besides, even if you find Alex, it's a waste of time. You can't, for one minute, believe anything he tells you." Cam crossed his arms, adopting his stubborn cop stare all over again. "He's a bastard, he's lied to you the entire time you've known him, and you gave him back the love poems, so he's not afraid of you anymore."

"Love poems?" Riles asked, and the derision in his voice poured like caustic over a wound.

"I have *copies*," Bobbie Faye pointed out, ignoring Riles. There was just really no way to explain how a gunrunner had actually gone to college and had once thought he might be a poet, until he realized where that left him on the pay scale of life. "Loophole! I never promised I wouldn't put them up on the newspaper's blog."

"I don't think the threat of local exposure as a poet is enough incentive to make Alex cooperate," Cam said, his eyes narrowed, thinking . . . strategizing. "Remember, he'd have to cooperate with *you* and no way in hell will he do that." When her head started to do loop-de-loops off her shoulders, he put his hand up to pause her. Cam smiled, wide, crooked, her fellow conspirator. Oh, the petty school dictators they'd toppled together when he smiled like that. He could take over the world with that smile. "I think I should call Gregory Browne over at *USA Today*. He owes me a couple of favors."

"National embarrassment. Perfect."

They high-fived, and Riles turned away, utterly disgusted.

"No, you're not allowed to place bets on how far Bobbie Faye would bounce it she fell off the state capitol. Even if it is very likely."

—Advanced math teacher Christina Cross
to her tenth-grade class

Seven

It wasn't true that V'rai was entirely blind. She could see some lights and darks (if the light was bright enough), and she had some idea if there was a doorway in a wall (especially if it was open, light streaming in). Other than that, though, her world was pretty much without form.

The visions, though, were a completely different problem. She couldn't control them and saw them in brilliant colors, with dimension and a roaring soundtrack. She was never sure, when one ended, just how to explain to people what had just happened. She'd always had visions, and by now, at age sixty-two, her family had gotten used to her going completely still or fumbling something she had reached for, her being a little bit zoned until the imagery passed. She lived through them with a quiet resignation.

What she hated was knowing she absolutely could not take any action to prevent the vision from coming true without making it worse. Often, much much worse.

"What was it this time?" her brother, Etienne, demanded.

She came to, realizing she was still sitting at the table of Etienne's RV parked in the yard where her brother was re-building the old family home and the mill. Aimee (their oldest sister) and Lizzie (second oldest) ate in silence, but she could feel them bracing for the battle.

Etienne was getting crankier and crankier, and the man had never been anything but crotchety and hell to live with anyway. On his good days. (Come to think of it, she really couldn't remember any good days.)

"Nothing, *chèr*," she answered. "Just tired."

"Don' mess with me," her brother warned her. "You saw it again, didn't you?"

He'd caught her at a weak point yesterday after she'd had a vision about his daughter. Bobbie Faye had been killed in that vision. V'rai had made the mistake of telling him about it. The imagery had been so vivid, so upsetting over how real it felt, so much more jarring than any other vision she'd ever had, and she'd had plenty of difficult visions.

So much of what she saw usually came true, and the few times she'd tried to change the events, whatever disaster she'd "seen" became a full-out nightmare. But today's vision? More confusing since it contradicted the previous one. V'rai couldn't remember ever having contradicting visions before. In this new one, Bobbie Faye was hurt. Bad hurt. Dying hurt. But not all the way dead.

So did that mean Bobbie Faye would live if they intervened? Or die?

"*Mais, non*, Etienne, leave it alone."

"Have you called Bobbie Faye?" Aimee asked Etienne, and V'rai kicked her under the table, then realized she'd kicked Aimee's prosthetic shin.

"Hell, no," Etienne snapped.

"Hush," V'rai said to Aimee, who had inhaled, clearly about to take up the badgering. Aimee had been on a tear.

"Tut, Boo, I won' hush," Aimee said, "when he's shootin' off his foot to spite his nose."

"*Sacre merde*! Dat's enough!" Etienne shoved away from the little table, caged in, not having the room to pace and throw a regular-sized rant. "*Je n'apprende un mot!*"

"Well of course you don't want to hear another word," Aimee snapped. "You never do."

But he probably didn't hear a bit of that as he slammed out the door and the entire RV rattled. It took a moment for the RV to settle as Etienne crunched the gravel, storming away.

Quiet.

"That went well," Lizzie said.

"The idiot should call her," Aimee griped.

"Oh, *chère, ma fille*, she is not going to talk to him," V'rai reminded, "not even a little bit."

"He's her dad."

"Is he?" Lizzie asked, hinting at the old scandal in the family that had caused Etienne to distance himself from everyone; V'rai could not only hear Aimee's disgust, but feel it, too.

"Don't you say such things," Aimee warned her sister.

"She *did* shoot him," Lizzie pointed out.

Gi-freaking-*normous*. The new casino boat on Lake Charles dazzled, bright lights against the black sky, soaring above the dark glassy mirror of the lake at night. There were multiple decks, like a wedding cake on steroids, and Bobbie Faye felt an innate hitch of annoyance from the wasted wealth she saw framed in the yellow amber glow of the big picture windows.

Three gangplanks—fore, and aft (the service entrance), and center—rose from the bank of the lake up to the boat in wide, welcoming, well-lit paths like whitewashed roads to Oz. As she, Cam, and Riles strode up the service entrance, Riles's grumpiness grew by some exponential factor of Stupid, which Cam seemed to think he needed to match in Protective Assholery, and really, if she could kick them both off the pier and into the lake? Incredibly satisfying. Like, deep dark chocolate over strawberries satisfying.

"I'm stunned they don't have your picture with a slash through it out here somewhere," Riles muttered. "That's a class-action lawsuit begging to happen."

She met Cam's gaze and then glanced away, grateful he disliked Riles enough not to elaborate on the fact that Bobbie Faye had been officially banned from the entire marina for life. She resisted peering over at the dock that had to be rebuilt after the yacht fell through it from the dry dock crane. It was not her fault the owner had asked her to man the levers moving the boat when she was supposed to be christening it. And wow, who knew a boat could splinter into so many pieces?

Cam looked away from her, frowning. Technically, he was supposed to enforce the ban, not help her bribe her way onto the boat. Thank God this was going to be a simple in-and-out. Find Alex, a little shouting, probably a few staff members having a heart attack, and she'd leave. Easy.

"Tyrone," she said, approaching the guard. The man was as wide as he was tall and all muscle, and he managed to appear menacing, if Menacing ambled and winked. He broke into a wide smile at the sight of her.

"Aw, Sugar Girl," he teased, giving her a hug and a peck on the cheek. "How 'ya doin'?"

"Sugar?" Riles asked. "You have some sort of good twin running around here, right?"

Tyrone frowned, but she waved dismissively at Riles and said, "Ignore the Booger Eater, he's just got indigestion. Got a gift for ya," she said, pulling a couple of tiny deep blue vials out of her purse.

Tyrone's eyes boggled a bit. "Is that what I think that is?"

"It's the *extra-strength* version," Bobbie Faye told him. She could see his fingers itched to snatch them out of her hands. "Go on. Ce Ce sent it with love."

Tyrone picked the vials up, in awe. "This is a whole year's supply."

"Yeah. You might need new shoes before it's over."

Riles snorted. "You can't be serious. What is that? Love potion?"

"Tap-dancing potion," Bobbie Faye said. "Ce Ce's been supplying it to several of the nation's best dance companies for years."

Tyrone dug three badges from his suit pocket—badges which would get them past security into the boat. "I think Suds is in the bar," he said, marveling over his good luck, so totally thrilled, he'd clearly decided not to remind her that even though Suds liked her, he'd asked for an advance written warning before she ever came back into his bar.

They eased past Tyrone as he held one of the vials up to the sunset, admiring the cobalt prisms of light it cast. Once they were out of earshot, Riles said, "That is the dumbest thing I think I have ever seen." Then he looked pointedly at Bobbie Faye. "Oh, wait. I stand corrected."

She waved the chicken foot bracelet at him. "Don't argue with the juju."

"Certifuckingfiable."

She watched as Cam scanned the kitchen and the security staff milling through it, the sheer enormity of the kitchen indicating the vast size of the boat. Which meant several thousand people, minimum, milling around. Drunk, drinking, or agitated by their losses—a complicated environment— and that was before they even took into consideration where Alex was, and how many of his men he had with him. Or how armed they were.

Of course, Alex wasn't supposed to be armed, much less armed in a bar in a casino. She knew Alex didn't generally play by the rules, and Suds had tolerated him for years. Kinda like Switzerland. Suds had kept her from killing Alex. He'd also kept Alex from killing her.

It was neutral ground, and Alex knew it.

She also knew Suds, ex-Marine from twenty years ago, was still a crack shot, and no one dared draw down in his bar without ramifications.

"This," Cam had said, "is a really bad idea." Which he had, in fact, been saying from the time they'd left his home.

"Classic fuck-up," Riles agreed as they wove through the service room of the casino, where waitstaff lockers gleamed in a row. "We really shoulda cuffed her at your house."

"You'd've had to shoot her to do it," Cam grumbled as she elbowed him.

"I'm okay with that," Riles answered.

"You," she said to Cam, "just can't stand it when you're not in control of the ball. And you," she said to Riles before he could make ball comparisons, "are just whiny because we're at round eighty-three and you haven't won one yet. This is going to be quick and easy: I find Alex, I embarrass

Alex, he steps out of the room to shut me up, we find out why he thinks Trevor's life is on the line, we leave, we tell the Feds." When they both gave her what she thought of as the suspicious-professor-gazing-over-the-spectacles look— Riles because he thought she was Satan's Right Hand and Cam because he knew she wasn't exactly successful at being the planny type—she added, "It's not like Alex is going to volunteer this stuff to the FBI and I need specifics for them to listen to me."

There were three ways for this mission to go wrong this evening, and Trevor watched as all three of them walked through the door: Moreau, followed by Bobbie Faye, who was followed by Riles. Trevor had expected trouble.

He just hadn't expected to be engaged to it.

The contact had chosen the mahogany-paneled room in the casino bar (appropriately named *Suds* after its owner); Trevor would have never chosen a location with this few exits. It made backup a nightmare and he was mostly on his own until he got off the damned boat. He watched the three as they entered, the clink of glasses and scattering of poker chips, the laughter and voices all humming in the room, drowning out any possibility of him hearing what they'd said to the usher at the door. Crystal glassware caught and reflected the light at the bar, and the player across from him nervously wound a chip through his fingers as the player next to him tapped the table, checking on the river card in a high-stakes Texas Hold 'em game.

Trevor called, not bothering to glance at the cards he held; his plan tonight was to lose gracefully. And lose a lot. He needed the contact happy and interested in what Trevor was selling.

Bombs. More specifically, the C-4 and detonator caps necessary to do a helluva lot of damage.

Bombs that rumor had it the contact wanted for a Louisiana target.

Bombs that Nina had been sniffing out on her part of the investigation as she closed in on the supplier.

Rumor had it that the contact had already purchased a few detonators, that some of the bombs may actually be in place, but the contact wanted more. And that's where Trevor had hoped to come in—as the "supplier," to lure the contact out into the public, and not just his lackeys here at the card table.

But all of his undercover work was gone to hell and back the minute that trio had walked in the door. Trevor knew his cover had to have been blown. There was no way Bobbie Faye and the Crewe of Idiots (he expected a hell of a lot better from Riles) would just happen to show up in the casino where he happened to be undercover. He didn't even need to ask how Riles had completely lost control. That reason was currently interrogating the bartender. Sonofa*bitch*.

And frankly, Trevor expected better of Moreau, expected the man to have some goddamned common sense, but Moreau had been working overtime these last four months to sweep Bobbie Faye back into his corner, and the cop had obviously lost his mind in the process.

"Call," the man named Brian said on Trevor's left.

On one level of consciousness, Trevor knew every move, every slight physical gesture made by the men at the table, whether they contemplated their cards, fiddled with the chips, drummed fingers, or simply stared, stone-faced. He knew every detail about what they wore, where they carried the weapons they thought no one knew about. He could judge who could handle themselves, and who'd probably run for the door. He'd known how many people were in the room, who left, who returned, and which women or men they were eyeing.

On another level, though, he focused on Bobbie Faye's fear. There was a grim set to her mouth and tension in her shoulders, and the fear radiated just beneath the bluster. Moreau, on the other hand, seemed cockier than usual, slightly more possessive toward Bobbie Faye. Trevor saw it in the way Moreau stepped in closer, crowding her slightly, and Trevor knew from the infinitesimally small way Bobbie Faye inched away that something had happened between them. Something more than just an argument, because Trevor had witnessed plenty of those, and she typically responded with more of an intense desire to drop-kick Moreau into the next week instead of . . . discomfort.

He was going to be damned lucky if he could manage not to kill that man.

Trevor sat with his back to the wall, Alex one man over, to his right, and Trevor knew Alex hadn't looked up yet, and therefore had not seen the tornado on the other side of the archway, across a very large room filled with people, and completely out of Alex's line of sight. Trevor wasn't sure he understood how any man could not be aware of her presence—he'd know if she walked into any room, anywhere, even if she'd been dead silent and he'd been blinded.

No, check that—what he really did not understand was how in the hell Bobbie Faye had gotten past the agent outside at the pier and Yazzy posted inside, undercover. Nobody had warned him, which was a fucking nightmare. They'd had a contingency plan in place. There were ways to have handled this, including arresting anyone who wasn't supposed to be on that boat.

The subset of which was entirely made up of Bobbie Faye.

Bobbie Faye knew the bartender was lying to her as he wiped the glass faster and faster with the cloth in his hand, in rhythm with his blinking eyes, and she was about to go across the bar and really scare the bejesus out of him when Suds came out from an adjoining room, a genuine smile on his lined face, his white hair still in a buzz cut after all these years.

"You causing trouble, Sugar Girl?"

He rounded the end of the bar as he asked, waving the bartender off, and Bobbie Faye barely reigned in her frustration, resisting the urge to use her purse as a battering ram against the mute bartender.

"Hey, Suds," she said, still distracted by the guilty expression the pipsqueak bartender had as he ran toward the alcove, glancing at her over his shoulder. "You're hiring chickens now?"

"*Sugar Girl*?" Riles said. "Seriously, exactly what sort of hallucinogenic drugs do you give these people?"

She ignored him, turning back to Suds, who picked her up a foot off the ground, hugged her and said, "You aren't planning on tearing up my bar again, Sugar, right?" Suds had maneuvered them a bit to where they were standing alone, where no one could overhear.

"I promise, Suds. That last time was a total accident."

"Honey, you took a chainsaw to three booths."

"They beat up Lori Ann after school."

"I know, Sugar, I'd have held the idiots down for you, but the *booths* were innocent."

"I really am sorry about that," she said, turning away from where Riles was glaring at Cam with the most disbelieving, *I cannot believe you're letting her walk around in public* stare possible. Riles had an entire repertoire of "skeptical."

"You paid me back. But if it weren't for the fact that I was your mamma's friend," he glanced over her shoulder and she followed his gaze, "I'd have been a mite upset."

There, behind the bar, were side-by-side autographed photos—one of her mom in a pink ruffled dress, one of Bobbie Faye in jeans, boots, and a tiny little t-shirt, each wearing the family heirloom tiara made from old iron, each with a "Contraband Days Queen" sash that made Bobbie Faye's eyes itch, and each signed, "To Suds, With Love."

"Is that there to ward off evil?" Riles asked.

Suds set her down, his brow quizzical.

"Don't mind him, he didn't take a Personality Pill today. I'm looking for Alex."

Suds held her chin in his hand. "I thought you were engaged to Cam here," he said, jerking his thumb toward Cam.

Riles bristled up into a fine hedgehog that would do the species proud, Cam crossed his arms, eyes narrowing, and Bobbie Faye knew she'd just turned beet red.

"She should be," Cam muttered.

"I'm engaged to Trevor, Suds, remember?"

"We're having scorecards printed next week," Riles offered, "complete with a 'player to be named later' blank."

Suds raked Riles with a military glare, his right hand spinning his wedding ring around his ring finger. It was the glare of an old military war dog to a young one, clearly saying that Suds wouldn't have a single problem taking Riles out behind a barn and hurting him if he kept it up.

God, what she wouldn't give for the chance to stick her tongue out at Riles, complete with a *nanny nanny boo boo*.

Riles had the decency to look properly chastised.

"Sugar Girl, Alex is bad news." Suds turned to face her again, "You did good getting away from him. You need to stay away."

"He has some information I have to have. I'll make this quick and clean and then we'll be outta here. Give me some time before you call the cops."

Suds gazed pointedly at Cam, and—thank goodness—she thought fast enough on her feet this time to *not* say "he doesn't count" and, instead, managed to say, "Cam's helping."

Suds turned to Cam, saying, "You carryin', son?"

"Yes, sir. This is work related, so I'm technically on duty. So's Riles here," Cam nodded toward Riles. "Delta Force, Spec Ops, snipers."

"Don't tear up my bar."

"I'm just going to go embarrass Alex, so he'll talk. That's all." She tried to do a "Scout's honor" pledge thingie. (Cam reached over and bent down the extra finger.) "Swear."

Suds kissed her on the forehead. "Right. I'm calling my insurance company. Alex's in the back room, playing poker."

Cam nodded, and Bobbie Faye turned toward the room in question and led the way.

There she was, arms swinging, storming across the floor toward Trevor's table, though she hadn't seen him yet, waitresses wisely clearing a path in front of her as she looked pissed off and scared. And determined. He loved her determination.

If he didn't kill her for it first.

Because just as she crossed the room, his tablemates registered her approach, though no one had glanced at her directly. He felt their tension, felt the subtle undercurrent in the air, felt them shift in their seats to better enable them to reach for weapons they weren't supposed to have in the casino and he knew . . . *knew* . . . suddenly, his intel hadn't been entirely correct. He'd worried that this meeting had come too quickly, too easily, that there may be some ulterior motive, and the Bureau had not wanted to look a gift horse in the mouth.

There definitely *was* an ulterior motive. A target—and she'd just walked into the room. He could feel the way the men shifted, the way they seemed to *expect* her. The way they seemed coiled, waiting for her to draw nearer.

No way would his own office have told Bobbie Faye where he was, so she wasn't there searching specifically for him (and she wouldn't have been, if she'd known he was there undercover). While he hadn't been able to call her, he'd sent a couple of coded texts telling that he was going to be delayed. She'd have hated that he couldn't come home earlier, but she wouldn't willfully blow his cover . . . so then what was she doing here . . . ? Fuck. *Alex.*

She still had not seen Trevor. Instead, she lasered in on Alex, who was sitting two chairs over. Alex, who had been forced to assist this mission or rot in prison, something Trevor had not been able to tell Bobbie Faye. Alex, who clearly would like to fuck up anything the federal government was doing, who knew Trevor and the Feds probably wouldn't have ever found his hiding places in the swamp if Bobbie Faye hadn't led them (inadvertently) across Alex's secret pathways in and out of south Louisiana. Secret pathways which had made his black market arms business incredibly successful.

If Alex was responsible for pulling Bobbie Faye here and into jeopardy, then in the not-too-distant future, there were only going to be parts of him residing in a federal prison somewhere. Very small parts.

The nightmare situation played out, slowly drowning him. He'd wanted her safe. She'd been through enough, she'd been hurt enough, and he fought back the anger at whoever had compromised her. The seconds ticked out as if God had decided each click of time would stretch to eternity before it snapped back, taking all sound and feeling with it, slamming home in a rush, a projectile intent on killing.

"It's a steel box the size of a room." "Yeah, isn't it great?"
"How on earth are you going to market something that insane?"
"We're calling it 'The Bobbie Faye Survival Kit'."
"Dude. You'll never keep up with the orders."
—Zachary Steele and Russ Marshalek on *Facebook*

Eight

She'd expected to cause a scene.

The one thing Alex hated? Was a scene. If she had to throw in a couple of trapeze artists and a monkey fucking a football to draw attention, she would have.

And Alex was here. In her sights, across the main salon, at the back of a little poker room just through the archway; he hadn't seen her yet—he was watching the dealer as he shuffled the next hand.

He'd placed bets with Nick against Trevor. And had not thought to hide.

She wasn't sure when he'd gone completely delusional, or when his survivalist instinct had self-imploded, but she was already writing the condolence card in her head as she approached. She noted that these men at the card table weren't his regular gunrunning buddies. For one thing, there were far fewer tattoos and no one was avidly staring at the ESPN footage of some car race on the big flat-screen TVs ringing the dark-paneled room, or dipping snuff and spitting in a spittoon, or wearing an "I shaved my balls for this?" t-shirt. What *did* register was how way-the-hell out of his element Alex was, especially if the thousand-dollar suit a couple of seats over was anything to judge by. Then she noticed the guy's diamond cufflinks, and if those suckers were real, the suit probably cost ten thousand, and she couldn't compress the little thrill of delight at the thought that Alex might, just once, get his ass handed to him. Wall Street Guy was looking down, checking the time on his diamond-encrusted watch when Alex caught the ripple of attention in the room and turned, frowning her direction.

Which is exactly when she felt Cam and Riles pull up, their steps stuttering, not keeping time with hers, and she could have sworn a lightning bolt of shock and dismay ran straight through them. They'd taken up subtle, defensive stances on either side of her, scanning the crowd. From Alex's and their body language alone, she knew, somehow, that everything had taken the Express to The Land of Dumb Ideas.

There was something different in the expression in Alex's eyes in that split second, that *holy shit, we're screwed* expression that she'd only seen a couple of times before. (Once, she remembered, was when she caught him with one of her friends from college going at it like bunnies in her car. She had a vague memory of a sledgehammer and his prized Corvette being involved after he'd explained that her car had more room.)

She glanced around the bar to see what had caused her skin to prickle, and she had the eeriest feeling that she'd seen something she should have registered. Alex leaned back in his chair, disgust practically oozing from his pores. His dark Cajun looks were mesmerizing, but that was like saying water was slightly wet. Half Cajun, half Cherokee (or so he claimed), still wiry, and with angular, harsh planes to his face that somehow made him angrier-looking than she remembered. If there was a World Record for Mean and Nefarious, Alex held it.

"Alice Michelle, you shouldn't be here," he snapped.

Alice Michelle? Shit. Calling her any other name had— long ago—been his signal for "pay attention, dumbass." Back when she thought "dark and dangerous" were cute and having a boyfriend who needed to talk in code was adorable, rather than a clue to illegal activity. Or maybe he knew her well enough to *know* she was going to cause a scene and he was trying to distract her because he was evil and . . .

"We . . ." Her body vibrated, hummed, and the back of her neck tingled; what was off . . . off . . . what? Something was definitely wrong and her body shivered with awareness, sudden anxiety curling through her toes. ". . . uh," losing all forward motion, trying to assess what had caught her in an undertow, "we need to talk."

Well, *that* came out forceful and scene-making. Call the Oscar people, quick.

His black eyebrows teased together in a puzzled question, like she was supposed to understand something, but why in the hell should he start expecting her to understand his non-verbal cues now when she had never understood the man before? He'd always been nonverbal and clandestine at heart, too much the poet mercenary, and she didn't do subtle all that well. Alex glanced over to the Wall-Street Guy and said, "Third stupidest thing I did."

The first, he'd once said, had been to date her. The second had been to teach her to shoot.

He'd already turned his back to her, dismissive. Fine, he wasn't going to talk to her voluntarily? She would blurt out the first lines of the love poem (she was going with the worst one first). But before she got out the first sappy line, Riles closed a hand around her elbow, pulling her back away from the table, and Cam maneuvered himself between her and the rest of the room. Neither man had said a word, and Riles's bald lack of scathing commentary amplified her own pinging radar.

"Hang on," she told Cam, "the plan was to—"

"You are *never* planning anything *ever* again," he snapped, low and harsh.

They had eased one—and only one—step back when a barely twenty-one-year-old heavily tanned waitress plopped a tray down on a table, pointed a French-tipped finger at her, and griped, "I know you!" in the same tone most people would use for "There's a clogged sewer drain!" She stepped between them and the door, and as Riles reached to move her out of the way, she dodged, shouting, "I lost three hundred dollars buying a really crappy car because of you! You used to do all of those car commercials for Zippy Ed's Car Emporium. You're Bobbie Faye!"

And as the waitress shouted her name and took a swing at Bobbie Faye, Alex and the men from the poker table came out of their seats. Poker chips flew, cards fell, drinks spilled, chairs tumbled, and nothing, not the poker-playing men from Alex's card game who were now reaching for her, not Riles throwing a low kick blocking one of them, not Cam elbowing the other in the face, not Suds ratcheting a shotgun behind them, *nothing* compared to meeting the eyes of the Wall Street Guy as he came up and over the table.

Trevor.

She had looked straight at him, and hadn't recognized him.

"Go!" he shouted, but she stood rooted to the spot. Relief, fear, *shock* jammed her body, riveting her in place.

He was, in a word, stunning. His short hair, neatly styled, the suit even more beautiful as she saw him in motion, its charcoal color emphasizing the lines of his shoulders, the shirt a crisp pristine white, the tie impeccable, the mustache goatee framing his grim line of a mouth—nothing, *nothing* seemed the same except his wild blue eyes, which expressed, now that she met his gaze again, *hellified pissed off*.

Relief surged through her, swamping her body, threatening to take her legs out from under her as the determination that had kept her standing and moving forward abated with a sudden ferocity. *He was alive.* He was okay. He was . . . shouting at her to *go go go* as he came toward her.

Oh holy goatfuck.

She'd just screwed up whatever undercover op he'd been running, and now at least two men from the table seemed intent on grabbing her, and for the life of her, she couldn't fathom why. Riles and Cam dragged her backward, people shouted, bodies tripped and fought and plunged, and through it all, her eyes locked onto Trevor's, the shock of having not recognized him burning through her.

A distinctive smoke smell filled the air from somewhere

nearby and the fire alarm blared a sharp, jagged screech through the plush-carpeted rooms, and a second later, overhead sprinklers spewed water in overlapping circles. Suds shouted instructions as waiters and ushers and casino staff scrambled to regain some semblance of calm for the frantic mob of disoriented gamblers. Trevor sliced through the crowd even as Riles and Cam yanked her backward. The men Riles and Cam had downed had risen again, heading for her until they caught sight of Trevor; they both reversed immediately, out of his reach, moving opposite directions as they melted into the swarm.

"We can split up," Riles suggested, his stare tracking one of the men as Trevor arrived at her side.

Trevor shook his head and she felt an odd dissonance— no long hair shaking in its wake. "No idea how many there are and I don't want to get picked off—we get out," he said, one hand on her elbow, having taken Riles's position as Cam led and Riles followed, guns out. All she needed was a flag and a sash draped across her chest, Miss National Without-A-Clue, and the debacle would be complete.

He was safe.

She hadn't recognized him.

They pounded through the soggy main salon, weaving through people who ran and shouted and Crap on Toast, did she ever owe Suds again. He'd poured her mom into more cabs than Bobbie Faye could count, had called her dozens of times when Lori Ann had ended a night at his old place, too drunk to drive home, and this is how she repaid him.

She was pretty sure that the all-purpose formal apology she had learned from Mrs. Russ in high-school English wasn't exactly going to work this time.

The lights flicked off and the place paused with a startled hush. Then the low emergency lighting blinked on and Bedlam said, "Hi, honey, I'm home," as everyone went Officially Batshit. These, clearly, were the kids who didn't pay attention during school fire drills because they were probably off playing hooky, necking behind the bleachers. At least four felonies occurred in her peripheral vision as gamblers-turned-thieves took advantage of the chaos, scooping up chips from abandoned tables and relieving wealthy, distracted women of their jewels.

"You got in here *how*?" Trevor asked as they moved through the rooms.

"Tap-dancing serum."

He didn't take his eyes off the room. "Well, of course." The Sahara couldn't pretend to that level of dry, antagonized wit.

White-hot fury streamed from him.

Geezus, she deserved it.

She wanted to reach over and touch him, reassure herself, but she held back. Even wet, his suit ruined, he was beautiful. Sure, technically, this was the same man she was engaged to. She hadn't had nearly the consternation the last time she'd met up with him in the middle of an op (back when they'd first started dating). He'd disappeared then, too, only to show up again with fake tattoos and long hair and biker clothes. That was fine. But this . . . sophisticated look? Freaking her out.

She shivered.

And her shirt was soaked. She looked down. And nearly see-through. Oh, crap. That was *it*, she was banning every light-colored shirt she ever owned. Wearing anything white was a guaranteed all-expense-paid vacation into Humiliationland. Between the arctic cold of the casino (the better to lure the tourists in from the sweltering heat and humidity) and the overhead sprinklers (which finally shunted off), her goose bumps were in full contact-sport mode.

Trevor pulled off his jacket as they turned through the kitchen doors, running past empty stainless-steel workstations. He slipped the suit coat over her arms, pushing her forward at the same time. They all halted in front of a large security monitor at the checkpoint inside the service entrance as a ten-by-ten set of security images rotated, displaying the many external camera angles: Tyrone and the other security guards were now out on the two main gangplanks, trying to help the screaming mob exit safely. Which left the service entrance free.

On one of the images, they could see the lights of the high-rise hotels that faced the lake—and the casino.

"We'll be sitting ducks," Riles griped.

She stole a glance at Trevor's profile.

He and Cam discussed—okay, quietly seethed at each other with about six billion veiled threats between them—just how there were too many people trampling each other at the main gangplanks and there was too much risk of not seeing someone come at them from out of the crowd if they tried to exit through either of those choices. They'd have to take the risk of the wide-open service pier.

As they headed to the exit, Riles and Cam took the classic two-man sweep, checking each doorway, then each room, as they crossed. Where in the hell had those two men in the casino gone? She hugged into the jacket. Trevor's scent clung to it.

"I'm sorry," she said as he leaned close, pulling her around a rolling cart blocking their path. "Your crazy girlfriend strikes again."

He frowned at her as he folded her into him while Riles and Cam checked the exit. "Fiancée. Soon to be *wife*."

She leaned back and gazed up into his eyes. "I see you're not correcting me on the 'crazy' part."

"The crazy works for me." He looked past her to where Riles and Cam had gone.

"Can I have that in writing?" she asked as Riles motioned that the passageway was clear.

"Yes," he murmured in her ear so she could hear over the still-blaring siren. "Pick a damned date."

"How do you know I didn't pick a date?" He slanted her a *yeah, right* glance and she grimaced. "You say that now, but when the cake blows and takes out half of your family, do not say I didn't warn you."

"When you meet my family, you'll realize that statement is actually an incentive."

He turned away, leading her through the doorway Riles had cleared.

They'd taken a few steps past locked doors and down the dark hallway when someone wrenched her backward.

The noise level had disguised the intruder's sounds as he slipped up behind them, or maybe he had dropped down from somewhere, all Spider-Man–like. She had no way to warn Trevor other than the fact that she was jerked clear out of his grasp.

The blare of the sirens stopped, and the following silence was louder, hurting her ears with the sudden whoosh of absence.

"Fuckin' back off," the man said as Trevor whirled to see what she was doing. "I'd not be likin' to shoot her, but by jazus, I will."

Cold sweat ran down her back. The man shoved something hard into her right side. From the shape of it, she'd say it was a Walther, but that was just a guess.

"I should just mark that spot with Day-Glo paint," she said, letting Trevor know where the gun was shoved.

"Like hell," Trevor said, so low she wasn't sure anyone caught it but her.

The passageway was narrow and they were lined up like ducks. The emergency lighting blinked, casting a surreal disco effect across the faces in front of her: Trevor, and behind him, Cam, and then Riles re-entering from the direction of the exit, having gone a few feet ahead, recon, making sure there was no trouble there.

Because *nooooooo*, it was back here, thank you, since Trouble had apparently stapled a GPS to her ass.

And before the next blink of the emergency light, Trevor yanked her forward, practically throwing her beneath him toward Cam as he sailed up and over and into the guy with the gun. The fight was fast and brutal and hard to tell exactly what she was seeing with the lights throbbing on and off. *Blink* and Trevor's arm sliced the space between him and the man and *blink,* darkness, then *blink*, the gun slid up into the space and *blink,* darkness, and *blink,* Trevor's strong fingers slammed forward into a choke-hold as the gun kept moving and *blink,* darkness and *bam.*

The crack of the gunshot split her ragged hope, echoing in the narrow space.

She jumped out of her skin, trying to move forward, stopped by something immoveable, holding onto her.

"Sonofabitch," Trevor swore as the man sprawled beneath him, dead.

"Shit, are you hit, LT.?" Riles asked, falling back into combat mode. He'd pronounced it "Ell Tee," and he'd said it with respect and admiration.

"I'm fine. He's dead. He unintentionally fired his weapon."

"Operator errors *suck*," Riles opined.

Trevor checked the dead man for ID and found none. "I don't know him. I knew two at the table, so there are still at least two—" He heard a gasp and looked up. Bobbie Faye had gone ghost white and frozen to the spot, one of Cam's hands clamped on her to keep her from moving forward. She didn't seem to be trying—instead, she stared, and when he glanced down, he realized the man's blood had spattered across his white shirt. "Not mine, Sundance," Trevor said, standing, reaching for her ice-cold hands, pulling her out of Cam's grasp. "C'mon. Let's get out of here before we get cornered."

Cam closed his cell phone. "I called this in and they're sending help. Foot patrol is trying to address the panic out there. We've got several people injured when the crowd started trampling each other on that lower walkway."

Riles opened the exterior exit door and two rounds drilled into it just to the right of his head. He slammed the door shut, locking it, and jumped back into the small passageway, keeping low, moving back toward Bobbie Faye.

Sean was not going to be happy. Lonan watched the people pouring down the walkway, running, all mayhem and madness. No Bobbie Faye.

This was supposed to be a simple snatch-and-grab, right in front of the Fed. It was all perfectly calculated. Sean had wanted it done this way. Grab her, toss her in the ambulance, none the wiser if she screamed—she'd look like an anxious accident victim and they'd have been gone. All while rubbing the Fed's nose in his failure. Perfect.

Well, not exactly. They didn't have the woman.

He sat in the cab of the ambulance they'd purchased and re-decaled to match the local district. Zimmer was in the driver's seat. The kid was twenty years old, all angles and frizzy hair that stood up as if he was in permanent fright. Lonan's phone rang and as soon as he saw which one of his men was calling, he knew it was bad news.

"Liam's dead," Brian, one of his better soldiers, said. "His gun's gone, too. Whaddya want us to do?"

"I want that fuckin' woman."

He punched off the phone, eyes still on the brightly lit walkways and gangplanks. Sirens blared from fire trucks a few blocks away as smoke poured from the forward section of the boat, and police and firemen couldn't be long.

How difficult could one woman be?

Blood spatter on Trevor's shirt.

Someone had shot at the door.

There was a dead guy in the hallway.

Bobbie Faye's brain hopscotched around those facts like a bunny on acid and not a single one of them was a safe place to land, especially not the one where she'd thought, for a second, that Trevor had a bullet in his chest, that she'd been the cause of him getting shot. Her vision went soft and fuzzy and she could feel the recoil of the SIG she'd used when she'd shot her cousin Mitch. Feel the yank against her hand, the weight of the metal, hear the crack as the bullet sliced through the distance between them, him standing in the yellow glow of the lights of the Old State Capitol, red blooming across his chest as he sank to the ground. She expected Trevor to sink any moment now, just any second, and she couldn't do a damned thing about it, couldn't stop it, couldn't breathe—

He shook her. He'd been talking and she finally met his gaze, quit staring at the blood on his shirt and caught the determined expression in his eyes—his very much alive and worried eyes.

"I'm okay," he said again, but she wasn't so sure she was.

They had taken an intersecting hallway, and she didn't know where the hell they were, she was so turned around and confused and maybe in shock. Lot of shock. Smoke seeped and rolled from beneath a second exit door as Trevor felt of it, yanking his hand back. They were soaking wet, there was a shooter behind them somewhere, and their secondary exit was on fire.

She nodded back toward the dead man. "Did he sound . . . Irish to you?"

"Bobbie Faye drinking game! One shot for every fire, two for every explosion."

—Michele Bardsley

"Girl, there is just not enough alcohol in the state of Louisiana for that game."

—Renee George

Nine

"MacGreggor's in Winnipeg." Trevor moved down toward another exit.

"Yeah, but he could—"

"I'm already on it." He glanced back at her, where her obvious doubt flashed in giant neon letters over her head. "I'm on it. I've called in to the Bureau every day. If you jump to conclusions, you're more vulnerable."

"Right, because it feels so much better to think that there might be *two* homicidal maniacs out there who want me dead."

"As opposed to all the regular people who want you dead?" Riles asked.

"Shut up." She appreciated what Trevor was trying to do—alleviate the stark-raving freak-out boiling inside her, which would burst right on through like that awful shot in *Alien* when that thing slammed out of that space guy's chest. She wasn't entirely buying it, but it was nice of him to try.

She saw a sign in the dark hallway and tapped Trevor's arm. "Ballroom." She pointed.

Riles kept up the rear as they checked the entrance. The blinking yellow emergency lighting flicked, slow and dim, like a TKO'd fighter who was knocked out on his feet, down for the count without quite knowing it yet. This, she noted, is where the serial killer would jump out at the girl who'd tiptoed into the dark with a pair of tweezers and a butter knife and then she thought *oh, dear God, did I just think* se-rial killer *to the Universe?*

She should just go dance on someone's grave while she was at it.

They crept single file, Trevor leading in the near-dark, the cooler air a relief as they studied the expanse of the multi-decked room, which was eerily devoid of people. The casino had an atrium center—multiple decks stacked like glittering bracelets around an open showcase of luxury: crystal chandeliers the size of small houses dotted the ceil-ing and though they weren't lit, they still caught the lights streaming in from the awakened city outside the massive picture windows that ran along both sides of each floor. A ten-thousand-gallon aquarium hogged the center of the ground floor below them. Surrounding this were tables fes-tooned with white (now wet) linen tablecloths, fine silver-ware, crystal, and quite a few half-eaten meals, all abandoned when the fire alarm had sounded.

Smoke curled near the ceiling, fire-truck sirens screeched outside, but there was an exit sign, diagonally across from them, faintly glowing green. They had to skirt around the balcony, but in no time flat, they would be out of the open "Hi, let's paint a target on you" airy room and into a nice, safe hallway that would take them to the exit marked "You Can Go Home Now, Dorothy."

"Too open," Cam said.

"No choice," Trevor countered, eyeing the way they'd come.

"Multiple places for a sniper," Riles cautioned.

They ran, hugging the outer wall of the wide large-capacity balcony. They were far enough away from the railing that the balcony above them protected them from most shots from a floor above, but the angles wouldn't have been impossible—and they didn't know where the shooter . . . or hell, shooters . . . were.

One quarter way, good. Halfway, great. Three quarters of the way and the glass banister exploded, bullets ripping into it, coming from in front of them. More shots, now from behind them. Cross fire—and then there was a distinctive *crack* and everything hushed for a second while the Universe said *gotcha* and then fuck of all fucks, sound pounded back into Bobbie Faye's ears as a cymbal-crashing clatter of glass shattering—a crescendo of bad news as the cross-fired shots sliced several rounds into the aquarium.

Water thundered out, thousands of gallons roaring a deep bass sound as it roared and slammed into them and their side of the boat. A wall of water, heavy with fish and turtles and momentum and volume poured down, and the boat lurched with the sudden shift of all that weight sloshing toward them.

One of the windows next to Cam shattered as he held his gun above the water flow—and more gunshots snapped into the wall near them as the boat tilted more and more with the rushing weight pinning them, flooding over them. Lake water raced in through hatches and doorways and things water should never race into on a boat. The wall was fast becoming the new floor, down was the new up, and one of the giant crystal chandeliers broke away from the ceiling, plummeting straight for Riles, who was battling the water and floating debris as Bobbie Faye yanked him clear and glass razored into the wall next to him.

They were capsizing. The gunmen had disappeared. No way to know where they'd gone, big turtle swimming by; holy shit, was that a baby shark? Couldn't go back—or forward—since either shooter could be lying in wait.

With a look shared between them, Cam, Riles, and Trevor aimed at the large clerestory windows on the outer wall of their balcony, firing, creating a hole at the same time the boat lurched again, throwing them forward.

Bobbie Faye slid into the blackness of the lake.

The boat pressed down, still sinking, the now-broken windows letting in more water to finish swamping it, and it bobbed up, then rocked downward on top of them, pushing them deeper into the lake, no air, fighting the damned coat jacket, sliding out of it while she looked around for Trevor.

She couldn't see, *couldn't see*, couldn't find him, couldn't tell which way was up, couldn't hold her breath that long, and then Riles tapped her, pointing. She followed him out, away from the boat, and up, where Trevor was swimming back down to find her. The casino rose for a moment, wobbling on the lake, a pendulum fighting a losing battle as Bobbie Faye and Trevor and Riles broke the surface . . . to Cam shouting and pointing as the boat groaned, slamming back down toward them and they dove and swam, hard. Inky blackness, muddy churned water, claustrophobia, lungs bursting, holy fucking *crap* she was going to drown, and then Trevor's lips pressed hers, air shoved into her lungs as he pulled her away from the sinking boat and upward, back toward the surface, this time out of the footprint of the dying boat.

They treaded water there for a moment, Trevor's arm around her. Lights of the fire trucks and police cars ricocheted along the bank of the lake as they stayed in place for a moment, waiting to see if any gunmen surfaced nearby.

Nina pulled the black silk form-fitting t-shirt over her head and smoothed it down her body; she'd already ditched the dress, and had donned her black skinny jeans and black boots.

Gilda paced the office in the penthouse, tense and rigid, phone plastered to her ear. Nina listened to her assistant's end of the conversation while she finished lacing up the boots. Gilda shook her head as she hung up the phone.

"They can't reach Trevor," Gilda said. "Apparently, he's a part of that incident at the casino boat."

"No fucking kidding." Nina clicked on the TV where there was a fuzzy shot frozen there of Bobbie Faye and Trevor, both soaking wet, leaning against a fire truck. The police had kept the paparazzi at a distance, but the photo was clear enough, and she'd paused it. "You were making the calls when it popped up."

"Oh!" Gilda said, stepping closer to the TV. "Wow. That's him? His hottie factor is much higher than his file photo indicates. And that's Cam, I recognize him." At Nina's questioning glance, she elaborated, "From the Bureau's background on Bobbie Faye." She studied the screen again. "Who's that?" she asked, pointing to the man who couldn't really be seen as he leaned against the cop car.

"That's Riles."

Gilda's *holy shit* expression was classic fan-girl enthusiasm. "Seriously? Doesn't he have, like, the most kills, ever?" Then she caught Nina's frown. "Sorry. Second most?"

Well, that depended on if Nadir counted as one kill (one event) or twenty-three (number of dead individuals), and if the latter, then Trevor—who'd had to take out the hostiles alone on that mission—technically edged both her and Riles out in the "total number of kills" department. Nina wasn't going to enlighten Gilda since that was light years above her clearance and pay grade.

Gilda realized her error and waved off the question as soon as she asked it. "Never mind." Her gaze strayed back to the TV and Nina's normally professional assistant was practically drooling. "Have you ever met him?"

Dear God, she was a groupie. Nina would have thought Riles's reputation as an asshole would have superseded that of his prowess in the kill department and would have deterred such google-eyed adoration, but apparently not.

"No, we've never met. We shouldn't be meeting now, if he'd done his damned job."

Technically, that was the official story—official, as in, for Bobbie Faye. Because how in the hell would Nina explain having once met Trevor's buddy, the sniper? Riles wasn't exactly the kind of guy who'd hang out on photo shoots in Italian villas or French bordellos, where Nina's S&M magazine would often shoot layouts. She hoped like hell Riles had one freaking brain cell working that remembered the official story. When she'd debriefed him once, he'd had a couple of bullet holes in him (one from her, his own damned fault, being in the way), and he had a startlingly asinine competitive streak that would just get him killed.

Gilda flicked a glance to the cameras located in the corners of the room. There were the obvious cams, and the ingeniously hidden ones, pretty much guaranteeing that no one entered or left work without proper reasons, without documentation filed and approved. Nina knew how rigid the company was. "The Company" because they were a deep-end-of-nothing, off-the-books little team that worked for NSA on loan to Homeland Security or whoever wanted them that week. Nina had worked for The Company since freshman year of college. They'd recruited her straight out of high school.

Nina had worked alone, mostly, all of these years, but she was a part of a hierarchy. She'd begun suspecting they had leaks. That last Italian job she'd done? Someone had known she was coming. Her main target had outmaneuvered her three times before Nina caught up to him. It cost her days, and the man did more damage—moving funding around for terrorists—before Nina could finish the job.

"They're going to be upset with you that you're leaving," Gilda warned, her worried frown marring the round lines of a face so free of worldliness and experience that it should have been on a twelve-year-old.

"Tough."

"We haven't been able to input this new intelligence through proper channels."

"This is the field, kid." She strapped on a black leather belt with hidden utility items. "I don't have time to sit around while this goes in coded, gets deciphered on the other end, they talk about it and brainstorm and then code in a plan of action." She put on her shoulder harness. She preferred her modified 1911 Colt with its precision sights. She wasn't quite the marksman Bobbie Faye was, but she wasn't far off. Too bad she'd never shot with Bobbie Faye on the range. It would have been great to have been able to share that love, that elation of nailing a target and beating one's best score, but Nina had been covert since she first went off to college. Bobbie Faye was supposed to think she was into antiques, decorating, men, and S&M. "By the time they make up their fucking minds what to do," she continued her rant to Gilda, "the bombs will have been detonated and a lot of people killed."

"You can't fix this by yourself."

"No, but I know one person who hasn't been compromised and who I can trust to have the resources to fix this."

"I'm not compromised!" Gilda exclaimed, innocence spilling from her like tub overflow.

Nina snorted as she checked her weapon: magazine, ammo, the chamber, spare magazines. All in working order. She didn't holster her weapon and Gilda's sharp eyes hadn't missed that cue.

"Kid, I don't know who exactly sent you and set you up here. Maybe it was our direct boss, and he's telling the truth—we have a leak in our computer software and you'll be able to find it and fix it. Or maybe you're a plant and are running something covert for someone else in the Company—or who knows, someone on the outside. Maybe you're part of the leak and you intend some nefarious harm. Or maybe you've been sent to keep me out of the action, or slow me down. Here's what I know: I'm going out that door and I'm helping Bobbie Faye. You've got a decision: help me or get out of my way."

Gilda's worry frown increased, and she looked like a put-out toddler. Nina bit back a laugh, reminding herself that this young woman was definitely much older than she appeared and, to be at the level of clearance Nina knew her to be, well trained.

"They're going to know you left," Gilda pointed out. "That you didn't wait for orders."

"I rarely wait for orders. You should know that by now."

They faced off, the computer monitor showing the room where their bomb-talking guest still resided, between them. The man was asleep—from exhaustion, first, and then the drugs Nina had administered.

"You know they'll track you," Gilda said, her voice pitched low. "You leave here with information about bombs—and our friendly overseas buyer—that you didn't wait to call in, and they'll assume you're the leak. That maybe you're helping the bombers—that you talked our boss into this S&M clubhouse cover as a way for you to set up an elaborate attempt to keep The Company from finding out exactly who the seller was."

The detonator parts. Extremely high-tech. Sold by her white-haired gentleman in room three to none other than Sean MacGreggor. The information they'd needed . . . weeks ago. Now was almost too damned late.

But Gilda wasn't just spouting party line—she was thinking.

"Here," Gilda said. "I think I have a workaround."

She nudged Nina out of the way so that she could get to Nina's computer; she pulled up a security checkpoint program and began typing something in rapidly. Nina watched and holy *hell*, the kid was good. Too good. She'd turned off security, keyed to Nina's thumbprint, and made it appear to be a cascading error in the program, not just Nina overriding it.

"Now," Gilda said, "with a system error and override, you couldn't trust anything that came or went out on the computer for another couple of hours, at least. It'll look like you had no choice but to go out with the information you've got, to get to the best person you know."

Nina reappraised the young woman standing before her, and saw in the eyes of an eager-to-learn young agent that Gilda was telling Nina just how much she trusted her. A young agent with the ability to slice and dice one of the most expensive and complex security systems The Company could buy.

"Who the fuck are you?" Nina asked.

"A friend," Gilda answered, and Nina knew that's all she would get.

Nina assessed her for a few more seconds, and then realized: "You're supposed to be my replacement." Gilda didn't deny it. "A little forced retirement?" Still nothing. Nina laughed. Oh, holy hell. "What changed your mind?"

"I think you're who you're supposed to be, and I think The Company's wrong to doubt you."

"Or you could just be giving me enough rope to see if I hang myself."

Gilda grinned. "Well, yes, there's that, too."

"I could just kill you," Nina said, subtly shifting position.

Gilda's light brown eyes twinkled and Nina wondered again just how old she really was. "Well, ma'am, you could try."

"Ma'am? That's just mean." Nina chuckled. "I wish I'd have known sooner. I think we could have had a lot more fun."

Then she left. Hopefully, she'd be in time.

Ce Ce stared at the TV news: the casino boat listed on its side, slowly sinking into Lake Charles. She didn't even have to see the headlines that an "unidentified woman" had been seen running through the interior, or hear the news update about the gunshots, to know Bobbie Faye had been involved. Ce Ce wore the twin to Bobbie Faye's chicken foot bracelet. Right then it was pumpkin brown. At least it wasn't red. Or black. Brown was way better than black.

Maybe she should sprinkle a little bit more of the anti-juju juice on it and double up on the spell, just to be safe.

"Oh, my *word*," Monique babbled behind her. "I won?"

Ce Ce turned to see her friend on her cell phone, dancing the Snoopy Dance, if Snoopy were freckled, demented, and had really bad rhythm.

"I won! Ceece," she said, moving the phone away from her mouth a little, "I *won*."

"Won what, hon?"

"LSU tickets. To the game! Tomorrow! They've been calling for a week and I keep forgetting to check my cell phone! They were almost gonna give my tickets away!" She stopped to listen to something on the phone, then in a rush, said, "I have two! Oh, *oh*, oh! And Russ can't go, he's got to work and I can't pick one of the boys and not the other three so you get to go with me! Isn't that *wonderful*?" Back to the phone, "Thank you! We'll pick them up."

"Football?" Ce Ce asked as her friend hung up. "Where people run around, banging into each other? Why on earth would I want to do that?"

"You're not looking at this with the right perspective. Let me s'plain: men in very tight pants bending over. Running around. And bending over some more. And lots of men. In the stadium. You're always saying you don't meet any good, hunky men, and we're going to be in a stadium with ninety-three thousand people. There's apt to be at least one or two cute ones there."

"You had me at the bending over," Ce Ce said, and Monique squealed and jumped back on the phone, calling every person she knew under creation to brag about those tickets. Sold-out game; impossible-to-get tickets.

This could be a lot of fun.

Ce Ce snapped the twin bracelet on her wrist. No reason why she couldn't protect Bobbie Faye while at the stadium. Her gaze wandered to the vials she'd been finishing up. Some of the love potion vials sparkled under her office light. No reason why those things had to sit around all weekend, lonely, either.

Hell, she might as well make a super-strong batch, since she happened to have all of the ingredients handy. It would be a damned shame to let this stuff go to waste.

"I don't think Bobbie Faye has the hang of this whole "self-preser-
vation" thing yet."

—Homeland Security expert Rebecca Hinson,
in CNN interview

Ten

She'd sunk a boat. A whole boat. A boat that was bigger than
a house. Bobbie Faye had never sunk something bigger than a
house before. Where does that go on a résumé? Hobbies?

Bobbie Faye frowned at the chicken foot bracelet protruding from underneath the towel someone had given her: the
foot was orangey brown. If a big-ass sunken boat only rated
an orangey brown, she did not want to know what would
make the damned thing turn black.

She stood on the bank of the lake, watching the boat continue to sink, its emergency lights still blinking (yeah, that
was handy). Overhead, the streetlights cast a faintly yellow
glow and the perky red and blue police cruiser lights and the
red fire truck lights and the eight billion flashbulbs and lighting for news cameras all made it look like a twinkly demented Christmas card scenario. The Hallmark Apocalypse
line: When You Care Enough To Fuck Up The Very Best.

Trevor stood a couple of feet away doing whatever it was
agents do when their fiancées destroy things, although she
was pretty sure she was garnering her own set of pages in
the federal government's "Employee Spousal Code of Con-
duct" section. Cam was on the other side of Trevor, talking
to his own superiors, arguing the relative merits of putting
her *in* the jail versus putting her *under* the jail. Meanwhile,
Riles had casually leaned against a cop car and was glaring
at her, the kind of accusatory snarl that went far beyond the

garden-variety "you are a menace to society" glare—she'd gotten enough of those to be intimately acquainted with the nuances (everything from "you're the kind of person who makes someone want to kick puppies" to "eat nails and die." The latter being the standard glare given to her by the governor.)

Trevor and Cam finished their conversations and Trevor led her, Riles, and Cam away from the crowds until they stood in the shadow of a fire truck, the sound of its running engine masking their conversation in case any diligent agent with a parabolic microphone, or any enterprising bad guy, tried to listen in.

"I want to know what the hell made you two," he looked pointedly at Riles and then Cam, "lose your fucking minds."

She stopped Cam from speaking. "We thought your cover was blown."

"How? I text-messaged you and—"

"We haven't gotten a message from you since the second day," Riles interrupted. "I'd never have changed the mission, otherwise."

"Like you had a choice," Bobbie Faye said, but she saw Trevor's surprise and confusion.

"Maybe," Riles continued, ignoring her, "you need to tell your sister to do a little more R&D on her products before releasing them."

Trevor frowned.

"What R&D? Which sister?" What did that have to do with—

"So what," Trevor asked, subtly squeezing her to hold that thought, "pushed this over from mere concern into 'go fuck up' territory?" He tensed, a hurricane brewing, a whirl of danger aimed at Riles and Cam, at the same time putting his hand beneath her hair, kneading the tension in her shoulders. It had become a habit, his reaching for her, fingers dancing across her shoulders to make sure she was okay. When she wasn't, he was so talented at unraveling the tension, she could just slither into a pile of drooling goo and forget, entirely, about vague references to sisters and phones.

Yet, even in that moment when the warmth of his hand felt like heaven, she was aware of how rigid he held himself, how angry he was. He could be a man of stillness, and maybe it was because she knew him so well that she could mark the difference between stillness and tense rigidity. Outwardly, they appeared almost the same.

"I'm sorry," she said again before either Cam or Riles could answer. For a screw-up this big, she probably needed to have the Goodyear Blimp fly over with some sort of honking huge flag, apologizing. Her luck, the blimp would spring a leak and plunge into a crowd of toddlers. "You said 'worst-case scenario, three days' and it has been *seven*. No word, then we get a strange story from Nick—"

"The bookie?"

"Yes, I know. Not a credible source. But there were big bets against me, all of a sudden, and I wasn't *doing* anything except contemplating the myriad ways I could humiliate Riles at the knife throw and really, *seriously*, you should have given him a shock collar when you let him show up, what *the hell* were you *thinking*?" He raised an eyebrow and a grin twitched at his lips, but he didn't answer as she plunged onward. "There were also big wagers against *you* and Nick said it was Alex placing the bets. I didn't know if you were dead or what and I didn't know what to do because the Feds won't talk to me, and also? Please tell whoever answers the phone when I call to quit muttering "Demon Spawn" as they hang up on me, it's getting old, and anyway, I was going to find Alex and beat the living crap out of him and hang him upside down from something upside-downy and find out what the hell he was up to and why you and I were in danger. And then I was all 'I have a plan' and one of these days I'm going to learn, and I had no clue we'd be stumbling straight into what you were working on." He squeezed her shoulders, reminding her to breathe. "I really am very sorry about that."

He nodded, reassuring. A wealth of relief shivered through her. "I get it." He eased her closer to him, turning her so that she fully faced him, still subtly working his fingers into the knots. "But these two," he glared over her to the two men, "should have known better."

"It's not Cam's fault," she said before Cam could dig a deeper hole, holding up her hand, motioning for him to stop as she felt herself whiplash with annoyance. "So . . . I'm what? Four? I need a baby-sitter *and* you're gonna ream them out for something *I* chose to do?" She folded her arms across her chest, giving Trevor the squinty-eyed glare. He raised an eyebrow, looked past her to the hotel-sized boat now lying sloppily in the lake, destroyed, streams of water from the fire hoses meeting in midair to put out the fires, and then he focused back on her.

It was really hard to maintain righteous indignation when she'd sunk a boat.

She sighed. "I dragged them into this. I wanted to know if Cam could find out anything more from the Feds."

"And you agreed to help her walk into a situation where you," and he looked at Cam, his voice turning cold, murderous, "did not know if an undercover sting had gone completely wrong or if a federal agent was missing, either of which should have suggested *bad fucking idea*. Why would you two go in there without decent intel? Especially given that you could have been walking into a trap?"

"I'm pretty sure," Riles drawled, "that he'd have done anything she wanted after they kissed."

Fury. White. Cold. Coiled. *Fury*. Trevor felt its jagged edges slicing through his veins and he stilled his hands on Bobbie Faye's shoulders. He glanced from Riles's smug expression—and he'd have to deal with that later—to the strain of arcing pain lining her face. Her normally luminous green eyes were dark and wide and the pallor beneath them ripped at him. He knew she wasn't sleeping. Hell, she hadn't been sleeping when he was there, holding the nightmares at bay. He hadn't been there for seven nights, but he'd been aware of all of the changes in her the split second he'd seen her on that casino floor.

"You can't kill him," Bobbie Faye said, jumping between him and Moreau as Trevor felt his gaze go icy with the challenge.

Wanna bet? he thought, though he kept silent. He could think of several ways he'd like to kill the detective. Two he knew he could get away with, except for the suspicions of the woman in front of him.

"It's not what you think," she said, though he didn't have to see Moreau's body language to know it was *exactly* what he thought. "I woke him from a dead sleep," she continued, guilt radiating off her, "and he was confused."

"He wasn't confused when he offered a second kiss," Riles countered, and Trevor wanted to beat the living shit out of him. Friend or not, this was the wrong time, the wrong place, and the wrong way.

"There was no actual second kiss," Moreau said, leaving off the *you asshole* end of that sentence directed at Riles, because, Trevor suspected, he had no real room for superiority. "Yet."

Shredded. Pieces. Alligator bait.

"Shut *up*," she said to Moreau, and then turned back to Trevor. "You know he's just doing that to goad you because he's a total moron sometimes," which satisfied the hell out of Trevor as Moreau frowned, "and yes, he accidentally kissed me the first time when I was in his bedroom and he was sound asleep and I thought he was dead and then he flipped me over and I would have done some of those self-defense moves you taught me but he was naked and I could've really hurt him and he was—*oh*," her eyes went wide when he speared her with a fury heated to broil. "Shit, I probably should have mentioned the naked part earlier, except that it didn't matter, because as good-looking as he is—"

"Wow," Riles interjected, "huge surprise there are *multiple* ex-boyfriends."

"Shut the fuck up, Riles," Trevor said without glancing over.

"—he's not you. God." She sank her face in her hands. "I probably should've slept one of those days you were gone."

She met Trevor's gaze again. "But you have to know that he didn't mean to—"

"Yes," Trevor said, quietly, keeping his voice even, his eyes on Moreau's satisfied expression, "he did." He slid his gaze back to Bobbie Faye, who was one large ball of anxiety and exhaustion. "But you didn't."

She shook her head emphatically, exhaling.

"That's what matters," he said, pulling her to him.

It wasn't *all* that mattered, and the hell of it was, the fact that she wasn't aware of how she was putting their relationship in jeopardy was the thing which could destroy them. As Bobbie Faye buried her face in his shoulder, he seared Moreau with the dead serious *do it again and I'll kill you* stare Moreau deserved.

And he meant it.

Bobbie Faye sighed. Trevor leaned laconically against the fire truck—as laconically as a giant lion about to pounce and shred the stupid-assed antelope that had just wandered into its sights and mooned it—holding her and, no doubt, glaring at Cam above her head. When she'd sunk the boat, she hadn't known she could make the day worse, but she had. There were about three thousand things she wanted to say, and another six thousand she wanted to ask Trevor, but after thinking he might be hurt (or worse), the ability to just stand there and listen to his heart beat beneath her ear not only comforted her, it gave her a sudden clarity that cut through the personal hellish loop of *oh, shit, you have so screwed up here.*

"Why," she asked him, "was Alex there with you?"

She expected Riles to snark with something like, "Ex-boyfriend tic-tac-toe?" but he remained silent.

Trevor's heartbeat slowed as he held her close. "Bombs," he said, and she thought she might be sick.

"He's selling them?" she asked, leaning back to meet Trevor's steady gaze.

"We were trying to," he said, and she was lost.

Eleven

"Someone has been buying bomb materials," Trevor explained. "We've heard some rumors that the buyer wanted more detonators, so we put a plan in place. We could do it fast by using Alex, since he's known on the black market circuit, and there was no need to set up a cover for him. We were putting the word out—subtly—that he had something impressive to sell. A couple of reps of the buyer were at that table. They had seemed interested a couple of days earlier when we traded information, but today, they'd stalled."

"Because I showed up," she said.

"No, Sundance, they'd changed the venue twice—we weren't even supposed to be at that casino tonight. It sure as hell wasn't my pick."

"Too many people, too hard to defend," Cam said idly, and she resisted the urge to peek back at the boat. At least the fire was out. (And except for Hell, dear Sinners, how do you like the weather?) She hoped Suds was okay.

"How'd you know where Alex was going to be?" Trevor asked her.

"Roy. He said he knew where there was a high-stakes poker game, but Alex wouldn't let him sit in on it."

"Alex didn't talk directly to him. We were monitoring everything. We need to find out who Roy talked to."

"I'm stunned he even answered his phone the first time—he was tailgating at the game. There'll be too many women there for him to bother with his phone 'til probably Sunday. Maybe Monday."

"So you what?" Cam asked Trevor. "Nabbed Alex, threatened him with lifelong prison, offered him a deal if he worked for you, and you weren't prepared for the asshole to double-cross you?"

"Personal experience?" Riles jabbed.

"Moreau," Trevor said, "be careful."

"Like you've been? It's obvious they were going after Bobbie Faye. Alex was placing bets, against *you*—"

"Something we did not know—"

"Cam!" she warned him, but he kept going, pent-up frustration etching lines in his face.

"—and they jacked you around on the location. They wanted you out of the house, away from her, and they wanted her out of the house—"

"Unprotected," Riles interrupted, nodding in agreement and unhappy to find himself doing so. "Or more so than I could do while we were holed up. That's why they stalled."

Her own fury rolled, heavy as lead, in her gut. "You think the whole point of Nick's confession was to lure me out and away from your protection?"

Just exactly *when* did she become the Universe's personal chew toy?

"Could Alex have been the original buyer?" Cam asked Trevor.

"Not according to ASAC Brennan." ASAC stood for Assistant Special Agent in Charge, Bobbie Faye supplied mentally, wishing like hell she had some sort of Bureau crib sheet for their acronyms.

"Which just means the Feds fucked up when they offered him a deal, because he never planned to deliver the real buyer to you and he was using you to get a lower sentence," Cam said.

"And I created the diversion he needed to get away." She thunked her head against Trevor's chest. "Damn, I'm sorry."

"Just how *ex* was *this* ex?" Riles asked.

She stiffened, but worse, Trevor's muscles bunched.

"That's enough," he said, his voice almost too low to hear. "One more word and I'll drop you in that lake."

Holy cats, he meant it. She didn't need to see Riles to feel the hatred; the strength of it bore two holes in her back.

"We need to find this Alex asshole and find out who paid him to draw Bobbie Faye out," Riles said.

"He's gone to ground," Cam answered. "We searched for him for years, and that salt dome hideout y'all blew up was definitely not his sole hiding place. What we really need to do is find Roy and who fed him the info about where the poker game was going to be."

Trevor was quiet. The kind of eerie misleading quiet that happens when everyone thinks all is well, tra-la-la, rainbows, kittens, and then bam, nuclear meltdown. She put her left hand over his heart and, slowly, he ran his own hand from her shoulder to clasp it, playing with her engagement ring.

Though the tension did not leave his body for a second.

Trevor's distant expression changed suddenly. Focused. She cocked her head, watching him. "Was the name he called you some private barb between you?"

She shook her head. "He would call me by a different name when he wanted me to pay attention."

"How convenient. The point is, he's gone," Riles said. "He used the distraction," and here he hesitated and glared at Bobbie Faye, "to get away. I say we find him and find out why."

But Trevor concentrated on her face, and as they gazed at each other, he said, "He was trying to warn you off. You being there surprised him. He couldn't have told Roy where we were meeting—Alex didn't know 'til I brought him there."

"Oh, hell," she said with sudden clarity. "Nick said Alex was *placing* bets. As in, *recently*."

"He couldn't have," Trevor answered, the same epiphany dawning in his eyes. "We had him under house arrest, monitoring him 24/7 for the last month."

"Nick lied. That little *weasel*."

"We need to find that sonofabitch," Trevor snapped, and

she wondered if there were going to be pieces of bookie scattered all over some deep, dark bayou.

They ran toward Trevor's car until a familiar face swam up in front of her and big hands grabbed her into a hug.

"Sugar Girl!" Tyrone said, nearly squeezing the breath out of her. "You're okay. I was so worried about you."

"Oh, Tyrone! I am so sorry—I would have never called you if I thought this was going to happen," she said, hugging him back. Well, *trying* to hug him back—kinda hard to do when he was as big as a refrigerator.

"Hon, I knew that boat was toast the minute you showed up," Tyrone laughed. "You just have that way about you."

"Geez, thanks."

"It's all good, Sugar. We got everyone out. I had a lot of evac experience in Iraq, but girl, you can sure keep people on their toes. We've got a lot to deal with, but you were the only one I hadn't accounted for. I'm glad to know you're okay." He turned to Cam and said, "You take care of her," because Tyrone was a little behind the curve on exactly who she was engaged to.

"I will," Cam answered, and Bobbie Faye moved between him and Trevor, because Cam was not only a big antelope mooning the lion, he'd just drawn a "bite me" on his ass in big red letters.

"Are you fuckin' wit' me?" Sean asked him, and Lonan threw himself into a leather chair in the apartment's plush living room, face buried in his hands.

"Have I ever fucked wit' you, Sean?" His answer was muffled into his hands. He had a hard time looking at Sean without being reminded, all over again, of his failure before. Of not being there when Sean needed him. Sean bore too many scars, too many reminders.

He'd always been a rough, scrappy kid. Aiden had been the one with the looks, but Sean, a little older, had been the one with the weird charisma, the one the ladies wanted, even though scars littered his body, his face, and he'd turned into a stocky man who looked like he'd kill you with one punch. . . .

At least, he used to. Before the fucking FBI agent had shot him with several rounds, chopping up his left arm, chipping his right shoulder, breaking both of his hands. He'd barely healed when Lonan had finally found and coerced the right person and gotten Sean out of the hospital. He'd also gotten Sean a physical therapist who met Sean's requirements, and resembled Bobbie Faye a little too much for Lonan's comfort, but that's what Sean wanted. The therapist had proven useful for keeping Sean's temper muted. Directed.

He watched his boss and friend as Sean worked with some sort of ball, trading off squeezing it with each hand. He'd probably never lift his right arm higher than shoulder-height, and he looked like a fucking pincushion—the old barbed wire scar across his face where someone had once tried to choke him just one of many scars. It was when he got up to go piss that the damage was obvious.

He wore sweatpants. His hands couldn't grip the zipper of the combat khakis he preferred. He couldn't grip a pencil or squeeze a trigger.

Lonan had not been in the right place when they needed him. He'd have died on the streets if it weren't for Aiden and Sean. They not only made sure he ate, but they made sure he ate first. They sent him to school. He'd gotten a university education.

He'd failed them. Aiden. Sean. Robbie and Mollie—dead—too.

He stared at his own hands, perfectly formed, manicured. "I could've fuckin' killed her a couple a times t'night," he confessed. "I wanted to."

"That's not the way of it," Sean said, empathy creeping into his voice.

"I know, Sean."

"Too quick 'n easy, lad."

He sighed. "You're right. I know it."

"I'd have loven to have her from the start of this," Sean continued. "Would've made it sweeter. But we'll have her."

Lonan nodded.

"They'll both suffer," Sean cajoled. "Doin' her like we plan? Will tie the fuckin' Fed in knots."

"Then he dies."

"Aye, Lonan, then he dies."

Lonan was happy with the plan.

Trevor made her wait in the Porsche. A Porsche. Holy Hot Buttered Jesus, he'd lost his mind, letting her sit in a Porsche. Clearly, his cover was "upscale business guy," and clearly the Feds were hell-bent to make his cover perfect, but wow, they'd really gone the extra mile.

She wanted to step out of the damned thing before her bad luck leaked out all over it.

He'd parked it in their drive; he'd backed in, left the engine running. He'd had to make calls the short drive home. Spare phone in his glove box, he was back to being unreadable agent-guy.

Riles checked the house while Trevor finished a call, standing outside the car, his conversation classified. Cam had parked at the road and now patrolled the grounds. Everyone searched for traps, signs someone had been there in the few hours it had taken her to sink a boat.

"It's clear," Trevor said at her side window, and she jumped so hard, she slammed her head against the seat rest.

"Crap, make a noise next time," she griped, climbing out of the car.

He didn't joke about her jumping in shock, didn't laugh, didn't use the moment like he usually did to sweep her playfully into his arms and tease her. In fact, from the moment he'd learned about the kiss, he'd become nearly unreadable. There hadn't been a single hot, steamy gaze, though yeah, she couldn't entirely blame him for that last one—she smelled faintly sulfury-lake-like, and her hair had curled as it dried into something not entirely unlike a drowned poodle. She wished he would just *look* at her, and then her brain went off on a how-icky-a-drowned-poodle-would-really-look tangent which was *not* the place to go mentally as he tugged her toward the house without a *single* solitary smart-ass word, his grip on her hand strong.

He stopped immediately at the living room, the blue color sharp against the white trim, and he faced her, something fathomless in his expression.

God, he hated the blue. She should've stuck with the butter cream.

"I started with red, and then green, but Riles said you'd hate green because of the camo and then—"

"It's good," he said. Then tugged her forward. They rounded into the bedroom and he locked the door before she registered what was going on. He reached over his head, grabbing the back of his once-pristine, now bloodied white shirt, and peeled it off, not bothering with the buttons. He tossed it away from them and she stared at the cut of his muscles, the flow of his hands as he moved toward her. The low-slung hum of her body whenever he was around kicked up a notch, musical in its wanting, and yet, all she could focus on were the differences. His too-short hair. The goatee. The expensive suit pants.

"You've lost weight," she said as he pulled her filthy lake-stinky shirt off, disposing of it and her bra in one fluid move.

He skimmed his hand along her waist, gently fingering the scars there, like he was lightly playing an instrument from memory. "You've lost weight, too," he said, so husky-voiced, she yanked her attention from his arms to his eyes, and for a moment, they simply stood, breathing each other in. His gaze stopped at her mouth, frowning, as if he could somehow see evidence of Cam's kiss. Seething below the surface, fighting it, trying hard not to be angry at her. Needing . . . something . . . and she framed his face with her hands and kissed him softly on the corner of his mouth, and on his cheek, and then stood on tiptoe to reach the scar just beneath his eye, and his arms came up around her as he breathed out, jagged.

"Thank you," he said, low, his voice humming up through her veins, "for painting for me."

He tasted her then. She curled her arms around his neck and drew herself as close as she could, skin on skin, warmth, heat, hard against soft, savoring it, and he took his time, exploring her mouth, the nape of her neck, her cheek, kissing away the tears she hadn't even known had formed.

An abrupt clattering sound echoed from the kitchen and they froze.

"Riles?" Trevor called.

No answer.

"Get dressed, quick. I'll be right back."

He sprinted out the bedroom door as she grabbed the closest bra, the one on the top of her dresser, the see-through black lace one Trevor loved. She barely had it in her hand, the lace whisper-soft against her fingers, when he came barreling back through the door.

"Get *out*! Bomb, bomb, bomb, get *out*!"

He dragged her over the bed to the old French doors, kicking them, breaking the lock, and the doors slammed open, shattering glass against the exterior of the house. He'd grabbed his go satchel and was shoving her off their little back patio, the cool night air chilling her as she tried to latch the damned bra. And run. Across a yard full of stickers, barefoot, hopping on one foot like a wounded penguin on a pogo stick. He scooped her up and flat-out ran, heading for the barn on the back of the property.

It was very hard to put on a bra while crunched against a man's chest and running for their lives. Bra makers don't exactly think of these scenarios. And just who in the fuck came up with the brilliant plan that bras ought to be clasped *in the back*? Where you cannot get to the clasps unless you're standing perfectly still? And pretzeling your arms all bendy behind you? Even the front closure things required getting the little hook lined up with its keeper, and where the hell was the Velcro bra?

"Get back, bomb!" Trevor yelled to Riles and Cam as they ran around the perimeter of the house, moving toward them. He cradled her until they were at the barn wall and then stood her up, placing her protectively behind him as she finally slid her arm through the straps, and she thought, *well this is silly, I need a shirt, and don't bombs usually go* boom?

When it did.

The concussion slammed them to the ground, Trevor rolling to take the brunt of the fall as the house fireballed upward and out against the deep indigo of the night sky as if Satan wanted to juggle, with smaller explosions following . . . perhaps the lesser demons in the act. For a brief moment, time suspended and she felt like she hung there in the air, topped out on a roller coaster, just a heartbeat away from screaming her head off, and then the debris rained down around them, falling and pinging on the raggedy tin roof of the barn. The fire spread, flickering against the dark line of the woods.

She had no sooner sat up and seen that Trevor was moving, wasn't bleeding, and then realized, *great, I'm sitting here in my bra . . .* and then registered *my* torn *see-through bra . . .* as Trevor rose up. And in that moment, out of the corner of her eye, while Trevor reached for her to check to see if she was hurt, she saw Cam running toward her.

Staring at her.

And she felt the chill of a light breeze across her bare skin.

Then suddenly, Cam was there, yanking off his shirt and, bam, between one breath and the next, he was fitting it over her naked self. Cam bent over her, blocking her from everyone's view, even Trevor's, as he checked her for injuries with a, "Baby, you okay?"

Trevor planted a hand in Cam's chest and shoved and, in spite of Cam having four inches on Trevor and in spite of Trevor having to come off the ground, he moved Cam away, hard, tumbling him into the groaning barn wall. "Back the *fuck* off," he said, and turned to pull Bobbie Faye up. "Are you okay?"

"I think Bobbie Faye follows the Marines' slogan."

"Really? What's that?"

"Total destruction in thirty minutes or the next one's free."

—SWAT Sniper Nancie Hays to Firefighter Kaz
D'España at the casino fire scene

Twelve

"She needs—" Cam shouted, pushing back against Trevor, his voice rising above the noise of the house burning.

Trevor was going to go after Cam, she could see it as clearly as the fire as he said, "You have no fucking idea *what* she needs."

She pushed between them, and something inside her snapped.

"Stop it, you two." To Trevor she said, "Am I okay? Fuck no. Me and Okay? We are not friends anymore. I don't think I am even speaking to Okay right now because you know what? This is a Victoria's Secret bra and it's the first time I ever went there when there wasn't a sale instead of going to Wal-Mart and I saved up and *myGod* do you have any idea how insane those prices are?" She shoved her arms in the sleeves of the shirt Cam had slammed over her head and as she spiraled away from the details to try to grasp onto the big picture, she latched onto a slim threat of sanity. "And by the way, who the *fuck* blew up our house?"

Riles had moved immediately to set up with his back to the fire, guarding their one vulnerable position—the lake—guns in both hands, the barn giving them refuge from any other angle. She caught a brief glance of his expression. With Cam hovering just behind her, Riles didn't bother to hide his disgust as he went back to scanning the tree line, searching for danger.

The house fire roared behind them, pipes hissed, joists seared in half and fell, glass popped and shattered. She couldn't quite wrap her mind around that. There was their home. In pieces. Around her. Oh, look, over there. Some of the tile from the ugly backsplash. Good thing they hadn't been able to afford the new appliances Trevor wanted.

The bedroom roof fell in, sccccrrrrrinnnnching and cracking and thunking on their king-sized bed. That beautiful bed and that beautiful mattress.

"It'll be okay, Sundance. We need to get out of here, though." Trevor scooped her up so she didn't have to walk barefoot across the stickers and burning debris.

"Right. Do they cover bombings under homeowner's insurance? Because I have never had homeowner's insurance before and I have a feeling there wasn't a 'Sure! We'll be happy to pay for it when bad guys blow it up!' codicil and I still don't think it was funny that most of them wanted a psychiatrist to sign off on me before they would even *consider* insuring me and the one we signed with was the *only* company who didn't get a restraining order—"

"You know you're babbling, right?" he asked, as he detoured around what used to be their microwave.

"—and really, seriously, I still do not believe that our insurance agent was on vacation in the Congo every single time I called for two months. We just moved in the damned house and Jesus, Trevor, I'm sorry."

Riles snorted.

"What?" she asked him. "I *am* sorry."

"You don't have anything to be sorry about," Trevor said, both to her and to Riles, and he caught Riles's eye just as Riles was about to say something else. Trevor glared; Riles clammed up. She had a feeling. Riles's life was just chock full of warning glances. "Check the truck," Trevor told his friend as they approached the front yard and she frowned, confused. Trevor nodded toward the Porsche (slightly on fire) and Riles's Jag (tires slashed from debris). The only vehicle not obviously damaged was Cam's truck. "Riles will be checking for explosives, trackers," he explained.

She quashed down the need to babble, to fling herself away from the moment, as she looked in his eyes, and his pain, riveted in the here and now.

"If you'd have done a half-assed decent job," Cam griped, stepping around the burning card table lying in the yard, "she wouldn't have been worried and we wouldn't be—"

"Shut the hell up, Moreau," Trevor snapped.

"—here." Cam clenched his fists. "Fuck you. With your house in flames—"

"*Our* house," Trevor said, setting her down beneath a tree on the front lawn halfway between the house and Cam's truck, the reds, oranges, and yellows of the firelight flickering over them. "Ours. And I'll take care of it."

Cam nodded pointedly at the burning remains. "Good job so far."

She stepped between them, splaying a hand on each man's chest, and damn, they both didn't have shirts on, and Cam reacted with a sharp intake of breath, and she snatched her hand away and wasn't *that* awkward. "Look, I know this is pure Crazy Talk, but I think we may have some bigger problems than the testosterone poisoning."

Cam leaned forward and said, "You're going into protec—"

"No."

"—tive custo—"

"No."

"—dy. Oh, hell yes, you *are*."

"No, she's not." Trevor's voice slid low, menacing, as he dialed his phone. Where the hell? Pants pocket? Mystical seventh dimension?

"This is *my* crime scene. What if that"—he pointed to the burning house—"was a warm-up?"

"Our best clue is Nick, and I know how to flush the little weasely sonofabitch out," Bobbie Faye said.

"No. We don't need you to be the one," Cam said. "We have hundreds of cops—sheriffs, state police, city—we can find him. And you're in no shape—you're exhausted, you've lost weight, you've got circles under your eyes. You look terrible."

"Well, gee, Cam, thank you. I feel *much* better now." She felt waves of heat and anger roll off Trevor as he talked on the phone to someone—clipped, short bursts—and the tension from him was like a battering ram . . . and yet, he knew this was her argument, and except for his hand at her waist, he made no other move. "And meanwhile," she continued, "how long will it take everyone to get a photo of him, knock on doors, turn over rocks?" What she didn't say, what she couldn't say, was, "And how great of a job did everyone do when Sean escaped, *huh*?" Because she could see it was fear for her that was driving Cam. "Nick lied. He was doing someone's bidding to get me in the casino and we need to know why." To Trevor, she said, "He's not evil, just mercenary. I can give him a reason to come talk to me."

"We'll handle it—you're going into hiding. I'll make some calls and—"

"She's not going anywhere, Moreau, without me." Trevor had closed his phone.

"Because you've kept her oh-so-fucking safe."

Cam had leaned in too far this time. She felt Trevor shift, felt his leg muscles bunch against the back of her legs, and knew that he was going for Cam—and she shouted, "No, Trevor!" jumping, putting her back against Trevor, keeping him from strangling her ex. Because right then, Trevor was losing it. Whatever was said on the phone had made it worse, somehow, and he had lost his home, too. He'd been the one to find this place, he'd been the one to put up the security. He'd entertained her by walking the backyard, planning where he was going to put a deck and a grill one day, and a hammock. He'd already repaired the old sinks and two rooms' worth of old hardwood flooring. He'd done that in the two weeks they'd lived there.

And it was gone.

"You really *really* can't kill him," she said over her shoulder to her fiancé. He gazed down at her angled face, his eyes glittering red, reflecting the inferno behind her, and she felt him go just a little bit crazy inside, even though he didn't move a muscle.

* * *

The mechanic stood there watching the boat sink, his own clothes ruined from the oily film that had spanned the top of the lake water as the boat had sunk. He wanted to wash his hands, had to resist asking one of the ER techs handling hurt gamblers for a sanitizer, which would have been ludicrous. In light of how nasty he felt, one little sanitizer wouldn't do enough. And so he forced himself to stand there, arms crossed, looking for all the world like another victim, gaping at the wreckage of years of work.

Because it was a wreckage. It was not supposed to go this way. He'd watched it unfold, powerless to stop it. None of it should have happened—not Bobbie Faye showing up, not the men going after her, not her fiancé involved in that poker game. Tactically, he'd missed something.

He shoved his hands in his pockets, needing to keep them busy so he wouldn't focus on the oily feel of his fingertips, and he felt a few poker chips there. Chips he hadn't remembered shoving in his pocket in the melee.

Had he forgotten something else? Some small detail? Had he missed something obvious?

This mess would have killed Chloë, seeing these people hurt. Her whole life, her mantra, her motto, was about safety, protecting the general public. Public service. That's what she was about, that's what she gave her life for.

Only she hadn't known she was giving her life.

The bile of that fact rose again, burning his throat, eating him from the inside out, the same way grief had eaten his soul. He wasn't the man he used to be, he knew that. Knew the crisp, clear autumn morning when it changed, when they told him of her car wreck. A one-person fatal wreck.

The ache and pain of losing her slammed him all over again as he stood there and watched the engineers and marina owners and police brainstorm just what to do, and how to do it, to try to rescue the white behemoth of a casino lying in the water. It was never going to be the same, though. He could have told them that, that it was never going to be the same, no matter how much money they poured into it, no matter how much effort and railing at the gods they did, no matter what sort of verdict came down from a jury somewhere, it was never ever going to be the same.

People would forget. Their lives would go on and people would forget. Eleven years from now, it might be a dim memory, that time when the casino boat sank, and someone would mention it and someone else's eyes would get a faraway look as if they were searching in the vast amount of daily minutiae, through the latest TV shows and what their boss said two weeks ago and the scandal of a pantyless celebrity that had hit the airwaves, and they would finally call up some vague, fleeting glimpse of this moment and nod, yeah, and then move on.

That's what they did with Chloë's memory now—they moved on.

They wouldn't just move on once this was complete. They would have to pay attention, they would have to remember. There would be outrage and numbing pain and laws made and his name would probably define a new standard of the harm that could be done, but they would, by God, pay attention.

So he forced himself to stand there, ignoring his concern that other agendas may be at work. As long as his succeeded as well, he didn't really care anymore what others' did. He was beyond saving, anyway.

"Damn fool girl," Etienne barked, slamming out of the RV for the second time in two days, and V'rai, Lizzie, and Aimee froze. V'rai didn't know if this was just another effort of her brother to blow off steam—the sunken casino ship imagery was now split-screened with the house explosion.

"He really ought to talk to her," Aimee said again.

"Not yet, *chère*," V'rai cautioned. "If he goes over there now, she'll die. I know it."

"It's not like you're right all the time," Lizzie pointed out. "Sometimes you're wrong."

"*Mais, non*, not lately," V'rai noted. "The visions . . . they have been stronger. Somethin' 'bout our girl, she . . ." V'rai stopped at a loss for the right word.

"Amplifies it?" Aimee asked, and V'rai nodded.

That was it, exactly. Amplifies. Ever since Bobbie Faye had come back into their lives, the visions were stronger. Accurate. Deadly.

They heard Etienne's truck engine rev and he peeled out of their long gravel drive.

"Oh, holy shit," Lizzie said, peering out the RV's window. "I think . . ."

V'rai got very very sick to her stomach just then, and knew . . . *knew* this was the wrong thing for him to do. Wrong time, wrong thing, and especially when he was so angry at his daughter.

"We have to stop him," she told her sisters.

Lizzie grabbed her cell phone, started dialing.

"That's a waste of time," Aimee said, grabbing the car keys.

"Which way is he going?" Aimee asked V'rai.

She thought a moment, wondering if she should tell them everything. Then, finally, she settled. "Lafayette."

"Then we're going to Lafayette," Aimee said, jangling the keys as she walked awkwardly to the door, her right prosthetic leg giving her trouble.

"How?" Lizzie asked. "You can't push the gas or brake, V'rai can't see, and I sure as hell can't cross bridges." Lizzie had never been able to drive across a bridge again after she'd wrecked on one and ended up in a submerged car in a river.

"Old times," Aimee said, maybe a little maniacally. "I'll navigate, V'rai will do the pedals."

"It's dark!" Lizzie protested.

"I can't see anyway," V'rai said, standing to join Aimee. "If we hurry, we can catch him."

"I'm not leaving y'all to go do this," Lizzie said, grabbing her gun. "You don't need me to have my eyes open on the bridges, but I can still shoot."

"And pray," V'rai said. Lizzie was really good at praying.

And shooting, but luckily, she had more practice at the praying.

Dox watched the Bobbie Faye woman, the two Feds, and the cop from his scope. At forty, he was the old man of Sean's group, and he'd shimmied up the tree a hair slower than he'd planned. He'd gotten out of the house a hair slower, too, after setting up the bomb and the message; two seconds slower and the Fed would have caught him.

He could tell the sniper guy "felt" him—good snipers usually had a sixth sense of when they were being watched. Dox could have taken them out multiple times since the explosion if he'd wanted to. Change that—if Sean had wanted him to. Sean, instead, wanted them alive and on the run.

If it had been up to Dox, they'd already be dead for what they did to Aiden and Mollie. He probably should have included Robbie in that number, since Robbie had died, too, but Dox hadn't cared about the little weasel rat-faced bastard. But Aiden and Mollie? Good people. Solid. Kept the crew together in the bad times, they did.

He'd wished, for them, that Aiden and Mollie had found each other, the way they were. They flirted around the edges of it, but they hadn't had any bit of happiness, like they could have.

Dox knew it was a romantic notion. He was fond of Romance. Loved a good flick. His wife had dragged him to that Bridget Jones movie a few years back, and he hadn't wanted to tell her but he'd kinda liked it when the Darcy bloke showed up there at the end. He'd seen the way Mollie stole glances at Aiden when the man didn't realize. Kinda the way the tall bloke, the state cop, hungered for the woman.

Well, it wasn't going to end any better for them. He didn't feel bad about that. He waited, because Sean said to wait. And Dox wasn't about to question Sean. He'd seen the man beat the living hell out of a woman who crossed him, once, and that was before Sean became a twisted fuck. They'd all lived well, though. They'd lived, was mostly the point; if it weren't for Sean, most of them wouldn't have.

Dox simply watched the foursome as they checked the truck for explosives and drove away. Sirens blared, fire trucks on the way. A good minute or two out, but that was his cue to go. He knew Ackers would pick up the tail on the road out.

Cam had pushed the truck at top speed, the dotted white lines on the interstate whipping together, a blurred line stitching the dark road to the horizon as they headed east toward Lafayette, which was smack in the middle of Cajun country and proud of it, throwing a party for everything that had anything to do with being a Cajun at the drop of a hat. Hell, at the drop of anything. Drop a toothpick, they would throw a party.

Damned good ones, too.

If he could picture his own personal version of hell, though, this would be it: a sniper to his right, riding shotgun, and Trevor and Bobbie Faye crammed in the extended cab's jump scat behind him. His only consolation? Trevor seemed to be in hell, too.

"I could have gone in and gotten my own damned clothes," she griped.

"We're trying to not draw attention here," Cam said. "You know, pretty much the opposite of what you do."

They'd stopped at a gas station, and Cam was still shirtless—waiting for Riles to get a replacement for Bobbie Faye from inside the convenience store. Trevor changed clothes in the tight quarters of the truck, a shirt and jeans pulled from the go-bag he'd grabbed. Yep, Cam's definition of hell. He tried his dead level best to ignore the fact that Bobbie Faye was in the backseat with a temporarily naked fiancé.

"Riles isn't going to know what to get," she argued. "Besides, everyone will think I'm still at the fire. They wouldn't recognize me."

"Like you aren't splattered all over every news program right now? How can you be so self-delusional?"

"Watch it, Moreau," Trevor warned, but Cam ignored him. Cam had turned a little so that he could see her over his shoulder, and the undercurrent of his words bounced around inside the cab. She was the fucking *Queen* of self-delusional, what in the hell had he expected? But there had to be a point where she saw that, where she grew out of it. If it killed him, she was going to open her goddamned eyes and pay attention to her life. Her real life. The one she could have, the one right there in her grasp, if she'd just wake the hell up.

Riles returned to the truck before she answered and tossed a pair of flip-flops in the backseat to her, then handed over a t-shirt, along with bottles of water and energy bars.

Bobbie Faye unfolded the white t-shirt and said, "Oh, *fuck* no. I am *not* wearing this shirt."

Riles grinned. "It was either that or the 'my life is a drinking game' one."

"You're lying."

"I figured the drinking game one was too obvious. I went for *subtle*."

It was a BAMA RULES t-shirt. As in *Alabama*. As in archrivals, game day tomorrow, and Cam was sitting there, former LSU champion quarterback. Yeah, Riles was subtle, all right. Riles grinned, exceptionally pleased with himself.

Trevor grabbed the shirt, turned it inside-out, cut off the back tag with his pocketknife, and handed it back to her, all one fluid motion, all without a word.

She *still* held it out from her body as if it would make her lift off the ground, spin around, and upchuck pea soup. She met Cam's gaze and he knew they were thinking the same thing: wearing this was like committing some sort of unholy, unpardonable sin.

That's my girl, he thought, as she grimaced. To this day, she could probably recite the plays better than he could. For just that half-a-second, they were back there, the crowd screaming, people rushing the goalposts, confetti floating in the air, horns sounding, band rocking the stadium as he swooped her up and spun her around and they laughed until they nearly fell over, dizzy with exuberance.

Trevor shielded her as she pulled off Cam's t-shirt, then he threw it at Cam, disgust and annoyance cracking his supposedly super-agent shell. Cam slowly turned the t-shirt back right-side-out, the state police logo in the upper right pocket area. Cam didn't let his gaze waver, just stared straight where Bobbie Faye was donning the stupid shirt, while Trevor glared back at him, threatening to throttle him.

He'd really like to see the man try.

Cam put the truck in gear and they got back on the interstate. He glanced in his rearview mirror, catching Trevor's expression.

Under any other circumstances, he'd have probably liked Trevor. He'd have probably even considered him a friend. Now? He was a very dangerous enemy, one he had to work with, one he would beat. The man was a stone-cold killer. Licensed to do it, sure. FBI, sure. Former Spec Ops. Bobbie Faye had enough trouble, all on her very own. Hell, she couldn't walk across the street without causing trouble. He knew two libraries which had banned her—one still hadn't rebuilt the shelving she'd inadvertently broke and sent domino-fashion across the floor. But the very positively *last* thing she needed? This guy. Because Trevor thrived on trouble; he didn't grasp that he needed to get Bobbie Faye out of this mess instead of letting her wade deeper into it. And Cam knew she'd keep wading, and he knew he'd always go in after her.

If the sonofabitch didn't get her killed.

Ce Ce packed thermoses. Soup, in case there was a cold snap—unlikely, but it could happen. Everything they needed for grilling—hot dogs, burgers, buns, the works. The tool company—Mac Tools, Inc.—was giving away the tickets and doing a big promotional gig right there in the parking lot—complete with photographers snapping their pictures. Monique was going to bring all of the drinks.

They were tailgating.

Never in a million years did she think she was going to be tailgating at an LSU game, but it occurred to her that she could bring a couple thousand business cards for her voodoo sideline business. This could turn into fun.

Her cell phone rang. She glanced at the late hour, surprised, and snatched it up.

"Ceece, it's Nina. Where is she?"

"Oh, hey, girl, she's at home."

"Nope, Ceece, her house just blew up."

"What!" Ce Ce clicked on the TV. "When on earth?" And she watched the live footage showing the burning house and the crowds of police and firemen and reporters and on-lookers.

"A little while ago," Nina said. "I'm on my way in. The police radio traffic says she's alive and that she's there, but they're not letting me talk to her."

"I don't see her on the footage, hon," Ce Ce said, bending close to the screen and scrutinizing the crowds. "They usually do close-ups, but maybe she's answering questions? Or maybe Trevor's got her safe somewhere?" Ce Ce scrutinized the data scrolling along the bottom of the screen—it said no casualties. She checked the matching bracelet: orange. Bobbie Faye's house blew up and it was orange? "And the chicken foot isn't black," she said aloud to Nina.

"The cuckoo clucks at twelve?"

"Oh, sorry, hon. It's a protection spell. The chicken foot is supposed to turn black if she's in danger, and it didn't. She might've already worn out its power. I'm going to have to super-boost it. She's wearing its twin."

"I am not even going to pretend to understand that—but is there a downside to this thing?"

"Well . . ." Ce Ce hated to talk about the downsides of voodoo. People could get so fixated on negatives, and that bad attitude could sometimes undo a spell. Or create the very problem she'd been trying to prevent. "A few."

"Will she turn blue again? Because I am so bringing my camera if she is."

"No, no colors. If she takes it off too soon, it could magnify the trouble. Or it could turn into an aphrodisiac."

"You can make something people can wear that becomes an aphrodisiac?"

"Well, sure."

"Ceece. We have so got to talk about franchising."

Nina hung up before Ce Ce could ask any more questions. Meanwhile, there was no way she was leaving Bobbie Faye unprotected. That left boosting the current spell.

Not a problem.

Thirteen

"Oh, shit," she said, gazing down.

"What's wrong?" Trevor's long frame didn't fit in the jump seat, so he was sitting at an angle, which allowed her to lean into him. She felt his heartbeat ramp up as she snuggled against him. She was as close as she could get without climbing in his lap. He followed her gaze down.

"The chicken foot juju turned black."

There was a moment of total silence in the truck cab. The first real grin of the night quirked at his lips. "I'm not sure I speak 'chicken foot juju'—I think you're going to have to translate that one, Sundance."

She held up her right wrist with the ugly chicken foot bracelet.

"Um . . ." he said, looking it over, "I'd been trying to ignore that."

"Ce Ce said if there was really bad juju around, it would turn black. And see?" She waggled her arm and the chicken foot bands clinked together. "Black." All three men were silent. Pointedly silent. "After the casino sank, it was only orangey brown. Not black." Still. Silent. Even Cam, who respected the voodoo, looked back at her in the rearview mirror as if she were three bricks shy of a load. Trevor's lips quirked again, and she felt a chuckle roll through his abs to his chest, though he suppressed it. "Fine. *Mock* the bad-juju indicator. I put on this shirt, the chicken foot turned black. We're in trouble."

"Because sinking a boat and having your house blow up were too subtle for you?" Riles asked.

She smacked him in the shoulder. "Thank you, Obi-Wan. I am so encouraged now." She turned to Trevor. "You don't think we just had a conscientious bomber, do you?" If she could mainline Denial right now, she would. She still had the shakes over the fact that Trevor had run to the kitchen after the noise, seen an intruder leaving out a window, a bomb sitting in the middle of the stupid island, and a message in ketchup, of all things, spelling "GET OUT." Of course, he could've waited five more minutes and then she would've ended up *fully* nekkid in front of Cam *and* Riles. (She could practically hear the Universe laugh evilly and start planning.)

Trevor squeezed her a little. "You're thinking too hard," he murmured in her ear. "You should rest."

"You believe in the bad-juju indicator, right?" Because if she was going crazy? He was going with her. That was *the deal.*

"Of course I do," he said, hugging her to him, keeping his chin on the top of her head. She knew it was so he could laugh at her, but fine fine fine fine *fine.*

She sighed, settling into his chest (and her Hormones, which had practically been bludgeoned to death by the night's events, managed a weak *mmmmmmmmmmmmmmm* as she felt his abs beneath her arms). It was much easier to think about that than the fact that someone really wanted to toy with them—how someone made sure Nick gave her just the right information to set her Wig-Out Meter on overdrive and send her smack into the middle of Trevor's sting operation— that took some serious insider knowledge. That someone, she was pretty sure, wasn't Nick—but Nick would know who it was—and this time, she was going to make sure the slimy bastard told the truth.

Someone clearly wanted her—or them—off balance, wary,

off their game. If it had been the matter of a simple desire to have her dead, any number of ways would have done the job a lot better, a lot faster, and a lot cheaper. So why would they go to the trouble of warning her and Trevor so they could get out?

It made no sense.

She could feel Trevor spinning through the same scenarios. Of course, he probably knew classified information, and for a brief moment, she thought wistfully about how nice it would be to have access to multiple sources of knowledge, because she hated not knowing crap, but she damned near snorted at the idea. She'd have to be an agent to have that kind of access, and Bobbie Faye being an FBI agent was about as likely as Nina suddenly going to work for Homeland Security.

She tucked her face against Trevor's shoulder, grateful to have him back in his normal t-shirt and jeans, grateful to have the equilibrium just tucking into him brought her. "I'm sorry," she said, for his ears only.

He kissed her temple, holding her with one hand, running his fingers through her hair. He murmured low into her ear, "It's not your fault, Sundance. It's not."

For the first time that evening, she let herself feel the reality of the moment. She'd just lost *every* single memento. Every one she'd kept from her trailer. He'd lost photos and military medals and a few things that he held dear. There weren't many, but they'd been important.

They were gone.

She squeezed her eyes shut, and he held her, his head bent to hers, and her need of him seemed to ease his tension, knocking the corners off his fury over Cam. "We'll have our own place, Sundance. We'll have our home and our family. I promise you that. I did not come to play, remember?"

She remembered.

She needed that right now.

Because that damned chicken foot was black. She wanted to take it off and fling it outside the truck, but Ce Ce had given her dire dire warnings, very explicit that she not take it off until Ce Ce did the unbinding spell, that taking it off could be even more disastrous than Bobbie Faye could imagine. But the damned thing hadn't turned black when she'd sunk a huge luxury casino boat and her house had blown up. So what, in God's name, was it that made it turn black *now*?

Then she remembered whose life she was thinking about.

Great. She was going into the Apocalypse armed with a Chicken Foot Mood Bracelet for Trouble.

It started raining.

V'rai drove. Well, technically, V'rai worked the pedals. Aimee had scooted as close to V'rai as she could to help steer the old Oldsmobile, and was shouting out instructions and landmarks while Lizzie screamed in the backseat.

"Lamppost!" Lizzie shouted and V'rai wanted to cut the wheel, but she didn't know which direction.

"Got it!" Aimee shouted back. "Push down a little more on the gas pedal, hon."

V'rai felt like the world was rushing past her and through the car, wind blasting her from the open window, the smell of asphalt in the dying heat of the late night whipping acrid against her face, cornfields just beyond that, pastures. She felt like a NASCAR commercial, with cars zooming the other direction, loud and startling. And V'rai was a little worried about being pulled over. "How fast are we going now?"

"Um," Aimee leaned over to see the dials V'rai knew were on the dashboard. "Twenty-two."

"Oh, dear," V'rai said.

She stomped on the gas, the car lurched forward, hard, throwing her backward, and Lizzie yelled "Bird!"

It was going to be the longest trip to Lafayette V'rai had ever taken.

If Bobbie Faye had had any doubts whatsoever about the exact location of the horse track, the three billion signs plastered on every square inch of the buildings and roadside for the last two miles would have cleared them right the hell up.

"Built in the middle of a sugarcane business that went belly-up after Rita," Cam explained to Riles—mostly, she thought, to fill the silence.

And then they turned into the well-lit entrance; the central corrugated metal building, with its jazz-finger angles and strobing lights plunked slap in the middle of a field surrounded by stately magnolias and live oaks, looked like the slutty girl at the debutante ball.

Her brother's dad used to gamble here, back when there was a dirt track, a railing, a few bleachers, and the small, clapboard Baptist church two miles down the road that had every gambler's name and included each one on their weekly prayer list. (Her mother had a real winning streak at picking ultimate assholes who would abandon their children. It was the one thing she and Roy and Lori Ann had bonded on fast and early.)

She would have been soaked, running in from the parking lot, if Trevor hadn't had a rain slicker in his go bag.

Inside, the cold hush of the air conditioner chilled her newly damp skin, and the crowd noise fueled the adrenaline. Thirty-foot ceilings, however, did not contain enough air to disperse the smell of rain-soaked skin and sweat. Leather booths abutted a floor-to-ceiling glass wall that ran the length of the room and overlooked the track to her right, and a long ebony bar lined the solid wall to her left. The entire club was cantilevered over the regular stands; a window seat gave the impression of floating on air.

Or in this case, water, since rain trickled down the glass.

There were big flat-screen monitors on every wall; just because the horses weren't racing here didn't mean they weren't racing somewhere in the world, and this group was drinking to it. Raucous laughter and chatter echoed in the room; there were easily a thousand people crammed inside. One quick glance told Bobbie Faye that this clubhouse catered to the wealthier clientele of the racetrack—the crowd reeked of money. From the designer clothes to the sparkling jewelry to the expensive, hand-tooled leather purses, it was all about people who had enough money to play with it.

The whole damned thing boggled Bobbie Faye's mind. She had exactly $2.38 in her checking account. She worked a lot of hours and made more than minimum wage, with Ce Ce insisting now on bonuses because her notoriety brought in a lot of customers. Those bonuses had enabled her to help have enough for the down payment on the house, but not a damned thing extra. How in the world did people have the money to play the horses? Or gamble on teams? Was there some sort of alien language or secret handshake that rich people had that made their money multiply?

She caught her reflection in the bar mirror.

Oh, hell, her hair had enough static electricity to power a buzz saw. Way to blend, she thought, tugging on it and trying to smooth it, 'til Trevor took her hand, his fingers laced with her own, and turned her so that she could see his expression: he dragged his gaze from her toes exposed in the flip-flops up her legs, pausing for a moment where her belly button showed just beneath the hem of the obviously-too-small t-shirt and then slowly up, and when he met her eyes, she recognized that heat burning there, that *if there weren't a thousand people in here, you'd be naked* heat.

Every. Single. Inch. Of her skin said, "hot damn" and "back 'atcha" as he squeezed her to him in the crowded room, one hand at the nape of her neck. He kissed her, possession and fire in spite of how she looked, and while she suspected that one of the reasons he'd kissed her right then was because her face was plastered all over every freaking TV in the entire room, with live footage of the casino boat and then live footage of their house (still burning, damn), there was absolutely no doubt in her mind that he'd wanted to do that for the last hour.

"Don't look," he said, when he broke off the kiss. Then he glanced over past Cam, who could have been carved in granite, he was so unmoving, so livid, so determined to gaze anywhere but at them, and Trevor asked the clubhouse guard, "Where are the fire exits?"

Before Bobbie Faye could turn around, Riles had blended into the gamblers and disappeared, heading for the exit on the other side of the room. Cam nodded briefly at Trevor, indicating that he'd have the entrance covered. As she and Trevor wove through the crowd, Bobbie Faye scanned the room, searching for Nick. She'd called over a dozen people when they'd first left the burning house, narrowing down Nick's location for the night.

But something was wrong. She knew it, could sense it. There . . . she saw it.

Nick. Sitting alone at one of the leather booths abutting the window overlooking the track. His attention . . . on her.

Then down at his hands flattened palm-down on the table-top. Nick did a really fine impression of hangdog guilt.

Bobbie Faye pulled against Trevor's hand, and he stopped short, following her gaze.

"That's Nick," she said. "And I'll be damned if he wasn't expecting me."

Trevor's sharp gaze snapped back to the man in the booth and then scanned the room. He pulled his cell phone out, hit speed dial, and said, simply, "They were expecting us. Tell Moreau. Spread the word."

The word, she presumed, was to be spread to the various backup and reinforcements he'd alerted on their way in. Cam had the Lafayette-based state police gathering at the perimeter of the racetrack, and Trevor had at least a couple of agents on their way in. Neither man was about to let Nick get away.

Except . . . he wasn't running.

Fidgeting? Yes. Sweating? Profusely. Even in the chill of the air-conditioning set to cryogenic levels.

"Oh, this is bad," she said to Trevor, who nodded, still scanning the crowd as she moved toward Nick.

Fourteen

Trevor pulled her back. "We're not sitting in front of that window." He motioned to Nick to meet them at the bar, and Nick eased out of the booth, careful to keep his hands at his sides, easy to see.

"I'm very, very sorry," Nick said as soon as he neared them. There wasn't a lot of room at the crowded bar, but Trevor maneuvered them next to the nervous bookie, all while checking out each person nearby, watching how they moved, their level of interest, or studied noninterest. "Really. Very. Honest-to-God, I'm—"

"Yeah. 'Sorry,'" Bobbie Faye said. "I get it. Groveling. Good move, but so really not going to save your ass."

"Very very," Nick continued, staring down at his feet. "Very."

Trevor tamped down the urge to slam the man's face into the bar, and he felt his ripple of tension go straight through Bobbie Faye. He tamped down harder. Trevor leaned forward just a hair, and Nick wisely stepped away. The pitch of Trevor's voice clicked into *you are completely dead* territory. "That was our home, you sonofabitch," he said, nodding to the footage still playing, "so you'd better start talking." He did not add the "if you want to live" on the end of that sentence. The likelihood that this asshole was wired for recording? Within the realm of possibility. But Trevor had no problem *communicating* that threat, and the bookie blanched and swallowed hard.

There was nowhere this bastard would be able to hide when this was over. Not a single fucking place. Trevor knew he'd been set up the second Bobbie Faye had walked into that casino. The sting he'd been called in on was well-planned, well-manned, and everything about it still seemed . . . off. They had enough information to know that they shouldn't have had that much information. The multiple changes in venues alone was suspect.

"I don't know anything," Nick said. "I mean, I—I know that this guy threatened my family. He had surveillance photos of my mom, my dad. Look, all I know is he said I had to take these big bets. And I had to warn her." He turned to Bobbie Faye. "You. I had to warn you. I don't know why, but he said I had to say Alex was the one making the bets."

"You met him?" Trevor asked.

Nick shook his head. "No, the pictures were delivered. He called—made it real fucking"—he blanched again, turned to Bobbie Faye—" 'scuse me." Apparently, he was a very polite bookie. "The guy made it clear he could get to anyone, and I believed him. I never got into this for the big stuff. I swear, Bobbie Faye, really. It just started as a joke a few years ago, that time you ended up on the JumboTron."

"Geez, thank you. My humiliation for the night wasn't quite complete, but I think that wrapped it up nicely." When she faced Trevor's quizzical expression, she turned a deep red. "Um, naked footage of me, skinny-dipping. A hacker managed to broadcast it up on the big screen at an LSU game."

Trevor bit back the urge to ask "alone?" because no one goes skinny-dipping alone, and the way she most definitely avoided glancing in Cam's direction told him just who that other someone had been.

"And," Nick had continued, "one thing just sort of led to another and we were doing a Bobbie Faye board like you do a football board and it kinda exploded." He took a small step back from her because she had bristled up like a porcupine.

"Sorry! Bad word choice. It grew. But I never really set out to make this some big money-making scheme. It was just kinda easy to keep taking the bets.

"Now, he's threatening my family. That's all I know. I don't know where he is or who he is, but I'm supposed to give you a phone number to call."

"How in the hell would someone know we were going to meet up?" Trevor asked him. Riles had moved into position a couple of feet behind Nick and, like Trevor, scanned the room for anything, anyone, suspicious. "We didn't even know until tonight." Not to mention that Cam had made sure that the police band was still broadcasting that she was on the scene at their burning house.

"Dammit," she muttered. Then turned to him as Nick shrugged, wide-eyed, innocent. "My phone calls to find Nick. Or else they're following us."

He and Cam and Riles had all watched for a tail, but it wasn't impossible, if someone had enough money, to hire four or five cars instead of the usual two—each one picking them up as the previous tagger dropped back.

"Or," Trevor said, eyeing Nick, "someone knew we'd come looking for you, to find out more. That I would naturally want to question you, and that's why you've been camped out here, waiting. If we hadn't started making those calls to find you, what would have happened? Would you have called," Trevor supplied without giving the man a chance to lie, "to drop some hints about something else that you knew? Or would we have gotten a convenient phone call of an eyewitness that placed you here, bragging about some information you knew?"

Nick studied his feet.

"Give me the damned number," Trevor said, and he dialed it as Nick called it out to him. "Meanwhile, you're under arrest. There's another agent on his way in here and if you move one single hair, I'm going to call that resisting arrest and I'm going to have a fucking field day on your ass, you get me?"

Nick nodded so hard, Trevor was mildly surprised the

man didn't give himself a concussion. And then he heard the damned Irish lilt of the man's voice when he answered the phone.

Nina rode the black Ducati, the 160 hp of pure Italian racing engine roaring between her legs, right where it belonged, tearing down the interstate, the roar of the engine humming through her as she wove in and out of heavy traffic. The miles stretched out in front of her, nothing but the bleak darkness of swamps on either side of the interstate; there was barely a small town or occasional farm between Baton Rouge, headed west toward Lafayette, to break up the monotony. Beneath her black helmet, her headphones were connected to a voice-activated cell, and her call to Trevor's phone kept going straight to voice mail.

Fuck.

He'd called in a location change—from the casino to the racetrack—and that's when she knew her information was correct. But she had to get it to him, and she didn't trust anyone else. She wasn't about to call it in, letting it wind its way through channels, battling out between his agency and hers (hers being nonexistent on the government's books, which just did not bode well for interagency communication).

She checked her watch. Twenty minutes. At top speed, she could get there in twenty, and then she'd find them. Tell them.

"Did you enjoy my gift for you, then?" Sean asked, and all Trevor had to do was pitch Riles one look, and Riles moved in close, his hands on his guns, ready to draw, scanning the crowd. Bobbie Faye went cold, dead rigid—hearing Sean, despite not holding the phone herself.

Goddamned sonofabitch.

"You're a dead man, MacGreggor." This time, he didn't fucking care who was recording him. "It's just a matter of time."

"Ah, but Cormier, me lad, you see, that's the thing you'd be doin' wit'out, is time. Of course, you could make it all a damn sight easier on yourself and give me the girl."

The mother lode of adrenaline raced through Trevor's veins and he curled Bobbie Faye toward his chest and plastered her against his own body, putting her next to the bar, himself between her and the crowd he steadily scanned in the mirror above the bar, and said, "Go fuck yourself. You're never getting her. Ever. I don't care *what* it takes, you're dead."

"Ah, but you'd be repeatin' yourself, and the thing is, you'd be wrong. We're goin' to get to a point, us two, where you'll just hand her over to me sweet as pie."

Bobbie Faye stiffened in his arms. He knew she was listening as best she could in the crowd—she'd laid her head against his shoulder, appearing to any interested audience that they were a couple where the woman was tired of waiting for her guy to get off the damned phone—but she was catching the gist of it. He hugged her tighter.

He'd waited on his belly for three days for a strike against a tango—a terrorist. He'd lived for months in squalor that made this country's garbage dumps seem pristine in comparison because that was where he had to be for the mission. He'd slit the throat of a pretty young woman who had a backpack of bombs, all set to destruct as soon as she reached the café in Bagram filled with women and children and soldiers. He'd had to come up behind her fast and silent, no negotiations possible, and end her with a quick move. He'd been the guy who'd had to take out a school, where all of the children were supposed to have been removed by his team. Only they missed one. A little girl who'd hidden, who understandably didn't trust the men in the scary uniforms and masks, who'd popped up in the window as his laser lit up the building to guide the smart bombs already en route.

He wished his memories of death and destruction weren't all just a blur. He should still be able to see the details of that little girl's face in that window, but his memories held too many things. Too many.

He hadn't realized how numb to the world he'd gotten. He hadn't realized how much he no longer cared, how he no longer *felt,* 'til he'd met Bobbie Faye. He'd gone through Quantico as a request from much farther up the food chain, and he still hadn't cared. He'd become a good agent, driven to find the answers, but it was instinct, survival, nothing related to caring. He became exactly what he'd detested about his parents: detached. Though their reasons were much simpler—they had never cared to start with. They were polite, professional, courteous, and both locked in their own worlds, only dimly aware that children orbited around them. It was just the way of it.

Then he'd surveilled Bobbie Faye for months for the op, because they had to know for certain just what, if any, involvement she had with the perp. (Turned out? None.) And the more he'd watched, the more he'd wanted to meet her. Just to see if it was possible that she cared as much—as tenaciously—as it seemed.

She'd cracked him wide open, and she hadn't even meant to. It was more than he'd expected. He'd felt, too much. It hurt, the wanting, sometimes, but he *felt.* And loved. And laughed. And he wasn't fucking losing her.

"You seriously underestimate me, MacGreggor," was all he said.

"Aye, that's possible," the man answered. "But you maybe want to ask yourself, if I've gone to the trouble to fuck ya around this far, d'you really think I had no plan?"

"I think," Trevor goaded him, "that you're nothing more than a bastard who got lucky." That wasn't what he thought at all, and it wasn't in the negotiator's handbook, that was for hell sure, and even Riles snapped his attention back to Trevor on that one.

"D'you think you can keep a fuckin' security team on everyone she loves and all your own family, too? You might have a pile of money to keep 'em all protected for a wee while, but I've got more."

Bobbie Faye heard the threat and nearly bolted out of his

arms, she was so angry, wanting to have at MacGreggor, and not having a target.

"My family!" she hissed at him when he held her in place. And then the second half of MacGreggor's comment registered. "Wait. Sercurity? You put security on them?"

MacGreggor chuckled. "Oh sure, I don't think she knew about that, did she? There's a fuckin' lot we need to tell your lovely fiancée about what you've been up to. And I'm sure lookin' forward to watchin' her reactions; even in that shirt, she's a real sight to see. . . ."

Trevor craned around. MacGreggor—or one of his men—had to be nearby.

"You sonofabitch. Why don't you come after me?"

"You fuckin' moron, I *am*."

And the truth slammed home for Trevor: MacGreggor was going to do all he could to hurt Trevor the most, by hurting Bobbie Faye and the people she loved.

"Give me the girl, and you'll save a lot of lives. That's your job, right?"

"Over my dead body."

Bobbie Faye gasped, her arms going around Trevor, and he knew he was shedding control. That's the last thing you say to a potential hostage-taker.

MacGreggor laughed. "Oh, yeah, boy-o, it may come to that, but not 'til you've seen what I've done and not 'til I have the girl. If she wants to save your stinkin' life an' the lives of people she loves, she'll walk straight from you in a heartbeat."

"What is it you really want?" Trevor asked the man, knowing full well MacGreggor wasn't going to tell him. Not really. But Trevor's phone had piggybacked a counter-signal when he'd dialed the number Nick had given him, and the Bureau would be working hard and fast to triangulate that signal, and trace Sean's whereabouts.

He couldn't be far. He was either in the room or had someone there, but he was close by.

"Always ask, eh?" Sean said. "But I've told you. *I want the girl*. Now, I'm not all that interested in blowin' her up

just yet, but the people around you? I have no problem killin'. You'd best be gettin' 'em out of there if you expect 'em
to live. So it is. You've got ten minutes. If you're lucky."

MacGreggor severed the call.

Lonan shoved the back door of the ambulance closed, the
satisfying *chunk* rattling the quiet night. He radioed Sean
that he was in place with two clicks on the talkie, avoiding
verbal traffic; they were taking no chances of being overheard. He climbed into the passenger seat of the ambulance's cab, still seething. He checked the tracking units on
his phone: five of the bombs had been delivered that evening. Two more due to go out in the morning. He could
make good on his promise to Sean.

Zimmer's hair had frizzed even more than usual in the
high humidity, and the kid looked scared. Well, he should.
He hunched over the steering wheel, giving Lonan the wary
eye. The kid knew everything to know about cars, and gears,
and driving like Hell was hungry and he was marked as
lunch, and he was reliable. The way he'd been at that age,
raised by Sean and Aiden.

"Everything's fucked," Zimmer said, breathing hard.
Asthma acting up a bit.

"Nah, just delayed a bit," Lonan answered. "We were
goin' t' be here anyway. Torment the Fed." He waved his
phone at the kid. "Shots of the girl, trussed up like a bird,
the Fed not knowing to choose between her an' the crowd.
Now we'll just grab her, extra-like. You've gotta be flexible.
Everythin's subject to change."

"How do y' know for sure they'll bring her here?" the kid
asked.

"Because we'll be the first on scene, and Dox doesn't miss."

The laughing crowd, the noise, the packed space, the constant animated movement in the racetrack's clubhouse over-
whelmed Bobbie Faye.

"Sonofabitch," Trevor seethed, having already motioned
for Cam and Riles.

Ten minutes. Hell, there was no freakin' way to even get everyone's attention in ten minutes, much less get them out of the building in an orderly fashion. "Fire alarm, *now*," he bit out to the bartender. "Bomb threat," he said, lower, as the man reached for the alarm.

Nothing happened. Nothing.

Frantic seconds ticked by, and still, nothing.

"Shit," the bartender noted under his breath, tapping at computer keys, checking on the security and fire software. "It's dead."

They could shout, "Bomb threat," or even, "Fire," and people would get trampled, and killed. And Sean would sit there, wherever he was, however he was watching them, and gloat, hurting and killing people.

Wait.

Watching her. Not wanting to blow her up *just yet.*

Trevor and Riles and Cam were already issuing orders to the security team, the staff, ushering people to get out, fast.

"I don't want them to go toward the parking lot," Trevor said. "Too many cars there, one could be a car bomb. We need to get them somewhere we can watch." He glanced around, the rain barely misting now, and he saw the open ground of the track. "There."

She followed his glance—it wouldn't help if there were snipers, but there was nothing but a big water fountain in the center. Of course, getting a couple of thousand people, both inside the club and milling around the shops, all to stand outside in the mud?

No. Fucking. Way.

"How many agents on the ground?" Cam asked.

"Two on the outer perimeter," Trevor said, checking his phone. He must've GPSed every damned one of them. "Two more on their way in, but they're not going to be in position soon enough."

"I've got three state cops, two sheriffs," Cam said.

"One minute down. Nine minutes left," she pointed out, and the crowd laughed and drank and watched the big-screen TVs. The security and staff were trying to move out the people on the perimeter to keep the crowd from trampling each other, but they weren't moving fast enough.

"He's not going to blow *me* up," she pointed out to Trevor, climbing up onto the dark bar. The rounded brass pipe that ran along the outer front edge felt ice cold through her blue jeans. She wanted to make sure the fucker could see her, see what she was doing.

Both men paused as if they were about to argue. "We don't have *time*. Eight minutes left. No one's moving fast enough. He can see me, so maybe he'll be curious. Give me the phone. Let me talk to him while y'all get everyone out. Maybe I can stall him." She held her hand out for the phone, not giving Trevor a choice. He could fight her—and waste time—or he could work with her. He handed her the phone.

"You're out of your fucking mind," Cam snapped at him, reaching for her. She wouldn't be a bit surprised if Cam didn't try to tuck her under his arm and run the gamut of the crowd with her. The only thing stopping him before was the ingrained utter priority of the innocents surrounding them.

"Duly noted," Trevor snapped back, blocking Cam's hand. "Get these people out of here."

She hit redial as they moved away from her, herding the crowd toward the doors as the entire clubhouse morphed into organized chaos.

"Hullo, *àlainn*," Sean said after the second ring, "an' how are you this fine day?"

She stifled a shudder, aware that Trevor had kept her in his peripheral vision as he moved very argumentative people out of the building. Sean's was the voice in her nightmares. His voice, the image of her having to shoot Mitch, the image of Sean dragging her toward that helicopter. Odd, how none of her other disasters had clawed up her insides in quite the same way that Sean had.

She inhaled, shaky, and then pasted on her cheeriest voice. "Oh, fine, Sean. I always like panicking people and causing mass hysteria. Gets the old adrenaline pumping. I've heard that's good for the complexion. And how are you?" she asked politely. One should probably always be polite to a murderer.

That was probably in a "How To Talk To Bad Guys" rule book somewhere.

The chicken foot bracelet was not only black, it had started to vibrate.

He chuckled. "You're an entertaining woman, luv, but it's not goin' to help you."

"C'mon, Sean, you don't want to blow people up. You're really really pissed off at me about the diamonds and, um, that whole arrest thing, but you're free now. You've escaped, nobody has a clue where you are. You win! See! Go home"—she saw Trevor hold up three fingers: three minutes—"and have some whiskey. I'll even buy—uh, with my next paycheck. Nothin' but the best. Besides, there's gotta be something else out there worth stealing! Something to live for!"

Sean laughed. It was a warm laugh, liquid fire, deep and rumbly, which surprised her about the man, but it didn't lessen the flood of fear coursing through her. "Yeah, álainn, I've missed you. But that doesn't mean you're safe there on that bar. You best be gettin' out."

"Or! Better idea!" she said. "You could change your mind! Good karma points!"

He chuckled again. "Luv, you've bought the crowd one extra minute, for makin' me laugh. But you need to know, I do aim t' blow people up, and before we're done, you'll have to choose who you save. I mean to have you, álainn, in bits and pieces if I must. You tell that to your fiancé. You've now got two minutes left."

Fifteen

A red dot appeared just above her heart—a laser gun, sighting in on her. Lesson learned: bad guys lie. Great. Fine time to remember *that* one.

"Tell him, *àlainn*."

"Two minutes!" she shouted to Trevor, who worked far across the long span of a room to her left where he urged people to hurry. Riles was ahead of him, at the exit, and about a hundred people remained inside. And because she shouted, Trevor glanced back over his shoulder and saw the red dot just below her collarbone. He spun, running for her.

"Tell him to stop right there, luv. *Now*."

She put her hand up to warn Trevor, shouting for him to stop as she waggled the phone at him so he'd understand. He braked immediately, breathing hard, frozen. A hell of an eternity crackled in the twenty feet between them as he stood with his fists clenched, his eyes scanning the room, desperate for some sort of solution.

"Well, now, me luv, what d'ya propose we do about this? I could shoot your fiancé there. Or the cop—better tell him to stop movin', too, *álainn*, he's wastin' my time."

She bit out an order to Cam, who'd also seen the laser dot and was crawling toward her, and he stopped and swore.

Red dots appeared on Trevor and when she glanced to her right, on Cam. Both men were in jeopardy.

"Or," Sean continued, with no more rancor in his voice than if he were listing off potential grocery items, "I could cut yez in half wit' bullets. Might be a bit messy, though. Oh, sure, and then there's the bombs. You've got one minute. Choose."

Fuck. She was going to die wearing a BAMA t-shirt.

"Sean, I can't even pick out an ice cream flavor in one minute," she said, extending an index finger so that Trevor would know the time limit. She wasn't entirely sure he'd breathed at all since coming to a stop. "You gotta give me more time here." Trevor tilted his head slightly, indicating the space behind the bar, but she wasn't sure why.

The red dots did not even fucking quiver.

"And when you think about it, we just had a minor misunderstanding. Itty-bitty, hardly noticeable at all. Like, if you were one of my best girlfriends and I had your address—because seriously, some of them don't give me their addresses, which used to kinda peeve me but considering I'm about to be shot, again, I'm beginning to understand—I'd totally send you flowers for an apology. They might have to be discount flowers, because I only have about a couple of bucks in my bank account, but they'd be pretty. And really, you'd be all 'oh, you are so sweet, I don't even know what we were arguing about.' So, see? You *like* me. You don't want to do this, I promise."

How many years were in a minute? Two billion? Because it had been two billion years, staring into Trevor's eyes, seeing the absolute fear and fury he had washing over him.

Sean chuckled. "*Àlainn*, I do, at that. An' that's why, me luv, I'm givin' you the choice. So who's it to be?"

Riles got the last of the gamblers out through the rear exit as she stared back at the wall of windows and out toward the nothingness of rainy night and klieg lights around the track. She hoped maybe she was gazing toward Sean. If he'd wanted to destroy her, he'd found the perfect way to do it.

"Jesus, Sean, I'm begging you. Please don't."

"Choose, luv. Last chance."

"Then pick me."

"No!" Trevor shouted, and her heart seized to a complete stop as both men moved toward her.

"That's what I thought," Sean said, and the entire world cracked wide open as a gunshot rang out, a bullet slamming at the very top of the plate-glass window facing her, embedding in the wall behind her, above her head, where twin crashes broke the night: the window and the bar mirror. Giant shards of glass, daggers, dropped straight down and shattered, bouncing outward, with her and Trevor and Cam sandwiched between a thousand razors. She flinched, screaming, curling away from the flying glass, rolling toward the back of the bar. Trevor was suddenly there, vaulting one-handed over the mahogany counter as she landed, blanketing her as the bottles behind the bar jolted, rocked, and then rained down on their heads. Cam swore, and she hadn't even heard him move, hadn't realized he'd gone over the bar as well, that he'd landed on her other side, and they all three looked up, straight above her head where the wall was now drilled with a bullet hole.

"He missed," she whispered, shocked, as Trevor muttered extremely violent threats to every part of Sean's body, though he still had the presence of mind to pocket his phone that she was still clutching like a lifeline.

"Not by accident," Cam said. "I saw the laser track straight up."

Another gunshot, and glass crashed as the enormous window on the farthest end of the room near the entrance smashed into a million pieces. There was a sudden quiet, complete stillness, the hush of foreboding. A high-pitched whoosh sang into the room and something thunked, bounced, and then thudded.

Trevor glanced past her, past Cam's shoulder, and said, "Fuck. *Grenade*. Go!"

Gunshots fired and glass crashed in a near perfect synchronized ripple across the expanse of the room. Grenades slammed in each window in sequence, domino-style, chasing them as they ran. Trevor led the way, Bobbie Faye and Cam following as fast as they could hurtle the debris left behind by the crowds. Trevor's heart pounded out *sonofabitch sonofabitch sonofabitch* with each beat. He counted the seconds from the moment that first grenade had landed, one-thousand-one, one-thousand-two, expecting the explosions on one-thousand-three, and they were still two steps from the exit. One-thousand-four, one more step, one-thousand five, hit the door, slam it open, one-thousand-six, slide down the handrail, no time to explain, one-thousand *bam*, the first one exploded, and the building rocked, tossing them to the bottom of the stairwell. *Bam*, a six-second delay and the second one ignited as he rolled, pulling Bobbie Faye along, hearing Cam shouting something, glancing over his shoulder to make sure Cam was with them, *bam* the next one thundered, the concussion knocking them against the external wall. The world went white with dust as the next one *bam* blew plaster chunks down on their heads and he hit the outer exit door and *bam* the last one detonated, large pieces of wood and metal and ceiling tile showering the stairs behind them.

Open space outside the building, *keep moving*, and he scanned for cover as the crowds screamed away from the track, pandemonium every fucking direction. Lights, smell of rain and mud and horse manure assaulted his senses. Something in the building ignited and Trevor realized the alcohol stored on the premises was adding fuel to the fire, bottles *pop pop popping* like firecrackers. Trevor lifted Bobbie Faye and ran as a grenade landed in the grass where they'd just stood. Riles appeared and ran just ahead of them, his guns drawn, spinning and watching for anything that he could, but they were flat outnumbered, outgunned, outmaneuvered, and *fuck* they'd walked right into it.

The grenade behind them exploded, throwing up dirt and debris as they hit the ground.

Everywhere around them, people moved, frenetic, panicked.

The cops and agents on the ground shouted instructions

to one another to get the people away from the track alto-
gether as they herded the screaming crowd out to an empty
field beyond the parking lot, beyond the line of fire. An
ambulance raced up, lights flashing but sirens off. Trevor
gazed down at Bobbie Faye in his arms, her face drawn in
pain, her left arm bleeding from a dozen little cuts and
pieces of glass thanks to the fall over the bar. Blood soaked
her shirt on her left side, her jeans were ripped, and he could
see tiny slivers of glass embedded on the tops of her feet.

MacGreggor might as well have poured acid over him.
He couldn't have done a better job of hurting Trevor, than by
hurting her. And that was the point, Trevor realized. There
was no one else he cared about, not like this. Never like
this.

He had to get her to that ambulance, check the cuts, clean
the glass out, get her something for the pain—

He angled toward the horse barn as Cam motioned the
ambulance driver to meet them behind the structure. No
way were they stopping in the open, though MacGreggor's
snipers could have nailed them at any point since they'd left
the building, given the right rifle.

Clearly MacGreggor had something else planned, or he
never would have let them get out of that clubhouse, nor
would he have used six-second delays on the grenades when
three seconds were more typical. He sure as hell wouldn't
have given Bobbie Faye the extra couple of minutes that it
took to save the gamblers' lives.

Only when they made it around the corner of the barn did
Trevor slow and set Bobbie Faye down. He crouched, removing the glass from Bobbie Faye's feet and legs, barely
aware she was doing the same for his arms and shoulders.
What he *was* very much aware of as he brushed glass out of
the calves of her jeans was that Cam stood inches away, checking her. Touching her. Running his hands through her hair.
Murmuring "baby" over and over as she stood there, in
shock, starting to shake.

The rational part of Trevor told him that Cam's help was

a necessity, that they didn't know what MacGreggor had planned for them next, and the best thing he could do was to let Cam help, to make sure she wasn't hurt, and get moving out of there as quickly as possible.

The soldier part of him told him that he couldn't take the time to kill or just put Cam on the ground, hard, because the bigger, physical enemy was still out there and obviously wasn't finished.

The male part of him told the other two parts to go fuck themselves, and he looked up from his crouched position as Bobbie Faye wove her fingers through his short cropped hair and she read the fury on his face and said, "I'm okay."

"I'm not," he said. And he knew he wasn't. He could still see the afterimage of the red laser dot on her chest. MacGreggor had outmaneuvered him. Trevor had failed Bobbie Faye—just by virtue of her being in that goddamned room, by earlier, being in that house, by being a pawn in MacGreggor's game—he'd failed. Trevor would never burn away the image of the grenades landing in the room.

"Cam, stop, I'm fine," she said, following his glare at Cam, who damned well knew what he was doing. "Trevor— it's—"

He stood, a blur of motion, and kissed her before she could say "okay," before she could explain how Moreau was just helping. She did not need the heartache of him being petty right now.

"LT," Riles interrupted. "They were shooting from a water tower." Trevor glanced over to the man, who was keeping an eye on their six. "I can see the tower lights beyond those klieg lights. Perfect angle down into the clubhouse. If we move fast, we could catch them."

"Moreau," he said, holding her to him, "you're with me. You know this kind of terrain better than I do. Riles, you get her to the ambulance, and you stay there. And don't you fucking leave her, or go anywhere, I don't care if you have to take a piss, you use the tire. We'll be right back."

He knew Riles would follow his orders. Even though they

were no longer officially Spec Ops, even though he was an
FBI agent and Riles freelanced, rank ruled.

He knew Bobbie Faye would argue. But she'd be arguing
with air.

The only real surprise was when Cam nodded and set off
with him at a dead run for that water tower.

Ce Ce had never been to Tiger Stadium at night, a Roman
coliseum-type structure that was silhouetted against the
bright lights of the field. The stadium was massive. That's
the word that kept playing over and over in her head: massive. The game was about twenty hours away and the pre-
game tailgating was in full, insane swing. RVs (which
generally parked at the local Winn-Dixie up to a couple of
days ahead of time, because the best non-subscription
spots were first come, first served) were now parked in the
RV section. Everywhere there were awnings and TVs and
portable generators and cooking, the mouthwatering aroma
of spices and rice and smoked sausages and steaks and everything grillable under the moon wafted toward them.

And beer. Everywhere. So much so that Ce Ce wondered
if the beer companies' stocks dropped on rain-out days.

Alabama fans had traveled three hundred and fifty miles
and had set up in various spots in the middle of all that ram-
bunctious chaos. Rowdy, barbed, good-natured ribbing (and
a lot of betting) added to the hum.

The chicken foot—the one that was Bobbie Faye's
counterpart—hummed, but in the dark of the night under the
yellow umbrella of parking lights, she couldn't really tell if it
was black or just dark brown, and she honestly couldn't decide if it was vibrating because of the danger to Bobbie Faye
or if it was simply the psychic vibes of the excitement over
the game.

She hoped it was over the game.

Thousands of people milled around them. Monique had
already mixed mimosas, extra-strength, and they'd started
drinking the minute Ce Ce parked out on River Road. She'd

already finished her first by the time they got to the stadium and picked up their free tickets.

A few minutes later, she saw the group Monique was headed for: raucous, laughing, eating hot dogs while something—probably jambalaya—cooked in a big pot on a propane burner. But none of that mattered more than the big hunk of man standing next to the pot. At least six-foot-six and probably closing in on three hundred pounds, broad-shouldered, dark ebony skin darker than her own, and a warm, welcoming smile. She put him at maybe two or three years younger than she was, which was just absolutely okay with her.

She smiled at her friend, who was already grinning, and said, "Hon. You were right. I *love* football."

Eight minutes.

Nina blew by two cops with lights and sirens and she knew if they weren't already headed the same direction, she'd have had a chase on her hands.

Seven. She could make it in seven.

And then Gilda called her.

"Roadblock," Gilda said by way of hello. "There were explosions. The chatter coming in over the scanner is garbled and insane."

They didn't usually listen to the police scanner, though Nina wasn't entirely surprised Gilda knew to do it. This was, after all, Bobbie Faye.

"They've got a roadblock already set up on the entrance. I'm GPSing you. You'll need to detour."

Gilda detailed the directions and Nina thanked her and clicked off, focusing on handling the bike. It was light-weight, thank God, but she didn't want to hit a patch of gravel and spin out.

The detour was going to add at least three minutes.

Explosions. There had already been explosions.

Resetting her internal clock, she glanced at her watch: ten minutes now. She could be there in ten.

* * *

Trevor and Cam ran across the muddy racetrack lane, through the grassy center, and on across the opposite curve without saying a word. Adrenaline and fear and anger pumped through Trevor; his whole world was burning down and he'd walked right into it. Just fucking slammed straight into it, and MacGreggor was making sure he knew it. Making sure Trevor knew that what was coming next was going to be torture on Bobbie Faye. MacGreggor's game of forcing Bobbie Faye to make a choice between Trevor and Cam back there in that clubhouse was not coincidental, not some flip of the coin. MacGreggor didn't *do* coincidental. A fire alarm creating a stampede at the casino and a second fire alarm which failed to create the needed exodus at the racetrack weren't just ironic parallels to their last confrontation, when Bobbie Faye had used a fire alarm to her advantage. No, MacGreggor was toying with them. Taken together, the events today were probably a clue. A warning. *Fuck*, Trevor needed to think. To plan. He had to outmaneuver this bastard.

He wasn't going to lose Bobbie Faye.

Not to MacGreggor.

And sure as hell not to the man running beside him.

God*dammit*. Moreau just made everything a thousand times worse, being there. Moreau should have never let Bobbie Faye talk him into helping. He should have known better. He should have known that an agent in trouble meant *do not fucking enter*, don't make things worse. Now, when Trevor should be focusing on MacGreggor, on thinking the way the man thought, gaining ground, setting a trap, the images of Moreau waltzing into that casino, his body language smug and possessive, invaded and screwed with him.

They moved silently through a thin perimeter of trees, keeping low while they each kept lookout, guns ready for cover.

"She'd be a helluva lot better off without you in her life," Moreau goaded as they crouched in the high grass, watching for movement in the field and the woods beyond it. They were positioned back-to-back, giving them a 360-degree view, as best as could be had in the dim light emanating from the water tower in the center of the field.

There was no sign of anyone present around the base of the water tower, no movement anywhere around the tree line, no signs of tree cancer, that telltale blip of darkness that indicated someone flat against a trunk or a limb. But any sniper making those grenade shots, with that precision, wouldn't be making amateur mistakes, anyway. Trevor kept scanning, knowing this was not the fucking place or time to have this argument with Moreau.

But he couldn't let it go. Not with his imagination supplying the image of that kiss Bobbie Faye had told him about.

"You're hurting her," Trevor seethed, low. "And you're deluding yourself. She's chosen. Respect that and back off."

"And let you take advantage of her? When she's torn up over killing Mitch and can't sleep and isn't eating—yeah, I see the signs. I know her better than you do, you asshole." Moreau kept his voice pitched soft, deadly, directed at Trevor in a tone so low, Trevor knew the sound wouldn't carry. "What she feels toward you? Guilt. You're railroading her, and there's no fucking way I'm standing by when you're too goddamned selfish to see it or care."

They had a dozen yards to go before they would have to cross flat, open field, no trees or shrubs or high grass to use for cover. "She's going to be my wife." Trevor pivoted, and faced the man, because the rage pounding in his ears demanded it. "And if you kiss her again, I will fucking break you in half."

Sixteen

Bobbie Faye and Riles approached the street side of the empty stables, the barn doors standing open; several horses and their trainers, grooms, and owners, all clustered in an adjacent field a couple of acres away. She could hear the horses stamping and whinnying and could see the light-colored blankets thrown over their backs, and she could see the movement, but not a lot of detail.

The ambulance slowed to a crawl, navigating around the debris from the clubhouse grenade remodeling. The remainder of a flat-screen TV burned near a smoldering booth and mangled chairs thrown out in the explosions. Large sections of scorched tin from the side of the building dotted the area like ice floes in a sea of debris. While her arm hurt like hell and she'd be grateful to be in the competent care of a couple of paramedics—especially if they came bearing painkillers and Band-Aids—the slow speed of the ambulance was a good thing, because getting mowed down by an ambulance *while* wearing a BAMA t-shirt was just exactly the sort of thing to make the Lake Charles obituary writer's day. (Bobbie Faye already had enough issues with Erin Lugo over at the newspaper for the last three premature obituaries she had published about her, especially the one where Bobbie Faye supposedly ate so many boiled crawfish, she had to be carried to the hospital where it sounded (from Erin's extensive description) like she'd died a rather prolonged, painful death.)

The ambulance crawled toward them, threading through broken bar stools and floor tile and Bobbie Faye forlornly eyed the distance between the vehicle and where she and Riles stood.

"I'm *not* carrying you," Riles snapped at Bobbie Faye after Trevor and Cam left them and ran toward the water tower.

"Don't worry, Barnacle, I haven't had a frontal lobotomy yet. I think you're safe from my cooties."

"Apparently, I'm the only one. What do you do? Put something in the water? With a girlfriend like you, I'm surprised Trevor didn't throw himself on a grenade just to get the suspense over with."

She stopped shuffling toward the approaching ambulance and turned to Riles, who was filled slap up to his eyeballs with wholly undisguised disgust. "Seven days." When he narrowed his eyes at her, she said, "I just figured out what my personal limit for asshole friends is: seven days. You've been nasty to me since the second you walked in the door. I haven't blown up or broken anything of yours or even come close to getting you arrested—yet—so you're gonna have to clue me in here, Riles, as to just what the fuck is bothering you. I'm used to people like Sean who are a teensy bit more direct."

"You cannot be that dumb."

"Let's just pretend for a moment that I flunked out of Stupid Guy Interpretation class, and I have no freakin' clue what your problem is."

"If you want to play it that way, fine, but I'm not buying. Trevor's a damned fine man."

"You think I don't know this?"

"He saved my life," he continued, ignoring her, "he saved several of his team's lives—he's done a helluva lot for other people because he has a good heart. If you expect me to just look the other way, lady, while you take advantage of that, you'd better think again."

She blinked at his raging animosity, and started to answer, just as Riles stepped a bit closer, getting in her face and seething. "Yeah, I know you're used to every guy slobbering all over you."

"Every . . ." she trailed off, not quite able to speak from sheer incredulity. She waved at the burning racetrack behind them. "How on earth would I possibly think that? What part of 'hey, Bobbie Faye, would you kindly go boom' back there did you not understand?"

"What I understand is that you'll just end up leaving him for the next shock jockey or adrenaline junkie that comes along, if you don't get him killed first."

"So I guess I should send back that BFF ring I bought you?"

"It's crystal fucking clear you don't know how to have a long-term relationship—hell, you don't even know how to let go of the guy two guys ago—and obviously you're one of *those* women."

"One of *those*? What? Breathing?"

"One of those women," he continued over her, having built up such a fury, his words jabbed at the air around her, "who uses men and then moves on. I might not be able to influence him in how he feels about you, but I can damned well try to protect him—you may rip his heart out, but at *least* you should have the decency not to roll him. Because I guarantee that within a few months, someone else will come along and you'll be gone, and Trevor will lose half of his net worth because he'll feel compelled to split everything fairly. I can't stop him from getting destroyed on a personal level, but if you cared about him half as much as you pretend to, you'd sign a damned prenup."

"A *huh*?" She felt whiplashed, disoriented. Could confusion *be* any more exponential?

"Don't play stupid. Where in the hell did you *think* all the money for the security detail came from?"

"Security detail?" Words floated in her head, snatches of conversation, zigzagging through her memory, until the kaleidoscope of words settled in a new order. Remembering Sean's taunt to Trevor. "What security detail?"

"You know exactly what security detail," Riles said, but for a split second there, his stare had turned wary. Unsure. "The detail guarding your friends, and your family."

She glanced back at the ambulance, which had slowed and seemed to be taking for-fucking-ever. Everything was . . . odd, and wrong and the glass in her arm hurt like hell and her head hurt and Sean was after them and Trevor and Cam were gone and she was standing there arguing with a veritable ad for birth control and not a damned thing *made sense*. "I didn't know about any security detail."

He crossed his arms, guns in both hands, and eyed her as if she were two bullets short of a full load.

"You jerk," she said, glancing back behind him at that ambulance, feeling edgy, out of sorts, disconnected from the sights and sounds around her. "Aside from the fact that today was brought to you by 'Grenades, One of the Top Ten Serious Turn-Offs for Your Future Partner,' you clearly got in the short line for Stupid when I wasn't looking. I'm sure Trevor's tried to get the Feds to occasionally check up on my insane family, but hello? If there'd been anything remotely like a 'security detail' on us, there would have been a mass exodus as Feds stampeded out of the state and Ce Ce would have been griping about the short supply of weasel entrails to use for the protection spells she'd be convinced we needed. I—"

She suddenly realized what was wrong behind Riles: the logo of the ambulance company. She'd been in too many of them. The logo was the wrong color. The paramedics climbed out of the cab and walked toward them and their expressions were wrong—somehow they were like double images of aggression, their right hands tucked behind their backs.

She glanced back at Riles, who was facing away from the truck; he'd tensed when she'd stopped talking midsentence and midexplanation. "Two, one on each side of the truck, guns, right hands," she said fast, and then before he could spin around, she purposefully threw her expression wide open and surprised and shouted, "Oh, shit, look out, behind you!"

The paramedics ducked.

She had to resist the urge to throw her hands up and yell,

"Score!" but there was no time for victory dancing. She and Riles both dove to the ground, a bullet cutting across his right arm just as he landed and rolled. They lay flat behind what might have once been a bathroom stall and *dammit*, she'd further ground glass slivers into her left arm when she tumbled. Riles tossed her his second gun as he shot—and the men circled, aiming strictly at . . .

Riles.

She and Riles rolled back up, shooting, keeping the "paramedics" pinned down as they made it around the far corner of the barn. A barn that was in the middle of a freaking *field* with no trees, no structures, nothing for cover. There was nowhere else to go, nowhere to run, except back toward the clubhouse or parking lot, both of which had plenty of innocent people and first responders.

Her life had seriously spiraled out of control when she knew that the best choice that she could hope for this evening was to make it inside a barn with horse manure and Riles.

Trevor and Cam noted four unique sets of prints leaving the base of the water tower—with no apparent effort to obliterate them. The tracks were made by four males in all likelihood, based off the size of the combat-boot-style impressions in the mud, and at least two of the men weighed more than Trevor did, judging from the depth of the displacement of the mud. They clearly weren't concerned with what Trevor and Cam would find, and MacGreggor had to know Trevor would investigate this area. He had to know Trevor and Bobbie Faye had made it out of the clubhouse, especially since that last grenade had landed near them outside—near enough to indicate MacGreggor's team had aimed it.

And there was a cell phone, lying in the mud in the center of the water tower.

With a smiley face drawn in the mud beneath it.

Trevor recoiled about the same time Moreau saw it and they both bolted back toward the stables where they'd left Bobbie Faye. MacGreggor had either seen Trevor and Cam headed this direction, or instinctively knew Trevor would investigate, and had left this evidence . . . to . . .

Sonofabitch. To distract him. Which meant MacGreggor must know Trevor had left Bobbie Faye with only one person to guard her.

The sirens stopped abruptly—every one of them—as if someone had given an order, and the eerie void that followed made Bobbie Faye jumpy as they dove through the dark barn opening. Dim lights rimmed the interior of the giant building, bathing everything in an eerie night-light glow, and despite the doors being open, smells permeated the place: leather, horse manure, horse sweat, and the fainter layers of saddle soap and barley. The long building was split in two, with stables lining the left side and tack rooms and offices lining the right. Bobbie Faye and Riles ran, her flip-flops slapping the concrete floor with each step, and they might as well have advertised, "follow me, follow me" for all the noise they made.

Riles sighed the sigh of the ultra-beleaguered, and Bobbie Faye figured if they got shot, it was his own damned fault. He was the idiot who bought flip-flops. Of course, they didn't exactly stock Nikes down at the Guzzle & Ride.

They raced across the building to the rear exit; as Riles toed open the back door, standing back from its opening, bullets ripped into the wood and he jumped back, shoving her down to the floor.

"No way those paramedics ran around the building that fast."

"No, that's an M110. Sniper rifle—just came out couple of years ago. Shoots 7.62mm. It's suppressed—that's why we didn't hear it."

"Duh. Because X chromosomes mean I'd never understand what 'suppressed' means. Thank you."

"Which means," he said, giving her a pointedly annoyed glare, "that they have help—that shot came from the woods across that field." He assessed the stables while she kept an eye on the door they'd entered. "We'll hole up, over there,"

Riles said, nodding to a corner which, to her, looked like a really convenient place to die: there were lots of saddle blankets to lean against when they were shot. "Don't worry," he said, "I think they only want to kill *me*."

She glanced at the chicken foot, which was not only black, but was vibrating and seemed to almost . . . pulse.

"Okay, ew?" she said, holding her arm away from herself. "What exactly does that chicken foot do, again?"

"Apparently, not enough, since you're still around."

"It'd take more than a chicken foot to get rid of me."

"I'll alert Colonel Sanders."

Which is the moment the youngest of the two paramedics eased around a large supporting column and took direct aim at Riles.

Trevor and Cam reached the stables in time to see the bullets lace up the door as Riles had toed it open. They lay flat on the ground behind the corral fencing, eyeing the woods where the shots originated; odds were, they'd just "found" MacGreggor's men. Trevor trusted Riles to stay low inside that barn, to keep himself and Bobbie Faye safe. Coming up on his left, though, were two cops who had heard the shots and were headed their way.

"Tell them to back off—last thing we need is someone thinking we're the shooters," Trevor told him, and took off, running for the woods.

Manure, horse sweat, hay and oats, old leather, and smoke from the burning debris just outside the barn battled her brain for attention. Smells always slammed Bobbie Faye in these moments. Sounds faded away to nothing, completely cotton-eared muffled, as if God had hit the giant Mute button, the better so that she could focus on just how bad having to shoot this kid actually was. Maximum heartache squeezed into the shortest possible time. Bobbie Faye saw the kid's gun rise up, aimed at Riles, his gaze steady, the decision already made. Probably made *for* him, an order from Sean.

The kid couldn't have been more than twenty, barely had time to live.

She eyed down the barrel of the gun, flying on instinct, a split second to aim, and it was her cousin, Mitch, all over again. The image of shooting Mitch overlaid this one of the kid, no time to think about how much she hated her cousin for having put her in that spot, no time to think about the deep razors of regret buried in her heart, no time to think about Mitch falling into a bloody heap, remembering Trevor's warning, "You're still hesitating."

No time to think about how this kid was going to be another bloody heap, because her gun was going up, up, up, and she shot, *bam*, without stopping, because the kid had already made the decision for her.

Trevor moved through the woods, silently, easing through the brush. The earlier rain made the deadfall on the forest floor soft and spongy, the limbs and leaves springy and quiet, but he still took no chances. His training took over: flowing through the dark woods like a creature of the forest, blending in with the trees and undergrowth, checking the sightlines, scenting the air, listening for even the faintest sound not generated by fleeing, scurrying animals. The dark felt like velvet out there beyond the lights of the racetrack, and the noises from the chaos decreased to a muffled hum once he moved a few feet inside the heavily overgrown brush. He kept a sharp lookout above him, on the low limbs— the shooter who'd hit the barn door had probably been elevated in order to make that shot.

There was a slight *schnick* farther in, to his left. A *schnick* like the scrape of a shoe against bark and then a soft *thud* as someone dropped to the ground, and Trevor risked being seen for the speed he needed to catch the man. He ignored the burn of brambles slicing into him as he raced, soft soft soft, flying through limbs that bit into his arms as he kept as much cover as possible. Trevor heard the heavy breathing of a man running hard, smelled sweat and the strong odor

of spilled coffee, and caught sight of the thin white strip of
skin—the back of the man's neck between his black cap and
his black shirt.

The man heard him and when he spun, Trevor was up,
airborne, a flying side kick to the man's chest, nailing it,
solid, and sending him backward to the ground as Trevor
landed and rolled through the wet loamy, rotting leaves,
springing up and onto the man before he knew what had hit
him.

He could kill the man.

He needed to keep him alive for interrogation.

Trevor *wanted* to kill him. Blood lust pulsed through him,
wanting vengeance for all of the hell they'd gone through,
wanting justice for their home, now just charred remains,
and his professional training barely held the rage in check,
like a fingernail grip on a cliff face.

The man fought back, sliding a knife out of a bandolier
across his chest, and the overwhelming silence of the woods
was broken by low grunts and thuds and fast quick quick
moves. Two heartbeats later, Trevor had the man in a death
grip, spinning him around into a takedown position, when
crack—a gunshot sliced through the night and the man in
front of him arched, hit, instantly dead, falling out of Trev-
or's hands.

Trevor dove for the forest floor, grabbing the dead man's
gun just inches in front of his face; he lay belly down in the
wet earth and scanned the trees for the second shooter, for
whoever meant to take him out and got his own man instead.

There. Someone moved through the brush, running low,
fast, silently and expertly and if Trevor hadn't rolled into
low-growing palmettos for cover, the man would have had a
tactical advantage. Then the sound stopped, the man frozen
in the deep shadow of a tree; Trevor lifted his gun, aimed,
had a silhouette—a headshot—in his sights when the man
moved a fraction.

Moonlight, slim, watered down, filtered through the
overhead branches and illuminated half of the man's face.

Moreau. Searching for him, one hairsbreadth of a trigger-pull from being dead. From being out of their lives. Forever.

And in that moment, he realized he could pull the trigger anyway.

Jesus Christ.

He eased off the trigger, dropping his head down to his forearm, wondering just when the fuck he'd lost his control. But he knew already. The moment those bullets had sliced through Bobbie Faye four months ago, he'd started losing it. He'd done everything he knew to do to keep her safe, to keep from losing her, and the disaster wasn't fucking over. It was only getting worse, and the man in front of him was hell-bent on destroying the very thing Trevor was fighting to keep.

"Moreau," he said, low, and Moreau turned toward him, surprise registering there in the pale light as Moreau saw the gun in Trevor's hand. They exchanged a look, and the man knew—Trevor *knew* that Moreau knew—he could have been worm fodder—the perp's gun, the murder weapon.

Moreau narrowed his gaze at Trevor, as if to say, "Wise move." Or maybe, "You fucking sonofabitch." Those two sentiments were easily confused.

Moreau met him and they crouched next to the dead man. "You should have kept him alive."

Trevor snapped his gaze back to Moreau. "I thought *you* were the shooter."

Moreau peered down at the man's head. The dead-center head wound was too perfect to be accidental.

The two men looked at each other, realizing just how very insane Sean must have become, to be willing to sacrifice his own man instead of letting him be caught and questioned.

Then they heard a gunshot echoing inside the barn, and a muffled, anguished scream.

They ran.

If Lori Ann had to hear one more thing about a carbur-something or an intake whatchacallit, she was going to bean Marcel over the head with the shiny ratchet he was admiring. They'd been there for hours in the fancy RV, and Stacey was now sound asleep in her little purple and gold cheerleading outfit, the plastic pom-poms sticking to her face as she used them for a pillow. The rowdy tailgaters surrounding them had ramped it up with every passing hour, drinking and having a ball the drunker they got and it was getting on her very last sober nerve.

To make matters worse, the RV's little built-in armoire held a new flat-screen TV (even Lori Ann was willing to concede Marcel was lying through his teeth when he said he had never made a dime off the whole gunrunning gig) . . . and the stories played back-to-back: Bobbie Faye sunk a casino! Bobbie Faye's house blew up! Bobbie Faye destroyed the racetrack!

It was hell having a hurricane for a big sister.

Lori Ann needed a drink. It had been 183 days, six hours, and (she checked the clock on the paneled RV wall) twenty-three minutes since her last drink. And thirty-four seconds.

She squeezed the pillow to her upset stomach and gritted her teeth.

"Hon," Marcel said, finally cluing in to the fact that she wasn't listening (she'd actually stopped listening about three hours ago, sometime around "fuel injection"), "it's been a whole four months since she blew something up. She was overdue."

V'rai somehow managed to pull off the road onto the shoulder and come to a stop. The pungent odor of asphalt mixed with a fishy smell from the swamp, which was just a few feet off the road, according to Aimee.

"We're all going to die," Lizzie screeched in the backseat.

"Shut up or we're all going to die in jail," Aimee snapped.

"Where is he?" she asked Aimee.

"Coming up behind us."

"*Chère*, this'll never work," V'rai said.

"Just tell him you lost your license."

"They run your name now," Lizzie said. "Don't you people watch *Law & Order*?"

"Blind here," V'rai reminded her.

"Ma'am?" a nice police officer said next to her door. "I'm going to need to see—ma'am?" V'rai attempted to pin his exact location with a smile, and she was rewarded with, "Over here, ma'am. Ma'am, have you been drinking?"

"Oh, no, *chèr*, I don't drink," she said.

"I'll need your license, registration, and insurance, ma'am."

V'rai turned to Aimee, who said, "So sorry, Mr. Officer, but we were in a hurry! We left without it."

"Then would you mind stepping out of the car?"

All that noise and traffic echoed around her and V'rai shook a little. She eased her way out of the car, keeping one hand on the dented fender as she made her way to the rear of the car. He'd stepped away from her and she couldn't tell exactly where he'd gone 'til she heard his own car door open again. She heard him on his radio, calling in the license plate on the car. Then there was a very very long pause, and the radio crackled again, but she couldn't quite make it out.

She heard the officer, however, crystal clear.

"Blind? You've got to be kidding me."

Nina parked the bike in the shadowed sprawl of trees; she could see the klieg lights of the racetrack haloed above the dark canopy. Going in without sufficient back-up or intelligence was a bad idea. But she had to tell them about the bombs. Trevor would need to know, they'd need to plan.

They were running out of time.

She eased into the woods, hating navigating a forest where every tree could be cover for someone with a gun aimed at her head. She was used to circling through Italian ballrooms and navigating elegant boardrooms, not sliding quietly through field ops, though she could. And she did.

Gunshot. A distance away, inside a building.

She picked up speed, keeping to the trees, and avoiding the moonlight. She didn't know who was surprised more—

her, or the three men on their way out of the woods who stumbled across her.

The oldest, carrying an M110 sniper rifle, looked straight into her eyes, his own eyebrows arching in recognition.

"It's the friend," he hissed to his colleagues and they all seemed wicked happy about that. Then he motioned to Nina with his gun. "And you're coming with us."

They were too close, too damned close, for her to pull her Kimber from her shoulder holster. One of the men struck at her and she twisted, planting a boot in his solar plexus, which threw him against the tree as the third sliced toward her with a knife and quickstep, she moved and twirled and defended—and she'd have been fine, she'd have taken the morons down if the older one hadn't backed up and pulled his pistol.

"Sean didn't say any-fuckin'-t'ing 'bout hostages," the one picking himself off the ground said.

"Yeah, an' he thought we'd already have the girl," the older guy said and she thought, *Thank God, Sean's men don't have Bobbie Faye, yet.* "We're improvisin'."

Nina had gone dead still as she watched how well the man in charge handled the gun. There were people who weren't comfortable with firearms, people who had never shot one, or specifically, never killed anyone, at least not on purpose, people who didn't want to even think about taking a life. Those kinds of people usually held the gun like a coiled snake that would curl back on them and bite them.

This man? Was not of those people.

"Get her weapons," he instructed the others and she weighed fighting against a bullet between the eyes as the other two pulled her gun and her knife from her belt.

He motioned, and Nina followed where they told her to go.

"I'm sorry, Governor, but the military will not call up an entire SEAL team just to deal with one woman. No, sir, no matter how much you cry."

—Gubernatorial assistant Gina Tallent

Seventeen

She'd *missed.* Bobbie Faye gaped at the kid, who was writhing on the ground, his shoulder bloody. He was very much alive. Because she'd missed her intended target.

She'd been off by a slight nudge to the right. And the bullet had sliced through the column—apparently made of Sheetrock and wood—which deflected it down and into the kid's shoulders instead of being the head shot she'd intended.

The last time she'd missed by that much . . . well, she couldn't remember the last time. She shot nearly every damned day for the last twelve years at the firing range. Give or take a day or two in the hospital.

Maybe Riles didn't maintain his guns like he should. Maybe the sight was off.

Yeah, right. He was a sniper. He lived and breathed gun maintenance. Hell, knowing Riles, he probably farted gun maintenance.

Maybe she was losing her control, her edge.

Then again, maybe the Universe was finally relenting just a tad, just a smidgeon, and taking her off its shit list.

With a glance, Riles stopped her from going to the moaning, groaning, whining kid and reminded her that there was still another of Sean's men inside, the other "paramedic."

"I just saved your life," she pointed out when he hadn't said anything. "Again."

"Are we supposed to bond now?"

"I think I've met my minimum daily requirement for Hell, thank you."

"I'm shot over 'ere," the kid yelled. "Do somethin'!"

Bobbie Faye and Riles couldn't risk stepping out from their protected position—Riles had chosen a spot mostly inaccessible to shots from other angles inside the barn. Someone would have to come right up on top of them—the way the kid had—to get a decent shot. She had to give Riles kudos for their relatively safe position. Although, if she'd put Riles on the kudos/demerit system, he'd be rivaling the national debt right now.

"Where's your friend?" she asked the kid.

"I don't know," he whimpered. He was sprawled behind the column, which blocked her view of most of his body. "He's gone."

"Yeah, and I'm a fairy princess," she said, "who's going to pop another one into your ass if you don't talk." Her hands shook. She hid them from Riles.

The kid went back to moaning and crying, and she heard a low bird call from somewhere to their right, over by the back door of the barn where they'd originally entered, and Riles gave three taps against the wall and grinned.

Trevor must be back. That meant he was safe. Except for maybe the second moron tooling around inside the barn. She figured the whole code thing with Riles was Spec Ops talk for "bad guy inside, watch your ass."

Trevor was back. She sat down on the floor, trying to hide the shaking. She just wanted to go home. . . .

Right. No home to go to.

"Chicken Foot," Riles said, watching for movement in the stables, "are you going to be all girly whiny tiara-wearing now? Because we still have a job to do."

"Fuck off, Barnacle."

"Right back atcha, babe. Don't let that kid get up and leave."

And with that, he slid out of their little hidey area and into the vast stables, and she couldn't hear anything, except for the kid moaning and swearing.

Lonan had his gunsights on the woman. She huddled down below a stall door, just on the other side, forgetting, he knew, that the thin two-by-four wouldn't protect her from a round. The odd green haze of the lights rimming the ceiling caught her white t-shirt and broadcast her position between the slight cracks of the stall.

He had a head shot.

The woman had shot Zimmer.

The woman *shot him*.

Stupid kid. Damned stupid, and it made Lonan sick. He'd hired the street rat two years ago. Gave him a leg up. Trained him.

Told him that he, Lonan, would take out the sniper.

Told the idiot to act as back-up.

Lonan could punch a hole through her right now. Easy. He'd seen the beauty of Sean's game: the revenge for Mollie and Aiden and Robby, and the revenge against the Fed, for Sean's arms. Lonan wanted her dead, wanted all of this to be over. They could go home when she was dead. She couldn't keep affecting Sean's judgments. His fucked-up choices. She'd be done.

He watched her stay completely still behind that stall wall—her shirt not moving, completely unaware that he had her in his sights. The urge to just pull the trigger anyway, just wound her a little more, clawed for dominance. Then the ambiance of the room changed, softened. In the hush, he knew the other men had returned. They would be circling through the building, trying to see if he was still there, trying to flush him out. He cast her one more glance. She'd pay for everything. Including Zimmer.

And he turned his gun on the kid where he lay crying on the floor and killed him with one head shot.

In the next second, he slipped out of the barn, and ran

into the darkest area of the woods. Dox and the other men
would be waiting in a boat not far away on a little bayou that
cut through the back of the racetrack property.

Bobbie Faye wavered there, on the floor, having to hold onto
the wall of the stall to keep from sliding onto the floor from
shock. The kid was dead. The gunshot still echoed in her
head and the kid *was dead.* He'd stopped moving and she
could see the blood spreading out on the concrete floor but,
luckily, not the actual head wound, and it had to be a head
wound—the rest of his body was still visible to her past the
column.

No way Trevor or Cam or Riles had shot him.

Sean was *insane.* Sure, she'd realized he was vengeful,
and hurtful and aggressive and all sorts of adjectives for *bad
motherfucker,* but this? Was *insane.* As much affection as he
had for his own men, if he was ordering them to be killed if
taken, then what the hell chance did she and Trevor stand
against him? He'd have no mercy.

The overhead lights flipped on and when she turned, she
saw Trevor running across that big barn toward her. He was
covered in mud and twigs and leaves and an expression of
ragged unshuttered pain permeated through him. She shucked
the flip-flops and ran, barefooted across the room and when
she got there, she leapt.

He caught her, and she wrapped her legs around his waist,
wrapped her arms around him, mindless of the mud and the
debris, mindless of everything Riles had said, mindless that
Cam came into sight, whole and well and safe.

She buried her face in Trevor's neck, his arms around
her, one hand sliding into her hair, thumbing the tension at
the base of her neck. She ached. Writhing pain, acid in her
heart, she hurt so much, all she could do was hang on.

"It's okay, Sundance," he said, as he kept moving, carrying her back to a safer location. "It's okay. Don't look," he
cautioned, turning her away from the kid. "Don't look."

She wasn't sure how long she stayed in his arms. He murmured for the longest time, one hand supporting her weight,

his free hand never ceasing to move, to trace over her shoulders, her side, her hip, as if he needed reassurance, too, and found it in their touch. She wasn't sure how many times he'd said, "It's okay," but she knew neither one of them believed it.

It wasn't okay. Sean was going to make sure it was never okay again.

"Is it a nice jail that we're in?" V'rai asked her sisters once the footsteps faded away. It smelled like musty files, Lemon Pledge, and Old Spice. And sweat, definitely sweat, but V'rai was having a hard time imagining a cell with Lemon Pledge. Maybe they just kept the bars extra clean?

"We're in the interrogation room," Lizzie explained, guiding V'rai over to a chair. "The jail's full—Friday night drunks—they didn't want to put us in there."

"This wouldn't be happening if he'd'a just claimed her," Aimee snapped. She'd been at it for the better part of a month, this anger over Etienne's bullheadedness against Bobbie Faye. "He should've claimed her a long time ago."

"Hush, *bebe,*" V'rai said, smoothing her palms over the cotton of her pants. It was colder tonight than she'd expected. Of course, she hadn't expected to light out of the RV like a bee on fire and drive the car, after all these years. She hadn't thought ahead, or she'd have brought a coat.

"You know it," Aimee continued, and V'rai could hear her pacing. "I know it, Lizzie knows it. Even Antoine knows it, but he's too chickenshit to say anything about it. He should've confronted Etienne when she was a kid. We all should have."

"We did, *chère.*"

"Not enough," she said. "It's our fault that girl is running around out there, not feeling like she's got family. Scraping by. She wouldn't have been in this position if Etienne had claimed her like he ought. He could've at least kept her from starving all those years."

Etienne had always had money. He was one of the most successful rice farmers in Louisiana and owned a mill. A mill that had burned to the ground recently after the last Bobbie Faye disaster, but still, a frugal penny-pincher like Etienne planned for bad years. He drove an old truck, owned the old car V'rai had driven this evening, the house was paid for (slightly burned to the ground, too, but luckily insurance kicked in). He didn't dress like a successful businessman with his worn shirts and cracked leather workboots.

No, his disagreement with Bobbie Faye's mother had never been about the money. He was a cheap bastard, but generally an honorable one who'd have paid child support if he thought he owed it. He hadn't thought so, though everyone told V'rai that Bobbie Faye was the spitting image of her, so she was clearly a Landry child.

But maybe she'd been Antoine's kid. Nobody really knew. For years, Etienne flat refused to acknowledge her, but V'rai had her own reasons for believing Antoine wasn't the father, though she had never taken sides, and as far as she knew, neither of her sisters knew the truth, either.

"I don't know why Etienne can't just accept her," Aimee muttered.

"Well, she *did* shoot him," Lizzie pointed out. Lizzie could argue either side of any battle and be perfectly happy with the outcome.

V'rai felt woozy, tired, and colors spiraled behind her eyes. She'd had the sight long enough as a child to remember how things looked. But she knew that some of the visions she had now were scarily visually accurate—too accurate to have just relied on a five-year-old's memories.

"She *should've* shot him," Aimee muttered, but V'rai heard Aimee moving back toward where V'rai sat. "V'rai? You okay?"

The darkness fell away and suddenly V'rai stood in grass. There were bright lights and a lot of screaming. A lot of dead people. Bobbie Faye crumpled at her feet.

She moaned and doubled over, barely feeling Aimee and Lizzie's hands on her cold, cold arms.

"We've started something here," she said. "She's in the wrong place. Wrong place. She's going to die because we can't send her to the right place."

Lonan entered the apartment, stepping between the two security guards who couldn't meet his eye. He'd failed to grab the woman. Twice in less than twenty-four hours. The casino should have been a surprise to her, and should have been easy. Lure her in to find her ex, anticipating one extra man with her—the sniper—but the second man hadn't been a part of the plan. The state detective was a surprise, and cost them a half-second in decision-making, and that half-second had been what it took for everything to go to ruin.

But the second time, in the barn, meant he'd failed at his own contingency plan. And then he'd lost Zimmer, and Emon in the woods.

He'd been made a fool of, twice. Twice meant he was as good as dead. You didn't disappoint Sean twice. But Lonan would rather face it, straight on, than run. Running never saved anyone from Sean's wrath—Lonan had, in fact, made sure of that in the past, and he had no doubt Sean would have someone else who'd do the same to him.

His anger at himself welled up and threatened to spill over into violence against the men around him, but it wasn't the lads' fault he'd failed. He did have one ace in the hole. Coming in behind him, with Dox and the men, was the prize that just might keep him alive. The best friend, Nina. She was cuffed, awake, and moving under her own power. Knowing as much as he did about the hellion that was Bobbie Faye, Lonan expected this one to be outraged, mouthing off.

Instead, she was cool. Completely, unequivocally. *Ice.*

Bobbie Faye had been debriefed, derided, discussed, dissected, denounced, decried, and detained, and those were the positives. Four hours after the kid had died, she, Trevor, and Cam were in a suite of the Holiday Inn, which, given the sheer volume of police, SWAT, and federal agents milling around or stationed on rooftops nearby, was now the safest location on the planet other than the White House. Riles had gone off to check God-knows-what for Trevor. She was just thankful he was not off glowering at her from a corner or reading up on the How To Mummify Your Best Friend's Fiancée.

Daylight streamed into the room from around the edges of the closed heavy drapes. She stood there, still barefoot, still in the blood-and-mud-covered inside-out BAMA t-shirt, watching Trevor and Cam interact with FBI (and ASAC Brennan was on the phone with the UCO, which she'd learned was Undercover Operations, as well as having the Terrorist unit conferenced in). SWAT, State Police, Homeland Security, and the local Sheriff's Department filled out every other square inch of space in the room. She was sort of surprised that the CIA wasn't present, but that waiter who kept bringing in coffee and room service seemed to be a little hyper-alert, so who knew?

Paramedics (real ones, this time, she was happy to learn) had finished doctoring her arm (lots of butterfly bandages but, luckily, no stitches).

"Try not to overdo it anymore, ma'am," the oldest said, country-doc sincere.

"Yeah, I'll get right on that." She smiled at him when he chuckled. "Thanks. Think these will scar?"

"Maybe a little."

Great. She was going to forever look like she'd leaned against a porcupine.

She caught Trevor's eye and nodded toward the bedroom— the last thing she wanted was to go missing for a minute and give him cause to worry. He had enough on his plate as it was. He nodded, and she knew that if he could, he'd escape in there with her.

She padded away from the noise, the comfort of carpet plush against her cut and bruised feet, and found an average hotel bedroom with bland hotel furniture. She blinked at the loud, ugly-print bedspread, the kind that always made her wonder if it wasn't some secret Rorschach test that she was failing.

But finally, there in the room: silence. Well, silence if she ignored the hum of voices from the living area. She sat on the end of the bed with her head down and her arms draped across her knees hugged to her chest, and wished she'd shut the door. Rectifying that now would require actual movement. God, she wanted to lie down, but she was filthy. And sitting there on that big bed reminded her of the one that was now charred remains. Her throat clogged and her head hurt, and she wasn't going to cry over a stupid bed when so much else was so incredibly bad.

Okay, maybe she'd cry a little.

She heard footsteps and felt the bop of relief that Trevor had broken away. She'd barely raised her head from where it rested on her forearm and peeked: it was Cam.

She closed her eyes, not wanting him to see her disappointment.

A padded chair scuffed across the carpet as he pulled it up and flopped into it, then propping first one, then the other, boot on the opposite chair. How many conversations had they had like this? Three thousand?

"Baby, you okay?" He rattled something plastic.

She pried her eyes open and he held out a grocery bag of clothes and tennis shoes. "Gracie brought these." Gracie was one of his sisters—he had a huge family, more siblings and in-laws than Bobbie Faye could count, and the majority of them loved each other and actually wanted to spend time together. They were weird like that. "She said these would fit. I don't know how you women know this stuff."

"Aw, c'mon. You don't have Benoit's jean size memorized?"

He smiled at the mention of their mutual friend who was still recovering from gunshot wounds. It was the first real smile she'd seen from him in a long, long time. It made her heart clutch and ache for him, and for the pain she saw in his eyes. He handed her the clothes. "Just his favorite color. I think that's enough."

"Let me guess: purple? Or gold?" LSU colors.

"You mean, they're two different colors? I thought it was all one. *Purplengold.*"

She felt herself smile. "Yeah, I think every LSU fan's a little freaked out that they bleed 'Bama colors. It's just wrong." She'd meant to keep the tone light, but the word *bleed* reminded her of the kid lying in a pool of his own blood in the middle of those stables, and she choked a little and put her forehead back down on her knees. She couldn't cry in front of Cam.

He stayed silent for minute, 'til she got it under control.

They sat for a while in companionable silence. She'd seen him do this with horses at his uncle's farm—wait quiet, just stillness itself, until even the most skittish colt relaxed and nuzzled him out of curiosity. It was a marvel to her, sometimes, how a man so bossy could also be a well of patience when he wanted to be. It was the same trait he'd used to such success on the football field, waiting for the right moment for the right play. She could feel him analyzing her strategically. She didn't even have to look up to see that his eyes were closed, and that he'd slouched down comfortably in the chair, his head against the back, arms crossed, resting, listening, waiting.

She could hear Trevor in the other room as he and ASAC Brennan issued orders and made phone calls.

She eyed the bag of clothes. "Did you check those for itching powder?" She had scads of suspicion where Gracie was concerned.

"Only poison. You're on your own if it's itching powder." He paused as they both remembered that summer she dubbed Sumac Insanity, when she tried to help in the yard *one* time, and ended up a walking billboard for Caladryl Lotion. And oven mitts, because Cam had had to tape them over her hands to keep her from scratching.

"I wouldn't put it past Gracie," she muttered, eyeing those clothes. Gracie had, after all, introduced Cam to someone who didn't "take" and she still blamed Bobbie Faye.

"You're always fighting someone," Cam said. She glanced

at him, saw he'd turned serious. "And I'm always going to be there."

"You hate that." She sank her face into her hands again. God, she was so tired, her head weighed a zillion pounds, and she hurt. Her chest ached. Her heart ached.

He grabbed a pillow from the headboard, put it nearer to where she sat, and then settled back in his chair as she struggled with whether to give in and accept the gesture or stay resolute, as if she didn't need the help. She gave in, finally, lying on the pillow, curling onto her side, facing him with her eyes closed.

"I'm sorry," he said, quietly. "I know you're tired. And I know you're hurting." He paused, then asked, "Remember the game senior year?"

The game. As if there were only one. But she knew which one he meant. He always referred to it as *the* game. It was the one that still ate at him. He'd played in spite of his knee swelling up twice its size.

"Remember what you yelled at me after the game?"

"I did *not* yell at you." She glanced up at him to see his classic *yeah, right* gaze. "I merely emphasized. Loudly," she amended.

"The entire student section ducked."

"Liar."

"You accused me of tunnel vision."

Oh, yeah, she remembered that. She'd accused him of reacting. Of playing the other team's game instead of his own. Of ignoring his instincts, ignoring his own training, and just *responding* instead of staying ahead of the game, playing his own strategy.

"Yeah, you sucked that game," she agreed, and he gave her the mock-hurt look he always gave her when they had this conversation. "Well, you did."

He'd gone on to win the SEC and then the national championship, so she didn't mind pointing out his one loss.

"Yeah? Well, you're sucking in this one."

She blinked. She thought for a second he was referring to this game with Sean, this cat-and-mouse torment, but she realized that, dammit, no, he was pushing her. He'd been pushing her for the last four months, ever since his declaration in the hospital the night she'd been shot, ever since she'd recuperated and Trevor had moved in with her, ever since Trevor found them a home.

"I don't want to fight with you," she said. "Can you wait 'til tomorrow to be a complete ass?"

He sighed, then scraped his hands across his face.

"No," he said, his voice soft, gentle. "Because you're *reacting*. You're not *choosing*. I know it, and I know you know it. You don't want to admit you were wrong, and you don't want to have to examine how you feel and dammit, you're too loyal for your own good."

"Bullshit."

"Yeah? Explain Alex to me, then."

"That's not fair." She'd dated Alex mostly to make Cam notice her. She'd had no clue Cam had thought of her as anything beyond a dear friend, because try as she might, she couldn't get him to ask her out. She would have asked him, except every freaking cheerleader and girly girl at LSU already fawned all over him and he'd griped about the women showing up at his apartment. She hadn't wanted to be just another groupie. She'd wanted him to make the first move. When she'd finally gotten frustrated and given up, she'd met Alex in a bar and realized, holy shit, attractive guy, someone who wasn't Cam, wasn't even in the same hemisphere as Cam (and therefore wouldn't be a constant pale reminder of what she didn't have), and bang, before she knew it, she and Alex were dating.

And fighting. Huge, loud, horrible arguments. Spiraling to the point where Cam had had enough as her best friend and showed up one day, moved all of her stuff out of Alex's place, threatened Alex within an inch of his life, and informed her they were now dating.

She'd have argued with him at the time, except she knew that he'd finally deduced how she felt about him prior to dating Alex. Or maybe he'd finally realized that if *he* didn't change their status of "best friends," then nothing would.

"You're wrong, this isn't—"

He kept his voice soft, though she could feel the tension pouring from him. "You didn't love Alex. You know it, and I know it. You stubbornly refused to admit that things were bad because you were afraid of admitting what you really wanted. I was afraid we'd screw up our friendship, which was the most important thing to me. But we took a chance. We fucked it up—I fucked it up when I arrested Lori Ann, the way I handled that—but we found our friendship again, when neither one of us thought that was possible. If you'd give us a chance, we could weather anything."

"Cam. No. . . . Trevor is not like Alex—"

"No? *Look* at it, baby. Cormier is *thisclose* to being so much like Alex, it's not even funny." He ticked the list off on his fingers. "He's got you as isolated as he can possibly get you without sticking you on an island, and I'll give him five minutes after this is over and be shocked if he isn't moving you offshore. He's dangerous, he's mysterious, he's never introduced you to his family, he kills people for a living, and he's a control freak. You feel grateful, I get it. You're in his debt and he's working damned hard to keep you there. He's—"

"Done enough damage yet, Moreau?" Trevor growled from the open doorway.

"A seven-foot-tall psycho in a hockey mask carrying a chain saw? I can deal with that. Bobbie Faye when she's on a tear? Any sane person runs for cover . . ."

—William Simon, Director, Homeland Security Tactical Division

Eighteen

Shit. Trevor spun away without an answer. He could not go into that room.

It wasn't just the words, though a knife twisted in his gut when she hadn't stopped Moreau. It was the history, the friendship, the intimacy. He just . . . he could not go into that room, not like this, not furious, not wanting to kill Moreau. Not furious that she was blind, or intentionally sticking her head in the sand—no—she didn't need that. Not after this night, and if he walked in there homicidal, he'd be no better than Moreau and *fuck,* giving Bobbie Faye the respect of space to choose the life she wanted was the only thing he could hold onto for the moment.

Breathing through the anger, he held himself in tight rein as he rejoined the team in the living room portion of the suite, where ASAC Brennan was on the phone to FBIHQ, talking to the Unit Chief. The SWAT commander issued orders on his own cell phone, activating teams across Louisiana—since the action had moved from Lake Charles to Lafayette in just a few hours, everyone needed a heads-up. MacGreggor was not done yet.

Controlled chaos—that was the feeling in the room as everyone picked up their laptops and supplies, maps and faxes. The entire group was relocating downstairs to a conference room where they could spread out. They were tripping over each other in here.

Trevor had hoped he'd have ten minutes alone with her. He needed ten minutes alone with her. And a shower. He stared down at the bag in his hand, ferried in by one of the field agents he'd sent to some local outfitters to get them new clothes.

"Trevor," she said behind him and he stiffened.

The way she'd lain there, curled in toward Moreau. The memory of her body language slammed down his throat and ripped out his heart.

"Not. Now. I'm working. You," he called to an agent so young, so scrubbed and shiny, he practically had "sun-ripened fresh" stamped on his forehead. "Get a couple of other agents and get on the phone to leasing offices—here and Baton Rouge and New Orleans. See what apartments have been rented lately for cash only. MacGreggor will want something nice, so start on the high end."

"B-but, you s-said to—" the young guy stammered.

"Fuck what I said, do *this*." Because when Trevor had glanced down at the clothes, he'd had the sudden realization that MacGreggor would want to set up somewhere permanently. Seeing the multiple people coming and going in this hotel room made it clear: MacGreggor had put too much thought into this plan to not have realized that logistically, being in an apartment or a house rather than a hotel would be an advantage. Hotels created issues—having to keep moving, worrying about being discovered by maids or bell-hops. Furthermore, a bunch of men with Irish accents camping out in one hotel for months, with all of the BOLO notifications floating around, would have aroused at least *some* suspicion. Houses in high-end areas were nearly the same problem: lots of nosy neighbors, neighborhood watch, guards at gates. If MacGreggor was just a man on his own? No one would notice. But they knew MacGreggor had more than a few men with him, and several men going into and out of a high-end home wouldn't be normal—and would incite suspicion.

Trevor was willing to bet money that MacGreggor wouldn't risk a house or an apartment in a slum or even a low-income area—too many rats who'd be willing to turn him in for the reward money. No, he'd go with a high-end apartment, probably something newly renovated, so the neighbors weren't as familiar with one another.

He hurled the bag of clothes and toiletries to the sofa. *Dammit,* he should have thought of this earlier.

"Trevor," Bobbie Faye tried again, positioning herself in front of him. "We need to talk."

He ignored her as Moreau passed by, exiting the room, nearly yanking the heavy hotel door off its hinges when he opened it, barely dodging Laura, a support staffer out of the New Orleans office, who was entering.

"Ten minutes," Bobbie Faye said, her right hand fisting his t-shirt, lightly tugging it 'til he met her gaze and he recognized that determined gleam. "We need ten. They have to get the conference room set up anyway." He looked away and she said, "Please."

Jesus, she was killing him.

Sixty seconds later, the living room was silent. Empty.

They glared at one another. He crossed his arms, waiting. He couldn't say anything—didn't trust himself to say anything. Moreau's list was true. Not entirely accurate, but true. It had been bad enough to know Moreau had kissed her, to know it wasn't theory or in the past. But when he'd walked in that bedroom and had seen how relaxed they were together, how intimately they were arguing—Moreau sitting so close, leaning forward, Bobbie Faye curled toward him—he could picture that kiss, picture Moreau's intent with heartbreaking clarity. It was all he could do to keep from obliterating the man.

He still wanted to obliterate him.

It must've shown in his expression, because she sighed, "Cam's just . . . stubborn. Could you please not kill him?"

The anger that throbbed through Trevor thankfully jammed the words he wanted to say and he *hmphed,* not an answer. How in the *hell* could she keep making excuses for him?

"Do you realize what he almost did today?" she asked

him, exhaustion and pain quivering around the edges of her eyes. He closed his own, blocking her out, and thought, *yeah, he almost came between us.* She continued, "When that laser sight was on your back, I thought I was going to lose you." She swallowed hard, staring at the drapes. "Then the kid . . . all that blood . . . Scan could've done that to you."

Gut punch. He planted the back of his head into the wall he leaned against as he realized she was now talking about MacGreggor, not Moreau. *Jesus Christ.* She'd been through hell and back in the last twelve hours, and that's what he should be thinking about. She'd been nearly killed more than once.

He'd almost lost her today.

He was losing her.

How could he explain that to her? How could he tell her she was everything to him, without adding to the pressure she was under?

There were no words. His chest ached, his heart rending into pieces at the pain in her eyes.

Thirty seconds later, he had the shower on, and in the next thirty seconds, both of them unclothed. They stood under the hot spray, holding each other, him leaning against the cold tile, feeling the length of her, the warmth of her, skin to skin. There was so much they needed to talk about. Things he needed to tell her. Things he needed to ask her.

He had to get downstairs, to the conference room. He had to stop MacGreggor.

He felt selfish with aching, broken jagged edges somewhere deep inside as he kissed her, hard at first, hungry. He wanted to burn himself into her memory, imprint so completely, she'd never think about anyone else, she'd never be drawn away from him. He cupped her face, as he pulled her against him, rough kisses, anger surging as he trailed down the softness of her throat, biting, kissing, biting again. She opened to him, tilted her head to give him access, vulnerable, her breath hitching as she twined her fingers in his hair. It was that slight tremor in her breathing that undid him. She was a woman ripped apart by compassion and love and the terror of what they'd been through.

He rested his forehead against hers for a moment. When he leaned back, he soothed the redness of the marks he'd made with his fingers, tracing the line of her throat up to her jaw, skimming her wet skin, silk against his palm, and she pressed against his hands, trembling. Her chest rose and fell in ragged breaths and he saw canyons in her eyes, a soul breaking apart. Breaking apart there in his arms, away from where anyone could see, worn down from the horrible things she'd seen, ground to a flat sheen by MacGreggor's constant terror and Moreau's constant pressure.

He'd warmed the tiles with his back, and he flipped her around, lifting her 'til her legs wrapped around his waist, needing to feel the pressure of his body on hers, knowing she needed to feel safe.

She closed her eyes.

He wanted to give her that safe place to turn to, be the safe haven for her, and ran his fingers along her side, tracing her curves, losing himself in her softness and angles.

The very compassion he loved her for could draw her away from him, could make her second-guess everything they had and destroy them. He tried to tell her with his heart, with the tenderness of his touch, how much he wanted her. He could not use the words.

She kissed him, frantic, drowning herself in sensation so she could forget, and he rode the swell with her, letting the sensation surround him, pushing them both with heat and ache and wanting, tasting her. He kissed his way to her breast with little bites, knowing he was marking her, knowing it was selfish, rasping the edge of a nipple with his teeth, and she arched and cried out his name.

She was what made him want to be a better man, she was light and toughness, laughter and goodness, and he could lose her. He kissed the other breast and she wriggled against his erection, begging, "Please, Trevor, now."

"Look at me," he said and her eyes flew open and held his as he thrust into her, the sadness in her eyes destroying them both as the water from the shower cascaded, framing her face, drops lacing her eyelashes. "Look," he said again, his voice rough with wanting, with longing, "at us."

She gazed at him then, the storms in the sea green of her eyes closing off some part of her, clouding over, and he thrust into her, battering back the rage, the wind and rain of her, fighting to save them both from drowning. The world fell away, and it was only her, only *feeling*, only the landscape of her neck, the sanctuary of the taste of her, and he thrust, wanting, keeping, needing, and she pushed against him, and they came together, shattering with sudden release and cries.

Reality faded back in, and she clung to him, leveraged as she was against the wall where he'd turned her, her face resting in the crook of his neck. She felt limp and loose and she shook with tears. Tears for the day, tears for the pain, tears for the loss of their home, tears for the threat to them.

He held her for years there, the hot water pressing on them, washing over their joined bodies as she leaned against him and cried. They had lost nearly everything today, but they were alive. Even if they made it through MacGreggor's gauntlet, they could lose each other if she didn't choose. He knew it, though he wasn't sure if she did, yet. He pressed a kiss to her temple, still holding her there, reluctant to let go, grateful for the spray of the shower so that she couldn't see his own fear.

"You want me to put superglue on *what*?" she asked, and from his grin, Bobbie Faye knew Trevor was enjoying a moment of fantasy. There had been toiletries in the bag (score) and underwear that fit (camouflage, someone had a sense of humor), and camo clothes (actually, a black t-shirt and camo cargo khakis, with enough pockets to store a sizeable Wal-Mart and still have plenty of room for the Von Trapp family), and black combat boots (she was sensing a theme here), but the one thing she was completely lost on was the tube of superglue.

"Your feet," he said again as they dressed. He pulled his

own black shirt over his head and wow, she ran her hand along his abs before he tucked the shirt in, and he grinned and kissed her. "It's an old field trick."

"Oh, sure it is," she said, holding up the tube, "because all of the instructions on here about not getting this on your skin should *totally* be ignored."

"It keeps new boots from rubbing blisters."

She eyed the tube, and frowned. "Is this one of those dumb things I'm gonna do because you talked me into it and then you're still going to be mocking me for when I'm eighty?"

He picked her up and set her on the bathroom counter, and for a split second, they both remembered the first time he'd done that. They'd ended up naked, then.

She had a real affinity for bathroom counters.

Trevor grinned, and she was relieved to see him smile. Relieved to know he was safe, standing in front of her as he took the tube of glue. "I'd be mocking you more if you ignored me and ended up with blisters." He bent a knee and she propped her bare foot there; he opened the tube, squirted the glue onto her foot, and then spread it (using the cap) onto her Achilles, the top sides of her feet—everywhere she'd have normally gotten a blister. He grimly avoided the small cuts from the glass.

She glanced over her shoulder at their reflection in the mirror and then turned back to him, grinning. Her first thought had been *thank God, I'm not going to die wearing a BAMA t-shirt,* but when he caught sight of the smile, he raised an eyebrow, and she decided to go with thought #2: "I look kinda ass-kickery in this."

"Ass-kickery?"

"Yeah, kinda all *Xena: Warrior Princess,* you know, except if Xena were into camo instead of all that metal breast-plate stuff." Even the chicken foot bracelet had turned back to brown, which had to mean that the threat was over. Or manageable. Right? She pretended to pull an imaginary sword out of a nonexistent back scabbard.

"Well, if you're not going to have the breastplate and the

clingy outfits and wear camo instead, then you're totally doing Sarah Connor . . . . with . . . what *are* you doing?"

She waved the invisible sword in front of him. "It's a sword, silly. We have really got to teach you how to do pretendsies."

He snorted, and checked her feet, touching the superglue to make sure it was dry enough for her to put on her socks.

"We'll get right on that."

"I could so totally see you with a sword."

He cut those blue eyes up at her, but a smile twitched at his lips and for that moment, everything was right with the world. She stopped mid-"sword" wave and placed it back in its imaginary scabbard.

He was too pretty, all cleaned up like this. The short hair still threw her; he looked so perfect, especially in the brand-new t-shirt and crisp khaki camo pants he wore. She missed him in his soft t-shirts and worn jeans, padding barefoot through the house.

"You were gone for seven days." He glanced up at her and she bopped him on the arm. "*Seven.* As in way more than *two.* Your math skills *suck,* mister. And," she said, taking the socks from the bag, "you left me with Riles, who completely manages to pull off the world-class feat of being in the dictionary under both *needs ass-kicking* and *total suckage jerkwad,* and probably a few others, and what in the *hell* were you thinking? I mean sure, I know you wanted him there for security . . ." and at the word *security,* Memory said *ding ding ding, we have a winner!* "And *oh, yeah,* what is all of this about security for my family? And Riles said you were paying for it? Just exactly *how* is that possible?"

"Riles told you about the security." It was a half-question, half-statement, but what chilled her was that his tone had gone flat and deadly. Not that she didn't want Riles's ass to be kicked because seriously, she'd pay for the privilege of a front-row center seat to that event, but she wasn't about to let Trevor veer off of the point.

"The fact that there actually *was* security to tell me about in the first place? Hello? Fiancée?" She pointed to herself.

"Think maybe I should know some of this stuff? Like the fact that you had to use your savings, and I hope to God you didn't use up everything, did you?" He scowled, shaking his head, and she continued, "Which—and don't get me wrong, I am super grateful that everyone was safe—but seriously, I should be paying for this. Somehow." And the enormity of what it must've cost to hire that many men to watch everyone suddenly hit her, and she swallowed hard. "And I'm going to," she said. She'd been offered a couple of spokes-model-type things, but they were sort of ridiculous and embarrassing (she was pretty certain the offer from the septic tank company was a new level of bad—then again, her standards for humiliation were now so low, a gnat couldn't limbo under that bar). "Riles was right about the prenup suggestion—we need to protect you and—" She halted at his expression. Holy *crap,* he'd gone from grim to murderous in a nanosecond. "Trevor?"

"Riles . . . suggested . . ." he repeated, and for the very first time, she sort of felt sorry for Riles, the way Trevor's eyes had gone from blue to the steel of a blade in a heartbeat. It was all she could do to keep from running out to find Riles and mock him with the ten-year-old singsong, "Ooooooooh, you are in trouble! You are in trouble!" Before she could follow up on the real point, the hotel room phone jangled, and she jumped, startled.

He crossed over to it, snatched it up. "Cormier." Whatever the other person said made him go completely rigid with fury and then he said, "*Fuck* no," slammed down the receiver, and backfisted the wall, punching a hole in the Sheetrock.

She gaped at him.

"Bomb threat," he said through clenched teeth.

"Sean?"

"Yes."

"A threat? Not exploded yet?"

"Not yet."

His reluctance to speak as they slammed on their boots scared the living hell out of her. Trevor grabbed his guns and they hurried out, blowing past the armed guard ASAC Brennan had stationed just outside their hotel door.

"What aren't you telling me?" she asked as they got to the elevator, an armed guard tagging along.

"He's threatened several bombs. Unless he gets what he wants."

He couldn't even look at her. His fists were white-knuckled and he was reining the rage in so tightly she thought he might spontaneously combust.

"What does he want?" she asked past the lump in her throat, crossing her arms, knowing it was going to be bad.

"You."

Riles met them at the door to the hotel conference room. "LT, you don't want to go in there, yet."

Trevor pulled up slightly, hyper aware of every move in the hallway, from the armed guards, to the agents on the other end of the hall carrying file boxes toward him, to the way Bobbie Faye barely breathed from the tension. Riles— who should never have said a single fucking word to Bobbie Faye about the security—and they would deal with that later—was wrong. He fucking wanted in that room. He wanted to see what the hell MacGreggor had sent over, what had ASAC Brennan practically climbing through the phone in alarm.

Moreau yanked open the door just as Bobbie Faye pushed inward and she fell . . . would have fallen directly into his arms, had Trevor not stepped into her path as soon as the door whisked open and caught her himself.

"'Bout fucking time," Moreau said, grabbing her hand and dragging her into the room. If Trevor didn't have a roomful of agents and cops as witnesses for the murder trial, he'd have slammed the asshole against the wall.

For all of Moreau's fears for Bobbie Faye, and for everything they'd all been through together, Trevor had never seen the man like this. Utter apprehension vibrated off the cop.

"Moreau." The cop's hands were now intimately bracketed on Bobbie Faye's shoulders. She hadn't said anything to brush her ex away as she gazed past him. Moreau scowled, but wisely backed off, removing his hands from Bobbie Faye. She stood still, shock playing across her face as she reached for Trevor subconsciously. Moreau nodded toward the big flat-screen TV at the other end of the room and time slowed as Trevor registered a part of the image he could see that wasn't blocked by ASAC Brennan.

And then ASAC Brennan moved, giving Trevor an unobstructed view of the screen and Bobbie Faye, next to him, said, "Oh my God, *no*."

Trevor moved her to stand in front of him, his arms enveloping her for support.

There, on the screen: Sean. Smiling, God help her, at the camera, with his unique barbed-wire scar tilted up at the lens, and the smile somehow mitigated how freaking scary he looked. He was almost *charming*. And his charisma would have worked, too, at least on some level, if he'd been the only person in the frame. But he wasn't.

Nina was behind him. Tied to a chair, clearly having been slammed around a bit, head slumped forward. Unconscious.

Bobbie Faye shook. Fury. Unfuckingmitigated fury.

"Welcome to the game, Cormier," Sean said, leaning a little into the camera. It was crap quality, something cheap and grainy, blown up big onto the screen. "I want the girl. And you'll give her to me, with a big fuckin' bow, or you'll be responsible for the bombs. There's more than one, and you can't stop them, though if you give her to me now, I might give you the way to stop the biggest.

"An' it doesn't matter, your bank account. You don't fuckin' have enough, not even with the thirty-or-so million, to pay me off. You can't guard everyone she loves forever. Besides, you fuck, your thirty million would barely scratch what I'd have made before, and what I'll make again. You'll give me the girl, or you'll be the death of many more.

"I'll call you wit' instructions, me lad. That'll be all."

He said that last bit to whoever had been holding the camera, and there was a heartbeat where he was frozen on-screen and then the picture went to black.

She didn't know what to focus on first. There were parts of her brain flinging themselves around like drunk kittens, battering the inside of her skull with exclamations of "Processing! Processing!"

Trevor had not moved a muscle as the video played, and she broke away from him, needing a moment, needing to try to pull oxygen in, and push it out again, because her entire system wanted to shut down from the shock of Sean's video.

"Thirty fucking million?" Cam asked. He wasn't looking at Trevor, he was looking at her, to see if she'd known. His grim nod a half-second later told her he knew the truth: that Trevor had not told her about his wealth. She felt her entire world shatter and fall away. It was dizzying, how fast the sound rushed out of the room.

Two thoughts collided and battered her chest, a hurricane of relationship debris thrown against her heart: *Nina's a hostage* and *Trevor did not trust me with something monumental.* She couldn't even begin to articulate the betrayal eating away at her, acid in her soul.

"We need to focus on how compromising this is," ASAC Brennan said, and she gaped at the man in his pristine suit. *Compromising.* What a fucking way to put it. He said the word with about as much emotion as he would've given to a canceled breakfast appointment. "That's my best friend," she pointed out. "I'd say we're pretty fucking compromised."

But there was something going on around her, some odd awareness buzzed in the air with some of the agents and SWAT and staff seeming just as puzzled over ASAC Brennan's choice of the word *compromised.* Trevor, on the other hand, did not look confused.

"We can't know for sure," Trevor finally said to the ASAC. "There's no way to know. He may have just grabbed her because she's Bobbie Faye's best friend."

"If he knows about her—" the ASAC began, then glanced at her and broke off the comment. Brennan turned to one of the staff and said, "We have the secure line up?"

We can't know what *for sure?* What the *hell?*

She faced Trevor and saw his imitation of granite had taken on a whole new level. The little tic in the muscle of his jaw worked overtime, driven, she could see, by a deep, unadulterated rage.

"What do you mean, we don't *know for sure?* What . . ." and she was just going to have to blow right by the notion of Trevor having thirty million like a freight train, because if she stopped to think about it? She'd spin completely off the planet . . . "*else* aren't you telling me?"

And he looked like he was deciding something, fucking *deciding* how much he could tell her when that was her best friend sitting there in that monster's hands, with threats of bombs hanging over their heads, with the only real leverage being that Sean wanted her—wanted her for revenge against Trevor, wanted to make them all suffer—and that's when ASAC Brennan was apparently connected to someone on that fucking secure line.

"Agent down," the man said to someone on the other end of that line and Bobbie Faye whiplashed around to Brennan and then back to Trevor again.

"Agent? Down? Who?"

Trevor got a nod from ASAC Brennan and nodded toward Nina's image that Riles replayed on the screen.

"When the hell did I step into the Alternate Fuck With Bobbie Faye Universe? Nina's an *agent?*"

"Not ours," Trevor said. "She's contract . . . to another agency. Has been since college."

Bobbie Faye glared around the room and Cam held up his hands in the classic *not me* way. "I always tell you the truth, baby," he said in an implied *I told you he couldn't be trusted* way. She could feel Trevor itching to step closer to Cam, the better to wring Cam's neck.

Riles didn't appear to be the least bit surprised, either, that Nina was an agent. Of course, Riles was the kind of guy that Satan probably had on speed dial, so he was probably good at disguising any human qualities like *surprise*. He stared at the video, now moving in slow motion without the sound. No doubt searching for clues as to their where-abouts.

"She's extremely high clearance," Trevor said, finally, when he focused back on her. "She has been for many years. You could not be told."

She reeled. The whole world tilted on its axis, bells clang-ing in her head. This could not be happening. She didn't be-lieve it. It just could not be happening. Nina was her best friend in the world, except now for Trevor, but she and Nina had been inseparable growing up. After they went to college, Nina had gotten all cloak-and-dagger with the S&M stuff, but Bobbie Faye figured it was a lifestyle . . . oh, holy *fuck*.

"The S&M thing. It's a cover?"

Trevor nodded and she spun back to the video, paying closer attention to the rerun. She felt as if she'd seen some-thing important the first time through, but had been so shocked at Sean's voice, at the image of Nina behind him, tied to a chair, she'd missed it.

Riles paused the DVD and Bobbie Faye started to pro-test, when he asked, "Does Nina know ASL?"

"Sign language? How the hell do I know? For all I know she quacks like a duck and levitates every other Thursday!"

Riles pushed PLAY and they watched the video advance. The camera angle barely gave them a glimpse of Nina's right arm, but the way she was leaning to the left with her head slumped exposed her right side. Her right hand's move-ments were so agonizingly slow, they almost seemed acci-dental. But there it was, unmistakable: Nina was using ASL spelling to sign something. Two letters were hidden as she turned her hand slightly to make them, but Bobbie Faye caught three: G D A.

Gilda. Her assistant. Bobbie Faye had talked to Gilda several times when Nina had been "tied up" at work.

"How fast can you get me to Baton Rouge?" she asked Trevor. She felt ice-cold, detached from him, and she recognized it as a rage so poisonous, she should come with a warning level.

"Fast. Why?" But before she could explain, Trevor saw Nina's movements. Knew, apparently, who that meant and where to go. He did not need her to explain who Gilda was. There were apparently worlds hidden in Trevor's silence, worlds he didn't feel necessary to disclose to someone as inconsequential as his own fiancée.

How could she ever fucking believe another word he said?

"Let's go," he said, and grabbed her hand.

She wanted to pull away. She wanted to walk out of that room without touching him.

And he knew it.

And he held onto her anyway.

The *sonofabitch*.

"Do you ever think that sometimes Bobbie Faye looks at her calendar and thinks, 'Wednesday—laundry, Thursday—dishes, Friday—destroy the state'?"
"Every. Single. Day. Of. My. Life."
—Deputy Lois Baron to Sheriff Linda Elliot

Nineteen

Everything Lonan had worked to arrange was spinning out of control. Just like that. The scapegoat for the bombs? Gone. Lonan had specifically chosen to help the mechanic with his plans to martyr himself with the bombs because once he was dead, the FBI, ATF, would all be satisfied that they had the culprit—and he and Sean and their men could slip out of the country, wealthy as fuck, without anyone the wiser. Sean would have had his revenge, they would have all made money on the futures they'd bought. It had been a perfect plan.

Now, everyone would know Sean and his men had set the bombs since Sean had gone the fuck ahead and announced it on his video. There'd be no crying bomber's final words—and Lonan knew the mechanic had made a tape of his own—whining about his wife on national TV, no idiot going on and on about how she'd been a safety inspector, she'd tried to nail Poly-Ferosia for safety violations that would've saved lives, and she'd been killed, and no one cared, boo-fucking-hoo.

Lonan had spent two months setting it up. Spent considerable money. He'd found four bomb makers, and he'd chosen the one who'd draw national attention away from Sean's group. They would get in, get the girl, torment the Fed, kill them, the bombs would blow, and they'd make a fortune—the perfect retribution for Aiden and Mollie and Robbie.

He'd thought bringing the best friend in would help lure the Sumrall woman into their trap. It was the only reason he'd gone along with it when he got to the boat and Dox had the friend. That—and he'd missed grabbing the Sumrall woman a second time. But now? Now Sean was going off plan. Off the fucking rails.

"Tell me we're still goin' t' blow the bombs, Sean," he said, standing up from the floor, wiping the blood from the corner of his mouth where Sean had backhanded him for objecting to the video.

"Oh, yeah, lad, we'll still blow 'em. An' the world will be watchin' and the Fed won't be able to do a fuckin' thing abou' it. I promised you—I promised you that you'd get to kill her family." Sean gentled his voice, put a beefy hand to Lonan's shoulder, and looked him eye-to-eye. "But I told ya that I aimed to keep the girl. Killin' Cormier fast isn't punishment enough. And he doesn't much care for his own life, but he does care about her."

Lonan felt his scalp crawl with apprehension. Sean wanted to *keep* the Sumrall woman when he got her. Lonan seethed. He'd heard Sean say it, sure, but he'd hoped Sean would come to his senses and realize that killing her was the best revenge against the Fed. But no, Sean was serious. He wanted to *keep* her.

"He'll track us, Sean."

Sean nodded toward Dox, who sat at the kitchen table cleaning his sniper rifle. "Dox'll make sure he can't. He'll be in a wheelchair the rest of his life, lad. Knowin' he's got nothin' she wants. Knowin' he gave her up to me."

Lonan gazed into Sean's weird amber eyes. He knew the smart thing was to nod in agreement. It was at that moment that Lonan realized that Sean, in his madness, believed Bobbie Faye would end up choosing to stay with him, even with her family dead at his hands. He probably had even invented a way to lay the blame at the Fed's feet. *Making the woman choose Sean over the Fed* was a challenge, a bona-fide, balls-down challenge, and Sean was *enjoying* it. Sean had always been attractive to women, particularly women who liked to walk on the wild side. He'd always gotten whatever woman he'd wanted, even if it had meant busting up marriages, and Bobbie Faye had become the ultimate red flag to the bull.

"How are goin' to pluck her out from under the Fed?" A heavily guarded, wealthy Fed, who'd stop at nothing to win. A man who was now forewarned.

"Oh, it'll be a great bit of craic," Sean said. "Since you lost her, lad, you'll help get her back. Because she's gonna ask to come wit' me."

She probably would—with her best friend sitting in the other room, tied to a chair. "Any exchange you set up, Sean, will bring the Feds raining down on our heads. You know they'll be waitin' for instructions—and as soon as you tell them where the exchange is, they'll have snipers and herds of fucking cops everywhere."

"Sure, they will. Which is why we're goin' to be the one place where they can't touch us."

Sean nodded toward the coffee table and there was the photo of the final bomb site and dread thrummed through Lonan. *No.*

"We're blowin' that one, Sean."

"We are, at that."

And that's when Lonan knew that ever since they'd missed Bobbie Faye at the casino, Sean had begun making secondary plans.

Then he saw the notes beside the photo, saw exactly how Sean had improvised, and it was bloody brilliant. He picked up the notes and the photographs, measuring just exactly what he had to do to convince Sean he'd had a change of heart.

"It's a fuckin' t'ing of beauty, Sean," he said, low, admiring it.

Sean clapped him on the shoulder. "Yeah, lad, Aiden would've loven it. And you'll get your justice, I swear it."

The mechanic paced in his workshop. Air squeezed in and out of his lungs and he knew his blood pressure had jumped.

His doctor would tell him to lie down and rest. Instead, he poured another Scotch—the good stuff Chloë had given him that last Christmas before he knew it was going to be their last—and he slammed it down. Good Scotch should never be slammed, it should be appreciated, but he didn't think he had the capacity anymore.

He stopped at his computer desk and rechecked his equipment. None of the GPS systems were working. Or—they simply weren't working *for him*. It didn't make sense that all seven bombs could just disappear from his screen at the same time. The bombs were not synched up—one shouldn't affect the other, even if there had been some sort of malfunction at the source. So, no, there had to be a malfunction in the tracking software, but he hesitated calling in his tech friend to track the error. Anyone else's fingerprints on this deal, even the slightest involvement, would ruin them.

He scruffed his hand over his short cropped hair and then rubbed the back of his neck. He wanted to pour another Scotch, but he needed to be able to think.

He had confirmed that all seven bombs were in place at the rental company at the precise moment they needed to be to be checked in and properly re-routed to the next job. He'd checked and double-checked with the precision he'd learned in the military to make sure each purchase order for the rental of that equipment was correctly executed. He'd made plans for every contingency. He'd checked to make sure each piece of equipment had actually gone out on delivery— he didn't want a stray hanging back at the rental company by mistake.

But when he fired up the GPS tracking system today, it was blank.

He rebooted his system and, while he waited, he walked the Scotch over to the shelf where Chloë's urn sat—the one sure thing to keep him from going near it again. The computer beeped its welcome screen and he turned back to business. He had seven bombs to blow. He had not worked this long and this hard not to succeed.

* * *

"She's freaking everybody out," one of the cops said to Etienne, who stood at the front booking desk signing a bond for V'rai and Lizzie and Aimee. Although when Aimee had seen Etienne storm in, she'd protested that she'd rather stay in the jail than deal with him.

Staying in the jail was not an option, however, since V'rai had upset several of the command staff. She'd only mentioned a few things from the various cops' experiences as children that she could see. Nothing from the future; she knew better than that.

"She was only telling them stuff they already knew," Lizzie said.

Etienne hadn't said a word. Bad sign.

"Yeah," the releasing officer said, oblivious to the little family war of glares and the undercurrent of anger between Etienne's and V'rai's silences. "She scared the hell out of Erin and Bea back in Records."

Another voice from a few feet away—V'rai thought it was the booking officer—chimed in, "Well, I think Erin wanted to shoot her."

"All V'rai mentioned was how Erin had three lovers in college," Lizzie pointed out.

"Yeah, well, she was married to one of 'em at the time," the cop answered.

Oops, V'rai thought.

Although V'rai had suspected that telling some of the cops' secrets would speed the whole get-them-out-of-here mentality along a little. With the paperwork signed, Lizzie took her hand and they followed Etienne out to his truck.

"Get in," Etienne said, snapping open the door to the cab and the single bench seat.

"We won't all fit," Aimee griped.

"Squeeze in and make do."

"It's not a long trip, *chère*," V'rai said to Lizzie. "Just an hour to the house. I'll sit in your lap."

They crammed in, and the old truck rumbled to life. V'rai held onto the dash, relieved. Until Aimee gasped and Lizzie stiffened.

"This isn't the way home," Lizzie said.

"Etienne!" V'rai cried. "*Mais non, chèr*! You'll get her killed."

"You don't know that."

"You have to take us home." All she'd wanted to do was catch Etienne before he'd made it to Baton Rouge and prevent him from interfering—and getting Bobbie Faye killed. Now they were plummeting down the interstate, straight toward her niece, and V'rai could feel the foreboding increase with every passing minute.

The truck swayed abruptly to the right and Etienne pulled over to the shoulder of the road; V'rai heard the crunch of gravel and they bounced along bumpy roughness of ground instead of asphalt for the second time that day. "You don't want to come? Get out."

All three sisters sat in hushed silence, knowing full well Etienne meant it. He'd make them walk home if they so much as squeaked disagreement. Finally, after a full five minutes and what V'rai suspected had been a staring war between Aimee and Etienne, she heard the gearshift engage and the engine roared again, accelerating back into the traffic.

"This is a very bad idea, *chèr*," V'rai said.

"Yeah," Etienne agreed. "So was havin' a kid."

"Mmmmmmmmmmmaaarrrrrrgarrrriiitaaaaaaaassssss," Monique said, pouring another portion into Ce Ce's glass from the gargantuan stainless-steel thermos she'd hauled to the tailgating party.

"Gooooooooood," Ce Ce agreed, clinking her glass to the thermos. She'd had no idea four or five of those suckers could be so happy. Happy-making. Making with the smiling. Smiling with the . . .

Oh, no. Ce Ce looked at the chicken foot bracelet and blinked to make sure she was seeing the blurry image correctly. She pulled it closer to her nose, whoa, too close, nearly had that claw in her eye, and she squinted. Maybe she'd had about six drinks. Margaritas, she thought. At some point, they'd switched to margaritas. She hoped she was drunk and imagining things, because if she wasn't, that chicken foot was striped red and black. Striped really could not be good.

She'd never seen striped before, not even stone-cold sober. She knew somewhere deep down inside there was a warning alarm blaring, but the rest of her was all warm and fuzzy and—

"How ya doin', darlin'?" The hunky man who'd been grilling when she and Monique had joined the tailgating party smiled at her. His name was Brand. Brett? No, no, it was definitely Brand. Or Briggs. She was pretty sure she'd already asked him a couple of times. He talked so sweet, a man that gorgeous should not know how to say things with all that glowy prettiness.

"Oh, I'm just fiiiinnnne," she answered, smiling back at him.

She took another sip of her margarita, trying to concentrate on that chicken foot, trying to think what it was she needed to do about it being striped now, trying to remember . . . something.

Brand handed her a plate of food. He seemed to always be handing her a plate of really good food. Last night and then breakfast this morning and ohmygoodness, was it already lunch? Her glass was empty. How on earth had that happened?

"Monique, hon, I need a refill to go with this gorgeous man, I mean, food," she said, and watched Brand-Brett-Briggs beam again.

Oh, yes, Ce Ce very much loved football now.

Too much too much too much her brain babbled as Trevor held on tightly to her hand, leading her out of the conference room, his fingers laced through hers. Bobbie Faye could have sworn her heart beat hard enough to make the earth bounce off its axis, and her pulse throbbed straight from her palm to Trevor's as he guided her down the hall, past the armed agents standing guard and a couple of SWAT guys who milled around in the lobby.

She flashed back to the video image of Nina in the background behind Sean, and her heart double-clutched, gears grinding, pain stabbing because *this just could not be happening.*

And the one person she wanted comfort from was the one person who had hidden himself from her. Hadn't told her the truth.

How in the hell do you build a real relationship without trust?

Just that thought—just that shard of the lack of trust wedging into her heart—made her double over, pain lancing through her limbs. Trevor squatted next to her in the lobby as she fought to get her breath back, trying to squeeze air into her lungs past the ache in her chest. He didn't say anything; he just watched her, holding onto her hand. Though he was close enough, he didn't run his hands up her arms or knead her shoulders or brush his lips against her forehead. There was no expression on his face, nothing but shuttered anger in his gaze. He didn't murmur reassuring words, didn't even volunteer that he'd explain. He might as well have been across the fucking universe.

She forced herself to pull in air, and the room smelled faintly of stale bagels and syrup from the brunch served earlier that day at a credenza on the other side of the lobby. She closed her eyes, refusing to meet Trevor's expression. It did surprise the hell out of her that Cam and Riles were silent, because if ever there was a time for absolute peacock-level strutting of "I told you so"s about her and Trevor not working as a couple, it was now. Cam could rattle on about how she didn't know this man she'd promised to marry and Riles could gleefully parade all of the sorority girls he thought would be good enough for Trevor. She ought to just have t-shirts made up so that when she met anyone new, they'd be forewarned with: "The Apocalypse is here now."

And overlaying all of Bobbie Faye's devastation Trevor's superior lack of faith in her: Nina turned out to be an agent of some sort. Her best friend, and for many years, her only friend, had been living a dangerous double life, and now was tied up in that monster's hands.

Anger throbbed through Bobbie Faye: living, swarming, biting, stinging *rage*.

Betrayal.

She'd believed in Trevor. In Nina. She'd believed she really knew the two people in this world she loved the most.

She thought she'd known them. She'd trusted them more than she trusted gravity to hold her down onto the earth every single day, and then to suddenly find out that there were all of these things she actually did not know? Things they hadn't trusted her to handle?

Ripped her guts out.

She stood and Trevor stood with her, watching, and she wondered if he even realized he was playing with her engagement ring again. She couldn't speak to him. Not without the anger coursing, burning through her, and she walled the angry words in. All she could manage was to nod that she was ready to go.

Cam and Riles followed them out, and as soon as they cleared the glass doors of the hotel, Trevor glanced expectantly at Riles over his shoulder; Riles tossed a set of keys over her head and as Trevor snagged them he turned to where Riles had indicated the car was. Police and agents hovered everywhere in the parking lot, though a bigger group clustered near the building.

Then Trevor stopped short ahead of her and his hand tightened on hers, holding her closer to his side. He laced Riles a glare of pure, unadulterated venom and she spun to see what had made him so unhappy.

"Your job was to grab us a couple of cars," Trevor snapped at Riles, fury riding every word.

So that's where Riles had disappeared off to when she and Trevor were in the shower.

"I did," Riles answered, defiance in his shrug.

"You just had to make a fucking point about the money, didn't you?"

She couldn't see what they were referring to—they were

tall enough to see over a gaggle of cops gathered in the parking lot.

"My job is to watch your back, LT, whether you like it
or not."

A car? Trevor was pissed off at a . . . oh. *Shit.*

An Audi R8.

It was sex on wheels and it looked like money. Lots and
lots of sleek, low-slung, predatory, purring *money*. The kind
of money people like her didn't have. She remembered a
man, once, who'd driven a fancy car, who had that kind of
money. He'd worn a suit and had tossed a hundred-dollar bill
at her when she was mopping up Boudreaux's, an expensive
eatery that catered to the execs at the chemical plants. "Get
something nicer to wear," he'd said. "You look like shit."

She'd thrown the money back at him. "Get a brain," she'd
said. "You need one."

She looked from the Audi to the grim, hard lines of
Trevor's jaw, the muscle working overtime, and she tried to
reconcile this kind of money with the man who'd fixed two
toilets in their home, who'd done all of the grocery shopping
while she recovered, who'd gone to sleep every night with
his hand splayed against her scars. The man who'd gotten
down on one knee and had gotten so choked up he couldn't
speak, he just gave her the ring with tears in his eyes.

The man who hadn't told her everything, who hadn't
trusted her.

"There are bombs," he said now, seeing her hesitate at the
sight of that car.

"Sbobbie Faye drinkingsss gamesh!"

"You already called that a while ago."

"I did?"

"Yeah, that's why you're on the floor with twelve empty shot glasses."

"Oh. At leash there's a reason thish time."

—Michele Bardsley and Renee George,
new Bobbie Faye fans

Twenty

It was amazing how much they could *not* talk about on their way to Baton Rouge. They could not talk about the weather, not talk about the rampant addictive evil that was HGTV (she'd caught him—twice—watching the macho Saturday glorified tool porn), not talk about the fact that certain celebrities reminded her of those skinny, shiny lizards whose sole proof of any discernable brain cells was the ability to change color, though "orange" didn't seem terribly wise. They could also not talk about the fact that Bobbie Faye's head was about to fling itself from her shoulders in complete psychic meltdown while she sat wrapped up in the all-leather cockpit of the Audi as Trevor hurtled them through space and time. (NASA should really talk to the Audi people. They'd be landing on Jupiter right about now if they had.)

Trevor's damned phone rang the minute they'd hit the interstate, and he bit off terse agency mumbo-jumbo as two cop cars escorted them so that their police lights could clear a path through the Baton Rouge pre-game traffic. Someone had stalled in the right lane; the cop cars swooped past on the left without any real warning and Trevor downshifted, the engines screaming, as he forced Riles—who'd followed with Cam in a suspiciously spiffy new Porsche—to back off. Trevor took the left lane, nearly kissing the cop cars' bumpers, and she had a brief appreciation for the fact that the air bags probably worked in a car that cost more than most people's houses, and she didn't have to rely on duct tape to hold the front right fender on as they slung past a couple of eighteen-wheelers.

Not that it was going to matter, since her heart quit beating when one of the trucks switched lanes and the Audi nearly slid *underneath* it.

Trevor hung up the phone in a cradle charger thingie and really, the fact that the car didn't know to anticipate having a robe, slippers, and pipe ready showed a clear level of slackery. There was enough silence in the car to fill the Superdome. If she clenched her arms any harder, she'd have bruises. She didn't know what emotion to deal with first. And even the fact that she had something other than her best friend getting kidnapped and, hello, *bombs,* to deal with just fucking pissed her off. Where the hell do you start with something like that?

She had trusted Trevor—she'd trusted that she could be herself with him, and that he would be just as comfortable being himself with her. This was the man she had been going to freaking *marry.* She'd known that she had a lot to learn about him, and that it would take years, probably, to discover all of those little details that made him uniquely him, but she'd never dreamed that he was a completely different person than he'd represented himself to be. The shock of learning he'd hidden his real history from her was worse than when she'd learned Alex was a gunrunner. She felt like she was in some sort of warped Dr. Seuss story, where up was down.

"I can't believe you didn't tell me about you—your—" Damn. She didn't even know what to call it. Money? Wealth? "How is it that you thought omitting tiny little details like, oh, say, thirty-freaking-million-dollars, was okay?"

"It wasn't a big deal," he lied.

Her eyebrows slammed against her hairline at that whopper and he grimaced at her gasp. "Are you fucking kidding me? Forgetting to tell someone you opened a Christmas bank account and you're squirreling away fifty dollars a month out of your paycheck is 'not a big deal,' bucko. And don't tell me you forgot to mention it because of the temporary amnesia brought on by my cooking that time you choked so hard I nearly had to do CPR. I'm not buying that one."

He knew everything about her. Every freaking thing. He'd surveilled her for months before they met, lived with her after that, and he didn't tell her *something this big*. Not just hadn't told her—he must've gone through serious fucking hoops to keep her from finding out; he'd kept her busy, with the buying of the house and moving and working out and sex.

"I don't have sole control over the thirty million—it's part of the company."

"Seriously? You're gonna try to make it sound like it doesn't matter because you can't run out to spend it on Big Gulps tomorrow?"

"Would you have given me half a chance if you knew?"

"What the . . ." she sputtered, not even able to complete full sentences. When had reality spun completely off its axis? "What on earth makes you think I'd hold something like that against you?"

"You. You flat-out refused to date several rich guys who asked you out before—"

"You're kidding me, right? You are kidding me. You'd have to be kidding me, because if you're not kidding me, that means you researched the guys who asked me out before you came along—"

"Just the year I was surveilling you."

She stared at him. He'd done background checks on everyone. *Of course he had—he alphabetized the fucking* soup.

Outside the painful little bubble of the Audi, the world raced by. She didn't know who had radioed what, but someone ahead of them must be clearing the left lane, because it was wide open. (And an inordinate amount of LSU fans on their way to the game were flipping them the bird from the slowed-to-a-crawl right lane.) The high-performance tires beat a rhythm as it hit the expansion joints in the concrete interstate, and the persistent echo in the silent car seemed to be whispering *no trust no trust no trust.*

Her hands went numb and her vision blurred and she wondered if this was what having a heart attack felt like. Because the world seemed very very far away, colorless. Worthless.

"You know, I knew when we first met that you were the kind of guy who had a lot of stuff in his background—you'd worked for the freaking government, doing God knows what, and there was going to be a lot of stuff you didn't want to talk about. Not just couldn't talk about, but didn't want to talk about. And I got that. That was fine. I saw the man you were, and I knew you. I fell in love with that man."

"I'm still that man."

God, the pain in his voice sliced her and she held herself tighter. "How in the hell am I supposed to know that? You lied," she choked out past the lead weight where her heart used to be.

"No, I didn't. I didn't elaborate when I should have"—he held up a hand, stopping her from interrupting—"and I know that's splitting hairs, but think about it from my point of view: I had fallen in love with you—but I'd had time to get to know the real you. I had inside information about you and an understanding of who you were when that first crisis with your brother developed. I knew *you*. Your heart.

"I wanted a chance. I wanted for you to make this choice based on us—not all of the other bullshit that can surround . . ." He paused, looking resigned. "Money. Look, Sundance, who you've seen is the real me. I live off what I make from the Bureau. Nothing else."

She waved pointedly at the car and he amended, "Usually."

"So let me get this straight . . . you had the luxury of getting to know me for a whole year when you did surveillance and then meeting me in person. Yet apparently I'm not smart enough over here for you to give me the whole truth? Is that it, Trevor? Or is it that you just don't trust me?"

They raced up the ramp for the Mississippi River bridge and Bobbie Faye had to close her eyes—taking that bridge in the best of circumstances, with no traffic and at a snail's pace, would have made her heart plummet into her toes. She was pretty sure they'd topped out over 120, and would have gone faster if the cop cars in front of them could have.

He had to focus a moment to downshift and manage the exit off the bridge, a sharp curve to the right.

"It sure as hell isn't about you being smart enough—you outthink most people I know. And it damned well isn't trust—you know I trust you with my life. You have this terrific sense of fair play," he said, "which can drive me fucking nuts sometimes. But it's who you are, and I get it, and that's okay. But I also knew that you would never in a million years say yes even to a date if you thought—wrongly, stupidly—that there was something completely uneven about us that you'd never overcome. My salary as an agent was bad enough."

"I'm not that bad."

"No? Are you kidding me? Do you know how much that card table in the dining room cost?" When she frowned and shook her head, trying for the life of her to remember, he continued, "I know exactly how much it cost. $49.95 plus tax, which came to $54.45, and you know how I know it? You insisted on going over to the goddamned ATM machine and pulling out the cash from your account and giving me half right there, before we left the store. I knew that put you down to less than five dollars in your account, and you stood there and calculated whether it was okay for you not to eat lunch for a week and make me happy by getting the table or to tell me you couldn't afford the goddamned table, and you picked *not eating lunch*. You wouldn't let me buy it if it was for 'us'—we had to split it, because that was only 'fair.' Well *fuck* fair. I don't give a good goddamn about fair. What I care about is you. You are my home. *You are it for me.* You make me laugh and you make me sometimes want to tear out my heart because it hurts so much with wanting you, but loving you is the only thing I can do. And you cannot hold it against me that my family happens to have money, Sundance. You want to talk about fair? *That's* not fair."

"That's a neat trick, Trevor, making it seem as if I would

hold your wealth against you. Yeah, it might've intimidated me, but we'll never know, will we? Did it ever occur to you that some of those guys who asked me out just might've been assholes hoping to call the Contraband Days Queen a notch on their expensive belts? And that they were so vain and obnoxious, they would've insulted a trust-fund baby? No, it didn't. So when were you going to tell me?"

"If I was really lucky, after we were married."

She turned in her seat to gape at his profile. She was agog. No, that didn't quite cover it. Her Agog had slammed completely up against You Didn't Just Fucking Admit That and lost in a complete TKO.

Holy breathing *hell*.

He reclined his head against the seat. "I realize now that was stupid."

"Ya think? Our dating, our being together, is not some damned mission, and you didn't have the right to decide what I am capable of knowing."

He scowled, his anger palpable. "Is that what you think? That I've manipulated you?"

"Well, *duh*. How in the hell am I supposed to know what is true about us when none of it's based in reality?"

"So you're telling me that you don't know how you feel about me? That you think what we have is only a result of manipulation?"

A thousand daggers sliced straight through her. Her skin burned, flames licking through her heart until she thought there would be only a pile of ash left on that leather seat. She wiped the tears from her face, rubbing them onto her jeans.

"Well?" he asked, his voice harsh, cracked.

He'll never really know. He'll always wonder, he'll always question her motives. The fact that he'd hidden his wealth meant that anything they had together emotionally was always going to be viewed under the microscope of manipulation. If they stayed together, would he think it was out of loyalty? Guilt? By not being himself with her from the beginning, not telling her the truth, would he always doubt that she could love him, the totality of him?

And now he'd manipulated them right into their worst nightmare: doubt.

She didn't know how to live with that.

"You should have trusted me," she said. "You should have asked for a prenup, then you'd know, then—"

"No."

The car slid easily through the nearly deserted Baton Rouge streets—game day, everyone was either at the game, tailgating, or at home, partying with family.

Oh, God. Family. She sunk her face in her hands. Trevor's family must think she was an absolute gold-digger. Geez. And Riles. No wonder he'd been such an ass.

Not that he was off the hook for his assiness, but at least she saw a motive.

"It's for your protect—"

"*No.*"

"I'm not comfortable with—"

"Then get over it," he bit out. "Get comfortable with it. Because I'm not starting off our marriage with some sort of contract that implies that somewhere down the line, we might not make it. There is no negotiation about that, Bobbie Faye. Not a single solitary damned bit."

"You have to at least have something for beneficiary purposes, so that if something happens—"

"No. Do you understand the word *no*? Because we're not going to compromise on this one. I will live in a hut with you, on a dirt floor, if that's what you want. I will live in a hammock or a tent or in a house with white walls and no furniture. I will eat bologna sandwiches with you for the next fifty years. We will live on our salaries and nothing else, but I am not, under any circumstances, going to be able to live with myself if I know you aren't taken care of if something happens to me. And in my line of business, it could. So everything I have, is yours. Everything. Because I want everything you have in return."

"Well, there might be some spare change in the sofa in storage, and I think I tossed in a box of toothpicks somewhere, but you've pretty much got the only thing I have, which is me."

"No, I don't. I never did."

What? What the hell? She whiplashed at the vehemence of his words, and her heart boomeranged, thudding with pain at the expression on his face.

He understood her confusion without her having to voice it, and his expression softened as the ache showed through. She knew he was letting her see into his feelings, that he was exceptionally capable of hiding from her. Seeing that amount of pain in him sent a rush of emotion that logjammed in her chest, and she couldn't swallow, much less talk.

"You have to draw the line for Moreau," he said.

She gaped at him—with everything else that he'd just admitted, how in the hell had this become about Cam?

He had to turn away from the shock in her green eyes. And the fact that she was about to defend the man, even now.

"He doesn't mean to—" she started, and his disgusted grimace cut her off.

"Yes, he fucking *does*. He wants you back. He's made that clear. He is, in a lot of ways, a good man. Jesus," he swore to himself, pissed off that they were having to discuss this. She was being purposefully obtuse.

"He knows the truth, Trevor."

Trevor pulled the car into a parking lot one building down from the S&M club, veering away from the two cop cars and Riles's Porsche, and parked. He faced her, his gaze sliding over her face, wondering if *she* even knew the truth of how she felt.

Was this her heart talking? Or her loyalty because she wore his ring?

She glanced down at her hands fidgeting in her lap.

"Cam will get used to it and—"

He glared at her. She was out of her mind. He counted to five before he could open his mouth and without telling her so. She crossed her arms and glared back.

"Quit defending him." He drew in a ragged breath. "I know us, together, and I know *you*." And he did. He knew her, but what he didn't know was if his faith was enough for them both. "But Moreau is trying to work every angle to come between us, and he's doing a damned good job. If he wasn't always present, I don't know—maybe . . ." And he had to think about this a moment. Had to allow himself to admit this, as galling as it was. "Maybe I would have felt a little safer telling you more." That was a low blow, and he could read it in the hurt in her eyes, but it was the truth and she waited for him to finish. "I want you to have your friends. Even if it's him. Even as much as it kills me that it's him, you've had a lifetime of friendship and I don't want that to end. I can deal with it, when it's platonic. But that's not what Cam wants and you know it. What I cannot deal with is him touching you constantly, reaching out for you to comfort him, or to comfort you, physically.

"If the roles were reversed—if that was a woman I used to sleep with, reaching out for me, how would you feel?"

Her face slacked, her frown receded and she stared at him. She was so used to thinking of others first, so used to trying not to hurt Moreau, that she hadn't thought she could hurt *him*. Christ, he'd been so determined to be so fucking strong for her, she had no clue how much he needed her.

"The line in the sand has to come from you." He softened his voice, and the raging pain shot through. "I need to know, Sundance, that there is a line, and that it comes from what you want. I need to know. Because this is who I am. Laid bare. You either want me, the way I am, or not. And it's killing me to feel like we're halfway and that you could change your mind."

She reached for him across the console and he backed away. "No. No. As much as I want to, no. You think about this." Jesus, he didn't know if he could do this. He'd been shot before, he'd been knifed, multiple times, he'd had shrapnel embedded in various parts of his body, and nothing compared to this pain. It was all he could do not to double over. It took every single ounce of will he had to climb out of that car, in that much pain, while she had tears streaming down her face, and not reach for her.

But that was the hell of it. He'd reached for her so often,

he'd fuzzed up her senses with sex, he'd used wit and charm and even understanding to manipulate her into where he wanted her. He had been, in his own way, a bastard, because he'd wanted her, and he'd pulled the full-court press to get her. And now?

Now he was going to pay the fucking price, because maybe Moreau was right.

Maybe Trevor had rushed her so much, so fucking scared of her not wanting to deal with the shit that was his family, the insecurity she'd have about his background, that the way she felt about him was all mixed up in gratitude and debt for the things he'd done.

Maybe he'd been lying to himself all along when he'd said he knew exactly how she felt.

Because maybe she needed an out.

"Tranquilizers?"

"It's Bobbie Faye season."

"You can't shoot someone with tranquilizers!"

"These are for me."

—Pharmacist Deborah Mundy to FEMA
coordinator Laura Gorton

Twenty-one

Trevor had barely gotten around the car when Bobbie Faye emerged and Moreau ran up. The cop's eyes narrowed down into cold hard hatred (aimed at Trevor) as Bobbie Faye wiped tears from her face, and Trevor braced for it—the *what did you do to her?* tactic. The asshole was going to use any advantage, and it was everything Trevor could do to not step between them and stop him. Moreau was going to touch her, to soothe her, to check to see if she was okay; he'd been using any excuse to touch Bobbie Faye, to re-create an intimate relationship with her, and now Moreau had a prime opportunity.

Trevor felt waves of determination roll off his own body, felt his fingers ball into a fist, and he fought it, fought it for her sake as she stepped past the car door and he shut it for her. A little too hard.

Braced for it as Moreau arrived.

"So, Duck Face," Moreau said to her, gruff, bossy, downright annoyed, "we gonna do this gig or not?"

Her eyes flew wide, surprised for a heartbeat, then she snorted, a quick laugh as she play-punched him on the arm.

"Jerk," she said, but the appreciation and relief rolled off of her.

Trevor couldn't see the humor, and then realized: it was something private. One of the hundreds of things they'd shared. Moreau had known the right thing to do in that moment when she was wholly upset by Nina and the bombs . . . and him. . . .

"You ready?" Moreau asked.

"Sure, Twinkle Butt, let's go."

Bobbie Faye started to explain the reference.

Trevor shook his head. He didn't fucking want to hear it.

"Hang on," Moreau said as he bent to retrieve his spare gun—a little Ruger LCP he had stashed—and as he pulled it out of his boot and fixed the jeans again, Trevor realized that he, too, should have thought to arm her.

Hell, he should have thought to make her laugh.

He shoved the heels of his hands against his eyes, forcing himself to think. He was reeling—the casino, the undercover op that was clearly a fiasco, their house blowing up, nearly losing her at the racetrack, and underlying it all, that kiss, and he couldn't melt down. He had years of training to work under fire, alone, in the dark or in the worst stink of the world, and right now? The possibility of losing her was worse than all of those situations put together, but he couldn't show it. Couldn't let it get to him. Lives were at stake, and by God, he wasn't going to fail her or them. Not again.

"You can't go throwing spitballs in there," Moreau said, as he handed her the gun. She checked the chamber, and the magazine, and just like that, she was back, tough as nails, ready to confront whatever came at them.

"I was not the one throwing spitballs," she said, as they moved toward the doors of the all-glass high-rise, and Moreau gave him a glance over her head, when she couldn't see.

This is why I've always been her best friend. This is why I'm going to win, the look said.

Trevor gave him the *fuck you* glare back, but without being able to put a bullet in Moreau, he wasn't so sure it carried the point adequately.

"You called ahead?" Trevor asked Riles as he came around the building—obviously finishing a quick scouting run. When they'd first left Lafayette and on the way here, he had talked to his own sources, but he wanted to hear Riles's appraisal. They'd operated together for too many years for old habits to die, and Riles liked recon. Even when intel handed him information, he triple-checked, which made him consistent and reliable.

"Yeah, LT, there are guards in the attached garage, two inside the front door, and one on the floor of the club. Those are the ones in uniforms. Since we're dealing with an off-the-books intelligence agency, you know there are others."

Trevor's phone beeped a message. He scrolled through the screens, and said, "Good. We've got blueprints of the building."

"Still no answer from ASAC Brennan?" Riles asked, peering over Bobbie Faye's shoulder as they all looked at the building plans on Trevor's phone.

"He says he's hit a wall—they," Trevor nodded toward the building, "don't exist."

"How can they not exist?" Bobbie Faye asked. "It's an S&M club. And a magazine. People are clients. The office is right there." She waved toward the building.

"The S&M company exists," Riles explained as Trevor paged down to another screen of blueprints, "but it's a very deep cover for an agency no one wants to admit responsibility for. It's too shady, too off-the-books to claim. Especially given how wet Nina's work has been."

Trevor subtly elbowed Riles, but not subtly enough for Bobbie Faye to miss it. "Wet?" She scoured Trevor's blank expression, and then the epiphany suddenly dawned. "Wet? As in, assassin?"

"Point is," Trevor said, "ASAC Brennan's hitting a wall, so we're not going to know if the employees in there are aware of Nina's status as an agent, if they're fellow agents, or if they're purely civilians."

"But Nina works for the government. And she's a fucking hostage. Are you telling me they aren't admitting that?"

"Her cover's been established for a very long time for some very good reasons. There are other agents' lives at stake, all over the world. If her employers pop up and suddenly claim her, MacGreggor will know exactly what sort of leverage he's got."

"Right now," Moreau added, "he may think he's only got your friend."

Trevor watched as she absorbed that, livid. He wanted to reach for her.

But he stood still, his arms crossed to keep from touching her. *Being together had to be her choice—not just because they needed the comfort of each other's touch.*

"Meanwhile, if anyone is even inside, they don't know we're coming. There's a tight security protection on their entrances and exits, which suggests they're not going to be welcoming. We also don't know who their clients are, what secrets they may be getting from those clients, and we don't want to go in there and arouse suspicion that the club is a government front."

"Why can't we just call Gilda and say, 'Hi, remember me, your boss's best friend? I'm worried about her—I'd like to ask you some questions?' "

"Sure we could," Riles said. "Aside from the fact that they're not answering their phone, we are not absolutely sure where MacGreggor snatched Nina—so we don't know if his people left something behind that could hurt us—and we can't guarantee one-hundred percent they're not inside the S&M club right this minute, holding the employees hostage. We're not about to walk into a really fucked-up deal. We have to assume the worst. You know . . . how you generally feel every single time you look in a mirror."

"You and duct tape, Barnacle, are going to become very good friends after this."

Moreau's phone rang, and while he talked, Trevor found what he'd hoped for on the building plans and he angled the phone so everyone could see. "There's a service elevator, east side. Direct to the employee entrance of the club above."

"Heavy security on that, I checked—video surveillance and a computerized entry, passcode and thumbprint—and that's a guess, I couldn't get close enough," Riles said.

"Nick's in custody," Moreau told them, hanging up the phone. "Lawyered up immediately. How about the stairs?" He leaned in to examine the blueprints with Trevor.

"There are two guards on each set of stairs. We'd have to split up," Riles said, also looking at the blueprints. "Two on the east side, one and"—he nodded to Bobbie Faye—"a half on the west side."

"Or I can use my passcode to the employee elevator," Bobbie Faye suggested.

"You have a passcode to the exclusive floor of an S&M club?" Riles asked. "That explains *a lot*."

Lori Ann's nerves multiplied, folded, multiplied again, and beat a rhythm against her stomach. Three hours 'til game time, and she and Stacey were wandering around beneath the stadium in one of the large parking bays—an area big enough to house visiting team buses and still have plenty of room for other vehicles and storage space for miscellaneous construction crap. They were waiting for Marcel to come back from the last-minute pregame Mike the Tiger check. Right before the game, the big cat would be loaded from his giant pen into the touring cage, right across the little tree-lined street, and then Marcel would pull the cage into this bay. At which point, she would try not to have a heart attack.

They were going to pull Mike the Tiger. Around the football field.

They were going to be a part of history, a part of this place she'd have liked to have attended. Maybe one day— maybe if she could stay sober, one day at a time, and Stacey was in school, maybe.

"Mamma mamma," Stacey chanted, her pom-poms going overtime, and Lori Ann had to haul her off the piles of concrete blocks someone had stacked up against the back wall of the bay. The wall that supported the stadium seating above it and the noise above them was already a low roar as people filed in to find their seats. Then she had to pull Stacey off the mountain of rebar and the boxes of tools, off the side of the giant generator, and then away from the orange cones tossed into a corner. It was little kid heaven and really, the idiot contractor should have picked a better spot for all of this crap. Of course, if they'd left it outside, it would have taken up precious parking spots—spots LSU charged a fee for, so what did she expect?

She pulled Stacey back off the concrete blocks, determined to interest the kid in something else besides practicing jumping like the big cheerleaders did. She scanned the room, noting a camera on top of a generator nearby. There was no barricade in sight to prevent someone from accidentally tripping on the construction supplies piled up there; a camera as a preventative safety measure wasn't really going to cut it, except maybe to show if someone was stealing the stuff. It was amazing how safety-conscious she'd gotten after having a kid—and being on the sidelines of Bobbie Faye disasters. Now, Lori Ann examined everything with the magnifying glass of "how dangerous is it?"—especially with Stacey determinedly taking after her aunt.

She smiled at her daughter, who was coated now with the sticky purple residue of the sno cone Marcel had bought her and, on top of that, the dust from the construction supplies. She was a big ball of sugar high, and Lori Ann was going to have to convince this kid to sit still in Marcel's truck for the trip around the field.

Yeah, like that was gonna happen.

The mechanic paced around his workshop, its pristine cleanliness a mockery of how he felt. He ran his hands over his close-cropped hair, wondering how the hell he'd not seen this coming. A quick glance at his watch told him the story: it was five minutes after the bombs should have blown. Five whole minutes. Still no GPS. He had not made his warning call to take responsibility. Without a computer uplink, he couldn't blow the bombs, and he did not know what the hell to do.

And the Irish were not picking up his calls. They'd bought the supplies, they'd left it up to him just how to make the bombs, how to get them into the plant, and he'd taken care of everything. The Irish had their motives, which was fine—they dovetailed with his: take down Poly-Ferosia.

He looked at Chloë's urn, and wished, for the millionth time, he'd taken her to work that day. He was supposed to drive her, but he'd been sick with a cold, and she'd made him stay home. They were supposed to go out dancing that evening for their anniversary and she didn't want him to be too sick to go.

A fucking *cold*.

He squeezed his eyes against the memory of arriving at the wreck after a friend called. Getting there as they'd pulled Chloë from the carnage that used to be her car, her body coated with oil and gas, burned 'til she wasn't recognizable. He'd reached for her, then. He'd pushed aside the fireman, pushed aside the paramedics, knowing it was too late, and he still reached for her, the oil and the grease coating his hands, burning in his nostrils with the horrid smell of burnt flesh. He smelled it in his sleep. He woke to it, every day.

A "one-car" accident. There had been a definite dent in the fender with yellow paint that he'd known hadn't been there before. Not enough evidence that she hadn't just had a fender bender in a parking lot somewhere, the defense attorney said. Not enough evidence for conspiracy that someone had run her off the road. Not enough to put those bastards behind bars, the bastards at Poly-Ferosia who knew she had evidence to nail them for all of their hazardous safety violations. Violations that would kill people if she didn't stop them.

Violations that would cost Poly-Ferosia millions.

He meant to cost them more. He meant to take this fight to their door. Eleven fucking *years* and his wrongful death case on Chloë's behalf was so mired in the court system, nothing was going to happen. Nothing. He could see it, he knew it, and all of that effort wasn't fucking *good* enough to nail the bastards for her death.

There was nothing on the news channel on the TV in the corner of the room. Nothing except the casino and the explosion at Bobbie Faye's house, her photo splashed on every station. There should have been photos of the plant exploding.

He found himself at his sink again, rewashing his hands. He didn't remember walking over there, starting the burning hot water, using the grit-laden soap again, the kind that scrubs away the oil and the grime, the kind he'd used so many times after Chloë. . . .

He turned off the faucet, grabbed a shop towel, and dried his chapped hands as he watched the news, his heart beating triple time.

The Irish.

The Irish.

He'd forgotten. How the fuck could he forget?

He stared at that channel, where Bobbie Faye's house burned, and he knew. He *knew* what they were going to do. It had to be the same Irish, the ones who'd been in the paper, who'd been after Bobbie Faye back in June, which was two months before they'd contacted him. He'd just gotten the word from his attorney that his latest effort had stalled on appeal, that it was going to take another round, another year.

Some perfect fucking timing.

He should have seen this. With his military training, he should have asked more about their motives.

Oh, dear God. He pulled Chloë's rosary from his jeans, and his hands flashed over the beads, second nature. He didn't know what to do. He couldn't let the Irish hijack his bombs.

He felt Chloë's disapproval. Felt it as if Chloë were standing in the room, her hands on her slim hips, her blue eyes flaring, feet apart in that fighting stance she'd get whenever she'd taken him to task, the same sort of fighting stance she got whenever she dealt with people who wanted to play fast and loose with the law for their own benefit.

Lucidity. He felt, for the first time in years, lucid. Really fucking clear, and holy hell, Chloë would kill him. She'd refuse to sit by him in their forever that he'd fantasized. He'd lost her, and he was going to lose her all over again, the part of her he'd kept in his heart, that he'd hung onto for years, because there was no way she'd have loved him through this.

He had no idea how to stop the Irish. Were the bombs even *in* Poly-Ferosia?

He dialed the Irish again, planning on a confrontation with the man, planning on getting him to slip up, to give a hint as to just what the hell they were up to. Threaten to go to the police. Threaten whatever he could.

The phone chirped that the number was no longer in service.

Twenty-two

"Izzy," Trevor said into his phone, "I need a ninety-second burst. Mark: 4:35. Can you do it?" Bobbie Faye watched him frown. "We are *not* talking about Mom now. No. Izzy, give me the fucking burst." He hung up the phone.

"Izzy?" she asked him. "Isn't she the sister who runs the family business?"

She needed something to think about, instead of the dead panic she felt over Nina being held, with the seconds ticking away.

They had set up in a perimeter around the building—Riles taking the east stairs, Cam the west, and she and Trevor taking the employee elevator. The poor security guards would be napping awhile—and would probably have a headache later from where Trevor and Riles had knocked them out. Trevor had noticed their check-in pattern with the head of security and planned an entry during a quiet interlude, hoping to buy them a few minutes before anyone in that clubhouse knew something was wrong. All of the access points, though, had security cameras, and Trevor wanted some sort of satellite doohickey to do something impressive that was going to take them down for a minute-and-a-half.

"An electronics business?" she added, remembering he hadn't given her a lot of details about the family business; she had assumed it was some sort of mom-and-pop store.

His eyes stayed glued to his watch, counting down to 4:35. "It's a pretty big electronics business."

He was annoyed—clearly not wanting to talk about something that focused back on his wealth, and from the anger simmering in his voice, she had a niggly feeling that "electronics business" should mean more than . . . She stared at the brand logo on his phone and *sweet fucking pink and yellow unicorns*, she just realized. "You're kidding me. Cormi-Co Telecommunications?" They were one of the largest, fastest-growing telecoms and had taken over her cell phone provider. A multi*billion*-dollar company.

"I have absolutely nothing to do with running the company, Sundance. Or with the hundred other things my sisters and my parents run—that's their thing. This is mine." He watched the time and said, "Go," and they sprinted to the service elevator security box. As Bobbie Faye plugged in the code Nina had given her over a year ago, Trevor stood near her—but not near enough. Not the way he'd have been standing the day before. His arms were folded, his hands weren't reaching out to touch her; it was as if he had completely withdrawn until he knew what she wanted—until she knew for sure and drew the line.

He wanted words. In the middle of this, Trevor wanted *words*.

The doors opened, they stepped inside, and he leaned against one wall, staring somewhere off into space, somewhere light years away from her, and she hated it. *Hated* this place between them.

"Your family—they have—"

"I don't want it." The elevator jerked upward as he met her gaze, flint shearing off him. "I have *every*thing I want in this elevator."

"You'd just walk away from all of that—"

"I already did. Many years ago. I've got my life. They don't like it, and there's a lot of pressure for me to participate, but I'm not going to. Izzy wants it; I hate it. And all I want is right here."

Her body heated to Inferno with just the sweep of his gaze, and still he held back. He didn't touch her, and it was wrong and empty and it made her angry, all over again.

He had not trusted her.

Still didn't. Not really.

She started to tell him just exactly what she thought about his stupidity when he put a hand up . . . the elevator stopped and the doors slid open.

"Thirty-two seconds 'til we have cameras again," he said, and eased out of the elevator into a beautiful kitchen area, his gun drawn, keeping her behind him.

They scanned the room—glancing into open doorways and pantries—and it appeared they'd interrupted meal prep. An Italian sauce simmered on the professional chef's stove and pasta boiled in a magnificent pot. Bobbie Faye noted clean dishes set out for a dinner—it was getting late in the afternoon—and there were six plates. She touched Trevor on the arm to direct his attention to the dining table, and with just her hand on his bicep, the electricity between them jumped and hummed low in her body.

He nodded, all business, moving away from her and purposefully toward a hallway. According to the blueprints, there was a large living room in the center of this penthouse "club." As he toed open the door, he hesitated at first, then he reached behind and slid his hand along her arm, tucking her closer behind him as if he needed the reassurance that she was there and safe. There were complete layers to the man that she couldn't fathom. The room they entered seemed empty and the whole place felt hushed—too quiet where there ought to be normal noises of people going about their day. Whoever had been cooking in the kitchen ought to be somewhere nearby, and the fact that the place seemed empty meant someone in the S&M club had seen them enter.

Trevor motioned her to follow and eased into the living space. From across the room, Bobbie Faye saw Cam and Riles enter from two different hallways, both shaking their heads—the hallways had been empty.

Trevor tapped his watch and motioned to his eyes—the

cameras were back up. There was one last area of the club to search, and as the four of them eased from the living room into what Bobbie Faye would have loosely described as the "work quarter," Trevor took point.

The door was locked. Definitely the pasta-cookers' refuge. Trevor backed off, taking one side of the door with her while Cam and Riles took the other. Trevor glanced at Cam, and they nodded: ready.

"Police," Cam shouted. "Come out. Hands up!"

Bobbie Faye jumped at the visceral, barking order—so definite, it made her want to put her own hands up.

An intercom snapped static into the room, and their eyes went to the panel next to the door, where a computer screen displayed a small, very young woman in an expensive suit leaning toward the camera projecting her image; her face was bowl-shaped and distorted.

"ID please?" she asked.

Cam held up his shield.

"Okay, we're coming out. We are not armed. And you've just violated more laws than I can count, so you stand still."

The door opened and a tiny wisp of a girl emerged. Bobbie Faye had a hard time thinking she could be more than twelve, but she wore an expensive business suit and carried herself with a rigid comportment that made Bobbie Faye wonder if the stitches had healed yet from the stick up her ass. It was the five women behind her which made Bobbie Faye bite the inside of her cheek to keep from grinning, though she noticed Riles did not have any such reluctance. They were all decked out in S&M gear—Amazon women in their high platform heels and leather outfits that had more . . . accesses . . . than actual coverage.

"Ohmygoodness," the small woman said as soon as she made eye contact with Bobbie Faye. "I can't believe we almost shot you! Nina would have kicked my ass." She saw Riles then, and practically started to drool. "Oh. Wow. You're. Wow. You're Mr. Rilestone. Wow. So great to meet you, sir."

If the twit genuflected, Bobbie Faye was going to bean her. Riles barely nodded and the woman could hardly tear her gaze away from him to look back at them. It was the worst case of crush Bobbie Faye had seen since elementary school.

"We're here about Nina," Trevor said. "We had to make sure this site hadn't been"—he was gazing past the women and around their inner sanctum, and Bobbie Faye realized he wasn't sure if they were agents or just employees—"compromised."

The woman assessed him, glancing from Bobbie Faye to Trevor and back again. And then something miraculous happened.

She seemed to age a dozen years, right in front of them, going from twelve to twenty-four or -five or so, instantly. It was a transformation of posture: a different way of holding her body, her facial features, relaxing into an expression that was more wordly, more jaded, less enthusiastic. It was the damnedest thing Bobbie Faye had ever seen.

"We're operational. I'm Gilda," she said. "What do you mean, you're here about Nina?"

"Nina's been kidnapped," Bobbie Faye said. "And she sent—"

"What!" Gilda said. "God*damn* it." And she spun on her heels, motioning them to follow her. "I've been GPSing her all day. She broke off communication last night, but I knew she was going in to find you—and I also knew that she couldn't reveal who she was," and with that, she glanced back at Bobbie Faye, "but obviously, you've figured that out."

"Not exactly with any help," Bobbie Faye said. She didn't have to see Trevor's scowl to know that it was a direct hit.

"We've got video," Trevor told her. "Your CO should have called, they should have gotten the word to you an hour ago."

There was a weird pause from Gilda. "I've been a little unable to work the computer."

They filed into a large computer room where everything appeared to be in perfect working order as far as Bobbie Faye could see—there were no blue screens of death on the monitors, and no actual smoke.

Trevor, on the other hand, studied the equipment like a pro and frowned at Gilda. "What's the problem?"

Gilda gave him a meaningful frown that Bobbie Faye couldn't quite parse, and Trevor's expression changed from confused to comprehension. They seemed to be having an entire conversation with only subtle eyebrow movements. It annoyed the living hell out of her.

"What's going on?" Bobbie Faye asked.

"Gilda here," Trevor explained as he watched the young woman's face, "has been actively avoiding contact with her CO because she's afraid that Nina's disappearance would imply that Nina's been compromised."

"Compromised? She's been taken hostage. Of course she'd been compromised."

"No, not just 'at risk,' but actually suspected of traitorous behavior." Before Bobbie Faye could protest, Gilda put up one hand to stop her and then went back to clicking on keys and pulling up screen after screen of video. "In our field, looks are deceiving. We've had a hard time finding the information we wanted, and our bosses began wondering why. There have been a couple of leaks"—and there, Gilda stopped and nodded toward Bobbie Faye—"this would so get me fired, if they knew I was telling you this, but you're with Trevor and she's your best friend. I think you can be trusted. Anyway, double agents have been known to stage their own deaths—or kidnappings—in the past. Our bosses had been wondering if she was the source of their problems, the leaks, and with this new kidnapping, if she wasn't creating an 'exit' strategy—a way to 'die' or 'disappear' without any of us having actual proof of traitorous acts."

"You're fucking kidding me?" Really, Bobbie Faye was going to have to get a whole new vocabulary to express *how flipping insane are you people?* Because clearly, she was wading waist-deep in cuckoo here. "You cannot possibly believe Nina would be a double agent."

"You've known her most of her life," Gilda pointed out, "and yet, you didn't know she was an agent. She's that good, so yes, it was a possibility." Gilda stopped Bobbie Faye from interrupting. "I don't believe she's anything other than loyal, but right now, her situation's precarious, and not just because MacGreggor's a sociopath.

"Which is why I didn't log in. If I stay off the computer, our bosses can't give me a terminate order on her," Gilda said, a little too carefully, and Bobbie Faye felt Trevor stiffen next to her.

"Why in the hell do I think your version of 'terminate' doesn't mean a nice farewell party with a bunny cake and pterodactyl cookies?"

Gilda scrunched the almost invisible eyebrows on her very round face at Bobbie Faye, then scowled at Trevor as if she'd just made a connection. "How in the hell did you get your SAC to let a civilian on this mission?"

"That's the first question you should have asked after you'd ID'd us," he chastised her, but without rancor—more like a senior agent to a junior, and Bobbie Faye had to remember all over again just who he really was. "She's with me," he said, as if that was explanation enough.

When Bobbie Faye frowned, puzzled, he leaned close to her and said, for her benefit only, "I pointed out that if you were gone, I was gone."

"You're breaking about seven hundred different federal codes," Gilda stated. "I'm sure they're going to have a field day with you when this is through. You could always come to work for us."

Trevor exhaled, *hmph*. "For a boss who's about to terminate one of his best people in the world?"

Gilda gave him a grimace, and then turned to Bobbie Faye. "Nina had information she thought would save your life and the lives of other people. She dropped everything to go there. She knew she was risking breaking cover, but she did it anyway. I hope you understand what that means."

Bobbie Faye swallowed, words choking her. Trevor took her hand in that moment, understanding her need, and simply did it, naturally. It was almost as if he thought better of it a second later, and he crossed his arms, breaking his grasp of her hand.

Gilda waved their attention back to the computers. Riles focused on one monitor and said, "Damn, you had infrared and weight-bearing monitors."

Gilda nodded at him, swooning a little again, then caught herself and jerked back into professional mode. "You broke the perimeter, but we get that all day with people walking around the building. It wasn't 'til you knocked out the cameras that we knew for certain something was up. We pushed the backup system and watched you, but you were very good at not facing the cameras. If you hadn't ID'd yourself—and if I hadn't been able to see Bobbie Faye behind you on the camera—we'd have implemented a couple of secondary systems you don't want to know about right now."

"You have Nina on GPS?" Cam asked. "Because I can't believe MacGreggor didn't check for that."

"He'd have to catch it at just the right microsecond to know where the signal was coming from." And then she proceeded to speak Geek with Extra Nerd thrown in about "microbursts" and "directional awareness" and something that sounded like "pink elephants," but was probably a tad more technical, and ended with, "ten-minute delays" unless something insanely annoying told the unit to go into hibernation mode.

"So this thing shuts itself off if it detects that you're trying to detect it?" Bobbie Faye asked.

"Not if *we're* trying—if someone else is wanding her. If they're actively checking for outgoing signals, the unit will hibernate for ten minutes. If there's no sign of active sensing, it'll send out a new burst. We haven't had a new burst in the last couple of hours, but Nina's been gone less than twenty-four hours, and the unit transmitted her vitals last burst—so she's alive. I had no reason to suspect she wasn't still undercover. She's disappeared before."

"She knows she's on GPS. That means she sent us to you so you could give us her location."

"We can nail Sean?" Bobbie Faye asked.

"Don't," Cam said, "even think you're gonna participate in that, baby. It's too dangerous."

"Hallmark really needs to make those 'Happy Lobotomy' cards," she muttered and she saw a smile twitch at Trevor's lips. Because no way was she not going to participate. This was *Nina*. She'd have to be dead to not participate—she'd already seen the blip on the GPS map pinpointing Nina's—and Sean's—location.

"You said information to save our lives," Trevor said. "What information?"

"Bombs. We had lured the seller of some high-tech detonator chips in here—we'd been working on uncovering who the supplier was, and how many he was selling. Or, in this case, had sold, because we got to him after the fact. I understand that you," Gilda looked at Trevor, "were working on uncovering the buyers, right?" At Trevor's nod, she continued, "Nina had gathered enough intelligence from some of the darker places she goes"—and that was the first time Bobbie Faye realized that this nicely lit, beautiful clubhouse was only a part of Nina's cover, that she'd probably trolled a lot less savory places—"that," Gilda continued, "she suspected this man of being the seller. If he hadn't had certain proclivities, she'd have turned him over to you and your tactics." She glanced at Riles then. "Or you. But she knew she could get information out of him.

"I think he felt an intense guilt, and I'm almost certain he knew he had a heart condition—I think he wanted to confess, which is why he put himself into a position of stress. Heidi," and Gilda nodded toward an excessively intimidating woman who was taller than Trevor, "managed to make him talk. He mentioned bombs. He's a huge U.S. patriot and knows that some freelance contractors to the government sometimes buy things off the books, to better facilitate off-the-books activities. He thought he was selling to a mercenary, former military, who was going to use his items overseas against terrorists. He overheard chatter—we believe from the buyers—that convinced him the detonator chips were going to be used here, in Louisiana—and it somehow involved *you*," she said to Bobbie Faye. "Today. The last thing we got out of him an hour ago was 'today' and then he went into cardiac arrest."

"Dead?" Trevor asked.

"Almost. He's in surgery now. We covered it up as over-zealousness. My boss will decide later if we want to use the seller's . . . proclivities . . . to blackmail him into testifying or working for us."

"Did he say how many bombs?" Cam asked.

"Seven. We aren't sure about that—he was pretty far gone by the time we realized what the problem was."

"*This* information," Trevor barked, no kindly mentoring tone now, "was what you should have said first. *Sonofabitch.* You need to learn field ops—you protect the public before you save your ass. Or anyone's reputation. Goddammit, we've lost too much time and you knew he sold detonators for seven fucking bombs? Set to go off today?"

Seven. Bobbie Faye met Trevor's gaze. Seven bombs.

Trevor had shot Sean seven times. To save *her.*

There was a soft knock on his door, and the mechanic crossed his workshop to answer it. His assistant, Pam, eased in with a batch of paperwork in hand.

"I've been trying to call you," she said, softly, knowing he hated any of his employees to come into his personal shop. Her eyes averted after landing momentarily on Chloë's urn. "I'm really sorry to bother you, boss, but you've got to sign these."

"Not now, Pam," he told her, his eyes going back to the TV.

One bomb. Detonated. In the wrong fucking location. How in the hell had the delivery gone wrong?

"But it's the insurance forms, and the casino's on the line, wanting to know how you want to proceed with the salvaging of the bar?"

It took him a moment to come back to this place, this place where he was something other than the mechanic who'd created death, where a very nice woman was trying to help him; Suds turned toward her and she stepped back from the fury he was sure showed plainly on his face.

"I know that you loved the bar," she added hastily, "but we'll salvage and rebuild and it will be better than ever."

She thought his lack of interest was despondence over the destruction of the bar. About losing what so many thought of as his life's ambition. The bar that had kept him sane after Chloë died.

He'd been a mechanic before he went into the military, determined to get away from the grease and grime; he'd grown up a mechanic's son, and for most of his young life, thought he didn't have a choice. Then he'd enlisted, and had an aptitude for fine, detailed work. They trained him as a bomb tech. And he used the signing bonuses to save up for his dream: the bar.

He'd met Chloe at his first little place. She was his second waitress, and he'd known the second she'd walked in the door that she was it. She could've had the whole thing signed over to her in five minutes, if she'd wanted to sweet talk him, but she was a hard worker. He couldn't even count the number of nights they fell asleep, mop bucket in hand, cleaning after the long nights. But it put Chloe through school, bought their home, built their dream. He expanded. He thought he had everything.

He bit back a reply—Pam didn't deserve his fury. She didn't know that his life had ended with Chloë, in that wreck. She—none of them—would ever really understand. Revenge had become his only ambition.

"Not now. You decide. You're officially promoted— manager, whatever the hell runs everything. Get the papers drawn up, and I will sign them. You are in charge." He checked his watch. "I'll call my attorney and tell him to expect the paperwork from you." She would learn, later, that he'd already drawn up all of the documents that made her the boss, including a will.

"Suds! It's not that bad. Really, it's water damage and we lost stock, and yeah, it'll be a couple of months for everything to be repaired, but the casino's going to spare no expense and I've already got a contractor lined up and—"

"Stop. I don't care. Just do whatever you think works." He grabbed the paperwork she still held and signed it quickly. "Just do it."

She eyed him, worried. She was a kind woman, a beautiful woman; if his heart hadn't died so long ago, he'd have thought maybe her eyes held a little hope, too. But there was none. Not now.

As she left, he looked back at his TV, at the footage from some news helicopter flying near enough to the twisted pipes and fire and black smoke pouring out over southern Lake Charles. The wrong fucking chemical plant. If all seven had detonated there, the place wouldn't still be standing.

So where were the others?

Bobbie Faye Repellent Sold Here!
SOLD OUT! SOLD OUT!

—sign on the front of the local WalMart

Twenty-three

Trevor strapped a bulletproof vest on her, fussing with it, adjusting it. He'd been silent since they'd left the S&M club.

Waiting, she realized, for her to walk away from him.

They had driven across town in silence, back to the river to where the GPS signal pointed. They were now a block over from the location of the signal source, and it killed her that they'd been just a couple of blocks from Nina when they'd crossed that bridge earlier, and had not known.

They stood in the back of a little coffee and sandwich shop—leave it to cops to set up where there was a steady supply of food, they weren't idiots—that had the welcome, worn feel of a place that had survived a lot of bad times with plain good functional food. The café squatted downtown amid crusty, ornate buildings from the 1900s, tall glass and steel and marble structures from the mid-nineties, and stucco and concrete buildings from the turn of the century. There was something soft and warm about the place—small round dark wood tables, scarred from years of use, pale yellow walls, faded and bleached from the sun streaming in the big wrap-around plate glass windows that faced the corner—windows where decrepit metal slats of blinds that were probably as old as the building itself hung raised to half-mast.

Cam hurried over to them, closing his cell phone. "Another bomb—this time in Morgan City." Morgan City was a growing industrial town near the Gulf. "That's two of seven, and you," he addressed Trevor, "cannot be fucking serious, putting a vest on her. You cannot think you're going to let her help."

"I'm standing right here," she said to him, "with ears and a brain and everything, and I'm not stupid—I know this is an official deal, you're all going to go to Sean's apartment, but I'm going to be here—waiting—and Trevor's trying to keep me safe."

"You'd be safer at—"

"Where, Cam?" she asked. "Where, exactly, will I be safer? At some random hotel somewhere? And then you'd have to pull police off this and everything else they're having to do, because you'd feel like I had to be protected, even though I'm a better shot than *you* are. I'm staying here. I'm going to be careful."

Cam glared at Trevor and said, "You already lost this argument, didn't you?"

"He knew better than to try," she snapped as, with his back to Cam, Trevor's fingers slid over the last clasp on the Kevlar vest. Trevor met her gaze and there was a long, long look—one that said *if I thought you'd be safer somewhere else, you'd be somewhere else.*

"Moreau, Cormier," a SWAT guy called, and they both peeled away from Bobbie Faye, Cam glaring at her one last time and Trevor reverting back to granite (she swore he had to practice that transformation in front of a mirror somewhere).

They were going up against Sean. If she knew him at all, Trevor would be leading the way.

"I really don't think we should go to Baton Rouge, Etienne," V'rai said, after the news had broken on the radio: two bombs in two chemical plants, both a couple of hours from Baton Rouge. It was all coming true. "I think we're going to make it worse, *chèr.*"

"I don't know how we can make it worse," Lizzie said. "This is Bobbie Faye we're talking about."

"I've got something to find," Etienne said, finally, after they'd ridden another five miles.

The eerie quiet of the street bothered Bobbie Faye. SWAT and the rest of the loosely formed takedown force had moved toward the rehabbed building in the nearly deserted downtown a few blocks south of the café. Baton Rouge on a Saturday was usually pretty quiet, one of the local state cops said—but on game day, it was a virtual ghost town.

Bobbie Faye stood at the makeshift command center, just inside the café, gazing out through the now-lowered blinds; she peered over to her right and saw the Old State Capitol and flinched. This had been the scene of the showdown with Sean, and she realized he'd picked this place on purpose. There were too many bad memories here.

Blood. And death. And bullets chewing into her.

Trevor's expression. That horrible moment when he thought she'd been killed.

She glanced down at the chicken foot—which was pulsing black and red stripes and still freaked her out—and then her gaze went to the gun Trevor had armed her with—she wasn't sure where he'd gotten it, but it was a Glock. He knew she was used to the weight. He'd made her practice with her own Glock every single day, and he knew she'd feel more comfortable with it over the Ruger Cam had handed her, though she kept that small pistol in the back of her jeans. Just in case. There were miles and miles of things Trevor seemed to understand about her. She'd gotten used to that. Used to his intuition not failing him.

She wondered if that was fair.

She glanced back out the coffee shop window, wishing she wasn't so tense that the smell of strong dark roast churned her stomach. Streetlights were starting to pop on outside—old-fashioned black iron bases, picturesque against the nightmare that was four blocks away. Trevor, going in, facing down Sean.

The earpiece Trevor had given her had little traffic, the police radio behind her was silent, and the men near her were quiet, too: the hush of hope, as if the world held its breath with her.

Something blond caught her eye. White blond, or else she didn't think her eye would have tracked it, and she leaned a little closer to the window to try to see what it was, as one of the cops said, "Get away from the window, ma'am."

But she knew that hair color. Reflected in the window, moving away from their position: L'Oréal Superior Preference 10WB.

Trevor moved quietly behind the SWAT leader, impressed with the competent, sharp team. The building was a classic turn-of-the-century brownstone, one of the few left in the downtown area. A metal awning had been constructed over the sidewalk and a Dumpster blocked most of the parking in front of the building—the entire structure was in the process of being renovated. SWAT had gotten the layout of the building. This whole city block was being rehabbed, so no wonder no one noticed a bunch of men going in and out of Sean's building across the street. If anyone had paid the slightest attention, they'd have assumed it was just another construction crew. There was only one finished apartment—only one place for MacGreggor's men to barricade themselves. As night fell—early—the glow from behind the blinds of the apartment windows on the top floor burned gold against the dark brown brick exterior and to Trevor, the lights were a dumb mistake.

MacGreggor didn't make dumb mistakes.

They'd thermaled the place: six men, one possible woman (in a chair)—classic hostage situation. The men moved between the rooms fairly frequently, and appeared to be armed. With the knowledge of the bomb threat, it was mandatory that SWAT keep the hostage-takers alive. At the same time, there was no time for negotiations. They couldn't risk a prolonged, protracted discussion with lame requests from MacGreggor, which would be nothing more than a delaying tactic, while he taunted them with the unexploded bombs.

The dumb mistakes kept adding up: holing up in a building

with only a front and back exit, a roof that was too far below the two rooflines adjacent to it to allow for an easy escape from above, no obvious transportation within easy grasp. SWAT had already breached the building, checking for booby traps and trip wires, using dogs to check for explosives, particularly in the apartments directly below where the perps were holed up. Everything was clear.

"I don't like it," he said to Moreau, who was right behind him.

"No shooters," Moreau agreed, nodding toward the empty rooflines on the streets surrounding them—empty except for the SWAT now positioned there. "We know Sean had at least three shooters at the racetrack."

"One dead," Trevor agreed.

"We're a go," the SWAT leader told them.

As much as they suspected this was a setup, they had to treat it like the classic takedown it appeared to be: criminals, a hostage, a breachable apartment. Trevor and Moreau would take up the rear of the breach team, not interfering with the well-oiled, well-practiced maneuvers of the men who had worked together many times before. Then suddenly the SWAT leader motioned everyone to hold: a message coming in to their radio frequency: "Confirm, another explosion. Harahan. Casualties. Call from a MacGreggor to 911 three minutes prior, warning of four more bombs, all in Baton Rouge."

Everyone went dead still. MacGreggor's information was not a threat—it was a promise, and Trevor knew it.

Trevor knew that there were agents—FBI, ATF, Homeland Security, and half the government alphabet—already crunching data, trying to figure out if there was a commonality between the bomb locations. MacGreggor was not a random kind of guy; there had to be a logic to his choice in victims, not to mention a reason he would deign to call them with a warning. MacGreggor always had a plan.

SWAT motioned go, and everything moved fast: breaching the building, the forward men continuously checking for nasty surprises as they all ran the stairs, keeping as quiet as humanly possible, taking the hallway, wiring and then blowing the door, fast fast fast, flash bangs exploding in the room, loud, bright, and he bit away flashbacks to Bagram as the noise and brief flash-blindness disoriented the hostage-takers. SWAT moving in, barely a heartbeat later, move move move, right, left, men sweeping the room, shooting, hostage-takers falling, not dead, wounded, shouting, screaming, the woman screaming, shrieking . . .

Shrieking.

Trevor knew without looking that it wasn't Nina. Nina would never have shrieked. She wouldn't have uttered a word.

She'd have known to expect breach protocol—she'd have expected the flash bangs and she sure as hell wouldn't have shrieked over dead bad guys. And just as he rounded into the bedroom where the woman sat tied, he saw what Sean had done: decoys. All of them. Holding guns, lying on the floor, shot by SWAT, and the woman, young, blond, not Nina. The belt with the GPS in it lying on the floor in front of her.

Four more bombs, in Baton Rouge.

And that's when he saw it: the drawing on the bedroom wall. Labeled INSTRUCTIONS.

"Trevor!" Bobbie Faye's voice piped into his earpiece. "I see Nina."

"Stay put," he ordered, already turning, already running through the doorway.

"Can't," she said, and then the radio went silent.

Twenty-four

"Bobbie Faye, location. *Now.*"

"Sir," an unknown cop voice answered in Trevor's earpiece, "we're following her—north of the coffee shop. Third Street. She's fucking *fast*, sir." Then, "Sorry, language."

"Bobbie Faye," Trevor repeated, "talk to me *now.*"

"I can see them," she said, "but they're two blocks ahead of me." He could hear her breathing hard. "I've gone . . . I dunno, eight, ten blocks. I can see the capitol."

Moreau, running two paces behind Trevor, snarled into his mic. "You'd better fucking stop, or I swear to God, I'll arrest your ass."

"For running?" she asked. "Shut up, Cam. Trevor, Nina's hands are tied, but they were running before they got into a car, so she's up and at least capable."

"I've got sight of your WMD," Riles chimed in and about damned time. Trevor had put Riles on the rooftop opposite the coffee shop as a lookout for Trouble, and she *still* got away from him. "They're in a car a block ahead of her—they're going slow, probably to not draw attention from local cops, low speed limit here—I don't think they see her yet."

"I've got a shot at the tires," she said, out of breath.

"Fuck," Moreau swore.

"Shit," Riles said, "she's taking the shot."

Trevor heard the pop echoing against the buildings.

"Damn," the unknown cop said, "she nailed a tire!"

Tires screeched a couple of blocks over, men yelled, and Trevor dug in, dug harder, grabbing for every single ounce of adrenaline and power because he was not leaving her alone for this. No fucking way, he'd go through hell first, and he and Moreau both angled toward the shot, running faster than he'd ever run in his life, buildings blurring in the dark. More pops, and he recognized the difference in sound. Someone else besides Bobbie Faye was shooting. Not far, *not far.*

"Shots fired, officer down!" Riles shouted. "One of the cops following her. Shit, she's still going after the car!"

"Sundance, stop. You can't take them all on your own. They'll grab you."

Bam. A gunshot echoed.

Bam. Another answered.

"Bobbie Faye?" Trevor shouted. "Answer me." *Nothing.* Dear God. "Riles! Goddammit, *update!*"

"Busy."

Three agonizing seconds later, he and Moreau caught up, bursting from Third Street onto a boulevard, and there in front of him, his nightmare: Bobbie Faye, down. Riles was dragging her in a dead man's pull to get behind one of the mammoth oaks growing in the median. Trevor's vision tunneled to Bobbie Faye, everything around her limp form going dark and leached of all color, fear punching holes where crisp hues ought to be: an officer down, another man down not far away, two officers running after MacGreggor's men, who'd stopped a pickup truck and yanked the people out at gunpoint, using the civilians to shield them from the officers as they slammed into the cab and stomped on the gas, damned near running over the old ladies they'd been manhandling. All he really saw, though, all he really cared about, was the way she'd crumpled where Riles had stopped with her; no resistance, no fight.

"Suspects fleeing scene," one of the cops radioed, "license Bravo eight-niner-eight-one-two-two-three, red Ford stepside, and a blue Town Car, partial plate Alpha-Bravo-niner. Headed east to the interstate from North Boulevard."

SWAT and officers flooded onto the scene, but Trevor saw nothing of the details except for her pale face as he reached her and Riles. Her eyes were closed; she looked unconscious.

"She's alive," Riles said as Trevor knelt, his heart so ripped to shreds, he couldn't have spoken if his life depended on it; he searched for blood. "Center mass, vest caught it," Riles continued. "That one"—he nodded toward the man lying in the street, blood pouring from a head wound—"came after her. One of MacGreggor's crew. She popped the tire on their car"—he nodded toward a sedan idling in the street with a flat—"and they piled out. That one recognized her."

Moreau leaned over them both, checking her pulse at her wrist as Trevor undid the vest. She was breathing. Shallow, but breathing.

"He saw the vest," Riles continued, "shot right at it. My guess is to knock her down, keep her from shooting him so he could grab her. I wanted to keep him alive, but I took the shot I had."

Trevor moved his hands to check beneath her shirt, but there were definitely no entry wounds. He glanced over to the downed officer, who was sitting up now with his shoulder bleeding.

Her eyes fluttered open and she moaned. Then her hand went to her chest. "Owie."

"What the *fuck* were you thinking?" Moreau demanded.

"Oh, I don't know, Cam," she said as Trevor helped her sit up. "I guess I was thinking, gee, I'd like to have a *fais do-do* on the boulevard, let me wander around with a gun and see who shows up."

Her hand clasped tightly onto Trevor's shirt sleeve, needing an anchor, twisting her knuckles into the sleeve, his own vest blocking her from getting closer. Trevor met her gaze and felt her starting to shake, aftershock from the adrenaline. She was clinging, hard, her eyes not leaving his as Moreau continued to rant.

"Moreau, shut the fuck up."

The harshness around her eyes softened, relieved.

"*You* let this happen," Moreau hissed. "You're going to let her get herself *killed*."

"Cam," she snapped before Trevor could answer, turning a blistering glare on her ex, "if you talk about me one more time like I'm not smart enough to make decisions for myself, I am going to fucking drop-kick your ass into next week, and then shoot you." She turned back to Trevor. "It's going to get worse, isn't it?"

He remembered MacGreggor's instructions drawn on that apartment wall.

"Yes."

The drum cadence of the LSU Fighting Tiger Marching Band ramped her heart into overdrive, and Lori Ann knew this was going to be a night to remember. The band stood in formation outside of the stadium, purple and gold uniforms in military perfection, a band that took her breath away, and Stacey jumped on every other beat, jackhammering her little body to the intoxicating rhythm. The cadence echoed and reverberated off the concrete walls of the stadium and between that and the chanting, cheering, screaming crowds— she and Stacey stood in a bowl of sound so complete, it annihilated the ability to hear anything else. The gasp of awe on Stacey's face made Lori Ann grin so hard, it hurt.

Marcel paused from buffing the truck one last time and came and draped an arm over Lori Ann, his other hand ruffling Stacey's blond (very dusty) hair, which had long ago fallen out of its pigtails. Together, her family, Lori Ann thought.

She thought to check her phone then—she'd forgotten to call Bobbie Faye back—and when she realized Marcel was chuckling, she had to laugh, too. No way she'd be able to hear a thing 'til after the game. She'd call Bobbie Faye then. Tell her about getting married, ask her maybe to be her maid of honor. Provided Bobbie Faye wouldn't kill the groom. Not killing the groom would be an important duty for a maid of honor.

Lori Ann eyed Marcel, wondering how a tux would look over a Kevlar vest.

Trevor helped her to her feet, making sure she was steady.

"They still have Nina," she said, and he nodded.

"I cannot fucking believe this," Moreau said.

She whirled as his own gaze jerked up toward Moreau, but Moreau wasn't looking at Bobbie Faye—for once. He was already running toward the people whose truck was stolen, and Trevor and Bobbie Faye followed at a quick jog. Then stopped, abruptly.

Three old women and one old man. Old Man Landry was how she referred to him.

Her dad.

"What the hell are you doing here?" Bobbie Faye asked V'rai, as her dad glowered. "They stole your truck!"

"Don't you fuss at your aunt," her dad said. "You fuss at me, you want to yell at someone."

"Do I *want* to?" she asked, whipping around, furious.

"Sundance, we don't have time for this," Trevor said as she reached for him. He wasn't even sure she knew she was doing it, her hand landing on his arm, sliding down 'til she had his hand in hers, fingers intertwined. He wondered if she understood what she felt. "We have to go," he continued, forcing the personal out of the here and now. "We've got bigger problems."

"Bombs," Old Man Landry said, and every single one of them stopped and gaped at Bobbie Faye's father. "Four more," he said, and Trevor felt Bobbie Faye tremble as her dad said, "I can find them."

"Etienne! *Mais non*!" V'rai exclaimed.

"Why not?" Bobbie Faye asked.

"You'll die, *chère*," she said. "You'll die if we go down this path."

"She'll die if I don't," the old man said.

Moreau leaned forward into the old man's space and said, "You'd better not be just screwing with her."

Landry looked in Moreau's direction. "You know I can do it. I helped you find what you lost."

Moreau grimaced, and Trevor was instantly sure that the old man had somehow helped Moreau find that engagement ring he'd bought for Bobbie Faye and had thrown in the lake behind his house in a fit of anger.

Trevor could not go there. Not right now. They both had too much to lose, and the clock was ticking. He'd seen the instructions, she hadn't. She had no idea.

"Let's go. And you," he said to the old man, "had better not be slowing us down because if she gets hurt again from something you've done, there won't be a single place to hide."

"She's going to get hurt," V'rai said. Landry turned to the old woman, who had tears streaming down her face and both her sisters supporting her where she stood.

"V'rai had a vision," Lizzie offered.

"A couple of them," Aimee added.

"We're just making things worse, *ma petite*," she said to Bobbie Faye. "Much, much worse."

"Where's th' whahoozie stuff?" Monique asked as Ce Ce dug in her purse for . . . something. Fuzzy. So very fuzzy. Must remember to tell Monique . . . something. Strong margaritas. Yeah.

She couldn't remember what she was digging in her purse for, and it was hard to hear Monique, even with her shouting in Ce Ce's ear, especially with the band blaring. Really good blaring, but holy pickles, it was loud.

Maybe it was the margaritas that made it so loud. Or sitting so close. Bad breath close, and she really needed mints for the kid on the . . . some sort of horn.

She squinted at the clock on the big JumboTron counting down to the game: one hour, twenty-three minutes. To . . . the ball thing. Kicking it. Lots of bending over. She was looking forward to that part.

The cute grill guy was seated next to her. He'd traded seats. For here. Near the student section. End zone. Mike the

Tiger, grrrrrr, oh yeah, she was searching for something. He smiled and she felt around in her purse. For . . .

What was it again?

"Binoculars!" Monique reminded her, and she gripped something round and out it came, but it wasn't binoculars. It was juice. Icky-looking stuff.

"The whahoozie juice!" Monique said, grabbing it and shaking it up and Ce Ce's adrenaline spiked and she grabbed it back.

"Careful, hon! Dangerousss stuffs here. Big with the danger." Then she focused on the chicken foot bracelet she wore and adrenaline slammed into the base of her skull so hard, it might as well be a cast-iron frying pan.

The chicken foot was not only striped, it was *moving*.

She blinked, stared at it, turning her head sideways a little, wondering if margaritas could make her hallucinate. She held it up to Brand-Brett-Briggs, who hadn't drunk anything stronger than lemonade, from what she could remember, and she asked, "Is this . . . moving?"

"Shit," he said, jumping back a foot, leaning away from her arm, "what the hell is that thing?"

"Chicken foot," she said. "Is it moving? Because moving would be very bad."

"Holy shit!" he said, moving farther away.

And aw, damn, he was going back to his original seat. Cute ass, though.

Not that she could worry about that right then, because the foot was *moving*.

If she could just pluck her heart out and put it in a Ziploc bag and store it somewhere, she could deal with this pain. Anxiety waged a game of doubles with Anger, and so far, they were pretty even up. Her skin felt taut and stretched over infinity, and pain stabbed between her eyes. Every part of her ached. Her *hair* hurt, how the hell?

Bobbie Faye stood in the corner of an old dress shop, sawdust thick in the corners of the concrete floor where someone had hastily swept construction debris. The Feds and cops had moved the joint command center to the building across the street from Sean's apartment and the remodeling job had barely made it to third-date earnest on this side of the street. Three people had tried to get her to eat one of the sandwiches someone had brought in, but she'd just throw it up, so there was no point.

Trevor handed her some sort of drink with electrolytes; sometimes she'd swear he materialized things out of thin air.

He should have taken it for himself.

"Drink. Don't argue," he said.

She studied him as she sipped it, wondering when the last time it was he'd slept. Eaten. He conferred with one of the billion people crammed into that storefront, where the worry was nearly as palpable as the sweat; she looked at the lines of his shoulders, the way he held the angle of his jaw, and saw he was exhausted, in pain, and determined not to show it.

She picked a back corner where she could watch the room. Riles had, at some point, leaned several abandoned tattered, silk-dressed headless mannequins in a front window.

She hoped the "headless" audience wasn't an omen.

The street had been cordoned off and the amber glow of the streetlights seemed tinted a queasy green in the big plate-glass windows. Bobbie Faye had no idea how the impromptu command had been set up so quickly, or how the sheer volume of people had squeezed in there to do whatever it was planny types did during crises. Police chiefs. Sheriffs. A mayor or two. Homeland Security. Someone had set up tables on sawhorses, taped a big city/parish map of Baton Rouge on the wall, and laptops and high-tech equipment she couldn't identify were scattered everywhere.

She wrapped her arms around her shoulders, pressing in, feeling as if she was going to fly in bits across the room from the sheer rhythm of *Nina Nina Nina* at the base of her brain; she felt like one of those black holes that just suck the life out of the universe, the center of all destruction. Nina. Nina held captive by a madman who'd think nothing of torturing her to get what he wanted. Nina. Her best friend who was practically a stranger to her. Who'd lived some sort of covert life all of these years.

She closed her eyes, leaning her head back against the freshly painted wall. Nothing made sense anymore. If she'd woken up yesterday morning and thought, "Hey, I'll go bungee jump off a short building," it would have made more sense than this craziness.

Nina. The one rock-solid relationship she'd had most of her life. Who wasn't at all the woman Bobbie Faye thought she was. Who had probably known where Trevor was when Bobbie Faye had gone stir-crazy, painting, thinking he might be dead somewhere and nobody telling her.

A band of pressure, a hurricane front of emotional wreckage bore down on her heart, inexorable, waylaying what little had made sense in its path. How in the hell had it become okay for people she loved to not tell her the truth? How do you move forward with a relationship based on half-truths and the other person constantly gauging and deciding what you could and could not know? And the question that made her sick: Why hadn't she been aware enough to know that people were lying to her? What kind of person was *she*?

Was there something she'd done to communicate to the two people she loved that she couldn't be trusted?

She watched her fiancé as he braced on his fingertips, leaning over a table, his hands on either side of a laptop. Everything about him screamed *poised* and *lethal*: tense muscles, corded sinews, dead-angry expression. He and Cam coordinated with SWAT and ASAC Brennan. Trevor had been on the phone since they'd left Sean's apartment, dealing with a thousand things at once. When Trevor had led her, Cam, and Riles into this makeshift command center, she'd seen the shift in the room, the confidence the other leaders had in him as they analyzed and attacked the problems.

He suddenly met her gaze as if he'd felt her watching him. She knew that he was listening to what the SWAT leader said, and simultaneously tracking the movements of everyone in the room, but those clear blue eyes softened, asking, in his way, if she was okay. She wanted to say *yes*. Just to give him some peace of mind while he had so much to do. She wanted to do that, because it was their second nature to reach out to each other. It had defined them as a couple. As a team.

He'd know she was lying.

But were they a team? Not really.

His expression shimmered from concern to pain, a mawing abyss of hurt, for her, for them both, and then he shuttered it down, and *just like that*, all emotion shut off from her, though he held her gaze. She wanted to close her eyes and look away, but not even that would bring relief; closing them would just mean that Fear would hopscotch from one pain to the other: the instructions written on that wall in Sean's apartment, burned in her memory, black words scrawled like disease against the white wall.

She closed her eyes and saw the image all over again:

> *1 hostage*
> *4 bombs*
> *thousands dead*
> *demands @ 7:00*

She saw the chair where Nina had been tied up. Saw the blond hairs a crime scene tech had bagged already. She'd almost thrown up right there, right in the middle of Sean's apartment, right in the middle of a crime scene.

"She shouldn't fucking *be* here," Cam had snapped at Trevor, who'd kept one hand on her shoulder, beneath her hair, his thumb kneading the knots there, and she leaned into that hand.

"Not knowing is much worse for her," Trevor had snapped back, and Irony wanted to walk up and smack the crap out of him, though she admired his own restraint. He wanted to hit Cam. No doubt about it, but he held back. After she'd stared at the message for five million years, he walked her back to the command center where, she threw up, twice, in the bathroom in the back of the store. The SWAT commander's voice brought her back to the present, and she opened her eyes to see Trevor still watching her.

"Twenty-six teams, feet on the ground, another four forming up," the SWAT commander was saying, and Trevor turned his gaze back to the man. "We're pulling in everyone, but we don't have enough dogs." Bomb-sniffing dogs, she realized, were breaking down the city and surrounding areas into sections of most likely versus least likely to attract Sean's attention.

There were dozens and dozens of chemical plants in and around the Baton Rouge area. Any one of them could be the target. So far, three plants in other cities had been bombed, and no one had tied them to one central concept or common product. It was too early to know exactly how Sean had gotten the bombs in place, but every single plant in the area had been put on terrorist alert and evacuations were underway.

Major corporations were shutting down. Billions of dollars were at stake. No one had a single idea where Sean would strike next, but they knew his threat was utterly credible.

"And he could hit anywhere in the state," SWAT reminded.

"I can't pull teams out of the outlying region 'til we have a more credible threat here," SWAT continued. "He may be trying to draw us away from some other area, just so we don't find what he's really up to."

"Landry's got a vague hit," Cam said, nodding toward Old Man Landry, who sat in the opposite corner. Bobbie Faye was as far away as she could get from her father without having to leave the room. Even from this distance, he looked as worn as old paper, crumpled and faded. His once-black hair had gone completely silver and she squinted, trying to remember when that had happened. The man who'd been her father when she was five had been tall and redwood-straight, a broad-shouldered, black-haired knight.

He stared into space, in some sort of "zone," frowning,

and the FBI agent taking notes next to him was obviously frustrated. From the consternation on the old man's face, Bobbie Faye thought Old Man Landry was about to have a heart attack, except he was too mean to have an actual heart, so that was out.

Thank God Trevor had ordered her aunts to be taken to a hotel two blocks over where they were being baby-sat by two agents who had been told that, under no circumstances, were the wily old women to be trusted.

From the table in the center of the room, the mayor, crisply dressed and as big as a bear, said, "I'm not putting this city's well-being in the hands of some sort of hocus-pocus. I don't care *what* the old man's track record is. I can call up the National Guard."

"And put them where?" Trevor asked, glancing at his watch. "MacGreggor's going to call in three minutes. He'll have a plan, and you can bet he's going to strike fast. He has no reason to delay, because there's nothing you can give him that he wants." He turned to ASAC Brennan. "MacGreggor said *the money I* will *make* in the video. So far, the three bombs have hit chemical plants—are we tracking any sudden jump in futures? Anything related to the petrochemical industry?"

"Or he could want to ransack your company," Cam pointed out, and Trevor glared at him a moment. "You have to admit, it's where he could strike at you and make money at the same time. And it's clear he wants you to hurt."

The muscle in Trevor's jaw worked overtime as he kept perfectly still, his gaze meeting Cam's as Bobbie Faye started to interject that Cam wasn't just being belligerent this time. Instead, Bobbie Faye gritted her teeth and saw that Trevor realized Cam had a valid point. "Yes, if I gave a damn about the business," he said. "If MacGreggor's done his homework— and he has—he'll know I resigned from the board the day I signed my commission."

"Concrete bunker," her dad said suddenly, interrupting everyone, and then he glanced around, startled, as if he'd just realized where he was. "The biggest bomb's in a bunker

of some sort. Lots of concrete above it. Doesn't make sense.
There's one moving—I can't tell you where it is."

"You can't seriously be going to listen to this man?" the
mayor said, waving hands as big as sails, sweeping aggrava-
tion toward Landry.

"But the third and fourth," her dad continued, ignoring
the mayor, "I got a place. It's in Poly-Ferosia. Look for rental
equipment."

"Concrete bunker?" she asked. "Describe it."

The old man looked at her then. First time he'd looked at
her since they'd left the scene of the carjacking.

"You need to get your butt out of here, *chère*," he said.
"Go check on your aunts."

"Describe the fucking bunker."

"I gave you what I know to be true," he said to Cam.
"That's all I got. If you had any sense at all, you'd make her
go home."

"Yeah, because bossing me around has been so effective
for you in the past," she said to Cam before he had a chance to
open his mouth and make things worse. "Don't even try it."

In Cajun, Old Man Landry said to Cam, *"You need to
make her go—she hasn't got a speck of sense."*

"She's tired, she's hurt, and she's not thinking clearly."

"So make her think clearly, you couyon, *she's got to go."*

"Cut it out," she warned them both. "English. Or shut up."

"She's going to come to her senses when this is over," Cam
said, watching her steady, aware she was picking up most of
the Cajun.

"Not another fucking *word*." She bristled and practically
vibrated in place with fury.

"Watch your mouth," Landry snapped, "or I'll wash it out
with soap."

Bigfoot could sidle up to her right now, dressed in a tutu
and asking to valet park the reindeer, and she wouldn't
have been more floored. "You've got to be kidding me. You
gave up that right when I was five and you stopped being
my dad."

"Baby." Cam tried to intervene and she put her hand up and stepped back from him as he reached for her.

"Don't. Even. Think. About. It."

Trevor watched them as he conferred with ASAC Brennan and SWAT.

Riles appeared at Trevor's side—he'd been working the phones on the other side of the room and she hadn't had a chance to fully appreciate his absence. The Universe so fucking owed her.

"LT," he said, "I think we have a problem." He nodded toward her. "Her crazy family."

Everyone in the room stopped to listen and they stared at her and the old man and she said, "Seriously, Riles, your firm grasp of the obvious is just impressing the hell out of me. My family's been crazy since birds had wings."

"Not *just* crazy. They're at LSU. At the game."

"No way. Lori Ann would never go to—"

"She's there," he said, turning to Trevor. "With her fiancé. And so's her boss, Ce Ce, and her friend, Monique. Add in her brother—who we haven't found yet, but rumor has it he's already slept with two women and gotten into three fights while tailgating—and that puts all of her main core group, except us, at the game."

"How the hell?" she asked just as Trevor asked, "Why the fuck didn't the detail report on this sooner?"

Oh. The *security* detail Riles had mentioned earlier. People Trevor had hired to watch her family.

"LT, the detail was supposed to make sure they were safe. They *were* safe—they're just in the same place, and none of the guys realized it 'til just now, at check-in."

"No way could MacGreggor get a bomb into LSU," SWAT said. "Not with the extra security around that place before a game. Not with the two hundred-plus cops we have, and the cameras. Not possible."

"No way should he have been able to get bombs into the plants he got them into, either," Trevor reminded him. "Not with all of the security hoops everyone with a backhoe or rake has to go through to get into a plant. He's found a loop-hole somewhere."

"Or had serious inside help," Cam suggested.

And then Trevor's phone rang, and as he grabbed it, she angled to see the watch of an FBI agent standing near her: 7:00.

"No, MacGreggor," Trevor said. "You are not going to talk to her. You can talk to me."

Twenty-five

The LSU drum cadence magnified and echoed back from the field to the mouth of the bay where they waited in Marcel's truck. They were at the student end of the stadium, parked facing the field, and Lori Ann gawked through the windshield, in complete wonder. She'd never been inside Tiger Stadium before, but she had thought she understood the enormity from what she had seen on TV.

It wasn't even close. The TV version was like looking at a copy of a copy of a copy. It was absolutely *nothing* in comparison to the sharp colors of purple and gold (and one section of Bama red), of bodies painted with purple lettering, of the frantic, manic *movement* of the fans, all arms and foam fingers and tiger stripes.

The cheering jarred her bones, and she was sitting *inside* the monster 4×4 truck, with the deep, glossy, gleaming Eye of the Tiger on the hood reflecting the enormous lights banked against the night sky. Word had come in that there was a record-breaking crowd, and the event coordinator who'd been running everything smooth as glass signaled Marcel that it was time to pull the big cat in the cage behind them out onto the field and circle once. As soon as the truck nosed out of the bay at barely five miles an hour, the crowd went *insane*.

Lori Ann gazed back at her daughter, strapped in a car seat in the extended cab, expecting to see those pom-poms going ninety-to-nothing, but instead, Stacey's jaw dropped, and she gaped, mouth open. Then turned to her mom and smiled the biggest, happiest smile Lori Ann had ever seen.

As Marcel eased the truck the rest of the way out of the bay, TV cameras dollied alongside them and the big pacing cat.

The roars were deafening. God, no wonder it was called "Death Valley." The noise alone could kill you.

She reached back and squeezed her daughter's hand, hoping this was going to be one of those moments as a mom that made up a little for the times she'd been drinking and gone. Emotionally gone. This was going to be one of the best nights of their lives.

"Fuck you, Cormier," Sean said, "you'll let her talk to me, unless you wan' t' be known as the agent who got thousands of people killed."

Trevor gripped his cell hard enough to hear the plastic casing crack. The last fucking thing he should have done is tell a hostage-taker "no" and he could see the SWAT leader was already furious. But Trevor knew the way to drag out the call and to possibly get a triangulation on Sean's cell phone location was to deny him the one thing he wanted: to talk to Bobbie Faye. He'd known Sean was going to ask for her. Two of his agents were at the computers running the signal.

"Bad move, Cormier," MacGreggor said. "You'll be on a call right about . . . now . . . and there's the fourth bomb. I have three more."

Old Man Landry held up two fingers to Trevor and whispered, low, "That was Poly-Ferosia—he's got another one there."

Shit. MacGreggor was trying to lure first responders in there to kill them. Several cell phones rang in the room: the SWAT CO answered his and scowled, scratching a note to Trevor: *Poly-Ferosia. Geismer.*

Sonofabitch. Geismer was on the outskirts of Baton Rouge. MacGreggor was circling in toward the city, a long, slow spiral of bombs.

Trevor glanced over at Yazzy and the other agents working on the signal. They shook their heads, motioning that the call signal was scrambled. *Goddammit*. Izzy's technology was supposed to be able to piggyback signals, and punch through the scrambling effort. MacGreggor could be fucking *anywhere*.

Trevor had taken a gamble. And lost. Which, he knew, was what MacGreggor wanted.

"The next one kills dozens, Cormier," MacGreggor's Irish accent purred, unhurried and unperturbed. "Thought I'd give you a fightin' chance, ya see. But I'll blow it now, if you don't put her on the line."

"I'll put her on speakerphone, MacGreggor. That's the best you're going to get."

He slapped the speaker on before MacGreggor could make another demand and Bobbie Faye stepped up to the table where the cell phone now sat. She regarded it with the same wariness he'd seen her apply to snakes and certain members of her own family.

"Well, hell, Sean, I'm here," she said, and Trevor looked up at her, hearing a solid determination in her voice he hadn't heard in a while. "You've been busy."

The man chuckled. "Sure, lass, I have. I'm noticin' you're frettin' a wee bit about your friend, here."

"Sean, I'm 'frettin' a wee bit' about the ozone layer, so that doesn't quite fucking cover how I feel about my best friend, and you know it. So let's just cut to the point here, because first and foremost, you're a businessman."

Holy fuck, she was taking charge of the call.

This could not be good.

"That I am," MacGreggor said.

"And you're pissed off at Trevor here, and you want revenge."

"You're runnin' out of time. The next bombs're on a timer, so you'll be wantin' to speed up?"

Trevor tapped his watch, and she followed up with, "How much time, Sean?"

"Your point first, lass."

"I want my friend back, alive, and unhurt. And I'm pretty pissed off, too, but I figure you can handle that, right?"

"You've kept me amused, *àlainn*. What's your point?"

She leaned down to the phone and pitched her voice with mischievousness. "Trade ya."

Trevor froze. She could not possibly be considering—

She wouldn't meet Trevor's gaze, standing across the gulf of the table, with the cell phone between them like poison.

"I want Nina and for you to tell us the locations and defuse the next three bombs."

Oh, dear God, she was—

"And I'll give you two things you can't get anywhere else."

"Fine, *àlainn,* now you have me intrigued. What would you be offerin'?"

"Gold." Everyone in the room froze, confused. Trevor frowned at her as she continued. "You want to make a butt-load of money and make the state suffer, too. Fine. I get that. I can give you something worth your while that'll more than make it up to you for you to not explode the last of those bombs. I know where the old pirate treasure is buried. Lafitte's treasure. Gold, jewels, and a huge historic significance. The state would have a cow if it fell into your hands. I know how to find it—but I can't do it alone, and Trevor here won't because legally, he can't. He's kinda a straight arrow like that. But you're not."

There was a heartbeat as MacGreggor listened. He'd obviously done his homework and knew her tiara—her mother's old iron tiara that had been made by Lafitte himself—was a map to the pirate's treasure. A treasure worth hundreds of millions by now.

It was how Trevor had met her, when a black market art dealer funding arms went after the tiara to get to that treasure. A tiara that was now lost in the Mississippi River.

But Trevor knew she didn't know where it was, and when he furrowed his brow at her, she nodded to her dad.

"Hell, no," her dad said.

She turned to the old man. "Hell, yeah, you will. You'll

do it," she said, "because that tiara belonged to me. And you owe me, old man."

Of course, if the old man had the sight, if he *really* could find anything, he could find that damned tiara. And she'd known this all along. Trevor wasn't sure who was unhappier about this: him, Moreau, or the old man.

"Sure, and you said two things," MacGreggor said. "What'll be the second?"

"*Me.*"

"Oh *fuck* no!" exploded from Trevor at the same time she heard several epithets (frankly, more than she knew existed) . . . amid Sean's chuckling.

"I take it this isn't an 'officially' sanctioned idea."

"Like hell," Cam snapped, stepping forward, his hand on her arm as he reached for cuffs from one of the other state cops.

"Get your fucking hands off her, Moreau," Trevor shouted, vaulting the table, blocking the cuff from her wrist as Riles and two other men she did not know helped form a wall between Cam and a couple of state cops and *every freaking one of them were armed* and yelling. Trevor's gaze locked with hers. And then to her, he ordered, no room for doubt, "*No.* You're *not* doing this. MacGreggor," he snapped toward the phone, "forget it."

"He's got *bombs,*" she mouthed, low so Sean couldn't hear.

"I'll be takin' the lass up on it, Cormier. Get over to LSU. Be at the north stadium entrance, one hour. No vests, no guns. I'll text you wit' instructions."

"Wait!" she shouted, and she prayed Sean was still listening.

"Aye, *àlainn*, second thoughts? Because you'll walk to me of your own free will an' you'll not be comin' back from this one."

"I have to see Nina's safe, first. That's the deal. You give her the bomb locations, you trade her for me. We have to know the bombs are defused in time, Sean, or the deal's off and you don't get to rub it in Trevor's face that you won. You'll always have lost to him, you got that?"

Sean chuckled, and said, "Oh, I'm goin' t' enjoy you, *àlainn*. You remind me of me."

He hung up and she saw Trevor check with the agents tracking the call.

"Nothing, sir. Unless he's in the middle of Beirut right now."

The steady rhythm of the helicopter's blade chopped above him and Suds stared at the bright glow of the laptop in the dark cockpit, knowing that his system failure was not a mistake. His gut wrenched and crawled. He'd built in a back door, a way to signal his bombs and reset the timers, in case there were many innocent civilians at the plant.

He'd have still blown them, of course.

But he'd built in that fail-safe, a back door, a disarming signal that he hadn't ever planned to use, to give him total control. As soon as he'd seen the news reports on the first two bombs having been blown—and in the wrong location— he'd tried to activate the signal to control the rest.

Someone had figured out how to override his shutdown signal. The Irish, no doubt, had the money for such a high-tech gadget.

Suds didn't have much time. Maybe he could get there before they could blow the last three.

"There" being Baton Rouge. The call had come in—any retired bomb squad desperately needed. His ex-military history had put him as an immediate asset to SWAT.

He was on his way. A friend was flying him in via helicopter to Baton Rouge when the tower request came over the headset, changing their course to an LZ, a landing zone, on the LSU campus. It was the next sentence that chilled him: "LZ hot. Terrorists suspected on site, repeat, terrorists suspected on site. Standby on channel three for additional instructions."

"Roger that," his pilot answered, and Suds wanted to throw up.

He'd become Chloë's worst nightmare—the man who figured out how to bypass safety regulations for personal gain. And now, nearly a hundred forty thousand people's lives were hanging in the balance, because of him.

She'd never forgive him.

He could not live, knowing that.

"It's a goddamn huge fuckin' setup, Sean!" Lonan warned, standing just out of arm's reach. "You got to know that."

"Sure, I do. And we have a good contingency plan and we have leverage—we have bombs. They don't know the locations and they can't do a thing about 'em if they find 'em. Besides, you've gotta admire th' lass for her gumption."

Lonan had not worked *this* long and *this* hard to throw it all away. He knew Sean was mad as kettles, but he'd never fully believed he'd sacrifice everything just *to get* the girl. Had he deluded himself? Fuck, they could grab her another time. They could blow the final plant, make their money when the prices for those products skyrocketed—they'd bought futures, so as soon as the price went up, they'd sell at a steep profit. Then they'd be gone. They could *always* come back another day when she least expected it.

"You're losin' faith, me boy, and that's a terrible sad thing," Sean said as he oversaw the loading of the equipment. "And you're losin' the fun of it."

"You've got to be kiddin' me," Lonan answered, unguarded, and then regretted it at the flash in Sean's eyes.

Sean paused a moment, checking his weapon and Lonan stood, waiting.

"Lad, I think of you as my baby brother, and I intend to see that you're taken care of. You'll be missing Aiden." Sean looked up, looked him in the eye. "I do, too. We had us some fun."

"So let's come back for this woman another day, then," Lonan argued. "You've got t' see that you can get your revenge later."

"Sure, I could. I could slip in, wit'out 'em noticin' and shoot the Fed and strip him of the girl, but it's not the same.

When that fucking bad business went down, they had cameras on us, and all the world saw that man, shootin' me, and her, jumpin' in front of bullets for him. I'm not goin' t' slip in, lad, in the dark of the night like I'm scared of 'em. It's not just gettin' the girl—it's rubbin' his nose in it, like she said. Him knowin' that his reputation's ruined on national TV— fuck it, on international TV—that he couldn't do a damned thing to change the outcome, and him sittin' at home, alive, fuckin' paralyzed, knowin' that I have her and knowin' that I'll use her every day in every way I want, to remind him he lost her, 'til I'm tired of her and maybe a good bit longer."

"You said they'd die, Sean."

"They will. When I'm good and ready. And you'll get to do the job."

"You're not . . . not in love wit' her?" he asked, horrified at the thought. Maybe he'd completely misread the gleam in Sean's eye.

Sean laughed. "She amuses me. She'll be a fighter, an' a fine piece of ass, an' then revenge."

Lonan nodded, measuring exactly what Sean said. And hadn't said. He hadn't said, *no, lad, I'm not in love wit' the bitch*.

"Time to load up," Sean said, and he motioned Dox to go retrieve the blonde.

Trevor wasn't entirely sure where he had made his first mistake. He thought maybe it was telling her, on their way between the apartment and the command center, that MacGreggor would likely ask for her when he called, would want to jerk them around, and for her to keep him on the line—to stall him—so that Izzy's tracing program could track him.

Not that he'd told her to *fucking* trade *herself*.

But no, maybe the first mistake had been when he got the phone call about the bombs. The Bureau wanted to force Alex to cooperate with the sting and needed Trevor there to rein Alex in and make sure the sting worked, and he agreed to go.

No, that wasn't it.

Actually, backing up, his first fucking mistake was to have not told her about himself, about his resources, which he could have explained to her while they were naked on a damned tropical island beach somewhere where no one could touch her until his own private army, laws be damned, had hunted MacGreggor down. She'd have been pissed but she'd have gotten over it. Or killed him first, which, at this point, would be *fucking preferable* to the idea of her offering herself as a trade to MacGreggor.

Bile rose in his throat and he choked on the anger, the fury. Moreau wasn't helping a goddamned thing with all of his shouting at her from three feet away. Riles and his men were barely holding the man off. Moreau would have cuffed Bobbie Faye and taken her to a jail somewhere in a heartbeat, and while that was *extremely* appealing in light of her offer, the fact of the matter was that MacGreggor could get to her anywhere, any time. They'd have to do witness protection in order to hide her, and he knew Bobbie Faye would never go for it.

She didn't have "run" in her vocabulary.

No, she wouldn't hide, especially knowing that Sean had Nina and had three bombs somewhere and could, very fucking *easily*, kill thousands of people, just to destroy both Bobbie Faye and himself. MacGreggor'd do it in a heartbeat.

He was having a hard time breathing, his chest was so constricted. The SWAT commander and his team and everyone else had jumped into high gear to assess the tactical situation. Trevor really needed to listen, even though he knew the odds, the impossible odds, against them finding those bombs before MacGreggor had his revenge. She stood in front of him, her big green eyes imploring him to understand. "You realize that he's lying," he said, choking on the words, fear driving a stake through his soul. "He's never going to give you Nina, and he's never going to give us the location of the bombs, and I *can't protect you* if you are in a crowd with that maniac."

She stood so close, he wanted to pick her up and carry her out of there, but she framed his face and her thumbs smoothed against his skin and he laid his hands over hers. She seemed calm . . . oddly, weirdly calm, but then he looked into the nearly fathomless depths of those green eyes and he saw how truly, deeply, hell-hath-no-fury pissed off she was.

"He has bombs, Trevor. You knew it was going to come to this. He'd already made that clear earlier at the racetrack."

They stood like that for what seemed like a billion heartbeats, and it wasn't enough time. He enveloped her in his arms, and hers went around his waist, her face buried in his chest, and he hoped to God this wasn't his biggest mistake of all.

"You *cannot* be fucking *serious*," Cam shouted at Trevor. Bobbie Faye realized he'd been arguing there on the other side of Riles for the better part of the last two minutes. "You're encouraging her! She doesn't know the odds, but you do!" Cam finally got enough leverage to push Riles out of his way, and he was *right there*, his hand on her shoulder, pulling her away from Trevor. "She's not trained, she doesn't understand that this is *certain death*. Or *worse*. But *you do*."

"Moreau," Trevor said, threats rattling in his voice, "move your fucking hand off her. Last time I warn you."

"Cam." She turned toward her ex as he pulled, and she grabbed his hand and held it, forcing him to look in her eyes. "He could blow the bombs *right now*. He's only waiting because he thinks it gets him something. That buys us time—time to find the bombs, time to disarm them. We have to use whatever we can to stop him from killing innocent people. Do you understand me? I'm not asking you for your permission. I'm *telling* you. I'm not going to stand by and be all damsel in distress while *innocent* people die. Whatever it takes to stop him, I'm stopping him. Don't tell me 'no' because I don't *do* 'no.'"

"She does suck at it," Riles agreed, standing between

their little group and the rest of the state cops (who were not happy campers).

"He will *kill* you, baby." Cam's voice ground out jagged and sharp. "He will grab you and if the sadistic bastard doesn't kill you on the spot, he'll make sure to do so much damage to you, you'd wished he had."

"Moreau!" Trevor said, stepping around Bobbie Faye, pushing the man back. "Now." And before she realized what Trevor was doing, he had hauled Cam out the shop and onto the street.

"Not my fault. Blame free will."

—God

Twenty-six

Moreau tried to fight him on their way out the door, but Trevor held him and propelled him onto the sidewalk. "Think!" Trevor snapped just loud enough to echo off the dark buildings along the street, moving Moreau out of Bobbie Faye's line of sight. "There are *bombs* out there."

Bobbie Faye's ex twisted away as Trevor released him, pushing off hard, but not following through with the punch Trevor was expecting. Even in the dark, outside the tepid glow of the streetlights, it was obvious the cop was ready for battle: muscles bunched, fists clenched, defensive stance, his chest heaving with heavy, adrenaline-soaked fury.

"We're running out of time!" Trevor said. "I don't fucking want her to do this any more than *you* do, but you're hurting her. *She's already made the offer*. We have to think tactically! Now!"

"You can't do this," Moreau ordered, his voice harsh, knife-edged. "You just fucking *can't*. She'll be dead." He paced, gestures sawing the night around them. "Do you really think letting her do this is going to stop him? That he'll abide by his agreement? Because if you do, you're a bigger fucking fool than I thought."

"No, it's not going to stop him!" Trevor exploded, then took a second to drag in his control from some distant recess of what used to be his professional ability. This was the last thing he wanted to have to do, but he'd do it. "She needs you right now. Hell, *I* need you right now—get your fucking head in the game."

Moreau's eyes narrowed and he breathed hard, itching to swing at Trevor.

"She *needs* you," Trevor said again. The clock was ticking and he had to get through to the man. "Her friend. For God's sake, you don't have time to fight me. You have to support her."

"You're not the only one who loves her." Moreau's words cut harsh, staccato, jabbing the air, his fists clenched.

"I know that," Trevor bit out. Heat lightning flashed in the night sky and the planes of Moreau's face stood in sharp relief against the hollow shadows of his eyes and Trevor thought of old samurais, swords drawn. "I *know* that," he offered again, quiet, his own chest tight with the effort.

Seconds ticked by.

"You could stop her," Moreau said, abruptly, as if all the fight had gone out of him. Then softer, aching, lower, his voice cracking, "You could, Cormier. She'd listen to you. She'd stop if you told her to."

He heard the heartbreak in that statement. Heard the man's voice shake, and it made him pause as Moreau scraped a hand across his face and Trevor turned a little, giving him a semblance of privacy.

"God knows I want to stop her," he told the man, matching his honesty. "I'd rather die than lose her, but if Nina gets killed or people die, she'll be destroyed. The toll of her killing Mitch last time . . . God, I've been watching her hurt so much. She was just starting to come back from that, but if she loses people because she didn't try to help? The woman we both love will be *destroyed*, Cam. Is that what you want?"

"Cam's right," Riles murmured as Bobbie Faye snapped her attention from where Trevor and Cam disappeared into the night. "I know you ride the Crazy Bus," he continued, "but this is certifiable."

"Riles, we really have got to work on this bashfulness issue."

"You're a complete raving moron."

"Would you do any different?" she asked him, pissed off. "Seriously, Riles, if you thought for one second that he'd take you instead, if offering yourself would keep him from killing people, wouldn't you do it?"

"I'm trained. And he'd never take me alive."

"Well, we'll just have to make sure he doesn't take me alive, either."

Riles stopped moving and zeroed in on her with a gaze so acute that she thought it'd bore a hole straight through her. But, God help her, she had a plan—and she needed to have Riles on board.

She'd already caught the gist of what the SWAT and other strategists behind him were saying. Even if they knew for a fact that the bomb was in the stadium, there was no way to evacuate the stadium in the time they had. And even if they had a prayer of evacuating in an orderly manner, any sort of announcement would cause a stampede, or worse. (Bobbie Faye shuddered from images of people drunkenly hurling themselves off the top of the stadium, trying to get out.) At best, after a game, it took several hours to get everyone out of the stadium and into their cars. There were at least thirty to forty thousand people in the parking lots, tailgating and watching the game on their big-screen TVs, and another nearly 93,000 inside.

And the bomb could be anywhere. Or it could be a complete bluff, and the bomb was somewhere else.

She glanced over at her dad, who looked tired, his face haggard and gray, and his arms folded as he watched her.

"Do you know where it is?" she asked him, and didn't realize until she'd spoken that her body language mimicked his with her arms crossed, fists clenched. She slammed her hands in her pockets, and asked, "*Tu fait à-rien*?" *Will you do nothing?*

"*Bouche ma chu*," he said—*kiss my ass*—his vehemence bouncing the words like marbles off the walls. "It's not here," he said, tapping his head. "I don't always get a whole picture. It's not like I have a GPS homing device up my ass,

chère, and it's not like I can think *à t'disputé avec moi.*"
With you arguing with me.

He closed his eyes and she wanted to argue that he'd managed perfectly well to find *her* for Cam once before and perfectly capable of finding insane things like T-Boy's lost hunting dog who'd gotten stuck on a barbed-wire fence four miles out in the bayou away from any known humanity, but if a little tiny thing like a bomb was eluding him, maybe he just had a fucking problem with priorities. But then again, she'd always known that, ever since he'd walked out. . . .

And now was not the time. She could not go all fourteen-year-old *oh woe is me* on his ass right then, because people were frantically working through every possibility for a bomb location, looking for access and egress points, straining to set up superfast and coordinate with LSU officials to try to keep thousands of people from dying.

She looked back at Riles, and said the thing she'd never imagined saying to him, ever, and it absolutely sucked to have to say it now.

"I need your help."

"I don't have a Rolodex big enough for all of the psychiatrists you need for help."

"Yeah, well, I don't need another psych eval to know I'm crazy. Shut up, don't even touch that one," she said. "I just need to know which guns you like best. Because you're gonna have to shoot me."

Trevor and Cam thrust through the shop door right at that moment and they stopped and gaped at her, both men going pale. Identical stares, and she couldn't decide if she should be more shocked over them both being in one piece or that they seemed to be in synch. Her last statement had clearly, instantly, given them both second thoughts about trusting her.

"I have a plan," she said to Trevor.

Riles shrugged at Trevor's glare. "So far, I'm pretty happy with it."

"He is *not* shooting at you," Trevor said, "and if you even *think* about it again, *I'm* going to lock you up. Don't argue."

"If you ladies," SWAT intoned behind them all, "have kissed and made up, we've got some instructions coming in."

Cam gave her a soft, unreadable look, and she knew he was hurting, badly, from not being able to stop her. She knew he'd intended to have her best interests at heart. She knew he loved her. He'd marry her right that second and whisk her out of there, if she said to. He'd even forgive her Trevor, because he thought he'd pushed her away—if he'd been willing to talk to her the times she'd tried before she'd met Trevor, then she and Cam would not be here right now, at this heartbreak. She knew he'd learned. He'd learned the hard way. She could see the pain radiate out from him, see that he would do whatever it took to make the two of them work.

"I think Old Man Landry," and she glared at the old man, "can 'see' some of the area where the bomb is, but he doesn't recognize it, but maybe you will? You know the campus better than anyone here."

Cam nodded, broke the gaze, and shuttered the pain and whatever it was he and Trevor had discussed outside. Instantly he was focused and back on task as he moved straight to her dad. A concrete bunker didn't sound familiar to her—though LSU had a large number of basements which were designated as fallout shelters. Then again, so did the state capitol buildings.

"Jesus," SWAT swore behind her.

Trevor grimaced as he moved to see the instructions coming in by text and then his grim expression just got worse. He had an expanded scale of *grim* expressions—from "annoyance" to "craptastic" to "stupid squared." Currently, he seemed to be displaying the "and now nominated for the Darwin Award . . ." disgust.

When he turned the phone so that she could see the text Sean had sent, her heart sank. She skimmed through the main instructions because yeah, they were bad and she'd expected them to be—she could tell from his expression Trevor had, too—but it was the very last directive on the page which fucking pissed her off . . . the bastard had gone way beyond acceptable bad-guy asshole code: He'd told her she had to wear one of the skimpy, itty-bitty, barely there, do-not-breathe-or-the-girls-will-pop-out cheerleader costumes. So he'd "know if she had a weapon" on her.

That was just damned mean.

Ce Ce wasn't entirely sure if she could handle the game if she sobered up. The noise was ear-bleed level, and when it did occasionally subside (commercial breaks), she thought she'd gone temporarily deaf. If LSU huddled, people cheered. If the other team in the red uniform huddled up, people screamed, shouted, and stomped the stands about a thousand times louder. This effort was apparently an attempt to make the other team forget whatever play it was they were about to call. Heaven knows that the very act of bending over and having nearly a hundred thousand people yell at her on national TV would have caused *her* instant amnesia and she'd have wanted to stand up to check to see if her dress had caught in her ass or worse, so maybe there was logic to this plan.

On the other hand, there was lots of bending over by young men in very tight pants, and she was pretty happy with the net results. She was not, however, happy with the chicken foot. It pulsed and throbbed and there was a rising pain in her right arm, a numbness tingling up to her elbow. She thought maybe it was the result of using that arm to lift so many beers (she wasn't entirely sure when they switched from the margaritas), but from the way the foot was twitching, she was pretty sure it wasn't just the drinking. She'd already performed two booster spells (she had been a teensy bit worried—not that she wanted to say that out loud, and tempt fate or anything, but boosters couldn't hurt, right?). Even so, in the last few minutes, the chicken foot's behavior had taken a turn for the worse: it was trying to crawl up her body.

"Honish," Monique slurred, "tha' looks really grossh. I dink you need to stoo, shtoo. Do. Shomething."

Ce Ce nodded, trying to blink away the brain fog. Monique

had a point. She had to do something. Another plain ol'
booster wasn't gonna cut it. She needed the superbooster.
She needed help.

She looked around at all of the people screaming and realized she had exactly what she needed. Mostly. Sort of.

The problem with a five-year-old on a sugar high, Lori Ann
had tried to explain to Marcel, was the five-year-old-on-
a-sugar-crash aftereffect. Two purple sno cones, a pack of
M&M's, and one massive box of sugarcoated lemon drops
(which Marcel kept sneaking her), and it was not pretty.

LSU maneuvered their spread offense into a Dash Right
93 Berlin and the instant the wide receiver broke free, the
place thundered. Cam would be proud. He'd used that same
play in a game against the Gators and won. (One advantage
to being the little sister of the girl who dated the star quarterback was enough LSU trivia to be a hit at every sports
bar. For life.) But the Gators game was the one where he'd
gotten hurt, where his knee had been hit so hard, he almost
didn't recover in time for the SEC championship game.
Where he got hit again.

Knee surgery had ended his career. And saved her life,
because he'd become a cop. He'd told her that she was his
little sister-in-law as far as he was concerned, and he sure as
hell wasn't letting her drive around drunk off her ass. He'd
arrested her when she wouldn't stop drinking and driving.

She gazed down at Stacey clinging to her like kudzu and
realized she owed Cam Stacey's life, too. Cam had never
told Bobbie Faye that Stacey had been in the car when he
arrested Lori Ann. He'd called his own sister, had her pick
up Stacey and bring her to his mom's house, had filled out
the police report that no one was in the car, and had irrevo-
cably changed all of their lives, and she knew Bobbie Faye
didn't know about Stacey.

Everyone screamed and danced at the extra point, and
Lori Ann sat still, holding Stacey in her lap. If she was brave
enough, she'd go ahead and tell Bobbie Faye. Cam had said
not to, and Bobbie Faye hadn't understood why he'd done it,

why he'd defied her request to "let her handle it" and gone ahead and arrested her sister.

She put her chin on Stacey's golden curls and closed her eyes, the deafening cheering blanketing her. If she'd been a decent sister, she'd have told Bobbie Faye anyway. If she hadn't been completely chickenshit scared. After years of being the biggest lush this side of the Mississippi, she'd barely gotten back Bobbie Faye's respect and trust. Barely. One very feeble day at a time.

LSU kicked off to Bama after the touchdown. She and Marcel and Stacey had "box" seats—which was not a box after all, but the row in front of the big bay opening below where the truck had driven through—so no one sat in front of them and she watched the game through the goalposts at the north end of the stadium. Marcel turned to hug her—every good play got hugs—and he frowned.

"Hon," he said in her ear, "she looks really tired."

Lori Ann rolled Stacey a little in her arms so she could see her face—Stacey, who had three lemon drops stuck in her hair, and wasn't *that* going to be a joy to get out—and sure enough, Ms. Cranky-Takes-After-Her-Aunt-Pants had fallen asleep against Lori Ann's shoulder.

"You want to go stretch out in the truck?" he asked.

"Yeah," she shouted in his ear, nodding hard for emphasis. The crowd roared again as the defense recovered a fumble and LSU had the ball again.

It was going to be a great night.

She reached for the keys as he dug them out of his pocket and he shook his head. "I'll make sure you get in there okay," he said, and he followed her out the row as four people behind them belly-butted and high-fived.

The sound dampened down to low-level-nuclear-bombardment as they walked into the coolness of the big bay. Thank goodness. They wove past guards, event staff, and LSU personnel, having to show their special passes to get back to the truck, which was parked toward the back of the bay (just beneath the bleachers), near the generator. The cheering went unabated and Lori Ann wondered how on

earth anyone who worked there wasn't permanently deaf.
She wouldn't be able to call Marcel when Stacey woke up.
Between the vibration of the stands and Marcel bouncing
around shouting, he wouldn't even feel it vibrating.

"I'll come check on you at halftime," he shouted and she
nodded as he unlocked the back door, moving the car seat
and bunching up a windbreaker he had for a pillow. She
kissed him bye and he made sure she was safely tucked in,
stretched out, feet out of the way of the door as he closed it.
Stacey curled on top of her like a kitten. A very big sticky
purple and gold kitten, but one who was, thankfully, asleep.

"I'm going to die wearing *bloomers*," Bobbie Faye said as
she pulled on the tiny little white short-shorts that the cheerleaders wore under their uniform.

Trevor worked on putting a couple of his gadgets in her
bra—and had a serious time concentrating there for a
moment—while she wriggled the bloomers on.

"For the love of God, be still," he said as he lost the tracking device in her cleavage. They were in a bathroom just inside the stadium entrance, and he'd appreciated how quickly
the LSU head of security had managed to grab a cheerleader of the right size and shape and get her out of her uniform just as Trevor and Bobbie Faye had arrived. "Dammit,
I've lost it again. This bra is crap."

"Sports bras suck," Moreau intoned over the earpieces—
communication sets Trevor had gotten from the local Bureau.
They'd switched over to a secondary channel while Moreau
searched for what Landry had described as the bomb location. "They smush you down too much."

She gasped, shocked, gaping at Trevor as if she couldn't
believe Moreau had just said that in front of—

"And in," Trevor agreed, seeing where Moreau was going, distracting her. "It's like the cleavage that ate Detroit."

Her head nearly popped off her shoulders. "You two are
not talking about my cleavage. I am *not* remembering this as
my last conversation. Geez."

"Fine," Moreau said, and Trevor could hear him running. "If you die, we'll talk about it at your wake."

"I have resources to pull that JumboTron video. Make still photos," Trevor added, giving her a wicked grin. "Or I'm sure I could dig up one with the SHUCK ME shirt."

"A collage," Moreau offered, the crowd noise louder over his mic, nearly drowning him out.

"Okay, now you're making me long for the death-by-bloomers."

"Shit," Moreau said and Trevor stopped, his hand on the zipper of the tiny white suit she now wore, knowing this was bad. "I think I found the bomb."

The crowd roared, another good play, and Moreau's voice was drowned out.

Twenty-seven

Nina fought off the grogginess and the pain in her right shoulder. She wasn't entirely sure what the asshole had stuck her with, but it was designed to keep her just alert enough to know she was in trouble, but not alert enough to be able to marshal any sort of defense.

The lights from the city blurred as she looked out the window, and the whir of the engine and talking of the men blended into a disjointed mix. They'd been jamming that damned needle into her since they had grabbed her, almost overdoing it when she'd fought back the first two times.

She was pretty sure her jaw was fractured. Two broken fingers on her left hand. And her right knee had started to swell after this last go-round. But two of MacGreggor's men were now unconscious.

She knew what Bobbie Faye was going to do. She knew it, and hadn't been able to stop it. Her best friend had to know by now that she'd lied to her all these years. She had to be furious, and hurting.

But she'd still walk straight into MacGreggor's trap because she thought she could save Nina. The world got blurry again and Nina bit the inside of her cheek, using the pain to focus.

Suds's helicopter landed on the parade grounds in the heart of LSU; he leapt out, body bent beneath the blades until he'd cleared them, and met one of the officers as he ran from the machine.

The cop handed him a communications unit and he plugged it into his ear.

"You're already connected, sir," the cop said.

"Any other bomb techs here?" he asked, wanting to know just who'd inspected his handiwork thus far.

"No sir. They're on the ground in several other places—they've got to clear the refineries. There's another bomb in Poly-Ferosia—there were two there, one detonated, the other intact. The contact officer here is Detective Moreau—he's the one who found it."

This just gets worse and fucking worse. Cam was a good kid. Man. Hell, he felt about Bobbie Faye the way Suds had felt about Chloë.

"Moreau's off the radio," the young cop continued, but Suds knew Moreau knew the job and would follow protocol: get people away from the bomb, no radios, no cell phones, nothing that could potentially trigger anything electronic on the bomb, establish an inner perimeter—where the worst of the damage would be done—and an outside perimeter, and get help.

"Where is it?"

"Stadium. North bay. Right below the student section."

Fuck. The crowd's stomping alone could set the damned thing off. Suds dug in harder, ran faster.

Cam eyed the enormous generator tucked into the back of the huge garagelike bay area, and he knew they were in big trouble. There was a camera on top, and there was absolutely no reason for there to be a camera on top of a generator. He'd moved fast, clearing back to an outer perimeter, pushing everyone out, locking down the area. No cell phones, no police radio. No staff, no overzealous fans, nobody.

Except for the minor detail of a few thousand people in the bleachers directly above him.

He couldn't see a bomb apparatus on the generator. But

this fit the description of what Old Man Landry had seen, and so far, that man had been unerringly right.

Cam had to wait 'til a tech got here. One was supposed to be on the way—and he needed someone with more expertise than he had to check this thing and see if there was a bomb inside. No one wanted to start a dead panic, no one wanted hysteria.

He scanned the bay again, remembering what Landry had described—the eye of the tiger, he'd said. He'd kept seeing a tiger eye, but it wasn't the actual tiger, or even the eye painted on the field. It turned out there was a tiger eye painted on the side panel of the big monster truck that had pulled the cage. It was parked close enough so that the generator was reflected in its gleaming paint job, and at the right angle, the compressor's image was so sharp that it and the tiger eye seemed to overlap like a double exposure.

He moved further out when one of the stadium cops motioned to his earpiece that Cam had an incoming message. He couldn't take the call close to the generator—the wrong frequency and the place could turn into dust. It was a pure judgment call as to where that outside perimeter ought to be; how big was the bomb? The whole generator? Probably not, he thought, cocking his head, assessing the machine. It had been rented, he'd guessed, as a backup generator. Useful after hurricanes or, ironically, in case of an emergency. He'd seen the rental company logo—LSU would have never let something like that in here without it being authorized and inspected. So whatever bomb it held had to be hidden well, something no one would normally see. Or the paperwork allowing it to be delivered had been forged.

Once he'd moved past the stadium walls to what he hoped like hell was a safe distance, he activated his radio and the earpiece crackled.

"Moreau here," he said, dispensing with codes. They were of course using the Incident Command System (ICS): keep it simple, stupid. Multiple agencies had to respond to big emergencies, and had to keep in contact without possible confusion. He'd remain the contact on site, in command of the area; LSU security staffed the command center, but Trevor was in charge as the most tactically experienced person on the site.

"Moreau," Trevor said via his earpiece as he turned on his unit, "the LSU staff says that piece was rented a few days ago and was delivered yesterday. Paperwork says it passed sweep inspection at the outer perimeter before being allowed on site." He was referring to the security sweep done with bomb-sniffing dogs that was always performed before the games. "Are you sure it's the one we're looking for?"

"Not a hundred percent. The description matches. But what worries me is that there's a small camera on top of the generator—and it swivels. I'm pretty sure it's live and able to track motion."

"Shit," Trevor responded.

Yeah. No fucking kidding.

"I've got incoming. More instructions." There was a long pause and then, "Fuck."

The pause lasted too long. Cam stood there, his arms crossed, assessing the bay area, trying to catalog in his mind everything he needed to do, a checklist, willing away the stress and allowing himself to float in that hyperfocused state where nothing mattered but the task at hand and remembering his training.

"Fuck. Moreau, he knows you're by the bomb. He says you have to move back next to it or he'll blow it. We'll coordinate evacuation."

Sonofabitch.

"No!" Bobbie Faye's anguish snapped through his earpiece.

"Baby, I'll be okay. Just don't let the bastard get you."

He signed off. No good-byes. She could decide later which bastard he meant.

He headed toward the generator just as a young cop ran up, with Suds following.

"I'm your tech," Suds explained before Cam could even ask. "Let's get to it."

Thank God, Cam thought. Finally, someone he could trust. Maybe, just maybe, something about today was going to go right.

"He wants you *where*?" Bobbie Faye asked Trevor as he barked orders over his mic. He had his hand at her back, guiding her up the sidelines as the seconds wound down toward halftime. "You can't," she said when he didn't answer, didn't elaborate on the snippets she heard. "If you're up on that stand, unarmed, you might as well paint a big-ass target on your back."

Sean had Nina, he'd pinned Cam to a bomb, and now he'd instructed Trevor to be up on the drum leader's stand—which would put him head and shoulders above the field. He leveled her a furious gaze, because that's exactly what she'd done to herself: drawn a honking big-ass target on her back.

Just once, just freaking *once*, she wished she was up against a really stupid bad guy. Someone along the lines of Moe Moe Balentine, who tried desperately to rob the same bank repeatedly (the one where his sister worked) by using a handwritten note on the back of his deposit slip. Or Winky the Wonder Clown, who thought it was okay to rob the store where he bought the mask. Could she get someone like that? No, indeedy *not*.

Trevor's hand rested on her shoulders, and her hands on his waist as he talked, coordinating with what he kept referring to as ICS. Everyone had moved fast, snapping into some sort of hierarchy they all understood as if there was one big Group Think, trying to get everyone into position as the last few seconds of the half wound down and LSU made a play that she couldn't see for all of the players standing on the sidelines between her and the field.

It really didn't matter if there was a hot pink polka-dotted Jesus standing out there right then, because Trevor was about to have to climb up onto the drum leader's stand. She memorized his face, everything about him, particularly his singular determination. She had a glimpse then of the leader he'd been in the field in Spec Ops: cold, clear, calculated.

There was a knife's edge to him. He was precise, relentless. Ice.

The only thing warm about him in that moment was his hand on her shoulder. His fingers slid against the muscles just beneath her hair, and she thought, *I am his one point of weakness.*

She was going to get him killed.

He'd held back the truth about himself because he didn't know how to trust her with it. He had not realized yet that he could. She knew he'd do it again, if he thought it meant protecting her.

The band had lined up, per normal halftime routine, and they were getting their new instructions. She watched a wave of confusion ripple across their faces as they digested the information. Many were clearly upset—they wanted to march onto that field at halftime and perform the show they had undoubtedly practiced an insane number of hours to perfect.

The halftime buzzer sounded, the cameras swooped away from the field to the end zones where the teams headed and she knew the network would be cutting into close-ups of the coaches giving their pointless content-free halftime reports.

"Where do you think he's set up?" she asked, knowing that Trevor and his men had been scanning every inch of the stadium, searching for Sean. He had to be there somewhere, and yet, there was no way Sean could have gotten into the stadium with weapons—the security was intensely tight at these games. On the other hand, he didn't have to have weapons; he had the bomb, a trump card, pure and simple. The fact that he *might* be able to set it off would keep SWAT at bay until Cam could assess the bomb threat.

The fact that there was still another bomb, somewhere, with an unknown location, meant Sean had two trump cards, really. He could even have the second bomb with him. Wherever he was.

She followed Trevor's gaze as he scanned the crowd; people moved to the aisles going for bathroom breaks, concession breaks, or visits with friends, although many were glancing out onto the field, wondering why the band hadn't started playing. Neither the LSU nor the Alabama band had moved into position, and she could see from the restless crowd that they were starting to notice.

She wondered if the LSU band still played the Darth Vader song when the defense rallied on a great play. "The Imperial March," was that what it was called? They really should, if they didn't still, because that song would just be so fucking *fitting* right now. Hearing that song would make this disaster unfolding in front of her feel like a big halftime show, an act, and she could pretend that none of this was happening. She wanted to pretend that the last few hours were simply fiction on a movie screen in front of her, that this man, *her world*, standing next to her wasn't giving her a final look, one that held his entire heart, one that said his biggest regret was not going and finding Sean and killing him when he'd had the chance.

He'd wanted to. It wasn't legal and he was an FBI agent and she'd reminded him of that, over and over. She'd dissuaded him from acting on his own. She'd made him promise, because she knew it would ruin his life, because she knew he would have killed Sean to protect her.

He'd do any damned thing he could to protect her. Any. Damned. Thing. He'd sacrifice everything.

And suddenly, she understood. She *understood*, and he had already started to move away from her and climb that stupid stupid *stupid* drum major platform and she grabbed him and kissed him, hard.

"If you get hurt," she said, "I'm going to fucking kick your ass. In front of everyone."

He grinned and said, "Good to know." Then he frowned at her. "And follow the plan, do you hear me?"

Yeah, she nodded. She heard him.

But he ought to know by now she wasn't really the planny type.

"We've got incoming," one of the SWAT team on the outer perimeter—the bank of the Mississippi just west of the stadium—said on Trevor's earpiece, toggled now to the open circuit where he could talk to everyone and hear status updates. "Three helicopters. JetRangers."

Trevor fully expected them. MacGreggor favored helicopters. What he didn't know was which parking lot MacGreggor would choose to land in, what sort of danger the various tailgaters would be in, and which entrance he'd try to use. Everyone on the LSU staff had strict instructions to not try to stop the man—for one thing, Trevor didn't want the staff shot and for another, there was the other bomb. He wouldn't put it past MacGreggor to have more than one bomb on site and blow one just to make the point that he could.

"Overhead!" another SWAT said into his mic. "He's coming in over the stadium."

And holy hell, he was. They came up and over the walls of the stadium, giant black locusts with blades chopping the air, and dipped immediately down, riding too close above the crowds, so close that people ducked instinctively. The birds split up—two circling the stadium, staying just above the crowd, just far enough above to be dangerous but not create a tremendous amount of backwash. No shots fired. No way to take them out without killing the crowd below them. The third hovered in the center of the field, just south of the fifty yard line, facing the sideline where he and Bobbie Faye waited.

He finished climbing to the top of the platform when MacGreggor's call was patched through to his earpiece.

"Nice to know you can follow directions, Cormier," MacGreggor said. "The lass is wired for sound?"

"I'm here, Sean," she said. "Where's Nina?"

"First off, lass, I want you in the middle of the field where I can find you easy."

"Well, isn't that just like a man, can't find anything by himself," she muttered, her absolute utter fury so clear in her tone of voice, she might as well have placed a FUCK YOU sign on the overhead ESPN blimp. "Seriously, Sean, do you think you could be any more of a big hairy wuss?"

Trevor froze. Every fucking member of his team froze. SWAT froze. She'd just called the bomber a *big hairy wuss*.

The helicopters were black and big and loud, circling just above the sea of gold and white and purple t-shirts. Panic hammered her chest the moment they had appeared, and like ants following a picnic, so had Adrenaline and Shock.

She clenched her fists; she had to get a grip. She could flip out later. Right now?

Pissed fucking *off*.

One helicopter hovered over the field. One of the other helicopters that had been circling overhead came to a hover position just behind Trevor. Bobbie Faye didn't have to even look to know just exactly how not good this was. But she looked anyway, and saw what she thought was that M110 sniper rifle protruding just enough from the opened door on the side of the helicopter to mow Trevor down where he stood. Her Aunt V'rai could make a head shot from that distance.

"Center of the field, *àlainn,* or you'll not be havin' a friend left to find."

She started walking out toward the center of the field, her peripheral vision registering the JumboTron, on which some enterprising agent or cop had managed to get the words SWAT DEMONSTRATION for the crowd's curiosity and nerves.

"Cormier, I don't believe I said you could evacuate the stands. Leave the sheep be."

"Are those. . . . M&Ms the governor's gorging?"

"I think those are Xanax."

"Right. Bobbie Faye Day. That explains the crying."

—Senator CJ Lyons to Roxanne St. Claire

Twenty-eight

The hotel penthouse lights were turned low, just as she'd requested. Her private butler had arrived a few hours ahead of her, and she saw that Henry had everything prepared: the glass of wine, a perfect '74 Château Latour, poured and waiting. She'd eaten on the jet already, her personal chef having created a magnificent tuna tartar, and she was easing onto the beautiful Louis IX settee, the silk of her suit rustling as she slipped off her Manolo Blahniks, when Henry appeared.

She hated to be disturbed during her evening wine, but he quietly held out her cell phone with a slight bow. "Madame, Mrs. Claire for you. She insists it's important."

Claire. Her dearest friend, but sometimes, tedious.

"Yes?" she asked. Claire knew her routine as well as Henry.

"Andrea, dear, you need to turn on this channel. This"—she heard Claire rustling—"this sports network."

"Have you—"

"Lost my mind? No, dear. It's very important, or I wouldn't have called. I don't know how to tell you this, but there seems to be an incident unfolding."

Incident. Andrea felt a chill sweep through her, though to see her, one would never know. She leaned forward and picked up the remote, clicking on the television in the armoire across the room. She usually closed out her evenings watching the financial reports, so Henry had the armoire open.

"I believe it's channel twenty-eight there in New York."

The image flicked on with a vast sea of people in a stadium, purples and golds (horrible color, what on earth were they thinking?) and there were . . . helicopters . . . flying inside the stadium. The station cut to a commercial and she muted the sound.

"What is this about?" she asked her friend.

"You know how William likes his sports," her friend said. "He follows everything, I believe. Except, possibly, cricket, though I wouldn't put it past him. Anyway, he'd bet heavily on this game and had the channel on—oh. There it is. That's from a couple of minutes ago—"

But Andrea didn't hear another word of Claire's babbling. She turned the sound up and leaned forward.

Her son. Standing on . . . some sort of platform.

"Holy fuck *holy shit* holy fuck," Kyle, the sportscaster, muttered and then, finally, presence of mind struck him dumb but his mouth hadn't quite caught up, and he probably looked like an overactive guppy. He slammed it shut, cutting a gaze to the man next to him in the newly remodeled control booth at the LSU stadium.

"We threw to national a couple of seconds ago," his producer, Colby, said in his earpiece, and he nodded, relieved. He sure as hell didn't need the FCC breathing down his neck. "They've been instructed by someone pretty freaking high up that they can't allude to anything going on here."

"What are they saying this is?"

Colby pointed to the JumboTron's message of SWAT DEMONSTRATION, which, frankly, was insane.

"Nobody's gonna buy it," Kyle said. "We've got to get on the air." They were sitting on the freaking largest sports story in . . . decades. He could see his producer salivating at the prospect as well.

Colby tapped the screen embedded in the desk in front of them—one of the overhead cameras had a close-up of the cheerleader running out to the center of the field. A lone cheerleader, and this was a woman, not a kid.

"You recognize her?" Colby said low, peering over his shoulder to a SWAT guy standing a few feet away as he co-ordinated with someone over his own earpiece. When Kyle shook his head, Colby leaned over to another console, clicked a couple of keys, and sent Kyle an image isolated from the casino boat disaster which had happened the night before and was still all over the local news. Colby zoomed in on the image and Kyle toggled between that one and the live feed of the woman jogging to the center of the field.

Holy shit. Little Miss National Disaster was about to guarantee him the highest ratings *ever*.

Ce Ce had sobered right the hell up. She didn't know you could get whiplash from sobering up that fast, but as soon as she saw Bobbie Faye step on the field, she knew this was the bad bad bad that the chicken foot was trying to warn her about. The claws were opening and closing, like the damned thing was trying to run away from her arm—now it was giving off an eerie blue-black light.

She uncorked the last of the bad juju concoction and poured it straight onto the claw, knowing she really should have taken the time to pour a little into a container and then just dip the outer talons, not pour it dead center on the whole foot, but she wasn't entirely sure she should touch it directly. And she hoped the chicken foot did not amplify the glassy-eyed shock of the people around her and send it back to Bobbie Faye. From the way that helicopter closed in on her girl, she couldn't handle any more bad.

"You saying a whahoozie spell?" Monique stage-whispered, as if the chicken claw could hear her.

It wriggled. Hell, maybe it could.

Ce Ce nodded, chanting low, shaking her arms low, then high, then low again, all a part of the incantation. Several drunks behind her thought it was a new cheer and eyeballed her, trying to imitate the motions and the words. Two spilled their beers, one going down her back and running the length of her arms, dripping onto the foot. She couldn't stop, though, to whip their asses. She just kept going. Breaking the incantation at this point would be far far far worse, and she didn't want to take *that* chance. The drunks were completely oblivious to the spillage, though one wondered out loud who'd drank the rest of his beer. The other kept following her motions, repeating them himself, as if it was some new line dance, and when she finally looked up, she realized a few other people near him had caught the motions and joined in.

Oh, holy hell. What kind of karma was she sending Bobbie Faye with a bunch of drunk auras funneled through the chicken foot? Drunk, horny young men's auras?

She had no clue, but she didn't dare stop.

The freaking chicken foot juju bracelet creeped Bobbie Faye out, and she could have sworn that with every step she took onto that field, the damned thing pulsed harder, 'til it throbbed, a bone-deep ache. It had been opening and closing now with such a regular rhythm that she'd almost gotten used to that part, but the throbbing sent sharp, electrical pulses through her until she felt as if she'd grabbed onto a 110-volt wire and couldn't let go.

If Bobbie Faye got fried by an overactive chicken foot, she was so going to have words with Ce Ce, assuming she made it into the afterlife. Hell, she'd haunt Ce Ce. Then again, as bad as Bobbie Faye's own personal luck had been, *death by deep-fried chicken juju* was probably the least she had to worry about.

The LSU drumline began a cadence—another of Sean's instructions. He was going balls-out for drama, and as soon as Trevor had realized that, Bobbie Faye had heard him send instructions to block the television feed nationally—to do whatever they needed to do to loop it locally only, in case Sean had some sort of TV receiver in one of the helicopters. Trevor didn't want Sean to know that the whole world wasn't actually watching, afraid that losing the national stage would so aggravate Sean, that he would prematurely blow the bomb.

But neither could Trevor risk that bomb exploding live on national TV, so he'd made the move to allow the halftime show to be aired to any satellite receivers, on the off chance Sean was watching the game to see if the cameras were catching his activities.

She was almost to the middle of the field when she heard Sean again. "Lass, you're not supposed to carry weapons."

She held up the pom-poms Riles had thrust in her hands when she'd come out of the bathroom, and she grinned. "I don't think I'm gonna cheer you to death, Sean. They're pom-poms. But fine, look." She flipped them over to where anyone in that helicopter that hovered over her could see she didn't have a gun hidden under the poofy poms.

"Drop 'em," he said.

She released them at her feet, and stood there, hands on her hips, watching the helicopter on the ground in front of her—though there was no guarantee Sean was in that specific helo, since its windows were tinted and she couldn't see who was inside. She glanced back at the other helicopter behind Trevor—it still had the rifle trained on the back of his head. He stood ramrod still, aware that at any second he could die, and he gave her subtle hand signals—status reports they'd hastily worked out when she'd been changing into the uniform. *Cam's not done yet, bomb's still active.*

Wonderful.

"Where's Nina?" she asked, keying her microphone.

"Right here beside me, lass," Sean said, and the helicopter set down as the second one swooped in toward her.

"Which 'here' would that be, Sean? The helicopter on the ground or the one that's chickenshit, flying around me like I'm booby-trapped? And really, seriously, Sean, I thought you had more balls than this."

She could see Trevor go completely pale from across the field. And then insanely *furious*. Well, he had said to stall Sean, because they had a plan.

Dollars to donuts, Trevor was gonna be a little more specific about "plans" next time. Assuming she lived to see a "next" time, which was, seriously, probably not going to happen. She'd made peace with that.

Though there were some people she really wished she'd gotten to say good-bye to, like her sister. Stacey. Roy. (Though at the rate Roy was screwing up his life, he was going to hit the hereafter about six seconds after she did.)

"You're baitin' me, lass, though I wouldn't put it past you to be booby-trapped," Sean chuckled. "Before I'm willin' to make the trade, you'll have to prove you're not."

"Well, then, Sean, watch," she said, and she reached for the zipper of the cheerleader outfit and the *entire* fucking stadium went silent, except for one group doing some sort of woo-woo dance, and she stripped off the uniform. Cameras flashed from the sidelines, and not those little bitty cell phone–sized suckers, either, but the great big stinkin' cameras with zoom lenses strong enough to determine that she probably should have plucked her eyebrows a couple of days ago.

Maybe she could put in for an order of Dignity in her next lifetime. All she had on was the skimpy sports bra and the too-short white bloomer things that, God help her, wouldn't even qualify as a scrap of material at the Wal-Mart bargain bin. "You think you're the only one with scars, Sean MacGreggor? Well, I've got scars, and I'm not hiding in a helicopter like some big whiny baby. Seriously, if you think I'm going to walk away from a man with balls like that," and she waved toward Trevor, "to a man like this," and she waved at the helicopter, "then you need to have a complete testosterone work-up, because you wouldn't deserve me choosing you. And the world's gonna know it, too, because by now, there are probably penguins up in the arctic circle who're tuning in on TV or YouTube. They're all gonna know, Sean. Hiding behind guns and bombs? Holding a gun on an unarmed man? Putting a bomb below a bunch of children? *Any fucking coward* can do that, Sean, and you never struck me as a coward. So you want me? You want your revenge? You really want to hurt him?" She gestured back to Trevor. "Get your namby-pamby ass out here and *get* me. They can't shoot at you because they can't risk missing and taking out a bystander in the crowd and you know that. No-body's gonna rush the field, and you know it. You got us where you want us—you really want to win? Do you really think shooting an *unarmed* man *in the back* makes you tougher than him? Show some freaking *balls*. I thought the Irish had some, but then again, maybe I was wrong."

"Trevor says to give you a heads-up," the young cop at the edge of the inner perimeter said. He'd been running out to the outer perimeter where he could use his radio to keep Cam and Suds informed. "Bobbie Faye just called the bomber a namby-pamby baby with no balls."

Cam and Suds shared a look.

"Well, that's good," Cam said, "because I don't think this was quite fucking hard enough."

Suds pursed his lips and went back to work.

"Also," the cop at the perimeter added, returning already, "they've found the second bomb at the Poly-Ferosia plant and want to know how you're doing on this one."

"Tell them to watch for multiple traps," Suds said and then he reeled off a lot of technical jargon.

Cam sharpened his gaze at Suds, apprehension warring beneath the surface with the relief he'd felt that he'd had someone with extensive bomb-tech knowledge show up. If he'd have had to describe everything to someone off-site while trying to follow instructions on how to diffuse this bomb, Cam wasn't sure he would have been able to do it, as tricky as it was. He knew he wouldn't be nearly as far along as Suds had already gotten, especially since Cam would have to have a cop there to run out beyond the perimeter to get every instruction and then relay it back in to him, since he couldn't use his cell phone near the bomb. The time delay alone would've been a nightmare. No, he'd been thrilled when Suds arrived.

Except . . . Suds was describing stuff about this bomb that they hadn't uncovered yet. Traps he hadn't seen yet. Traps in the other bomb *he couldn't possibly know about*.

How?

He was about to ask that question when out of the corner of his eye he caught movement. He glanced over at the truck parked twenty feet away from the generator and nearly died, right there on the spot.

Stacey was waving to him from the backseat of that truck.

"Isabella," Andrea said into her cell phone. "I know you're the only one your brother is still talking to."

"Mother, I'm busy."

"Busy monitoring the feed from the football game. Don't bother to deny it."

"What do you want?"

"Henry's at my laptop, and I want you to send me a routing line so that I can watch the live feed from there. The local station has apparently stopped broadcasting nationally. I can suspect on whose orders."

"Trevor wants absolutely nothing to do with you, Mother, and you haven't bothered in years. The last thing he'd want is for you to use this—"

"Route it now, Isabella, or the next board meeting will not be pleasant."

Andrea hung up. She knew exactly how her son felt, and she'd always been fairly certain that he'd mellow with time. Instead, he'd become worse. And now, if her eyesight hadn't played tricks on her, that helicopter that the camera had captured hovering just behind him as they cut to the sports desk halftime show had had someone inside with a gun pointed at her son's head.

"We have the feed," Henry said.

Lonan could feel it. He could feel something unnatural washing over them.

Something dire and hot burned in Sean's amber eyes, and Lonan hated the look of it. It didn't bode well. He glanced over at Ian, who still controlled the laptop with the codes. He knew Ian had overrides, in case Sean changed his mind about the timing. Or lost his mind, as was, clearly, possible.

It was Lonan's job to blow these bombs, and to make sure the timing was right, and he wasn't going to fail Sean again.

"I'm comin' to get you, *àlainn*," Sean said. "You've got style, lass. I'll give you that. It'll do you no good, in the end."

He signaled Sean and they both muted their microphones. "It's a trick," he told Sean, but he knew he was wasting his breath.

"What're they gonna do, then? Shoot me in front of millions? This is the nation that got all squirrelly over a fuckin' wardrobe malfunction. They haven't the stomach to do anythin' wit' any balls. Not on national TV.

"Set her down," Sean instructed their pilot, Denny.

The woo-woo dancing grew in the stands, and Bobbie Faye had no doubt whatsoever that Ce Ce was somehow behind it. Every single time those arms pulsed upward and shook their demented jazz hands, the chicken foot clenched and reached for something, and she had no clue what, but it *hurt*. The shimmying had synched up with the boogie of the cadence the drum line paced—and the dancing seemed to be spreading to a second section. Heads bobbed, bodies gyrated, the rhythm and *feeling* throbbing through her like a raw ache, a claw hammer to her heart.

The helicopter in front of her lifted off and circled around to exchange places with the third helicopter flying around in circles. She so wanted to tell Sean he needed MapQuest to find his ass from a hole in the ground, but the dancing in the crowd pulled at her attention as the swaying spread to yet another section. The thump-thump-ratatatatatat of the drums filled the stadium and echoed back again, swelling and beating and pumping adrenaline into her pores. She fought against the weirdness that seemed to swamp her, taking over her body, and she ground her teeth and clenched her fists, battling for focus.

She looked over to where Trevor stood, his arms crossed so he could key his mic without being seen. The notion slammed into her all over again: he had not trusted her.

Trust was a damned fucking hard thing to break open and

live in. Breaking trust open and living in it, living in the give and take. The give of . . . the *give*. And maybe it was the swaying of the crowd, or maybe it was the bright lights making her dizzy, or maybe it was all of the stress highlighting what was at stake, but the epiphany she had as she gazed at him nearly slammed her to her knees. It was as if her perspective had shifted or had focused, like clear lenses when she'd been blind. With the chanting crowd and the rolling drums and the helicopters moving into their positions, she suddenly realized that love wasn't always about *what you get*. Love was not just about what you felt, but about what you were able to give, what you ought to give. What the other person needed.

He was standing there, giving her the most important thing he had: being a partner to her in his plan. Trusting her to hold up her end, believing she could do something exceptional in a time of crisis. His life—their lives—depended on her part in this, as well as his.

Faith. He needed her faith in him. In who he was, who he had become, what he'd done with his life, and what they could be, even with mistakes and misunderstandings. He had not fully opened up to her. But she hadn't fully opened up to him, either. How do you have faith, unless you simply choose? She could see where his fear had come from. See what had held him back, but when she thought about it, he'd shown faith in her over and over again, in the way he treated her, in how he respected her opinion, her abilities. He wasn't perfect. Thank freaking God, he wans't perfect. And he needed her. He needed her faith. It was such a startling revelation, she almost turned and ran off the field, just to get to tell him face-to-face, to see the look in his eyes.

Instead, she tapped her leg twice for him to switch to the secondary channel they'd set up. She fiddled with her bra strap, taking the moment to surreptitiously switch channels herself. Trevor's fancy phone could monitor Sean's channel while talking to her. *They had maybe ten seconds.*

"I'm done being stupid," she said.

"From the woman who just called the bomber a big pansy? Sundance, you want to fucking narrow that one down?"

"Good point. I get why you didn't tell me about you. I get you might've had reasons to be afraid. And I'm going to give you an earful of grief later, buster, so don't think you're off the hook, but I understand. It's completely within the realm of possibility that I might've overreacted in a knee-jerk sort of way—not that I do that, but mind you, it's within a statistical possibility that—"

"So you're saying I was right?"

She had to fight off a wave of dizziness to answer. "I'm saying I'm pissed off that you *might* have been right, which is an *entirely* different thing and you can't hold me to that, I reserve the right to totally recant when I'm not standing in my underwear in front of a hundred thousand people—"

"Plus the TV audience—"

"And I'm pissed off that you didn't know for sure how I felt."

"*I* knew for sure you *felt*, Sundance. I just didn't know if *you* did."

She thought about that for a second as he grinned. He fucking *grinned*, with a gun at his back. *God, she loved this man*. She fought against another wave of *crazy*, a feeling of being swamped by a fever as the crowd's undulations seemed to vibrate through her; she hoped he couldn't hear the disorientation in her voice. "November eighth. One month. You'd better be there."

"Just try and stop me."

As Sean's helicopter landed in front of her, they both switched back to the main channel, and heard a woman on the line. A woman Bobbie Faye had never spoken to before, but the utter control of the voice, the simple command she had, sent chills down Bobbie Faye's spine, chills that danced to the rhythm of the drums. Rolling, moving, living, breathing, *drums*.

"No," the woman was saying. "I am Andrea Cormier, and as I've said, Mr. . . ." they heard her speaking to someone, "MacGreggor, according to my DOJ resources, you're a businessman. This is a business deal. You name your price."

"For your son?" Sean laughed. "You don't have that kind of money, luv."

"Oh, but you don't know that, do you? Name your price. Half right now, in a Swiss account, the other half when my son is safe."

"Get the *fuck* off this line," Trevor said.

Bobbie Faye gaped. First at Trevor, then back at the helicopter.

Oh. Holy. Hell.

This was her future mother-in-law.

"Fine, luv. I'll play your little game."

"No fucking way," Trevor said. "How in the hell did you—"

"Izzy, dear. It's simple—she caved, pretty quickly, too. She tapped into your frequency. Our company built the little Cor-Tech 940 units you're using to communicate, and we tracked your phone. I'm on a live feed of this arena, Mr. MacGreggor," she said, re-directing her conversation back to Sean. "My information from the Department of Justice indicates you've been a profiteer for many years and this action is outside of your normal methodology. I haven't followed all of the dynamics, but given that you have my son unarmed and his fiancée on the ground, I believe your goal is humiliation and then suffering. What better way to accomplish your goal than for his hated mother to rescue him? So. Name your price."

"Mother, you will *not* fucking do this."

"Language, darling, language."

"It's Saturday, luv. You can't get the money moved."

"I can."

"A hundred million."

She laughed, a light and feathery brush of something that was just as deadly as it was soft. Bobbie Faye had to practically lock her knees to keep from sinking into the ground because the woman *chuckled* at handing over a *hundred million dollars.*

"Done."

"I keep the girl," Sean said.

And without missing a beat, the woman said, "Of course."

"Well, for my team, I pick Wolverine, Terminator *and* James Bond."

"Fine. *I* pick Bobbie Faye."

"Mom!! Kelly's cheating again!"

—8-year-old twins Dotty and Kelly

Twenty-nine

"Sonofabitch," Cam swore, moving toward the truck. "Stacey, be still," he said, tapping the passenger window to wake Lori Ann. "Lori Ann—don't touch anything. Don't open the door—y'all sit still. Do you understand?"

A bleary-eyed Lori Ann nodded, gathering Stacey to her lap. Stacey had a couple of lemon drops stuck in her hair . . . which meant the inside of that truck was about to be destroyed by the little nap-energized dynamo.

"Damn," Suds said from behind him, then muttered, "fuck fuck *fuck*," and Cam startled—in all of the years he'd known Suds, the man didn't curse. Whatever he'd found must be bad. He glanced at Suds, who was staring at the bomb in the generator, and not at the truck, where Stacey and Lori Ann had sat up. The man's expression had gone from strained to deathly pale.

"Do I need to get them out of here?" Cam asked, knowing that the friction from opening the door could be a big bad bang of a problem. He motioned again for Lori Ann and Stacey to be still.

Suds stared at the truck and then back to the generator. Then back to the truck again. A sudden dawning of realization and then a look of dread spread across his face that made Cam's tension ratchet up.

"Cam, walk around to the back and see if that truck's got a rental logo on it."

"With this paint job? Are you nuts?" he asked, walking around the truck anyway. And sure enough, saw the logo. "Holy shit, how did you know?"

As Cam puzzled over why in the hell a rental would have such a paint job, he saw a "win this truck" sign on the rear bumper—a raffle for a cancer charity sponsored jointly by the LSU alumni and the rental company. Cam looked from that sign to Suds, who had tears streaming down his cheeks. The man sank his face in his hands and mumbled something Cam couldn't quite make out.

"How the hell did you know this?" Cam demanded. "And what does it mean?"

"It means the last bomb's in that truck."

Cam felt every single drop of blood in his body pool in his feet. His gaze went back to Lori Ann and Stacey, watching him for further instructions. "How do you know that?"

Suds lifted his head, his gaze locked on Lori Ann and Stacey. "Because I'm the bastard who built the bombs."

Dox sat in the helicopter behind the scope on his M110, his breathing even, the Fed in his sights. His orders were simple: shoot the asshole the moment Sean had the girl. Sean wanted the girl to voluntarily walk toward him, because he knew the Fed would lose his mind. He knew the Fed would lunge toward her and that's when Dox was to mow him down, leave him sprawled out there, lying on the field, watching her climb in the helo with Sean and watching them take off, unable to move or do a damned thing about it.

In principle, Dox liked the plan. He had his finger on the trigger and he waited. Three pounds of pressure, and the man was a paraplegic, at best. With the vibration of the helo, the rhythm of the rotors, the velocity of the wind, the exact distance (his spotter had it measured), he knew exactly where to place his sights to achieve his shot. He'd been doing this too many years not to know the calculations by heart. Three pounds of pressure and all he was waiting on was Sean's signal. He breathed, even. Slow. Calm. A simple job.

* * *

There was no way Sean was going to abandon his plan for revenge just because someone threw money at him, and Bobbie Faye knew it. She knew Trevor knew it. Hell, she could go ask the third-grader in row seventeen, the one with the purple 'fro and tiger stripes painted across his face, and that kid would know it. If all Sean had wanted was money, he wouldn't be here right now.

No, this was about a helluva lot more than money. There was a helicopter in front of her on the field, and one hovering behind her, but the one that had Bobbie Faye barely able to breathe was the one still hovering behind Trevor, the propeller wash whipping at the crowd below—who seemed to be oblivious as they joined the woo-woo dance, throwing their hands up in the air in rhythm with the drums. The rhythm swayed her, filling her with dread and anticipation and she felt as if fire licked across her arm and down her chest, curling in her fingers.

She felt stranger and stranger as more people in the stands joined the dance, and it was as if . . . power . . . coursed through her, threatening to take her over.

"Sundance," Trevor said, low, almost a whisper, as he watched her while Sean, on the line, rattled off a Swiss bank account number to the world's scariest woman.

She shuddered, electricity rippling through her. Her arms flinched and jerked and she felt light-headed. The crowd swam, the drums pounded and filled her head to the brim, and from far away, she heard him say, "Sundance?" again.

"Bad juju," Bobbie Faye answered Trevor, feeling her body swaying. Swaying. On its own.

She stood in the middle of freaking Tiger Stadium with a couple hundred photo cameras, a few dozen TV cameras (no doubt still recording), God only knew how many cell phone cameras, and she was *swaying*. Twitching and swaying and starting to gyrate with all the grace of a drunk pole dancer stepping on tacks.

In her borrowed too-small underwear.

With her future mother-in-law watching.

Dear Universe:

> *Hate you. Hate your shoes. You have bad breath and I*
> *hope your hair falls out.*
>   *—the girl wearing the STUPID CHICKEN FOOT*

And as if from a zillion miles away, on another planet, Trevor's mother repeated the number Sean gave her, and then she said, "You realize the Feds are tracking everything you've just told me."

"No worries, luv." His Irish accent blended into the drums, slid into them and became a part of them as the rhythm filled Bobbie Faye. "You make sure the fifty is in there in the next five minutes and your son'll live. The money won't lie long enough for the Feds to touch it."

"Half now, the other half after you leave," she reminded him.

"Meanwhile, *àlainn*," Sean said, and Bobbie Faye saw him shove Nina to the doorway of the second helicopter, using her as a shield, "you're comin' to me."

"Give me Nina," she said, her voice slurred as strange lightning ripped the sky overhead, and the air crackled around her. Crackled and danced and seemed to live and she kept moving. Undulating to the hypnotic rhythm of the crowded stadium.

"What are you doin'? You don't have the power to negotiate, *àlainn*. Look up."

She had to force her body to obey, to look up at the JumboTron, and an image of Cam and Suds facing off appeared, the tension in their faces obvious in giant grainy detail. Then Bobbie Faye realized what she was seeing: the side of a big monster truck and inside it, Lori Ann and Stacey.

Lightning crashed down onto the field, not far from where she stood, and the crowd oooohhhed and the chanting grew louder, as if this was some demented halftime show: Almost-Fricasseed Bobbie Faye.

"Oh, God, it hurts," she moaned, and she didn't realize she'd keyed the mic until Trevor and Sean both said her name. How was it that the drums were so loud, so *loud*, so constant, beating into her? She had the dimmest idea that she was still moaning, that people were saying her name over the mic, but she wasn't entirely sure what language she was hearing anymore.

Because all she was, was the drums. Electricity snapped away from her in sparks. She was freaking *radiating* fireworks like a deranged Roman candle. Heat speared off her and she could feel the rush of the crowd's adrenaline. Her hips jerked, sliding to the right, drawing out the rhythm of the beat, the beat that pounded into her. She fought it, dammit. She reached for the chicken foot but just *thinking* about pulling it off her arm made it pulse with an electrical shock as her body convulsed forward, doubling over, and a grunt kicked from her gut. And then it forced her up again, and the fucking thing *took over*. Suddenly she longed for when she had simply looked like she was stepping on tacks, because now? Now she was dropping into a low stance and bouncing on one leg to the rhythm of the drums, and then the other leg, spinning, arms reaching for only God knew what, electricity shooting off her fingertips, burning, burning, the chicken foot screaming in her head, and she swore, if she lived, she was personally hauling her ass to Kentucky Fried Chicken and eating every damned drumstick they had.

Up in the control room, Kyle gaped. Next to him, Colby gaped. All of the sound techs gaped. The SWAT guy gaped. Not a single one of them could take their eyes off the . . . what would you even *call* that? Happening in the center of the field. Then the woman made some sort of move and they all dropped their mouths a bit more.

The entire stadium was getting into the act, but nothing was as . . . fucking *hot* as Bobbie Faye right now. It was like watching one of those belly-dancing women do a dance with scarves. Kyle suddenly realized he'd missed out on a helluva lot in life if this is how women danced here in the South.

"What the hell is she doing?" he asked Colby, not able to take his gaze off her.

"Winning us an Emmy."

* * *

The drums pounded. *Pounded*. And she hopped on one foot. In a circle. Gyrating. *On one foot*. There were too many ways to die of humiliation right then, so apparently the Universe felt the need to give her the Sampler.

"Bad . . . juju . . ." she gritted out through clenched teeth.

"Sundance," Trevor said now, alarm lacing through her earpiece.

"Lass," Sean said, equally confused, "what the fuck are you doin'?"

"I . . . don't . . . know . . ." she said, fighting for control as her body jerked and swayed with the roll of the drum. "Can't . . . stop . . ."

The drum line thundered, the bass pounding through her every heartbeat, every single fiber of her body. She felt her hips sway and her arms slide up her body, twining overhead, and cheers went up from the crowd as sparks flew from her fingertips and rained down around her, bouncing off the field at her feet. A river of sparks. The drums beat deeper into her, the chicken foot burned, and she closed her eyes, feeling the wash of the waves of the crowd pulse over her soul.

"Show me the helicopter moving away from my son, Mr. MacGreggor," Trevor's mother commanded, and within a couple of seconds, the helicopter hovering behind Trevor swung forward, above the field now, though the rifle inside still aimed in his direction.

Bobbie Faye registered somewhere in the back of her mind that she was distracting Sean from the helicopters and his plans. The lizard part of her brain that was all about survival wanted to focus on this, and focus on Trevor's plan, but the waves of the crowd—of the whole stadium—cascaded through her and she couldn't fight it. Didn't want to fight it. There were too many of them, and it burned too much. She thought she might turn white hot with flames and be ash any moment now, and still she moved.

"The money is now . . ." Bobbie Faye heard a clicking noise, computer keys, ". . . there, Mr. MacGreggor," Trevor's mother said, smoothly, calmly, not even giving the slightest indication of concern that she'd just sold off her future daughter-in-law or, apparently, that said future daughter-in-law had just turned into a Lite-Brite Barbie.

"Aye," Sean said, "the money is there, luv. Now, *àlainn*, cut it out, whatever you're doin', you've run out of time."

"I'm . . . trying . . . bad . . . juju . . ." But she couldn't move toward him. She was pinned there, in the center of the field, and behind her closed lids she saw flames, the center of a bonfire, circles of flames around her, and she danced. Wild wild lightning sparking through her, she danced, the drums and the crowd's noise screaming in her head. She knew without opening her eyes that the crowd danced with her. *With abandon.* This was what it felt like to be split apart into a million pieces and jammed back together again, electrified, a current running through her. The drums throbbed, the crowd roared, and she heard Sean's cell phone pick up Nina's words, dim against the crashing noise in her own head.

"She's wearing a bad juju bracelet—voodoo, MacGreggor. She can't control it."

"How are you makin' those lights, lass?" Sean asked, and there was trepidation in his voice. She didn't know *what lights*, with her eyes closed; she couldn't open them, didn't understand the heat shimmering inside her.

"It's a trick," another man said. "A fuckin' *trick,* Sean," and Bobbie Faye sensed . . . felt . . . Sean usher Nina out of the helicopter and climb out behind her along with three gunmen who fanned out in front of them, guns aimed into the crowd.

Drums. Rolling, biting, deep, burning. And there she was, flailing around like a deranged, drunk flamingo. Unable to stop. Drums . . . *drums . . . lost in the drums . . .*

"Now, *àlainn,* you've got a choice to make. Sixty seconds. What will it be?"

"Does . . . Nina . . . have . . . the . . . codes?" she bit out, her body bending to the beats.

"You'll lose the second half," Trevor's mother reminded

him, her voice crisp as a knife slicing through a head of lettuce, "if you kill the people in the stands or my son. Take the girl and go."

"Twenty seconds, *àlainn,*" Sean said, and then, apparently, to Trevor's mother, "and thank you, luv, for the extra fifty million. I've got no intention of lettin' people go."

Sean reached out and grasped her arm.

She opened her eyes, saw every one of Sean's men flinch at what they saw there, and she gazed down at his hand circled on her forearm just above the bracelet. With a twist of her wrist, her palm clasped his forearm, the chicken foot bracelet throbbing between them.

She looked into his eyes and saw the insanity there, saw the raging lust fed by mindless power, by revenge and lack of control. He could still blow the bombs—still shoot Trevor—and a pure raw raging inferno swelled from the crowd, rolling over her from all sides, as if she were standing in Hell's front door, and she leaned toward him and said, "*Very* bad juju."

Lightning cracked the night sky, clouds rolling as if the earth itself recoiled from the bad juju of the man standing in front of her, and then it reared back and slammed forward again, spitting rain as lightning and wind whirled around her.

"Got it, Trev," another woman's familiar voice said on the line. It was as if that voice was from another lifetime, a thousand lifetimes ago, and Bobbie Faye only dimly remembered that voice, remembered she was supposed to know what *got it* was about, that it was a part of something important. . . .

Except all she knew, breathed, and understood, was her connection to Sean and the utter *want* in his expression— the greedy abyss of black desire, the determination to blow those stands. She would end it, put an end to the two of them, right where they stood in the middle of that field, end *whatever* she had to end to take him out, and she reached deep, reached into the center of who she was and found herself again, that hard, glittering tenacity, that strength of knowing herself. Confidence. *There you are. Welcome back.*

She grinned. "*I win.*"

"*Now,*" the unknown woman on the line snapped.

"*Go,*" Trevor commanded, and that's when the entire place went black.

Suds noted the second the uplink disconnected from the bomb. Cam was holding a gun on him, which would blow them all to fucking pieces if he pulled the trigger. And for reasons he did not understand, the stadium lights had slammed off, but the lights in this bay remained on.

"The link's down," Suds shouted at Cam above the crowd noise, which had swelled to a roar that rivaled any thundering hurricane Suds had ever heard. "If it comes back up, if the server reroutes it, MacGreggor can pull the trigger on both these bombs instantly. We've got to get them out of here."

"You fucking *built* these bombs?" Cam seethed.

"I never meant them to be used like this. And we don't have time, Cam. You know I've always tried to help Bobbie Faye. You know I helped her mother. And those two—" He pointed to Lori Ann and Stacey. "You know I'm the one who called you when she was driving drunk with the kid. I did not mean this to be used this way. You can shoot me later. Lock me up, blast my head off, I don't care." He choked on the tears. "Let me fix this! We're running out of time. *We've got to get the bombs out of here.*"

He saw Cam battle with the devil's bargain: risk that Suds would pull the trigger on the bombs himself or pull Suds out of there—with no other bomb tech nearby—and risk the whole place going up.

Cam glanced over at Stacey, whose big blue eyes stared at Cam's gun, and Lori Ann, who shook violently. He holstered his gun and eased open the door to the truck, so very carefully, and cautioned, "Move very very soft, Lori Ann."

He took Stacey in his arms. Then he looked back at Suds and said, "I will follow you to Hell if this thing blows. The people I love are out there."

Suds nodded and Cam ushered Stacey and Lori Ann out to the perimeter as Suds rushed to dismantle the bomb on the generator. He could see the lights flickering on the miniature computer board he had attached. It was searching for a new signal.

"Yeah? Bite me."

—the Universe

Thirty

In the dark, Trevor heard the spit of a round from the sniper's rifle perforate the platform where he'd been standing a half a second ago: he'd flipped off it as soon as he knew Izzy had blocked MacGreggor's signal to the bomb. Then he heard two echoing shots and two cries of anguish from the helicopter.

Riles said, "Sniper and spotter down, LT," and Trevor didn't bother to glance up to the helicopter in front of him. He knew Riles was already zeroing in on the next problem—the men surrounding MacGreggor and Bobbie Faye. He had thought he might have to put an infrared homing signal on her somehow, for when the lights were out, to make sure he could find her.

But she fucking *glowed*. Sparks were flying off her as if she were a multi-thousand-dollar fireworks display.

He had no clue how she was creating the sparks, or when she'd planned them. He knew she had on nothing underneath that borrowed underwear and he also knew for a fact that she had not been fitted with some multi-thousand-dollar fireworks display.

Trevor sprinted toward her, snagging a SIG from one of his men. As he landed on the field, even in the mostly dark, with the nearly full moon melting out of the clouds, he could see her, see her and MacGreggor each with a grasp on the other's forearm, and she stood there, staring at her enemy. *MacGreggor had a hand on her*. Was a breath away from pulling her into that helicopter, and she stood there. Gazing at him.

Not moving.

Scaring the living hell out of Trevor.

"Someone's trying to reroute the signal," Izzy said in his ear. "They've got to have a laptop there somewhere. I'm countering, but I'm warning you—"

Nina, with her hands cuffed in front of her, took down one man; Trevor didn't blink when she broke the man's neck and laid him out on the ground, turning into the next one coming at her, who suddenly stopped, then arced backward, dead.

"That's two she owes me," Riles said as Nina ducked and dodged a third man.

Lightning flashed again, and on some level, Trevor knew it was starting to rain, but he didn't see anything except Bobbie Faye, standing between him and MacGreggor, and he didn't have a shot. She was standing there with that sono-fabitch's hand on her and Trevor didn't have a shot.

"No shot here," Riles said.

"Sean, *no!*" Lonan shouted.

Ian hit the send button on the laptop. He was rerouting the signal, because Lonan would be damned if they were stopping the bombs—when Lonan saw Sean move toward the woman. Moving like he was fucking *mesmerized* by whatever the fuck she was out there doing, and Lonan knew, then, that he had to save Sean.

Save him from himself. Save him from whatever spell the woman had cast on him, whatever had made him come back for her. And it couldn't just be revenge, he was too wrapped up, too . . . insane.

Lonan stood in the helo, his gun raised and aimed at the girl, and she was as good as dead. He had one heartbeat where he wondered if he'd get more satisfaction shooting her in the arms or legs first, to watch her hurt before he watched her die, and that one heartbeat said *die*, because the Fed was coming up behind her. The Fed, who was focused on Sean and not him, who couldn't have seen him standing in the dark helicopter with the field lights off, who couldn't have seen his gun.

A bullet struck Lonan square in the chest, knocking him back against the wall and the world went blank.

It took Trevor a million years to close the gap between them, coming up behind her as the lightning flashed again and his heart fell through the ground because *she kissed Mac-Greggor.*

Kissed him. Hard.

The third helicopter landed nearby and men flowed from it and Riles's sniper rifle cracked and men crumpled on the rain-soaked field, but she could only focus on Sean.

She'd seen the small remote in his left hand. She'd seen it and knew what it was. Power surged from the crowd, and she felt the fire . . . flames licking around her, a column of fire, burning, and knew, *knew,* what she had to do.

And she kissed him.

Lightning sizzled and thunder clobbered the sky, rolling in with the drums. Rain ran down her body as the burning current flowed from her and into him. All of it. It seared him, an electrical jolt he couldn't break free of; she felt his breath tighten, his body jerk, as the current burned. His eyes were open, shocked, and she knew the moment he dropped the remote, the blazing current making him forget entirely where he was, forget that Trevor was coming up behind her like the hand of God, forget that he'd lost, just now, he'd completely lost. She stepped back from him; his hands were raised, about to embrace her, and there was a moment, just one second, when he looked at her, where the flames shimmying around her reflected in his amber eyes and his brows went up in surprise.

"*Àlainn* this, *you asshole,*" she said, and she plowed the heel of her right hand into his chest. Power flowed through her, through her arm, down her wrist, and he rocked back, feet flying up off the ground as if a sledgehammer had swung and caught him. As he fell away from her, his hand flailed out and he grabbed at her, grabbed for purchase. His fingers snagged the chicken foot and yanked.

And as it ripped free, the crowd surged, the drums rolled, Trevor clasped her shoulder, and the world fell away, *bam*, a rolling iridescent, multicolored . . . *pulse* . . . emanating outward from Sean as he fell backward. The pulse rippled out, knocking everyone down on the field, knocking back everyone in their seats, like some sort of nuclear bomb and they were ground zero.

Silence thudding against her skin.

Silence as loud as the drums had been. Aching, deafening, slippery.

She could only focus on Sean, who was lying there, twitching. She didn't see it until it moved in her periphery: the rain glinting silver, slicing through the moonlight, and there in a flash of lightning was a gun rising up out of the helicopter. The man standing behind it was one of the "ambulance" drivers and he was saying something about this being for Aiden. The gun moved up and up and Trevor fired. Fired and fired again, and faster than she could count, he'd loaded two bullets into the guy and one in the guy with the laptop next to him. Trevor spun, tucking her under his arm, spinning her to his chest, his arm a band of steel, holding her up while the whole world tilted. Trevor spun again, firing like the wrath of God as he shot two more men who were rising up from the other helicopter to aim at them, and then rain crashed and lightning stabbed the dark and there was Sean, trying to sit up. His body smoked as he reached for the fallen remote, his fingers curling around it there in the wet grass, and without missing a beat, Trevor pressed her face to his chest, his hand shielding her eyes as *bam* he ended the demon who'd have killed them all.

Cam rode one of the police Harleys, lights and sirens, moving people out of the way on Skip Bertman Drive, which T'd into River Road. Suds followed in Marcel's truck, both bombs lying on the backseat.

They'd worked fast and gotten them out of the stadium.

Cam had radioed Trevor, but it wasn't clear to him what the hell was going on back there.

All Cam knew was that right now he had to get these bombs away from the stadium. If that signal came back up, they'd blow.

He flashed back to Suds telling him about his wife. His loss. Losing his mind.

Cam could understand that loss.

He focused on the task at hand. They were lucky in that most of the road had been kept clear for the mass exodus that would happen after the game was over. They were freaking unlucky in that there was nowhere to take the truck except down River Road. To the right—houses and then downtown. To the left, lots of cars and then fields. Crossing some of those fields and buried beneath the road were oil and gas pipelines headed out to the Mississippi River. And directly in front of him, the levee. An explosion there would destroy the levee and flood . . . and oh fucking hell, he couldn't think about it. It was too damned many people.

Instead, the image of Bobbie Faye lying in the hammock, out behind his house, came to mind unbidden. She was napping, curled up against him as he studied for an exam, the sunlight filtering through her hair as he gently rocked them back and forth with one foot, his forgotten textbook on the ground as he held her, just watching the way the light played across her cheek. Smiling to himself because even the Tasmanian Devil looks peaceful in sleep, and so, then, did she.

He hoped like hell his luck would hold. Because if that truck went, he was going to go with it.

"Wow," the drunk behind Ce Ce said. "That was, like, the best halftime show, ever!".

Ce Ce collapsed in her seat, exhausted, her body wracked with the pain she'd been channeling. Monique put her chubby arm around Ce Ce and hugged her.

"I saw what potion you used," Monique said, low. "That was the demon one."

"Don't be silly."

"Uh-huh. You didn't tell Bobbie Faye she was spitting into the anti-demon one, but I know." She waggled her red brows at Ce Ce. "How many did you get?"

"I'm not sure," Ce Ce said.

"Think you got any zombies?"

"I didn't want to risk it. Do you realize how many politicians come to the game?"

"Oh. Right. That'd have been a lot of bodies to explain."

"Exactly."

"Sanitize," Nina said, standing at Bobbie Faye's shoulder, having somehow gotten her hands out of the cuffs. "Trevor. *Now.*"

He opened his eyes—his face had been buried in Bobbie Faye's hair, and he was holding her so tightly, he wasn't sure who it was for—her, or him.

"It's raining," Nina reminded him, and he just then realized he was drenched. "Let's use it."

He didn't want dead bodies on the field, little kids seeing the blood and people he'd killed. Nina wasn't on a radio and so dispatch had not heard her—and he nodded. "Riles."

"Got it," Riles said, coming up on them.

They had maybe thirty seconds before the crowd realized something was infinitely wrong, and maybe sixty seconds before the press pushed their way onto the field. Trevor knew they were about to break six billion different laws, but the bottom line was, he was going to be responsible. He knew neither SWAT nor the state police nor LSU wanted to explain that there had been a massive gunfight in the middle of the field, that the children in those stands had stood right above a bomb, and *that they had not evacuated anyone.* Luckily, the klieg lights were still off and it was still softly raining.

He started to tell Bobbie Faye to go to the sideline, that she didn't need to see this, but one glance at her hardened expression, daring him to not trust her, to exclude her, and he nodded again.

"We're gonna have to amend our vows," she said, as she

grabbed MacGreggor's feet. "I'm beginning to sense that 'moving dead bodies' needs to be right up there with the whole 'love and honor' part."

He should have protected her from this.

"He was going to kill a lot of people," she said, understanding him as if he'd said it out loud. "If he'd lived, he'd have found a way to keep killing, out of revenge." She helped him lift MacGreggor into the helicopter. "We could not let him do that."

Then again, maybe he wasn't giving her enough credit.

Maybe he never had.

And it hit him, what a freaking fool he'd been not to trust her.

"Sixty seconds," he said, as Riles and Nina lifted one of the bodies and moved it into the door of the nearest helicopter. Trevor's other men had already begun lifting bodies behind him.

Forty-five seconds, and every body was accounted for and laid in a helicopter. Someone had instructed the band to start the LSU fight song and the crowd roared back to life as the stadium lights came back on. Nina piloted one helicopter, Riles another. He and Bobbie Faye climbed into the third, and they no sooner had lifted out of the stadium when an explosion blasted from about two miles away, a fireball rolling into the sky, the concussion rocking against them.

She couldn't breathe. Bobbie Faye watched out of the helicopter's front window and flames rolled up and out, a truck in the center of it, debris all around, and all she could think of was *Cam*. He'd radioed that he and Suds were getting the bombs out of the stadium.

The copter pivoted and raced toward the wreckage and as they got closer, all she could see was how very very bad it was, and she thought, *no, not Cam.* Her heart thudded and all sound ceased and her hand splayed against her window, and she wasn't sure if she was trying to reach out, or trying to push it away. All she could think was *Cam*.

Thirty-one

"Madame?" Henry asked Andrea, and she waved him away.

"Isabella," she said into her cell phone, "you cut off my signal."

"You were finished, Mother," her daughter said. "Anything else, and you'd have done harm."

Andrea thought through the implications. Then asked, "So what would you have done if Claire hadn't conveniently seen that broadcast at that moment?"

"What makes you think I didn't call her husband and suggest he change channels, Mother?"

"You two are clever," Andrea chuckled, "I'll give you that. I suppose you couldn't help that, given the genetics. But your sisters stand with me, Isabella, and your brother wants nothing to do with the company. You'll regret favoring him. But then, you always had a soft spot for him."

Isabella laughed, and Andrea frowned. Isabella rarely laughed. Like her brother.

"Mother, I think you sometimes forget I am your daughter. And I'll warn you now, which you will ignore, I know. Don't go after his fiancée. Not after what you did last time."

"Or what? He won't forgive me? I did him a favor last time and he has admitted that. The two of you, darling, will one day learn that I know what I'm doing."

There was a long silence, and then softly, so very softly,

Isabella said, "Mother, if you go after her, whether or not he forgives you will be the very least of your concerns."

Trevor set the helicopter down south of the burning debris, out of the path of the ambulances he'd called. She beat him out of the cabin, but only because he had to shut it down. And she ran, her heart in her throat, screams trapped in her chest, because she could see Cam lying in a field, twisted and unmoving, the carcass of the Harley a mangled heap not far away.

The closer she got, the more blood she saw.

Cam came to, blinking wetness out of his face, feeling submerged in more wetness. He was drowning. Or bleeding to death.

Trevor leaned over him from one side, Bobbie Faye on the other, and she said, "Cam? Cam? Fucking answer me or I'm going to beat the living hell out of you!"

"What the—" And then he remembered: Suds pulling off the road suddenly, plunging the truck through a fence and into a wide open field. Cam had stopped and turned his bike to go back when the whole thing went up in a rolling explosion. Suds had plunged into a field that didn't have a pipeline running through it, which had probably saved Cam's life. "Oh, *fuck*," he said, trying to sit up.

"Hold on, Moreau," Trevor said through gritted teeth, and that's when Cam realized the man had no shirt on and was, instead, ripping it.

"I'm okay," Cam said as Bobbie Faye grabbed his hand, and he reached for her and, God, she never looked so . . . terrible. "Why in the hell are you in your underwear?"

"She did a striptease in the middle of the field," Trevor said, turning a piece of his shirt and tying it in place on Cam's thigh, stanching a bleeder, and that's when the pain shot through him and he sat up, realizing he was lying on the ground, rain pelting down. He smelled like mud and cut grass and rotting leaves and coppery blood, and the light from the burning truck cast a glow on both Trevor and Bobbie Faye's faces.

"It was *not* a striptease," she griped.

"Then she danced the chicken dance," Trevor continued, overlapping her.

"Okay, that's just mean."

Cam looked down at his leg—still there, thank God, but both legs were bleeding from shrapnel cuts. Trevor had clearly been working on him for a couple of minutes. He glanced past them and saw a helicopter—and then closer, the wrecked bike. Cam could hear the ambulance sirens above the blaze of the truck. They all knew Suds was dead. Cam would have to tell them more. Later.

"A chicken dance," Cam said, glancing over her. "Is that as bad as I think that was?"

"Worse," Trevor said.

"It wasn't that bad."

"Chickens everywhere are gonna sue."

The ambulance approached, and they could see it weaving past the cop cars blocking River Road. As Bobbie Faye watched, more than a little stunned, Trevor offered a hand to help Cam up and, to her surprise, Cam took it and stood, dizzy for a second. When he swayed, she caught his other side and he wrapped his arm around her shoulders, leaning on her.

Trevor backed away, dropping his hands to his hips, giving her one of those unreadable gazes she hated.

The paramedics ran up, and as they helped Cam, Trevor said, "You need to go to the hospital with Cam."

"But I'm not hurt," she started, and then she and Trevor locked gazes, then he nodded toward the helicopter.

"I'm going to be a while."

She looked back at the helicopter. "Oh."

She could tell Cam was doing some quick calculations. He looked toward the stadium, where he heard cheers of the ballgame back in play . . . which meant no dead bad guys on the field . . . then glancing from her to Trevor standing there, which meant no bad guys running around. His gaze settled a moment on the helicopter, then on Trevor. "Is that as bad as I think that is?"

Trevor shrugged. "It's not as bad as the chicken dance."

And Trevor jogged away, without a touch, a hug, or a kiss good-bye.

"He stopped the signal *how*?" Cam asked as they rode in the ambulance, its shocks absorbing the bumps along the pot-holed asphalt road.

Bobbie Faye closed her eyes, trying to ignore Cam's wounds, which the paramedic was now checking, ignoring the bleeding, ignoring the smell of antiseptic and sweat and swallowing down the fear.

"His sister, Izzy," she said, trying to focus, "is the head of R&D at their telecom company. She'd developed a tracking program, something that they are using to try to pinpoint unregistered cell phones based on their signal."

"Like triangulation," Cam said, "where a signal can be isolated inside of an area bordered by three cell towers."

"Yeah, only faster, like caller ID, even if the signal is being bounced through a filtering device from towers all over the world. Apparently, in Nerd World, Izzy can trace a call from the end destination back to the origin, if she knows what the destination is going to be and when it's about to happen. Izzy helped Trevor set up his mother—who apparently doesn't mind dropping fifty million to get what she wants." She ignored Cam's scowl. "When their mother got the bank account number and repeated it, Izzy's software piggybacked onto her mother's signal, riding the transfer in to Sean's bank account and from there back to Sean's signal as he logged in to that account long enough to confirm the money was there and transfer it. She—"

"Traced it back to his computer."

"And was able to lock out that specific ISP footprint."

The medic finished checking Cam's cuts. "You're gonna need stitches."

But Cam wasn't focused on his cuts, or the pain. He was

completely focused on her, though he was muddy, bloody, and had dark circles under his eyes. "Let me get this straight—Trevor made sure his own mother made that call to Sean?"

"Yeah. Well, I think so. I didn't hear all of it, but he set it up while you were talking to my dad. I heard him tell Izzy to make the call, and Izzy apparently said she wasn't nearly a good enough actor, and that she couldn't be acting with Sean and trying to trace the call at the same time."

"So if Trevor's mom had not called?"

"I think he had someone else standing by, but I don't know if they could have moved the money as fast. He knew she'd drop the cash, even while he was telling her not to. Probably *especially* since he was telling her not to."

"So Cormier just double-crossed his own mother." She looked away from his *you are so screwed if you trust this guy* expression. "Did you know all this as it was happening?"

"Um. Not all of it, no. I knew why he'd called Izzy. And what he needed the signal for. I just wasn't quite sure what they'd planned."

"So the money is really in Sean's account?"

Yeah, that part made her sick. Not just that his mother had lost it, but because of those final words to Sean, that of course he could keep "the girl." It wasn't everybody's future mother-in-law who made no bones about preferring their future daughter-in-law dead.

Well, at least Bobbie Faye felt special.

Bobbie Faye wore scrubs that a nurse was kind enough to find for her, and was clean from grabbing a quick shower in the nurses' ward room, but she was too numb to think straight now; her brain was reeling with the events of the last twenty-four hours. She sat curled in the world's most uncomfortable chair. Why, exactly, did hospitals think they had to make sure you were in pain in a waiting room? Was it to drum up the extra business? Keep people from loitering and from all of the frolicking good parties going on in there?

She was waiting on the doctors to finish with Cam's stitches. They'd kicked her out of the room when they realized she wasn't family. Or his fiancée.

When she glanced up, she realized Old Man Landry stood at the arched entrance to the little room. They stared at each other for several long, mean minutes.

She couldn't stand it any longer. "Thank you for helping find the bombs."

He nodded. She didn't mention the tiara. He was never going to help her find it, even if all she wanted it for was because it was her mom's. He was convinced she would just do more harm searching for it—or getting it—and once he'd made up his steel-trap mind, she might as well chew off a limb as try to open it.

"I saw the dance," he said, looking away from her to the far wall, studying it for a century. Then, finally, "It must be from your mom's side."

"What? The Crazy? I think your side had enough of that to share."

A smile twitched for the briefest of a second, and then was gone again. "I meant the goodness, Bobbie Faye. Necia had that. People loved her. I'm glad you take after her, *chère*."

She gaped. In all her life, he'd never said something nice. And just like that, he spun and left, and there was a hole in her heart as big as the space where he'd stood.

Later, Lori Ann sat next to her in the little waiting room alcove while Stacey played hopscotch across the shiny linoleum tiles of the hospital floor. Bobbie Faye watched Lori Ann through her own half-closed lids, and her sister kept wiping tears from her face, her arms crossed stubbornly, but she didn't want to talk about it. That she even wanted to sit by Bobbie Faye spoke of her anxiety, wanting her sister for comfort. Bobbie Faye remembered the many times Lori Ann had vehemently insisted that she did not need a big sister to boss her around. Until she did.

But Bobbie Faye didn't know how to fix this one. She didn't know how to reassure Lori Ann that Stacey was okay—that ultimately, she wasn't going to be psychologically scarred from the event. The fact that the kid had just bamboozled another handful of candy out of one of the nurses ought to be a big enough indicator, but Lori Ann still shook.

It was learning about Suds that had her crying.

"Are you sure?" she'd asked Bobbie Faye three times.

"Yes. Cam told me on the way here."

"I can't believe it. I really can't."

And Bobbie Faye knew the feeling—she couldn't either. Apparently Suds had left behind evidence—he'd never intended to live through the bombings. He just hadn't realized he would be double-crossed and the bombs would end up where they could hurt so many people. At least, that's what he said to Cam.

"I don't really remember meeting Chloë," Lori Ann said.

"I think you were twelve when she died. And we were dealing with mom's cancer, so I don't think we saw her much—just Suds. But he loved her deeply. He was not the same for a long time after. Very angry, just . . . a very different person."

"He always seemed okay. Of course, I was drinking all the time, so what do I know?"

Bobbie Faye cut her eyes to her sister—she wasn't saying that bitterly. Just matter-of-fact. "I think you saw what he wanted everyone to see, once he got past the initial shock. I think he wanted to be okay. He found a way of going through the motions."

But even as she said it, Bobbie Faye couldn't quite wrap her mind around it.

Marcel rounded the corner and froze, seeing Bobbie Faye.

"Aw, *chère*," he said to Bobbie Faye, "I don' know how to tell you how sorry I am."

He looked positively . . . scared . . . that she was going to come up off that chair and beat the crap out of him for somehow driving the truck for LSU. But Sean had planted that truck, not Marcel.

"I've been making calls," he said, "trying to backtrack

just how exactly I got the gig to paint the truck and drive Mike around the stadium. It was a big win for my new business. I shoulda known it was too good to be true."

"It's not your fault, Marcel. I know you wouldn't hurt either of them," she said, nodding to her sister and her niece. Partly, she knew, because he valued his life and would not want her aimed at him.

And partly, if she had to be honest, because she could see how much he cared about them. She'd wanted that for Lori Ann. It wasn't who she'd have chosen, but if Lori Ann was happy, that's really all that mattered, wasn't it?

Lori Ann slipped her hand into Bobbie Faye's, lacing their fingers together. Bobbie Faye stared at their intertwined hands and it was like seeing double—it was the one physical trait of their mom's that they shared, and her eyes blurred a bit as she squeezed back the tears.

"Marcel," Lori Ann said, "could you take Stacey to . . . uh . . . go get something to eat? Or drink?"

Marcel looked between the two of them and nodded and called Stacey, who hopscotched happily over to him and took his hand with the clear-eyed joy of a child who didn't know that she was supposed to be all screwed up.

They sat for a moment in silence and Bobbie Faye held her breath. Lori Ann sitting beside her because she wanted to hear about Suds was one thing, but Lori Ann willingly talking to her was entirely another. Was Lori Ann pregnant again? Had she been drinking? Both? Whatever this was, it was going to be bad, given how her sister's hand trembled.

"So," Lori Ann said, wiping her eyes, "you know that night?"

Bobbie Faye frowned at her sister, her brows knit together. Puzzled. "Tonight?"

"No," Lori Ann said, her voice cracking. "*That* night."

Oh. The night Cam had arrested her. The night she'd point-blank told Cam a few hours earlier that she'd handle it, she'd make sure Lori Ann got into treatment. The night he'd explicitly ignored her and arrested Lori Ann anyway. The night their lives had changed, the beginning of the end.

"I'm familiar," she said. Dust bowls should be as dry.

"When Cam arrested me—"

"Lori Ann, no," Cam's voice said from the open-arch entrance to the sitting area.

Bobbie Faye snapped her focus to his face, the anguish there as he leaned on crutches, and she was pretty sure it wasn't just the physical pain she read. She turned back to her sister, her scalp tingling as she noted Lori Ann's matching anguish.

"He didn't tell you everything."

"It doesn't matter, Lori Ann," Cam said. "Leave her alone, she's had a rough night."

Bobbie Faye narrowed her gaze at Cam. "Yeah, like that's gonna work." Then she focused back on Lori Ann. "And?"

Cam hobbled closer, slowly lowering himself to a coffee table in front of Bobbie Faye as Lori Ann's anguished expression got as deep as the sea.

"Bobbie Faye," Cam said, "let this one go. I'm asking you, please."

Exhaustion and despair creased his face. Bobbie Faye turned from him to Lori Ann, and her heart lurched. What weren't they telling her? Then she looked back at Cam, and the fatigue of his arms, his shoulders, his eyes begging her to let it go. There was so much she could not give him, but she could give him this privacy. She nodded.

"Cam stopped me from driving drunk," Lori Ann blurted out. Bobbie Faye was about to toss off a *duh*, when her sister continued, "with Stacey in the car with me."

Bobbie Faye went completely cold. The police report had said Lori Ann was alone. That Cam had seen her swerving and had pulled her over.

"She was in the car with me," Lori Ann said, wiping her eyes with her other hand, never letting go of Bobbie Faye's, "and I was flying. Really flying—I don't know how fast I was going."

"Ninety-seven," Cam said when Bobbie Faye looked at him.

"The ticket didn't say anything about ninety-fucking-*seven*," Bobbie Faye said.

"Or about Stacey being in the car," Lori Ann reminded her. "I don't know how I missed the eighteen-wheeler, but I did. If Cam hadn't stopped me, I'd have probably flattened the car before the night was over. I was still drinking."

In the car. She'd been drinking *in* the car. With Stacey. And speeding. Bobbie Faye held Cam's gaze and started understanding a lot more. He had to have gotten Stacey out of that car and off that site—she'd *thought* it was odd that Stacey had been spending the night with his mom that night because she could have sworn that Lori Ann had said no to the offer. But Stacey had turned up there and Bobbie Faye had assumed Lori Ann had changed her mind.

Which meant Cam had arranged it, all from the side of the road.

"Why didn't you tell me?" she asked him. *Oh, how different their lives would have been.*

"I asked him not to," Lori Ann said. "I begged him, Bobbie Faye. I knew I'd lose Stacey. For good. And I deserved it, but I wanted to get cleaned up. I wanted a chance, and I knew I'd lose her."

"But *you* didn't tell me," she said again, pinning Cam with a glare. "As long as we've known each other, you knew that wasn't the sort of thing you should keep from me."

"I knew how you'd react," he said. "Which was astonishingly close to how you *did* react."

Because she'd believed he'd arrested her sister for spite. To prove that he, as the big bad cop, knew best. That his way was the only way anything could be done. She glared at him, and his glare softened into one of deep regret.

"I promised her, Bobbie Faye. I couldn't go back on that."

She turned to Lori Ann, who was frowning at the two of them. "So why are you telling me now?" She was pretty sure she knew, though.

"Because y'all broke up because of me, and you should know . . . you should know what a coward I was and that I begged him not to tell you. I wanted you to know so you could forgive him. And maybe have a chance together."

Bobbie Faye closed her eyes, breathing evenly, thinking carefully, remembering all of the things they'd said to each other over the year after that arrest. She wasn't entirely sure how long they sat like that, the three of them in the waiting room, but she knew, suddenly, that Trevor was at the entrance. It wasn't just Lori Ann's intake of breath or Cam's subtle stiffening, but the way her body hummed, reaching out for him. Connecting.

She opened her eyes and looked at him, leaning there against the entrance archway, waiting for her. Patient. Determined, but patient. There was a world of promise in a man like that, a man who wouldn't quit on them. On her. Who wouldn't let disagreements stop him.

She looked back at Cam, sitting across from her, bitter ache etched into his face. She wanted to reassure him, somehow, but she couldn't. Because the simple fact was, both men had lied to her.

Or, rather, omitted the truth.

Trevor, because he was trying to make sure she had the opportunity to be herself—her true self—for them to be together, and Cam because he was afraid of that same true self. And maybe it wasn't even that simple but her heart understood it.

More than that, she realized, she'd been able to fight with Cam and walk away. She'd already been able to imagine a life without Cam.

She couldn't imagine a life without Trevor. Didn't want to ever contemplate it, couldn't breathe with even the flicker of the possibility. She met her fiancé's gaze and wondered if he knew. She held her heart there for him to see and he nodded. Warmth from his eyes, warmth from his heart, wrapped themselves around her and he hadn't even moved an inch from where he leaned against the doorframe. She wasn't quite sure how he managed that.

She turned to Lori Ann, at the apprehension sparking off her as Bobbie Faye reached for her little sister, hugging her. "No, kiddo, we did not break up because of you. We broke up because of us, so don't take that on yourself."

She cocked her head and appraised her sister. Really *looked* at her. Lori Ann looked good. Healthy. A little heart-sick right then, but good.

"I'm proud of you," she told her and Lori Ann's eyes widened when she understood what Bobbie Faye had said, and she beamed as Cam stood up on his crutches.

Bobbie Faye stood, too, putting a hand on his arm to stop him from leaving. "I don't know if I ever thanked you for stopping Lori Ann that night." When he gave her an *are you kidding me*? look, she said, "I'll take that as a 'no.' But thank you."

He held her gaze a long, long moment, his own expression becoming unreadable, and she knew he was hurting in a way she couldn't reach. Shouldn't reach. Because she was only making it worse.

Then she looked over to Trevor, who was still waiting. "I'm ready to go home now," she told him, and she saw the understanding in his eyes, saw him grasp what she was telling him, though his expression remained quiet, calm.

"Bobbie Faye," Lori Ann said, confused, "your house blew up. Where's home?"

She hadn't taken her eyes off her fiancé, and when she said, "Doesn't matter," he nodded.

Trevor held her gaze and she knew he understood she was drawing that line. That he deserved that, he deserved her thinking of *him*, first.

Cam turned to leave and paused. He looked at Trevor, who met his gaze.

"I'm not stopping," he said.

"Neither am I."

"You wouldn't deserve her if you did."

Trevor nodded and Cam left, easing out on his crutches and then disappeared down the hospital hallway.

Marcel gathered up Lori Ann and Stacey and after they left, Trevor took Bobbie Faye's hand and they walked toward a back exit.

"Where are Riles and Nina?"

"Still being debriefed."

She and Nina had a lot to talk about. A lot of betrayal, a lot of years of double meanings to layers and layers of meanings and it made Bobbie Faye's head spin just trying to figure out the webbed tangles of their friendship.

She and Trevor moved together in synch through the hospital hallway, hand in hand, almost waltzing as they spun and dodged crash carts and EKG machines, trolleys of bandages and busy patients complaining loudly on their cell phones.

"Is Riles still griping that he didn't get to shoot me?"

"That was never going to happen."

"It was a part of the plan." He cut her a look like she was delusional. "Well, it was. If I couldn't get Sean to come out of that helicopter, Riles was going to shoot me—hopefully not something major—and I'd fall and then Sean or his men would—oh, hush," she said as he steadily cursed under his breath. "It could've worked. Riles seemed pretty bummed about me veering from the plan."

"There was no way on this planet I was letting anyone shoot at you. I'd have to be dead first. And even then, Riles would know to pull you out of any situation."

"You know Riles and I don't exactly get along, right?"

He grinned, and twirled her so that she was out of the way of a young intern barreling down the hall, her nose in a chart. "Actually, you get along with Riles better than most people. Most people try to kill him by the second day."

"Geez, *now* you tell me. I feel like I missed an opportunity here."

"Oh, I'm sure there'll be more. He's going to be my best man."

"Now that's just peachy. Does Riles have the same wedding handbook I have? Because in the *official* 'don't torture the bride' wedding handbook, the best man is not supposed to kidnap the groom to 'save him'—"

"He is *not* going to kidnap me."

"Or put one of those 'exploding altars' in the church—"

"He is not going to put in an exploding altar."

"Or have a team of psychiatrists standing by—"

"He is *not* . . ." he tucked her into him and kissed her as he danced her through automatic doors that swooshed open, "going to do *anything* to stop this wedding."

"Hey, he made a list, is all I'm saying."

"He made a list?"

"Color-coded." Then when Trevor arched an eyebrow, she said, "With footnotes. There may have even been pie charts."

"I'll have a talk with him. He'll behave." They passed the nurses' station, walking through a bank of patient rooms. "Or I'll sic Nina on him," he mused.

"He's afraid of Nina?"

"Most everyone in the black ops world is afraid of Nina, though she's only known by a code name."

"Really?" *Huh.* Now *that* could be handy.

"Most people don't ever get the chance to see her like you do. It's one of the reasons she needs you so much."

She felt the balm of that statement wash over her, a gift so simple, so needed, that she had to look down at the floor. Her vision blurred and she held onto his hand so he could guide her around carts and wheelchairs and random equipment lining the hospital corridor.

Then a thought suddenly grabbed her. "Hey, wait—why aren't you still there being debriefed?"

"Well, technically, I no longer work for the FBI. They're talking to my lawyers."

She stopped, her heart plummeting so quickly it hit her toes and bounced. "What?"

He looked around them, saw an empty patient room and pulled her inside, closing the door with a soft shush, and then he tugged the privacy curtain across the little metal window embedded in the door. Trevor cupped her face in his hands, his thumbs stroking along her cheeks, lingering on her lips. "I was going to tell you when we got somewhere private." He searched her eyes for anger, but she knew he saw, instead, her shock and concern. "It's okay. Someone has to be the fall guy for that disaster."

"What?" she asked again, barely coherent.

"It was a mess, the botched undercover sting, losing

Alex—who, if he has any sense at all, is halfway around the world right now." His hands went to her shoulders, his fingers playing in her hair, and he sighed. "And killing everyone . . ." His gaze drifted far away, past the hallway, past the buildings, and she clutched at his waist. He came back to her then. "It wasn't the right thing to do. Nor was moving the bodies. And technically, as far as anyone knows, we were airlifting those guys out for immediate medical attention, so we, again, technically, did not destroy a crime scene. But officially, someone has to scream, and officially, someone has to take the hit."

"But it doesn't have to be you!"

"Yes, it does, Sundance. It was my family they were after." He meant her. She was it. "And don't you dare feel responsible."

"Yeah," she interrupted him, "in a world of Top Ten Bullshit Things to Say, that just hit number one."

"This is on me," he said, slapping a palm into his chest. "*Me.* I could've wounded them instead of taking them out, and I knew it. But I wasn't giving MacGreggor another chance at hurting you or anyone else. I'd do it all over again."

They regarded each other and she said, very quietly, "Trevor, nothing, ever, is *just* on you. *Not ever again.* We're a team."

And she saw how hard that hit him, how much he needed her, needed to hear that. His eyes softened and he cupped her chin, his thumb running over her lips, unable for a moment to speak.

"What will happen?"

"Lots of posturing. It'll get ugly. But I can handle it."

"*We.*"

"*We* can handle it. And the thing with my mother—and really, the rest of them," he continued after kissing her gently, "is going to get *very* ugly."

"Trevor, I just danced the chicken dance in my underwear in front of the Universe. I think I can handle 'very ugly'—don't you?"

"Yes," he said, hugging her to his chest, his face buried in her hair, his voice choked. "Thank God, *yes*."

His phone rang and he frowned, then pulled it from his pocket, checking the caller ID and showing her.

"Ce Ce?" she said, answering it as he ran both hands down her waist and then up and under her shirt. Discovering (as if he didn't know) that she'd ditched the stupid wet sports bra. "What's wrong?" She listened for a second and then said, "No. Absolutely not. I'll call you later."

He paused from his exploring and she said, "She had a *great* idea." And Sarcasm said, *hi, I've* missed *you*. "She thought all of the bridesmaids should wear acorn head-dresses."

"Acorns?"

"I don't know, some sort of symbol of fertility or something."

His thumbs circled the underside of her breasts as he gazed at her and she felt her entire body say *home*. She leaned into him a little.

"Fertility's not a bad thing," he said, watching her carefully.

"*Practicing* it is not a bad thing," she agreed. "Little proofs of fertility can wait a while."

"I like the practicing part," he said, his thumbs now smoothing over her breasts, circling and teasing, rasping over her nipples and what were they saying? "Also," he added, bending to kiss her neck as he slid one hand down inside the loose elastic of the scrubs she wore, and between nibbles he said, "I am amazed you're not yelling at me. For not talking to you. About my past." His hand dipped between her legs, and his other captured the back of her neck, holding her to him, his lips against hers. "I deserve it."

"Um," she said, after a long while, trying to remember what she was supposed to be doing. Oh. Yeah. Answering. "Yeah. You do. Can we table the yelling for later?"

He tasted her along her jaw and then down her neck, whipping off her shirt, and then his whiskers scratched against her breast, his hot mouth closing around a nipple and she arched into him.

"Tabling. Duly noted," he said between kisses. The things he knew how to do with his hands. "But just so you know, I'm not going to do that again," he murmured, and nipped at her because she'd whimpered when his mouth had paused long enough to talk. Then he moved to the other breast and then down and as he kissed her scars, kissed the curve of her hip, he added, "Ever, Sundance."

"What?" she asked, regretting it because it would mean he'd have to stop that magic with his tongue and . . . oh . . . oh . . . and then from far away, he answered.

"Let anything come between us."

She caught his gaze in her own as he stood, and it felt like an oath. A vow. And she nodded, tears dampening her cheeks.

"Nothing," she agreed.

"Good to know." He grinned against her lips, his fingers working magic and her own hands undoing his jeans, sliding in and around and cupping him. Then she pushed at his shirt—and realized it was a clean one, no telling where he'd gotten it—but she didn't care, just that her hands were on him. She hummed with that power she'd felt on the field, felt that surge of electrical current heating up her body. And it didn't matter that they were in a hospital room, didn't matter that they had no specific address to go to. All that mattered was this, him, and then their clothes were on the floor and he lifted her, her legs going around his waist, and she felt pure joy breaking through the darkness inside her heart, the place where she'd been afraid, too long afraid, and before he kissed her again, she saw that same joy in his eyes, that same benediction. And as he slid into her, her entire body shouted *home home home home home.*

Acknowledgments

There are so many people who make a book possible, and not nearly enough words to thank them. I would like to mention a specific few who were exceptional help for the novel you hold here. If there are mistakes in this book, it is certainly not for the lack of the people listed below trying their dead level best to keep me from making them.

A very deep, heartfelt thanks to:

Kim Whalen, my most amazing agent. You've been a rock and you've kept me laughing throughout these books and you're the best.

Nichole Argyres, my extraordinary editor, who believed in Bobbie Faye from the very beginning and helped me make the dream come true.

Matthew Shear, Anne Marie Tallberg, John Karle, Joe Goldschein, Kylah McNeill, Ed Chapman, and everyone in the art department who made these covers rock (I love them)—thank you all. It's been one of my greatest pleasures to be a writer with St. Martin's Press.

Colonel Mike Edmonson for allowing me such great access to your troopers as I researched this book.

Captain Duane Schexnayder, who answered so many SWAT questions, I am forever in your debt—you were the epitome of professional and brilliant and I appreciated your suggestions more than you could know.

Detective Bart Morris, who was just flat-out cool, and

who gave me insight into the mind of the detective and helped me flesh out my instinct into real characters.

Sharon Naquin, Ph.D., Executive Director, LSU Division of Workforce Development, one of my dearest friends and without whom the above would have not been possible. You not only helped me to find the perfect resources, but you were a constant cheerleader and source of encouragement.

Special Agent Pam Stratton, for all of your efforts to help me grasp the hierarchy as well as the inner workings of the FBI and how it would function in this wild scenario; you, quite simply, rocked and were a joy.

Yvonne Hewitt, for your tremendous help in getting the Irish speech patterns correct in both *Girls Just Wanna Have Guns* and *When A Man Loves A Weapon*—as well as the terrific catches when I mangled the colloquial phrasing. I could not have done this without you.

Nancie Hays and Luke Causey, who both answered numerous technical questions about guns—especially for putting up with my emails that went along the lines of, "That thingie thing you told me that did that thing, you know? What was that again?" They both have the patience of Job, and a good deal more humor. I would've been lost without them.

Cap'n Bob Bernstein, for your wonderful sense of humor and help with brainstorming the casino boat scene. You were a phenomenal inspiration.

Jason Newman, Staff Sergeant, Air Force, who gave me detailed military background. Jason weathered some very oddball questions with grace and humor; any mistakes are my own.

Nick Lejeune, for the generous use of his name. Thankfully, the real Nick is a terrific guy and nothing like his counterpart in the book. (Well, except for the dimples.)

Kathy Sweeny, who answered random frantic last-minute attorney questions and tried to keep me from making grave mistakes in exactly who does what when, when it pertains to legal processes.

Jacob Causey, for all of the answers on fire and both Jacob and Nicole Skrintney for the answers regarding cars—and for drooling with me over the Audi.

Emilie Staat, who is an extraordinary assistant and who kept me sane. (Okay, *saner*, because "sane" may be stretching it a bit.) You were always an amazing, fantastic friend and a huge help.

Pam DuMond, CJ Lyons, Lori Chapman, Renee George, Michelle Bardsley, Terri Smythe, Amanda Causey and Jerry McGee, all of whom read drafts and were a phenomenal support.

Pooks. Patricia Burroughs, a woman of tough questions and great advice and lots of laughter and intense debate—thank you for being such an amazing friend and for holding my hand through that first draft.

Allison Brennan, Lori Armstrong, Roxanne St. Claire, Debra Webb and Karin Tabke, for all the late night freak-out Q & A sessions.

POVers (you know who you are) who've been friends and support for 15 years. Also, thanks to all of the fine folks over on Crimescenewriter and Weapons_Info (both Yahoo groups) for the wealth of information they dispense for writers.

Alabama football fans—you are what makes a school rivalry great—a good sense of humor.

LSU football fans—you are, of course, the greatest. (I may be biased.) Thanks to a crack LSU staff and team, nothing like what I've described has ever happened.

The Fans. The letters I have received have humbled me and made me so grateful for being able to be a writer. You've lifted me up, sustained me and made all of the years of hard work worth every single solitary minute, and I hope I get the chance to continue to bring you laughter and pleasure.

My parents, Al and Jerry McGee, my in-laws, Patsy and Marion Causey, my brother, Mike, my sons, Luke and Jake and their wives, Amanda and Nicole, and my granddaughter, Angie. (I am barely getting used to saying "granddaughter," but she is the cutest critter on the planet, so that makes it easier.)

Carl, my husband and best friend. You make me laugh every day, and happy beyond measure. I am the luckiest woman in the world (and no, you cannot remind me of that when I am grumpy). Thank you for putting up with all of the late nights of me staring at the computer and for all of the times you brought food into the cave when things were a little ragged and you probably should've been in fear for your life. You are my rock that I lean on and my heart.